ADVAN(

Confessions of a Neighbor

"Amazing scenery, vivid descriptions and intense emotions are just part of the appeal of Confessions of a Neighbor: A Mystery in Switzerland by Heather Nadine Lenz. In this hard to put down story, you develop a real attachment to Ella and suffer along with her as she deals with issues from her past, her insecurities about the future, and the everyday struggles of trying to live while following her dreams. Wonderful descriptions of setting and ballet add a lot to the realism of the story. Well done! Psychological manipulation plays a large part in the story and Lenz sets the scene slowly and deliberately, then shocks you when the trap is sprung. This is a book that is well worth reading on many levels."

-Reviewed by Melinda Hills for *Readers' Favorite*

"Confessions of a Neighbor by Heather Nadine Lenz tells the story of Ella, a hopeful 16-year-old ballet dancer whose dream is to one day be able to make a living as a ballerina. Fate, however, has other plans for the young woman who lost her mother as well as her grandmother far too early. She is lonely and ends up falling victim to an evil scheme. Fortunately, she also has someone who is secretly looking out for her well-being. But the eyes of that secret helper cannot be everywhere. I enjoyed reading Confessions of a Neighbor by Heather Nadine Lenz."

-Reviewed by Kim Anisi for *Readers' Favorite*

Confessions of a Neighbor

Heather Nadine Lenz

United States

heathernadinelenz.com

Plum Tree Press

Published by Plum Tree Press

First Edition November 2016

Cover design © Lisa Book

Editor David Yost

Book ISBN-13: 978-0-692-81008-8

Book ISBN-10: 0-692-81008-0

Printed in the United States of America

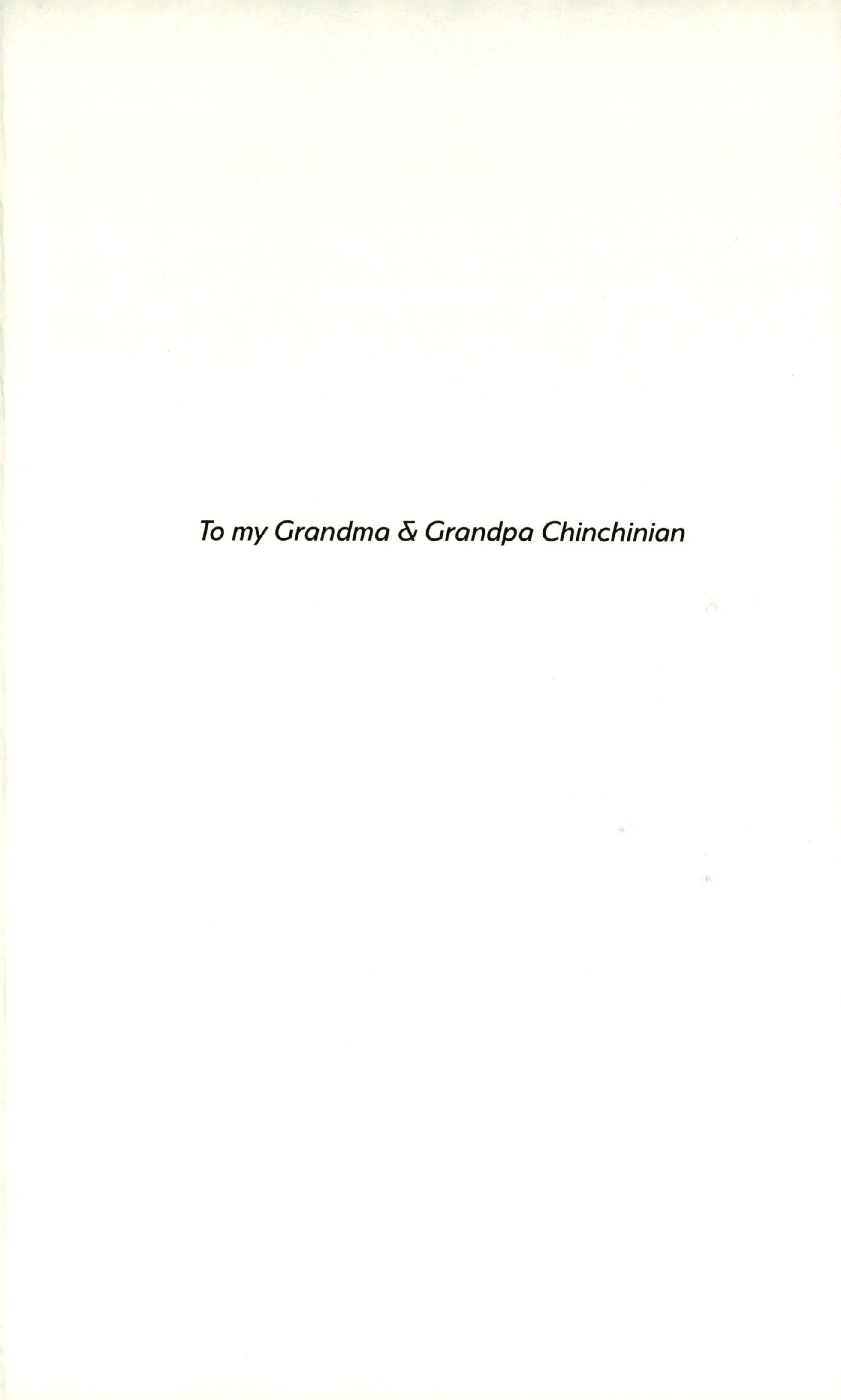

To my Grandma & Grandpa Chinchinian

Confessions of a Neighbor

Prologue

Heart racing, Ella opened her eyes. Black water was licking at her skin.

The sheer force of the pain in her ears caused her to inhale sharply, holding her breath, tears streaming down her cheeks. She went to bring her hands up to her ears. She couldn't. Ella was certain there must be needles or knives thrust into her eardrums, so sharp was the pain screaming in her skull. A weight lay heavy on her chest, weighing her down onto the stones grinding themselves into her back. She needed to push herself free.

But she couldn't move her fingers. It was dangerous to lie half-submerged in water in winter, and the cold was seeping its way steadily into her body.

You must claw your way up, out from under this weight, out of the water.

Ella went to scream for help, but then muffled her own cry. Was someone out there in the darkness? Waiting. Watching to be sure she had died? Who had done this to her? What had happened?

Her body began to shake, fighting a battle against the cold

water's leaching of the little warmth left in her frozen body. The indifferent sky stared down upon her, the stars glittering like so many jewels spread out across the blue oblivion of space. She willed her body to stop its shaking, fearing the slight splashing sound it made might give her away. He would come.

Ella prayed to every angel in the world to swoop down to still the trembling of her body and help her escape the icy claws of this monstrous lake. Her body went still. The gentle whispering of the waves against the lake shore was soothing her, hypnotizing her into submission. The stabbing pain in her ears lessened, and the urge to move weakened. Her thoughts drifted and danced, spinning like so many spheres of memory and delusion.

In the remote distance, the rumbling of a cargo train echoed out over the lake front. And then silence swallowed the world, save for the soft rippling of the water. Peace, a warm glow, spread through her, tingling along her skin. Her eyes were closing, the anguish of living and loving seeping out and away from her into the nothingness, the icy void.

Anneli.

Her baby.

A hunger was rushing into the void, an anger howling against indifference, snatching her awareness just in time from the sirens singing her toward permanent sleep. The heat of fury began scorching through the petrified body holding her hostage in the darkness. Move now, Ella, move now or you may never move again.

She managed to roll onto her side, her fingers still incapable of movement. For the first time Ella noticed the sailboat tied up a few feet away at the dock. She began crawling out of the water inch by inch, her clothes impeding her every move forward. Tearing at the wet and clinging shirt and jeans, she fought desperately to undress without the cooperation of her numb fingers.

At last freed from her garments, Ella tried to stand and fell promptly onto the ragged stones, cutting her feet, her hands, her knees. As silent sobs wracked her body, she crawled to the plastic dock, the pain of her bloody hands and knees searing through her with each inch forward.

At last Ella pulled herself up onto the plastic dock, lying bare beneath the dim glow of a sliver of moon.

Within seconds of stillness, the cold slammed back into her body, leaving her breathless, gasping for air, hollowed out by the force of its impact. Her muscles contracted. Lying rigid like a pale corpse in the moonlight, Ella noticed her long, blond hair had already frozen in the night air. She was running out of time.

Rolling onto her stomach, she inched forward, one knee at a time, her elbows her best vehicle for forward momentum. At last she reached out an arm for the side of the sailboat and, pulling with all her might, fell headfirst inside.

Face pressed to the floor of the sailboat, she saw the cabin door. *My only hope for warmth.*

She desperately wanted to open the door to the cabin and hide herself away from the leaching cold of the night. She lifted her hand up, and it slid uselessly over the handle. Panicking, she realized she couldn't grasp the handle, her fingers traitors in their numbness. She tried to open the door with an elbow, again and again and again. Her thinking was clouding, her mental ability to process the world around her oozing out with every degree of body temperature she lost. She didn't realize the door was locked until a gleam of silver caught her eye beneath the seat.

The key. The key was under the seat. Collapsing to the floor on her stomach in complete exhaustion, Ella stared at the key. The cold air was stabbing once again like needles into her ears, her body screaming on the floor of the sailboat. Through the cloud enveloping her mind, Ella had an idea. She took the large key in her mouth. Pushing her way back to the door, she pushed the key into the lock. Grasping the key handle with her teeth, she attempted to turn the key.

Bitter, metallic blood rushed to fill her mouth as the key cut her tongue. The key gave a click. The door swung open and Ella fell inside the cabin. The last ounce of energy she had went into kicking the door shut.

The force of the door slamming caused an oar to fall in front of the door, locking the door from within. There was a bunk above her, but Ella didn't have the energy to crawl up onto its comfort. Instead she pulled the blanket down with her feet, partially covering her bare body before fading away.

Chapter 1

Elation welled up within Ella as she took to the center floor. Every muscle warm, a sheen of sweat on her face, a wellbeing and inner concentration offset the pain radiating in her knee. She looked forward to this class during her entire shift of waitressing at Flavor.

"Gorgeous, Ella. Try it again, but raise your gaze. Yes. Great extension. Now, did everyone see Ella's extension from her center, and the way she made the move appear effortless? Okay, on to the next step," said the teacher.

Ella's attention snapped back into focus. Everything that had come before, all the uncertainty stretching out before her, the squishing of emotions inside her heart, the constant murmuring in her head, fell away. When she danced, she was weightless.

Ella gave a huge sigh of relief as she closed the door of her studio flat behind her. As she carefully locked the door and returned her things to their home on the shelf, the weight of the day fell from her shoulders. Rolling her head around, she made her way barefoot to the large windows of her apartment and opened them to the cool night air. Pausing at the window, Ella looked out over the city, enjoying the breeze on her skin.

Ella loved this time of day the best. The sun was sliding behind the horizon, taking her tension away with it, but not her loneliness. The sky was still bathed in pink, warm orange and grey blue.

She stood for a few moments, watching the moon in the distance rise, a few stars glimmering in the encroaching darkness. She gazed across the street. He was hugging her in their kitchen.

They were such a cute couple. Ella wondered if the wife realized how lucky she was, to have found love, to live in such a high design penthouse flat on the top floor, with a view out over the city, the lake, the Alps snow-covered in the distance. But above all, she wondered if her neighbor appreciated how lucky she was to be with *him*.

You could learn a lot about someone by watching them day in and day out. Most people are creatures of habit, and the neighbor was no exception. She knew, for instance, that he didn't watch TV and he spent very little time on the Internet. The first half an hour or so of his evening he spent talking with his wife, massaging her feet in his lap.

Afterward, he would read a book or work at the dinning room table, papers spread over its surface. In the spring and summer, he would come out onto their extensive terrace at around eight o'clock to garden in the raised designer boxes filled with vegetables, flowers, herbs, berry bushes and fruit trees. He was never lounging with guests in one of the sleek designer lawn chairs next to their cascading fountain. They never had anyone over for dinner or a drink, never.

Ella looked down at her watch. Good, it was a few minutes to nine. She would wait. At nine he stepped out onto the terrace. Ella watched him walk to the seven-by-twelve-foot endless pool, turn it on, and begin to swim into its river current. She knew he would swim for half an hour. Winter, ice, snow, rain or sun, it really didn't seem to matter.

He swam every day without fail, ever since she began noticing him across the street a year ago. She admired his willpower. Was the water heated? How did the water feel against his skin, his muscles straining with each stroke into the current? She could almost smell the chlorine, feel the air fresh on her face as she slid into the water with him beneath a star-clouded sky.

Ella sighed. The neighbor was a welcome escape from the fear crawling beneath her skin.

Nausea hit Ella, and she ran to the bathroom.

She had three days until her ballet audition. Money was so tight. The salary she earned waitressing was just enough to cover the rent, her other living expenses and her ballet classes. She hardly had enough to pay to travel to the audition. Tears slipped down her cheeks as she walked out of the bathroom. She leaned against the wall and collapsed down in a heap, her face in her hands. Why did she have to do this all alone?

Why did her mother and then her grandmother have to die, leaving her all alone at sixteen? Ella let herself fall into the grief, swim in it, until the sorrow lessened an inch. Taking a deep, shuddering breath, she rose from the floor. Wiping the tears away, she walked across the studio and placed a hand on the bar. It was time to take refuge.

She should practice. Instead, she opened the cupboard and took out a bottle of vodka, pouring herself a huge glass. She returned with her drink to the window.

"EXCUSE ME, IS THIS seat taken?"

Ella jumped. She had been daydreaming, staring out the train window. She looked up to see a strikingly handsome man standing in front of her, broad shouldered and muscular, his blond hair cut short.

Behind a pair of black glasses, intense green eyes looked at her, eyebrows raised. A slight smile teased at his lips.

Ella realized her mouth had dropped open, her eyes wide. He looked even better up close than she had fantasized.

"Listen, I won't bother you. I'm just interested in a cup of coffee on my way to work. Say, you look familiar. Have we met before?"

"Actually, I'm… um… No, we've never met." Every cell within her was vibrating. Her face flushed red. Oh god, she almost told him she was his neighbor.

Her hands began to tremble.

Of all the trains in Switzerland, why did he have to be on

this one, asking to sit at her table?

Pull yourself together, Ella. There is no way for him to know how many hours you have spent at your window, watching him.

"So why are you going to work on a Saturday?"

As soon as the words slipped out of her mouth, she regretted them. Of course plenty of people went to work on a Saturday, and anyway, what business of it was hers? Pulling off her hat and raking her hands through her hair, she realized he was still standing there, designer messenger laptop bag in hand, waiting for her answer.

She motioned at the chair, speechless, and took her favorite book out from her bag, pretending to be absorbed.

How could her neighbor be on the same train, in the same compartment with her? Didn't he work in Zürich? Shouldn't he be off somewhere enjoying the day with his wife?

"You sound like my wife," he answered with a sigh, sinking into the chair beside her and taking out his laptop. "I have to admit, I love my job. And when you are in phytotherapy research and development, the work feels limitless."

Ella looked up from her book. Her pulse was starting to revolve faster, like an engine revving.

"I've never heard of phytotherapy," Ella answered, tilting her head to the side and smiling.

A sparkle came to her neighbor's eye as he broadened across the chest and leaned toward her, hands on the table. "Phytotherapy is the evidence-proven production of plant-based medicines."

"You mean herbal remedies?"

"What? No." He slammed the table for emphasis, and Ella startled at his intensity. "My plant-based medicines are tested in clinical trials for the efficacy and safety in comparison to placebos as well as other standard treatments.

After passing clinical trials and regulatory approval from the health authorities, they are manufactured under the most stringent quality conditions." Owen gestured dramatically with his hands, emphasizing each point.

Ella decided there was something very sexy about a man passionate for his career, and yet his earnestness amused her at the same time. The man was gorgeous, with his blond hair and startling green eyes, not to mention the smooth, muscular physique. And he was taller than her. Most men weren't. But watching him from afar, she had imagined him, well, different. She had painted him as the strong, silent, smug type. A smile played at the corners of her mouth. He was kind of a nerd. She liked that.

"You sound very passionate about your work. I'll let you get back to it," she said, motioning to his open laptop.

Ella returned her eyes to her book, acutely aware of the presence of the man across the table from her.

"Would you like anything?"

"What?"

"Would you like anything else?"

Only then did Ella register the waiter at her side. "Oh, yes, a weizen beer please."

"We only have those in half a liter…"

"That's fine."

Ella knew she shouldn't drink, but her nerves were jangling like a huge loop of keys, and she wanted to quiet them before they attracted attention.

"Tell you what, bring me one as well," said the man across from Ella. "That's my favorite beer."

A moment later the waiter returned with the beer bottles in his hands and two glasses. While pouring the second glass, the train tilted and the waiter lost his balance, spilling beer all over Ella's hardback book. In a flurry of apology and napkins, Ella stood stock still, staring at the last book her grandmother had gifted her before she died. Two tears slipped down her cheek.

"I'll bring you a new beer, on the house, I'm so sorry," called the waiter as he returned to the kitchenette.

"It was a gift, wasn't it?"

Ella looked up and nodded at the neighbor.

"How did you know?"

"Because no one cries over an old book unless it has a special value to them, not unless it was a first edition or something."

"It was."

"It was what?"

"It was a first edition of *The Fellowship of the Ring*. And the last birthday present I received from my Grandma."

"Good grief, how much does something like that cost?" asked Owen. He was already reaching for his phone and beginning a Google search. "That book didn't really cost thousands of Swiss francs, did it?"

Ella just shrugged her shoulders in response. Of course she knew the book was valuable. She had all three hardback volumes of *The Lord of the Rings* in perfect condition. Well, perfect condition until today.

Ella gazed down at her beer-soaked book. She didn't care about the worth of the book. Its value was priceless. She was holding one of her Grandmother's most beloved possessions, a gift she herself had received from her father.

Every time Ella picked up the book, she could almost hear her Grandmother's voice reading aloud. How many hours did Ella lie nestled at her Grandma's side as a girl, listening to her Grandma read this novel aloud?

The waiter brought back a freshly poured beer and set it down on the table, and Mr. Gorgeous mumbled something. Ella didn't look up from her book. She was far away in a place where her Grandma's voice echoed and she was cocooned in safety and love. A moment later, the damp book was being taken out of her hands.

"Here, let me help you."

Ella sat with tear-stained cheeks as her neighbor carefully tore off ten paper towels from a roll, folded them in half with precision and placed them with care between the wet leaves of her book. As he was placing the last paper towel between the pages, he reached a hand across the table and said, "I'm Owen, by the way. Owen Meier."

Slipping her hand into his, she gave a strong shake and let go, wondering at the calluses on his palm and finger as she let go. Where did he acquire those calluses? She knew he gardened and swam, but that wouldn't produce those toughened hands. Her foot began tapping, her very being jolting with unspent nervous energy.

"How did you know how to salvage my wet book?"

"I googled it," he smiled, while tapping his iPhone on the

table. "You won't be able to get thousands for that book trilogy now. However, you will be able to read it just fine. That is, if you don't mind the smell of beer."

"Thank you." Ella glanced up at him from beneath her long eyelashes, and then smiled down at the table, her fingers playing with her hair. He winked at her while interlacing his fingers and placing them behind his head. But as he leaned back in his chair, relaxed power and superiority playing out of his movements, he knocked into the woman sitting at the table behind him, causing her to spill her coffee all over her lap and the white tablecloth.

Ella laughed at loud, the merriment bubbling up inside her, a sudden release for all her tension, worry, and fear. Owen turned around to the old woman. She noticed his ears had turned bright red, as well as the back of his neck, which he was rubbing while apologizing to the grey-haired woman behind him. Ella sat bemused as her neighbor handed the small woman a bunch of paper towels and insisted on buying her a new cup of coffee. He turned back to her with flinty eyes and a clenched jaw, but seeing the smile fade from her face, his features softened.

"Scalding a sweet old woman with coffee is funny?"

"What, no. No, I'm sorry. It was just the sudden change in your expression and the fact that it was the second beverage spilling in a matter of minutes."

"Yes, well. If they didn't put these tables so close together, it would have never happened. I've never read The Lord of the Rings books before by the way. Is it any good? I don't read very much. I don't have the time." He tapped his laptop.

"One of the best stories ever written," she said, her heart beating faster.

She didn't know what in the world he was talking about. He spent hours reading a book every week, usually with a glass of red wine in one hand. She had seen him. Her cheeks burned at the thought of watching him from afar.

What would he think if he knew how much I know about him? How can he be sitting across from me now?

"So where are you headed today?" Leaning in and placing his arms on the table, he caught her gaze and held it. "Looks like you are going on a holiday."

"Greenland." Ella gave a small start. Why did she lie? She was going to an audition at the Stuttgart Ballet Germany.

"Excuse me, did you say Greenland?" Owen furrowed his brow, tapping his lips with his finger.

"Interesting. Why Greenland?"

"I'm visiting my mother." Ella plastered a carefree smile on her face. She hoped it said, 'I am so excited and happy' instead of, 'my heart is beating so fast and hard it feels like an airplane engine just before takeoff.'

"Wow, that will be an experience. Where are you from by the way? You look familiar somehow."

The air whooshed out of her lungs. "Um," Ella looked out the window. "Zürich."

"Yeah? Me too."

She looked up from the table into his green eyes, and he smiled, a dimple showing on his cheek. Ella relished the nuances of seeing the neighbor up close. She couldn't see from far away what a seductive grin he had. How many times did she fantasize about meeting him in person, to see the color of his eyes, hear the baritone of his laugh, perhaps even feel the warmth radiating from his skin?

"So what do you do for fun?"

"I dance ballet."

He looked her over, and she blushed.

"Alright, sure, I can see it," he said, the lines around his eyes creasing when he smiled. "Long legs, long arms, long neck. You have prima ballerina written all over you."

Ella couldn't help but smile back, pushing her hair back from her face.

"And you?" she asked after a long pause. He raised his eyebrows at her, the smile still on his face. "What is your deal exactly?"

"I'm not sure what you mean," he answered, frowning. He leaned in, placing his elbows on the table.

She fought her instinct to lean back in her chair. He was so close she could smell his aftershave. "I mean, what do you do for fun?"

"Drink beer with pretty women, such as yourself."

Ella looked down at the table. Was he flirting with her?

Yes, she decided. She had experienced enough flirtatious banter while waitressing to recognize it.

"Okay, I swim. And row on a year-round rowing team."

Ella nodded. Well, that explained the calluses.

"Isn't it too cold half the year to go rowing?"

Owen ran his hand through his blond hair and winked at her, giving a satisfied smile. "Not for me. The cold doesn't stop me. Just call me a polar bear."

"Oh yeah, a real tough guy huh?"

She began laughing out loud. She wondered if he really did have a love for the outdoors, or if he was working to offset his nerdy side with athleticism and an attempt at being macho.

Ella thought she glimpsed flinty anger, a coldness behind Owen's eyes surface.

It was gone so quickly she couldn't be sure.

"Well, Kreuzlingen, this is me. Time to do some rowing."

"I thought you were going to work?"

"Yeah, I'll head back to Zürich to the office straight from rowing. It was nice to meet you, Ella," he answered, holding out his hand. "Maybe we will run into each other in Zürich someday."

"How do you know my name?" she asked.

"Oh," he answered while running a hand through his hair. "It's written in your book."

She stood to move her small suitcase out of his way just as the train came to an abrupt final stop, causing Owen to lose his balance and pitch forward into her arms, knocking the wind out of her.

"I'm so sorry. Wow, uh," he muttered, running his hand yet again through his hair. "You okay?"

"Sure. I'm tough like a polar bear."

Owen looked at her quizzically and then laughed.

"I enjoyed talking to you, Ella." He gave a dazzling smile. "Have a nice trip," he called over his shoulder, as he made his way down the stairs and off the train.

Ella watched Owen stride from the train. All of a sudden, he stopped mid-stride, turned, and looked back at the train with a hand shielding his eyes from the sun.

ELLA LET OUT A HUGE SIGH to expel some of her nervousness as she slid into the splits. She had been to numerable auditions in the past year all over Europe. Each time she had failed to secure a place in a ballet company.

A wry smile came to her face.

As a child, auditions were a source of gaiety. The pressure was minimal. There was a new leotard always waiting on her bed when she awoke on audition day. There was the post-audition ice-cream sundae celebration to look forward to with her mother and grandmother.

This was her fourth audition. She knew her technique was impressively clean and precise. And yet, she had already faced three rejections. She didn't know how she could take one more. Ella looked around the room at her competition as everyone lined up at the barre.

Why did everyone look so calm?

Ella moved to position herself so that she could clearly see the director at the front, but she was crowded back by other dancers. Lifting up on her toes to see, she was suddenly pushed from behind and fell forward with a crash on her hands and knees. Everyone turned to stare at her, before the director continued showing the steps for the dancers to execute. No one offered to help her up to her feet.

When it was Ella's turn to join a line of dancers and present the choreography, there was sweat beading on her forehead. Her palms were sweaty. What was she going to do? When she was sent sprawling on the floor, she hadn't seen a few of the steps of the dance. Looking at the dancers out of the corner of her eye, she improvised the few steps she didn't know. Her face was set in a grimace of concentration as she stepped forward on pointe while doing a grand port de bras into a powerful back bend.

After the audition, Ella drank in huge gulps of cold air as she hurried to the train.

She didn't need to wait in anticipation for the letter to come. She knew her performance had held no artistry, and her limbs, usually all grace and elongated body lines, had been tight and rigid with fear of failure. Ella hurried to the train station, the streets a blur through her tears.

A bone-aching fatigue pulled on her body as she slumped onto a seat in the train. Why were her shoulders clenched and her arm movements forced instead of ease and lightness? Fear had made her freeze up and dance like a novice, instead of a professional.

That was the last ballet audition she could afford, and she had failed. It would take her months to save up for the expense of traveling to another one. She closed her eyes. Maybe she should just give up.

ELLA TOOK A DRINK and refilled her glass with vodka. All at once, loneliness was running toward her, a pack of wolves in the moonlight gliding toward their prey.

One floor below her, across the street, Ella spied a faint outline in the pool of light emitted from a laptop in their home office. She was working again. No surprise there.

He was sitting on the sofa, reading something with a glass of red wine in one hand. She could see he was laughing out loud. A warmth filled her, and she smiled.

She liked a man who could laugh out loud at something in a book. She found everything about this neighbor attractive, from his blond, wavy hair to his glasses.

Ella let her cheek fall against the glass of the window. We want what we can't have.

CHAPTER 2

As soon as Ella took off her jacket and shoes, she crossed to the window. She let out a sigh. He wasn't home yet. Just then, she saw him enter her line of vision. She watched as he carefully took off his shoes and wandered in socks into the kitchen. Placing boxes of food into the fridge, he poured himself a glass of wine and wandered into the living room where he sat down on the couch, smiling. He took her feet into his lap, running his hands absentmindedly along her calves as they talked. He set his glass aside and began massaging her feet.

A thrill traveled down her spine, watching the perfect life playing out in slow motion across the street. He leaned down and kissed his wife's knee, then her inner thigh. He slipped his hands up his wife's dress, pulling pink-laced underwear slowly down her legs. He stood up, pulling off his tie, unbuttoning his shirt to reveal defined stomach muscles and broad chest. He knelt back down, where he kissed her ankle, his lips caressing their way slowly up her leg. He pushed her dress up.

Her heart pounding, Ella tore herself from the window and wandered over to the floor-to-ceiling mahogany shelf. She carefully refolded the cashmere blanket on her blue armchair. Ella went into the kitchen and downed a cup of vodka. She cut up some strawberries. The sweet taste of the strawberries was dulled by the alcohol in her mouth. The drink loosened her inhibitions and she couldn't resist. She crept back to the window to watch Owen make love to his wife.

Only they weren't making love. They were sitting on the sofa talking. From out of nowhere, the wife grabbed a large glass pitcher of water from the side table and slammed it against Owen's jaw. Owen backed away, holding his jaw. The wife picked up the scented candle from the coffee table and hurled it at Owen, the glass hitting him square in the chest. Hot wax splattered over his skin.

Ella watched, spellbound, as Owen ran bare-chested to the front door, grabbed his coat and shoes and slammed the door behind him on his way out. She peered down at the street, waiting. A few minutes later, she saw him walking up the street toward the lake front.

Ella shook her head, trying to free it from the horrifying scene of abuse that had just played out across the street. What had just happened? Did he hurt her while Ella was in her kitchen? Was the violence mere retaliation? But what could have provoked the wife?

ELLA RETURNED HOME FROM her long shift hollowed out of hope that her life would ever be anything more than isolation and waitressing. She missed opening the door after a long day and smelling garlic and spices simmering, fresh bread baking in the kitchen.

How many times was she greeted by a clattering of dishes and a tumbling of words stirring together as her mother and grandmother prepared dinner together? Tears dripping down her cheeks, she remembered what it was like to enter the kitchen, arms encircling her, the lavender smell of her mother and the clean soapy smell of her grandma, the feeling of being adored. She could almost feel her face being tilted up, a kiss whispering against her cheek.

You loveable, lovely girl, a joy to see you. How was your day? The same homecoming, the same question, day after day the same routine. Snacking on farm-fresh crunchy carrots, cucumbers and radishes as the dinner finished cooking. Conversation and laughter swirling about them as they set the table, lit the candles, and ate together. The soothing predictability of Ella washing the dishes each night and cleaning the kitchen as her grandma and mother relaxed with a glass of wine in the living room, reading. A comfortable, sleepy sort of silence washing over the room as Ella settled at the kitchen table to do her homework.

Whoever wrote that monotony is the bane to happy life never had her family to return to each evening.

Ella went to let fresh air into the stuffy room. That's when she saw him. He was on his terrace, standing among his potted bamboo plants, next to his cascading water fountain. He was looking up. Looking up at her? Could he see her? She ran and turned out the light before dashing back to the window. No. Certainly he couldn't see into her room, way up here in the attic, given the sharp angle of her tower to his flat. She could only see *him* if she stood with her nose practically pressed against the glass.

An abrupt step from the window, and with one hand she was pulling her bed down from the wall, fluffing the duvet and pillows in their bluebird eggshell blue.

Ella went to the bathroom to shower, stripping off her leotard and threw it into the lavender laundry bag. Stepping under the hot water, Ella thought of her neighbors while watching the soapy citrus bubbles whirling toward the drain.

Brushing out her waist-long blond hair, Ella returned once again to the window, pausing, the brush motionless in the air. He was undressing.

Her toes tightened, her breath caught in her throat as if he might hear her breathing. He always took his pants off first, folding them neatly and placing them on the shelf. Next came the shirt, button by button. He placed his glasses on his bedside table before he took off his socks, then his undershirt, revealing rippling muscles and a washboard stomach. In boxers, he started his push ups.

She counted fifty-five push ups, and then he lay flat, lifting his legs up in a straight arc from the floor to a ninety-degree position one hundred and five times. At last the boxers joined the rest of the laundry, and he changed into his swimsuit before heading toward the pool on the terrace.

Ella didn't need to look at her clock. It would be a few minutes to nine. Ella shifted focus to *Her*. She was curled up on the couch, watching something on the huge screen on the wall as she ate from a takeout box. She was far more unpredictable than he was. She almost never watched TV. Why tonight? The wife wiped at her eyes, pulling her hands through her chin-length brown hair. Was she crying? Was it something on TV causing her distress, or something else?

Ella's focus turned to the terrace, where she could see him swimming in the pool. His rhythmic movements, stroke after stroke, comforted her. Perhaps she should take up swimming.

She didn't notice the wife come out onto the terrace at first, not until she was beside the pool. Ella watched her press a button as he continued to swim into the current. The pool cover began to roll out over the pool. By the time he noticed the movement of the cover above his head, it was halfway closed above him.

He hurried to exit the pool, but he wasn't fast enough. He was caught between the cover and the pool wall, the cover pressing against his upper chest. She could see he was yelling at her, but she was doubled over with laughter. At last he managed to push the cover back a fraction and pull himself up out of the water. His hands on his chest, he fell to the floor, heaving.

His wife turned on her heel and walked back through the patio door, shutting it behind her and locking it. Eventually he grabbed a towel from the back of a lounge chair and went to the door, banging on the glass. Ella could see his wife. She had returned to her spot on the designer sofa, wine glass in one hand, bowl of popcorn in her lap. She ignored the man standing a few feet behind her and the noise of his fist hammering on the glass door.

Ella realized she had been holding her breath. She hadn't seen any provocation for what had just happened. Owen was being abused by his wife. Why did he stay with her? What was she missing? She turned away from the window, selected *Pride and Prejudice* from her bookshelf and climbed under the duvet.

She desperately needed to distract herself from the abuse playing out across the street. Why was he tolerating the abuse? She shouldn't watch them; she knew she shouldn't. Why was it so hard to pry her eyes away from the trauma playing out across the street? She knew the answer. She was infatuated with him, worried for him. If she called the police, what could she say?

Ella shook her head. She couldn't help him. Ella promised herself never to look out the window again. Tomorrow she needed to break out of her routine so she wouldn't be tempted to return to her voyeurism.

Curling up into her bed, cocooned in its softness, her body was heavy with fatigue. Reaching into the bedside drawer, she pulled out a bottle and sprayed her pillows. The scent of lavender wafted up, transporting her out of her city tower and to a field of flowers waving heather purple under French skies of blue.

Her mother's fingers curled around her own. The soft fabric from her mother's dress brushed against her bare arm. Her fingers were trailing the flower tops, her hair blowing free in the breeze. A lunch of French baguettes, duck a la orange and potatoes was awaiting her in the café in the village. She could almost hear her mother's laughter.

ELLA CLIMBED THE STAIRS to the top deck of the ferry and found a lounge chair in the sun. The water glistened in the sunshine, and a cool breeze blew in her hair as she sat down and put her long legs up on the bar in front of her. She gazed out at the snow-covered Alp chain bright white in the distance. It was a perfect day. A single tear slipped down her cheek.

Ever since the failed ballet audition, she was even more hollowed out by her loneliness. A raw, aching hunger had befallen her, set siege to her soul, making her ravenous for connection of any kind. Detaching from the world had begun as a defense mechanism when she lost first her mother and then her grandmother.

Day by day and echoing night by night afterward, she had avoided people as much as possible, only putting on a bright fake smile while waitressing each day. She had clung to the safety of isolation and her ballet training.

Now Ella was certain her need for connection was radiating from her, a lighthouse in the darkness, warning off any that might pass too close to her shore.

Each solitary day she spent increased her interest in the lives playing out just a fraction of an inch beyond her outstretched fingers, just a street removed from where she lived. It was sugar, spun sticky and sweet at the fair. A tiny taste, a mouth of air, an entire armful, it gave the delusion of satisfying her hunger. She knew better. It wasn't nourishing; it would leave her crashing into desolation, her head pounding, her heart racing. She shouldn't watch them anymore.

Ella looked around the deck. An elderly couple sat with content smiles on their faces next to her, drinking their coffees and enjoying the view of the sparkling water and the view of Zürich from the lake. A father was pacing with a crying infant in his arms while a toddler ate a croissant in her mother's lap. Out of the corner of her eye, Ella could see a young teenage couple kissing, oblivious to two women laughing together, sipping glasses of Prosecco in the sunlight.

Love and warmth were circling around her like so many dancers, and she was here in the center, still as a statue, unable to hear the music. Invisible and mute in the middle of a grand party pulsating out in merriment, in faces turned toward one another in sympathetic friendship, in adoration, in recognition, in love.

Why was it that you could sense the abundance of love or desperation in someone's life, just by looking at them? Ella decided people must give off either a positive or a negative charge. Those overflowing with love or meaning in their lives radiated a positive charge that attracted others, or at the very least set people at ease. It was as if they had a message branded across their chest: I need nothing from you and I wish you a lovely day. Those unfortunate individuals with a negative charge radiated a hunger, a need. And no matter how they dressed or acted to try to cover it up, their negative charge betrayed them.

Ella knew most people had a fear of need, or at the very least resented it greatly. Ella sighed. The negative charge within was becoming a black hole of desperation.

"Well hello there. I thought that was you. I took the liberty of ordering you a drink. So you didn't make it to Greenland after all, huh? On your way back home already?"

Ella looked up at the tall, blond man towering over her, two glasses of champagne in his hands. He handed one to her and relaxed in the lounge chair next to her, sprawling his legs out in front of him, his face turned up to the warmth of the sun. Ella panicked. What in the world was Owen doing on this ship? Where had he come from? What should she answer?

"No, um, my mother is gone. I will never see her again."

"Good grief, you can't be serious," he said, as he sat up and looked over at her. When she didn't respond, he reached out and patted her arm, his face showing concern. "I'm so sorry for your loss. Did it take you by surprise? Or was she already ill? You're not going back for the funeral?"

Ella didn't answer any of his questions. She continued to lounge back in her chair, gazing at the light dancing off the waves and the snow-covered Alps reaching up to touch the clouds in the distance. She didn't know why she had given that answer to Owen. Of all the excuses for canceling her trip, why had she used that one?

"My mother always said she didn't want a funeral. She said I should find a park bench with a beautiful view and always return to it when I wanted to mourn her absence from my life."

"So your family and friends, you will all gather together in Greenland and dedicate a bench to her memory?"

"I have no family. Nor friends. And I am never returning to Greenland."

Ella turned her focus from the waves and the Alps to the tiny Swiss villages and fields along the shoreline. She went numb. In theory, she should feel the heat of the sun warm on her bare legs, the rays on her face. But a cold, seeping outward from her bones to the surface of her skin, left her shivering and exhausted. She couldn't understand why she had provided those answers. Perhaps because they were true and she never was a good liar, unlike her mother. When put on the spot, a good lie never came to her lips.

Owen was looking out at the waves. Ella decided he must be thinking of how to disentangle himself from her company in a polite way. They had met once on a train. She was certain there was no reason for him to want to remain in the presence of a grieving young woman. That was what she had intended with her answers, wasn't it? To drive him away from her?

It was. There was a lump in her throat, though, and tears stinging the back of her eyelids. She was alone in the world

When this sexy neighbor walked away, she would fall back down into the pit of loneliness, its darkness crushing her spirit beneath its weight, making each step forward into building a new life a struggle.

If only there was someone out there in the world that she could flee to, one lifeline to hold on to as she struggled out from beneath the earth and into the light.

"Are you sure you are quite alone? No one in the world to comfort you?"

"No one," she answered, and then, shaking herself, she glided to standing. The faintest traces of a smile lifted his lips at her answer.

Why would he like that answer? Shouldn't it make him sad for her? Then again, most people react awkwardly to loss and suffering. They just don't know how they should respond. Was that the case here?

Ella realized that she had been so preoccupied at shielding herself from his searching questions that she hadn't asked him what he was doing on the ship.

What were the chances of them bumping into each other twice in less than a week, when she had never happened upon him all the years they lived across the street from one another in Zürich? Pressing her lips together an folding her arms, she scrutinized the man in front of her. The wind was playing with his hair, whipping it around and causing it to stand on end. She couldn't see his eyes behind his sunglasses.

"I'm cold. I'm going in for a cup of coffee. What are you doing on this ship anyway?"

"Oh, I have the afternoon free. I rowed with my team on the lake, and I thought I'd enjoy a bit of a lounge in the sun and watch the world go by," he answered. "What are *you* doing on the ship?"

"Being on the water is healing for me," she murmured, motioning to the lake expanding away from them.

"My sentiments exactly," he replied. He set down his empty champagne glass and leaned his head back in his hands. When he lifted up his arms, his shirtsleeves pulled up.

"What happened?" Ella reached out and traced the black-and-blue bruise covering his forearm with her fingertips.

Owen froze, staring down at her fingertips. Horrified, Ella snatched them away, heat flooding her cheeks.

"Rowing accident. Listen. I should check in with my wife, let her know what time I will be home tonight for dinner."

"Right, of course. Goodbye then." Turning her back, she settled back into her lounge chair. *Message received.*

"No, I'll be right back, beautiful," he said. "Can I get you anything else? A coffee? Another glass of champagne?"

"Coffee sound great."

Warmth flared along her neck, the heat pulsing along her skin. She traced her fingers from her flushed and tingling cheeks, down her neck and along her collarbone, gazing out at the mountains in the distance.

Ella knew he was a married man, but when her fingers caressed his skin, all she could think about was trailing her fingers down the muscles in his back, to push her hands through that wind-tousled hair. She wanted to tell him to walk away from his wife. She knew that bruising was not from a rowing accident.

"A café crème, black, just the way you like it," said a voice behind her.

Ella turned to see Owen making his way around the table, setting down two cups of coffee as he sat down on the chair opposite her.

"And how, pray tell, do you know how I like my coffee?"

"I guessed." He winked at her while stirring two sugar packets into his own as well as a cream.

"I know what it feels like to be all alone," Owen said, gazing down at his hands and shrugging his shoulders. "I'm sorry you lost your Mom. And your Grandma."

"Oh. Thank you."

Ella took the opportunity to examine Owen. He had pushed his sunglasses up onto the top of his head, and she noticed a black bruise under one eye. He looked haggard and tired. "How did you hurt your eye?"

Owen quickly pushed his sunglasses back down over his eyes. "Rowing accident, I told you. Don't worry, it looks worse than it feels."

He smiled at her, showing straight, white teeth. "So, when are you going in search of your bench? I can come with you, if you don't want to undertake the task all alone. I told my wife I will be home late."

"Wow, you sure are nosy for a Swiss man. Isn't there some secret law you learn while growing up Swiss that you don't ask private questions, especially of strangers?"

"I'm sorry." Owen shifted in his seat, fumbling with the empty sugar packets. "I don't pry. Really, I don't usually talk to strangers, let alone ask them private questions. I just thought we clicked in the train. It was such a stroke of chance to run into you again so soon and we both have suffered so much recently that I felt we had connected somehow. Besides, I grew up in Sweden." Owen rubbed his forehead. "I'm rambling. I'm sorry. Listen, I'll leave you to your own thoughts. It was nice running into you again." He licked his lips and ran his fingers through his hair.

Ella knew what he had suffered, but she was shocked he had hinted at it.

"You said 'we.' What have you suffered, Owen? Want to talk about it?"

"Did I? Oh."

Owen stared out of the window at a sailboat drifting by, its red sail billowed by the wind. He let out a huge gush of breath. "I've been having a bit of trouble with my wife." He ran his hands through his hair before crossing them across his chest.

"I'm sorry to hear that. If your relationship is a poisonous, well I think you should leave her and move forward alone."

Owen looked up. "I can't leave her." He grimaced. His face had gone completely white, and he clutched his arms across his chest even tighter. "She wouldn't allow it."

"What do you mean she wouldn't allow it? You just leave. File for divorce. Find a new flat."

"It's not that simple. You don't understand. I'm a man. I don't even think the police would believe me."

Ella took a deep breath. "Are you saying you aren't safe? What wouldn't the police believe?"

Owen shook himself, sitting up straight. "Listen, I don't know why I told you all that. Just forget about it, okay? I'm fine. It will be fine. I probably deserve what happens, like she says. I can be a real schmuck sometimes, you know? I'm always messing things up."

A beast began growling within her chest. Owen's wife was abusive, and he shouldn't stay with her. He didn't have to.

"You are handsome and intelligent. You seem like a kind person. No one deserves abuse because they 'mess up.' You have a choice, Owen. Your life belongs to you. You can leave."

Owen returned his focus to the waves outside the window. Ella sat in silence with him for over ten minutes. She didn't know if she had overstepped unspoken boundaries by offering him advice. But didn't she know what it was like to feel unsafe? She didn't want him to suffer anymore. She hoped he would realize it wasn't necessary. She noticed they were entering the harbor.

"Are you getting off?" he asked.

"No, I'm cruising the lake for the afternoon."

"Well, thanks for the kind words, Ella. I really needed them today. Maybe we will run into each other again someday," he smiled over at her, as if the intensity of the past conversation had never happened.

"I hope so," she smiled back at him. She stood up and offered her hand, but he stepped forward and kissed her on each cheek. He paused, looking into her eyes, still standing so close that she could feel his breath on her cheek. He looked as if he wanted to say something, but then thought better of it. He reached out and pushed a strand of hair behind her ear before saying goodbye and bounding down the stairs and off the boat.

As the boat headed back out onto the lake, she could see him striding toward the train station. She could still feel his lips on her cheek, smell the clean scent of his aftershave. She was quivering like new leaves in the breeze. Her senses sharpened, the colors were more saturated, the sun warmer on her face, and suddenly she was aware of the smell of freshly cut grass and blossoming flowers swirling around her in the wind. The man she had spent so many hours watching had just sat across from her. He had trusted her with his secret. He had kissed her on both cheeks.

What were the chances she should run into Owen twice in one week? After never meeting him in Zürich in all the years she had lived across the street, it seemed highly unlikely. Was this fate? Something was wrong. She couldn't put her finger on it, but something was off.

Ella hugged herself, rubbing her upper arms. A longing so intense it sent an ache echoing within hit her hard. She had been placed in solitary confinement and just had been allowed short visiting hours. It made it so much worse to get a taste of companionship, of the lightness of exiting in a world of connection, of love. Ella closed her eyes, trying to memorize the feel of Owen's lips on her cheek.

Chapter 3

Ella leaned against the front door of her studio. The scent of lavender, lemon and a touch of bleach engulfed her, and she breathed a sigh of relief. It smelled like her mother and grandmother. It smelled like home.

She had had every intention to stop at the market on her way home. Today was to be the day that she began following her Grandma's instructions.

She had even carefully written out a grocery list before work, tucking it in her coat pocket. Yet in the end, she had arrived home with a bottle of vodka and a frozen pizza.

She always had such hope in the morning. She had a deal with herself that when she first opened her eyes, she would leap out of bed, make it and fold it up to the wall.

For thirty minutes, she would clean and then carefully apply makeup, curl her long blond hair and drink an espresso and then eating a muesli. She left the flat for work at the exact minute each day.

She went and poured herself a full glass of vodka and walked to the windowsill. When was the last time she had curled up with a book? Every time she sat down with a book, she ended up rereading the same page over and over again. So instead, she often ended up drifting around the flat, gazing out the window. Like she was doing now. He was working at the dining room table.

She tore her eyes from the window and sat down in her reading chair in the dark, waiting.

She had thirty-three minutes more. At exactly nine o'clock came the knock on the door. Ever since her grandmother's death, a small old woman had climbed the steep stairs to her tower studio at ten o'clock each night and knocked on her door.

Ella had never answered, only peered through the peephole. She had just wanted to be left alone in her initial grief.

Yet today, the weight of loneliness was pressing against her chest, stealing the air from her lungs. She leaped across the room and unlatched all the locks at the sound of the first knock. A very old woman stood before her, her short white hair like soft cotton bobbing on the top of her head. Twinkling blue eyes looked out from a face lined with wrinkles. The smiling woman set down a basket filled with vegetables, fruit and homemade black bread on the ground and placed her hands on her hips.

"Where on earth do you go until after ten every night? And what on earth are you doing in there in the dark?" Mrs. Annikov clicked the light on at the door.

"Excuse me?" Ella took a step behind the door, using it as a shield between herself and the tiny woman standing on her doorstep. "Who are you? Are you sure you have the right apartment?"

"I have the right apartment, little one. I'm Mrs. Annikov. I was fast friends with your Grandma. She told me to come on up here every night at nine o'clock and make sure you are eating properly, ask you some questions and give you a goodnight hug. And by his holy grace, I have come up every night since her funeral, but you have never been home. So I've just left the food wrapped up in a bag on your doorstep. How have you been?"

Wondering how she should answer, she began twisting her mother's diamond ring around her finger. The day after her grandmother's death, Ella had stepped into quicksand. Grief and anxiety began sucking her down with each movement. Ella found the only way to keep her head above the surface was to stop struggling.

She was still paralyzed, neck deep in muck.

But Ella didn't want to explain herself, not to this strange woman, not to anyone.

So she did what came naturally; she directed the attention away from herself.

"You were friends with my Grandma?" she asked. "My grandma never mentioned a Mrs. Annikov."

"I sure did know your Grandma. To see her wasting away from cancer like that, it just hurt my heart. She made me promise to watch over you when she was gone."

"But she never talked about you. I don't remember…"

"Now that just can't be. We baked bread together every morning and then enjoyed our coffee," said Mrs. Annikov, her brow furrowing as her arms fell to her sides.

Ella's face lit up with recollection. Her Grandma had often mentioned a friend she'd made in the building, just after they lost her mother.

Ella realized those years between sixteen and eighteen were a blur from sleepless nights and agonizing days.

"Anna? Are you Anna?" asked Ella, her voice tight.

"Yes, that's right, Anna Annikov. Now, have you been eating the food I have been leaving you?"

"I, well, yes, thank you. I have eaten the food you left for me," stammered Ella, thinking of the rich black bread, the ripe raspberries, and the crunchy carrots she had eaten just yesterday from the wicker basket. Opening the door wide, she said, "Please come in."

"I'm sorry dear, I can't stay. I can't leave my husband too long on his own. Would you like to come down with me?"

"Oh, no, that's okay…" began Ella. Mrs. Annikov fluttered a hand at her, interrupting.

"That's what she said you'd say. Now that's just fine. You come on over here for your hug, and tomorrow and from now on will you open the door at nine for your basket and your hug? I am a woman of my word, and I made a promise to your grandma, lord rest her beautiful soul."

Ella stood helpless for a moment as Mrs. Annikov stepped forward, opening her arms. When was the last time she had been hugged?

Ella bent down and into the arms of the small woman, noticing the spicy smell of her perfume. After a moment, Ella let go and took a step back, just as Mrs. Annikov slipped around her and walked over to her kitchen island, where she took up the bottle of vodka and began emptying it into the sink. Ella was too surprised to speak.

"What would your grandma think, you drinking alone in the dark?"asked Mrs. Annikov, as she placed the basket on the counter. "Promise me you won't buy more."

Ella stood paralyzed with shame.

"I don't even know you," Ella whispered.

"But I know *you*, child, and I knew your Grandma, and *that's* the point. I am too old to care about ruffling feathers. Now, I have a letter from your grandma. I am to ask you a few questions," said Mrs. Annikov, pulling a pair of glasses out of her cardigan pocket and balancing them on her nose. "Ready? Are you taking care of yourself?"

Mrs. Annikov paused to survey the studio and looked Ella up and down. Ella remained speechless next to the open door.

"The answer is a definite yes. Alright then, now the second question, did you train today?"

Ella shook her head no and looked down at her feet. She hadn't trained since her Grandma died. She wasn't sure if she would ever dance again.

"Well, it doesn't look like you cooked today, so that is no to question number three as well. Now, let's see, did you learn something new today, and did you do something kind for someone else?"

Ella didn't look up from the floor. Her mind was racing.

Sighing, Mrs. Annikov carefully refolded the letter and placed it back in her pocket.

"I'll take that to be a 'no' to questions four and five. Okay, last question, Ella. Have you found a job?"

"Yes."

"May I ask what it is?"

"I'm a waitress at Flavor," Ella answered, lifting her chin slightly and standing up even straighter.

"Well, isn't that lovely. Now here is what we will do. Can you come over tomorrow night at seven for dinner?"

Ella tilted her head in consideration. Tomorrow she only worked the lunch shift. She nodded her head in agreement.

"Good, then we will talk it all over. I can support you. I know I'm an old woman, but I'll tell you something, little one: I worked for forty-four years with the International Red Cross as a nurse in countries all over the world. I did my part in helping people pull themselves back together after a loss." Mrs. Annikov paused, her face softening as she looked up to the ceiling, lost in thought. She shook her head, refocusing her attention on Ella. "And I will help you, too."

"Could I read it?" asked Ella. "The letter you have from my Grandma, could I read it? Could I… could I have it?"

"I'll tell you what. You can earn it. Can you make sure you are punctual for dinner tomorrow? I'll make one of your Grandma's recipes. Good night, Ella."

As Ella slowly closed the door, she could hear Mrs. Annikov muttering to herself all the way down the stairs. "Months of climbing these stairs. Dear me, I reached her at last…"

Ella stood motionless at the door, tears silently slipping down her cheeks. If only she had opened the door long ago. Ella was no longer alone. She slipped between her silk sheets and fell immediately into a deep and restorative sleep.

THE NEXT MORNING ELLA awoke to a pounding head as if she had drunk an entire bottle of vodka the night before. Only she hadn't touched a drop. Shaky, sweating, and rattling with anxiety, she thought of the insomnia and nightmares she had suffered in the night. She wasn't sure sloshing all her liquor down the drain had been a good idea.

She felt worse than ever. Ella longed for a small shot of liquor before her workday. Just to smooth herself out before she headed to work. It took all her willpower to drink a fresh-pressed orange juice instead.

She struggled through her shift at Flavor and showed up with flowers at the Annikovs' door on time, ghostly pale with dark smudges under her eyes.

"Ella, wonderful to see you dear. This is my husband Sergio," said Mrs. Annikov, the lines around her eyes creasing when she smiled, her blue eyes bright.

A spry man with white hair and piercing blue eyes walked over to the door and shook Ella's hand. "So this is Ella. Your Grandma was one of the most interesting, cultivated women I have ever met. I spent hours listening to her talk about how lovely you are, Ella. It is a pleasure to meet the star in person at last. When are you going to dance for us? We could just move the furniture to the side."

"Now Serge, don't frighten the girl, she just arrived. Come along into the kitchen and enjoy a nice hot tea while I finish the dinner, Ella. Serge, you can set the table and light the candles, love."

"Nice to meet you, Mr. Annikov," said Ella, before following Mrs. Annikov down the hallway.

Mrs. Annikov carefully extracted a letter from a cookbook and handed it to Ella. "Your Grandma told me to give this to you in person."

Ella unfolded the heavy cream envelope and took out a card featuring a stack of books, a cup of coffee and a bouquet of flowers on the front. She opened the card.

Dear Ella,

You told you me yesterday that you didn't know how to carry on all alone. Of course you can. You are a warrior. Think of all the dancers out there already living on their own at the age of fourteen with great self-sufficiency in the pursuit of training. If we were still at home in Russia, you would be at the Vaganova Academy, which takes dancers at age ten.

So I have written you this letter to help you move forward without me. I wish with all my heart it will help you. I have faith in your strength, goodness and resiliency.

My best advice is to establish a routine. It will move you forward each day when you don't have the willpower or strength to design your life toward health and success.

Positive energy flows in a clutter-free, sweet-smelling space, so invest time daily in cleaning your home.

Glamor is a fortifying force. Look elegant, especially when you will be spending the day on your own at home.

Eat regular, healthy meals. Cook yourself fortifying food- the recipes your Mama and I always made for you. You know our recipes by heart.

Spend time everyday training and stick to your daily ballet practice. Search out at least one way every day you can bring kindness into the lives of others. Giving when you feel like you have nothing changes everything. Learn something new every day.

I hope with time you can revel in the beauty and pleasures of day-to-day life: the first cup of espresso in the morning, a perfect rose, the sun warm on your skin after a swim in the lake, the best part of a fabulous book, the warm embrace of someone you love.

The Lord smiled upon me when he gave me such a lovely granddaughter. The best part of my life has been the honor of loving you and your Mama. I believe in you, Ella.

Sending you kisses on the wind, and praying your dreams come true, your Grandma

SETTLED ON A STOOL in the kitchen, a hot drink in her hand and the smell of homemade black bread and pumpkin soup wafting through the room, Ella let out a sigh of relief.

She may still feel trapped in quicksand, but a cool drink had been brought to her parched lips. She was thankful Mrs. Annikov wasn't pestering her with questions. A peaceful quiet lay over the kitchen, the ticking of the clock on the wall, Vivaldi playing in the background.

After a few more minutes, Mrs. Annikov turned to Ella. "So then, we are about ready to eat. Shall we go through your grandma's questions, or shall we wait?"

Ella swallowed too big a gulp of tea, the spicy contents burning her mouth as she nodded wordlessly.

"You look gorgeous, dear. And your flat is sparkling clean?"

"Yes."

"Let's see, the second was the training. You haven't started training yet, have you? There must not even have been time between work and coming here for dinner."

"Actually," said Ella, clearing her throat. "I woke up early and trained this morning."

"Good grief, what time did you wake up this morning in order to do that?"

"Five thirty," replied Ella, feeling a smile wash over her face. "I slept really well last night and woke up early, so I decided to change into my things and do some work at the bar. But I lost all concept of time and space and ended up training for a few hours. I was almost late for work."

"Good for you, Ella. I swore you seemed lighter this evening, brighter somehow. The training must have done you a lot of good," exclaimed Mrs. Annikov, clapping her hands in delight. "Now let's see, did you learn something new? Did you do something kind?"

"No, but I will tomorrow," answered Ella, the smile fading from her face.

"Never you mind, that isn't true. You are here, are you not? That is your act of kindness. And as for learning something new, well, you learned to step right out of bed and to the bar. That is a good lesson."

"I don't think that is what she meant. And it is kind of you to cook me dinner, not for me to be your guest."

Ella patted Mrs. Annikov's arm reassuringly. It was almost as if Mrs. Annikov had failed to complete her grandma's directives, instead of the other way around. She looked so crestfallen.

"Now that is where you are wrong," scolded Mrs. Annikov, shaking a finger at Ella.

"Sometimes accepting a gift or help is a kindness all in itself. It does a body good to feel needed. Now, we are ready for dinner. Please help me carry in the dishes."

Ella walked through to the dining room and admired the red roses on the table, the soft candlelight, the dimmed glow of the crystal chandelier over the table. Mrs. Annikov's fragrant bread and hot soup, the jokes Mr. Annikov told and the love of the old couple for one another warmed her from the inside out. Winding the scarf around her neck, Ella refused a second helping of dessert and gathered her things to go home. At the door, Mrs. Annikov opened her arms and Ella fell into them, wondering that such a small woman could exude so much warmth and strength.

"I have one bit of advice before you go," murmured Mrs. Annikov into Ella's ear. "I know you're still sad. And that's okay. But let the good memories of your mama and grandma flood back in too. They will always be a part of you, in every dance step you take and recipe you cook. Good night, little sun. I wish you sweet dreams."

Ella stepped in the door, and a heavy, peaceful drowsiness descended upon her.

Within minutes she had changed, brushed her teeth, pulled down and climbed into her bed. That night she slept better than she had since before her mother died.

"SUPPORT YOUR ARMS, ELLA. Relax your shoulders. Lift from the back, not from the shoulders! Yes. You need to turnout more, Marie. From the hips, Marie, not the knees. Did you hear me, Marie? Start the turnout from the hip socket, not from the feet. How many times have I told you this? Now you've shifted the weight too much into your heels. Distribute the weight more to the ball of your foot. Good, now practice that at home."

Ella felt eyes traveling over her form. How was it that she always knew when the teacher's focus was turned her way? Ella looked down at her feet. Why wasn't she turned out enough? She hadn't ever had this problem before.

"You need to pull in, Ella. You are over-rotating. Raise your gaze, look in the mirror. It's causing you to hyper extend your lower back. See me after class, and we'll talk more about working on some corrections."

Ella felt her fingers tingling. Her heart was racing faster than a gazelle fleeing a lion. What was so terrible that she needed to stay behind after class? She looked around and saw a few pitying looks. Ella shook her head. How could she go from the best in the class to the worst in just a few months of break?

At the end of class, Ella sat stretching as one by one the other girls left the studio. She felt betrayed by her body. She was finding it near impossible to lower into the splits. Sliding into the splits had always had always been like slipping into warm water.

How hadn't she noticed her body tightening, winding in, compressing, until today? Before her muscles had extended, they now felt taut and static. Where power and strength lifted and elongated, she felt a hollow emptiness.

"Ella? It's wonderful to see you again dear."

"I haven't danced in some time."

"Yes, that's what I wanted to talk to you about, Ella. I'm afraid I have to be frank with you. You have a slight version of lower crossed syndrome. Your abdominals have weakened, your hip flexors and lower back tightened, your butt needs strengthening. You were at one time our most promising dancer. But I can't welcome you back into this class in your condition. I'm worried you will suffer injury. And I would sincerely dissuade you from pointe work. Your feet have lost their strength. You need to go back to the fundamentals and work on your turnout and conditioning."

Ella walked out of the studio. Her ears were still burning. Laughter broke out behind her. A crowd of teenagers were standing beside the studio door.

"Not so self-satisfied now, are you, Ella?" asked Marie. "Now that your mother's gone, there is no one to give you an unfair advantage."

"Marie," reproached Anna. "That's mean. I'm sorry, Ella. You'll just have to work hard to catch up."

"So many hours of dancing every day? Like she ever will be able to catch that up," snorted Marie. "And don't act like you are above the rest of us, Anna. Don't tell me you're not relieved. Now you're the best dancer in the academy."

Anna's face flushed and her eyes turned toward the floor.

Ella ran from the girls in the hallway, ignoring Anna's 'wait, Ella' and flew down the stairs and out into the cold air.

Somewhere deep inside, Ella had held on to the belief that she never had any friends because she was the best. It was ballet; it was envy barring her way to a circle of laughing friends. Now she was the worst in the class, and that belief was punctured.

She was never going back. With each step, Ella's resolution grew, the safety of her studio flat beckoning. She needn't face those girls again, that teacher, or any teacher for that matter. At home she would be safe, alone in her four walls. Marie thought she had lost her unfair advantage. Well, she hadn't, not entirely. No one could appreciate the neuroticism of her mother. She had planned for every contingency, even her death. Hours of ballet class instruction were awaiting Ella at home. All she needed to do was press play. But first she had her shift at the restaurant to work.

Chapter 4

She was stressed. She knew it from the way Ella kept rubbing the back of her neck with her hand, the way energy spilled out of her, skittering out into the room via her tapping foot. She couldn't see Ella's face from where she stood, but she knew her brow would be furrowed, her mouth set in a firm line.

She had never seen a friend pick her up from work, nor family stop by the restaurant. Ella was always alone, which meant she could be the perfect target.

Her heart began beating wildly in her chest as Ella passed by the bar on her way home. Ella's shift was over. Would Ella recognize her? As per usual, Ella didn't look her way.

Outside the windows, darkness was descending, hurtling its weight onto the city, the streetlights buttresses holding out the gloom. During the day, the streets were filled with people like brightly colored fish, swimming their way along the Bahnhofstrasse, their footsteps drowning together into one wave of sound.

But the streets were quieting now, footsteps echoing. She couldn't follow her home.

She motioned to Nathan that she was ready to pay for his drink, but he smiled at her and shook his head on the way to serve a drink across the bar.

"It's on the house," he mouthed with a wink.

She returned his smile, left the restaurant and made her way out onto the street. Ella was gone. The lake front was empty. The luxury shop windows of the Bahnhofstrasse blurred past as she went through her plan in all its detail once again. Tomorrow she could spend the entire day lying in wait for her.

It wasn't enough to watch her at the restaurant anymore. She needed to know about Ella's every movement, both awake and sleeping. Then she would know if she was the perfect selection. There was work to do.

Chapter 5

Ella pulled up the collar of her wool coat against the cold. She wrapped her sky-blue scarf intricately around her neck in a warm knot before opening the door to the restaurant. Glancing at her watch, she realized she had just missed her tram home.

She decided to walk. As snowflakes began drifting down, she opened her pink umbrella and began the kilometer walk home. As she walked along the cobbled stone street, her muscles warm and loose from a yoga class, pride swelled in her chest thinking back on her past week.

Her hair smelled of chlorine from her daily kilometer swim at the indoor pool. She had eaten a healthy dinner every night at the restaurant across from her work. She planned to go shopping on Saturday and visit the farmers market. She was ready to start cooking her mother's and grandmother's recipes. All the alcohol had been poured down her sink.

Every time the bottle sang its sweet siren song, Ella had picked up her dance slippers instead.

Ella rolled her shoulders back, wincing. She was sore from the hours of barre work and dancing, despite the loosening effect of the daily yoga and swimming. Ella expected to feel exhausted. Instead she was revitalized, sore, but renewed. Even her boss Nick had noticed the change in her at work.

Ella turned the corner and paused in mid-step, ensuring

the new dance leotard she had picked up on her lunch break was in her purse.

That was when she noticed she was being followed. The hairs on her neck stood on end. She sensed eyes upon her. Ella scanned the street. It was empty of movement.

Then behind her: a muffled cough. In the shadows just around the corner from which she came, she stopped. The profile of dark figure was outlined by a street lamp in the darkness. She started walking, the heels of her boots echoing on the sidewalk. Footsteps echoed behind her. Looking over her shoulder, she saw no one.

She quickened her pace. Ella began to run and heard the steps matching her pace. Up ahead, the lights of the nursing home radiated out into the darkness, its windows exuding security. Ella sprinted down the block and up the stairs. Stepping through the doors of the nursing home, she looked out behind her at the street. It was empty.

A woman with dark hair pulled back into a tight ponytail sat behind the reception desk typing. She came out from around the reception desk when she noticed Ella standing in the front entrance.

"Excuse me? Are you looking for a resident's room number?"

Ella cleared her throat. She didn't know what to say. "No, I don't know a particular resident."

"Oh, then you must be the young woman who called earlier. I thought you decided against coming and volunteering with us? Or did you decide five evenings a week wasn't too much time investment for you after all?"

"What?" Ella hadn't called. But then again, she decided, it was a good idea, volunteering here.

"Actually, I decided I was interested. I mean, I am interested in volunteering. On a regular basis. This nursing home is on my walk home from work, so it would be very convenient."

Two soft, kind eyes looked back at her, and a warm smile spread over the face of the dark-haired woman.

Ella's shoulders loosened a bit, her breath slowing.

"Are you a nurse? Do you have and training in caring for the elderly?"

Ella just shook her head no. She turned toward the door.

Zürich was one of the most affluent cities in the world, but even Zürich had its share of the lonely, the poor and the marginalized. She would have to try somewhere else tomorrow, she decided. It would be a lot easier if she had a cell phone or a laptop like most people.

"Wait," called out the woman, "please don't leave. We have a volunteer position you could be interested in."

Ella turned back.

"My name is Alice. We are happy to have volunteers to provide companionship for our residents. Some of them have so few visitors, or none at all. Others have visitors, but they get bored. Are you willing to play games, organize crafts and other activities or read to our residents? We are looking for a volunteer willing to invest one hour a day, five days a week with us."

Ella paused, thinking.

"Yes. I would be interested in the position. I would be able to come from ten to eleven Monday through Friday."

"Very nice, our weekends are rather busy, but the weeks are quite lonely for many. The timing would also be perfect. Are you ready to fill out the paperwork tonight? It's just a page."

"Yes, certainly," answered Ella.

"Beautiful. We could use a fresh face around here to add some new energy to the place. When would you like to start?"

Warmth flooded Ella's cheeks. "Now?"

"Why not?" responded Alice. "Here is the form for you to fill out."

Ella carefully filled out the form and handed it to Alice.

"Now that's done, you can follow me to the dining hall. Where are you from, by the way? Your German is perfect, but there is an accent I can't place."

Ella realized she hadn't had to answer this question in years. That was one of the reasons she had isolated herself. Innocent questions such as this one were very difficult, and possibly dangerous, to answer. What should she say?

"I guess I am rather a citizen of the world. I have lived so many different places in my life."

Alice nodded. "You know what, I have a very good friend who feels the exact same way you do. He feels as if he belongs everywhere and nowhere at all. He said it is both liberating and disheartening all at the same time."

"I agree with him," answered Ella.

"So, here we are. For this first night, I will set you up with a game of Personality. It is many of the residents' favorite game. They will teach you the rules. Tomorrow I will leave it up to you to decide how you would like to share your time with them. The best would be if you could make a weekly schedule for me to post. Then those who are interested in your activity can be sure not to miss out on the action. Once I introduce you, I will leave you on your own. My shift is over and my kids are waiting for me at home."

"Good evening everyone," called out Alice to the hall full of residents. "This is Ella and she is a new volunteer. She would like to play Personality for the next hour with anyone who is interested. Now see you all tomorrow."

"See you tomorrow," replied Ella as she lowered herself into the chair at the table Alice set the game down upon. Six residents made their way to Ella's table. Some walked sprightly, some shuffled forward with a walker. As soon as all the places at the table were taken, a man took it upon himself to distribute the cards.

Ella took a deep breath and said, "Hi, my name is Ella. I have the privilege to spend the next hour to play this game with you. Who can explain to me the rules of this game?"

HOME AT LAST. Ella took off her shoes and carried her grocery bags into the kitchen. She extracted vibrant plumeria in yellow and pink from the paper and placed them in a crystal vase. The light sweet smell wafted up from the vase, making her smile. Free flowers were a definite perk of working in a restaurant. These would die the next day, but they were still pretty tonight.

Setting the vase of plumeria on the cherry wood table next to her reading chair, she returned to the kitchen and took one single bird of paradise out of the wrappings and placed it in a vase on her marble kitchen island.

Next she took out vegetables and herbs fresh from the farmers' market she had visited on her way home and put away the rest of the groceries. Tonight she would cook a real meal. At last a strength was rising in her. She was following her Grandmother's instructions.

As the smell of garlic and basil filled the room, she began kneading the dough for black bread, chopping up carrots, cucumbers, avocado, roma tomatoes and cilantro to add to her arugula salad leaves, dark and glistening. The heat of the room drove Ella to the window, opening it to let in a cool rush of night air.

The scene playing out across the street caused bile to rise in her throat. It was happening again. It was like watching a movie in mute mode. It was clear they were fighting from the way her neighbor was gesturing. As per usual, her husband was just standing there as still as a statue. The dark-haired wife picked up a wine glass from the glass shelf and threw it at her husband's head. Taken by surprise, he didn't have the time to duck. The wine glass hit him in the face, knocking his glasses to the floor.

As the wife picked up another wine glass, he fled to the bedroom. Either he had locked the door, or his wife decided not to come after him, because he stood in the room alone. He walked to the floor-length mirror and checked his face. From this far away, she couldn't make out if he was cut.

She wanted a drink. If you want a drink, then you will train, Ella repeated to herself. The mantra had provided an excellent alternate plan to handling her negative feelings. Two weeks after she had quit, her skin had a natural glow, and she was sleeping better. She didn't want to start again. She wondered when liquor would stop singing to her like a siren, luring her to the rocks with its song.

In the kitchen, she tossed the simmering garlic, butter, fresh basil leaves, salty black olives and roma tomatoes together with wholegrain noodles and diced prosciutto.

She set three glasses of sparkling mineral water on the table, along with her vegetable platter and the pasta dish. As a last thought, she lit candles in her grandmother's candlesticks, watching the glow of the candles dance on the wooden table. A few minutes later came a soft knock at the door.

"Ella, our little sun, how lovely of you to invite us in and cook for us in your beautiful home," said Mrs. Annikov while opening her arms for a hug.

"It smells delicious," said Mr. Annikov, handing Ella a Russian Napoleon cake.

"Thank you by the way, dear, for that flower you dropped by tonight on your way home was just exquisite, what is that called?"

"A bird of paradise."

"Well, how delightful."

"I am famished and it smells delicious." said Mr. Annikov.

"Yes, please sit down," smiled Ella, giving Mr. Annikov a quick hug. "Let's eat."

Once the Annikovs had returned home downstairs and the kitchen was clean, Ella sagged with exhaustion.

Yet despite the fatigue, anxiety was nibbling at her nerve endings, causing her short, irregular breaths. Changing into her leotard and tights, pinning her hair up, Ella's thoughts were of the neighbors across the street.

If you feel like a drink, then you will train. Repeating the mantra aloud, Ella began pulling off her work clothes and slipped on a leotard and her ballet shoes. Music poured into the room, filling her like a vessel, pulsing and expanding within her as she began her ballet exercises. Her thoughts turned to her mother, of all the evenings, her homework complete, they had changed into leotards together, pulling on ballet shoes.

She could almost feel her mother's presence behind her as she began to warm up at the bar. 'Head up, angel,' she could hear her whisper, 'neck long...'

Thirty minutes later, she stepped away from the bar, ready to dance. The music gathered her up, and she glided around the small space, joy flickering tentatively within her, daring to take hold.

ELLA OPENED THE DOOR to her flat and took off her shoes with a soft smile still on her face, the remnants of laughter glowing like embers on her lips and in her eyes. They had given her a cake tonight, to celebrate a year of volunteering. She wasn't sure who was helping whom at the nursing home. With each evening she spent with the residents of the center, the fissures in her heart were mending.

The Annikovs had noted the change in Ella immediately and they had encouraged her to continue her engagement at the nursing home. In turn, she had started cooking lunch for the Annikovs every Saturday and taking them out for a slow walk along the river afterward. Two weeks previously, they had started having lunch together with his wife Julie before the restaurant opened. A new life was starting to build up, once again filled with relationships that gave her life a richness and vibrancy.

Stretching, Ella quickly changed into her leotard and ballet shoes and turned on the music. The room was stuffy, so she went to open the room to the cool night air. Below her, the neighbor was sitting at the dining room table. Notes and papers nearly covered the wooden surface on which he rested his elbows, his eyebrows furrowed together in concentration. Ella noted that he had been working late into the night for weeks now. She wondered what he was working on. Where was the wife? She scanned the flat. Just then the wife walked into the room and over behind her husband, reaching her arms around him and resting her head on his shoulder, looking down at what he was reading.

Maybe things have improved over there, thought Ella, seconds before Owen sat up straight and pushed her arms away from him. The wife walked around the side of the table, obviously yelling something. He didn't even look up. For over ten minutes, Ella found herself glued to the window. The neighbor was yelling, her hands gesticulating, while he just stood there, continuing to make notes as if he were alone in the room.

Get out of there, Ella wanted to shout, as the wife walked into the kitchen, took the huge glass bowl of oranges and threw it as hard as she could toward the back of her husband's head. The bowl hit him in the shoulders before falling to the floor, shattering into splinters at his heels. Still, he didn't look up from his work. Ella was horrified.

The wife stormed out of the flat. He sat motionless. Craning her neck, she could see her neighbor striding down the street toward the lake. She turned her attention back to the flat. He was still just sitting there. Ella began to panic. Was he seriously injured? Should I call for help? A moment later, Ella watched him stand up, efficiently clean up the mess with a dustpan from under the kitchen sink and return to his work.

Ella turned on her music and began her daily hour-and-a-half long ballet training. The scene that had played out across the street fought for purchase in her consciousness, but she let the music fill her, focusing on the grace and fluidity of her movements, until all that was left was each breath, each note of the song vibrating in the room.

Ella strolled along the street on her way home, thinking over about the hour of private ballet instruction she had saved up for. She had been told she needed to work on her hip flexibility and develop her 'process of learning.' Whatever that meant.

Her core needed strengthening still, and her muscles needed lengthening. She made a mental note to join a yoga class once a week.

"Are you stalking me?" called a voice.

Ella looked up and into the intense green eyes of Owen. He was striding toward her from the opposite direction. Heat flamed in her face.

"Don't be silly. I could just as easily accuse you of the same thing. This is my street."

Owen paused in mid-step.

His body went rigid for a fraction of a second before he pushed his hands through his blond hair and laughed. "Very funny. Why wouldn't you have mentioned this is your street the past two times we ran into each other?"

"Why would I mention my address?"

"This is my street too."

"Is it?" asked Ella.

She hoped her act of surprise appeared genuine.

"Well, what a weird coincidence. Why haven't we ever run into each other before? It's good to see you."

"Right back at you, Owen," parried Ella. The interaction was making her uneasy. He was acting strange. Nervous.

"Shouldn't you be at work? It is the middle of the afternoon. Do you have the day off?"

"When I have a difficult problem to think through, I like to walk. Or go rowing. I'm free to come and go as I please. I just badge in and out so my hours can be totaled for the month. Often I work late into the night."

Ella frowned slightly, puzzled. Why was he lying to her? He was always home in the evenings, at the latest in time for his nine o'clock swim on the terrace. Or had something changed in the past week? Had he started working late to avoid his wife? Had she noticed that? Ella wasn't sure.

She had stopped her voyeurism most days. It upset her too much to see him mistreated and while she was powerless to intervene. Most nights she chose to avoid the window, visiting the Annikovs, dancing, or curling up in bed with a good new book and a cup of tea instead.

"Are you sure you aren't working late to avoid your home life?" Ella covered her mouth with her hand. "I'm sorry," she mumbled. "I shouldn't pry."

Owen shrugged his shoulders, looking down at his shoes. "Yeah, well, maybe you are right. It could be a bit of both, perhaps. Listen, I better head back to the office. But it was good to see you Ella."

Ella smiled. "Goodbye, Owen."

Just as she turned to go, Owen's fingers shot out and grabbed her hand. She looked back at Owen with raised eyebrows as he stared down at his hand holding hers.

"If you give me your number, I could meet you for a coffee or a drink sometime."

"You should come by my restaurant sometime. The food is delicious, and the terrace a delight. You could come by on your lunch break with your colleagues. It's called Flavor. Do you know it?"

"Your restaurant?" asked Owen, his smile almost a smirk.

"Well, the restaurant I waitress at anyway," said Ella.

Owen was giving her a quizzical look. "I thought you were a ballerina."

Ella sighed, looked down at her feet, then back up at him. He stared back at her, waiting for a response.

"Training to be one, anyway, but until then I have to earn money somehow."

"Well then Ella, I might just have to stop by and have the prettiest ballerina in Zürich serve me a cold after-work beer."

The heat in her face spread all the way to her ears. "Are you flirting with me, Owen something or other?"

Owen's face clouded over, and he adjusted his glasses on his nose while clearing his throat. "Of course not. I'm a married man. I was just, er, stating the obvious. So, hi ho, hi ho, I got me lots of work to go," sang Owen, swinging his arms and dramatically simulating a march. "Goodbye Ella."

Ella laughed out loud, taken by surprise by his silliness. "That's not how it goes. You really need to work on your English, Mr. Meier."

Owen laughed with her, "Oh yeah, do you know someone who could help me?"

"Yeah, me. My English is flawless."

"Are you flirting with me, Miss Ella something or other?" asked Owen, the grin reaching his eyes.

"Of course not," she answered. "Why would I want to flirt with an old guy like you?"

"What! Thirty-two is not old."

"Yeah, well it is if you aren't quite eighteen," responded Ella, pushing Owen on the shoulder.

"I'm afraid that is true. You win, beautiful. I will leave you to the immature, penniless men of your age group. Maybe I'll see you at your restaurant."

"Maybe I could give you my number…" began Ella. But he had already turned away. The gravel crunched beneath his feet as he walked away, leaving Ella standing alone in the wind, listening to his footsteps echoing in the void.

CHAPTER 6

ELLA PLACED THE FINAL GARNISH on the four huckleberry lemon vodka martinis and picked up the tray. Her face hurt from smiling all day at new customers. Her shoulders and neck hurt from carrying trays of drinks out to the terrace, and she was extremely hungry. It was going on seven at night, and she hadn't had a bite to eat since breakfast. They hadn't expected such a large turnout on a Thursday. Ella was almost through the door to the terrace when the bells of the front door to the restaurant chimed.

"Ella! So this place is in a great location. If the food is as good as the view, you have a new loyal customer."

At the sound of his voice, every inch her skin began tingling. Ella stood frozen for a moment before turning around.

"Owen, it is good to see you. Just let me deliver these drinks, and I will be right back."

On the way outside to the patio, Ella tried to take deep and even breaths, but her pulse was throbbing in her throat. Ella returned inside. Owen was standing by the door, looking around at the décor.

"I like the raw stone walls and modern steel chandeliers juxtaposed against the warm cherry wood of the tables and chairs," he said with a smile.

"Just wait until you see the terrace, my friend. It is an oasis of relaxation and rejuvenation," said Ella, beaming.

"Oh we are friends now, are we? You sure must have a lot of friends if every time you run into a bloke a few times you add them to your contact list," teased Owen.

"If we are friends, you best come and greet me properly."

Ella was at a loss for what to do. She just stood there. Owen bridged the distance between them; placing his hands gently on her shoulders, he leaned in and kissed her directly on the left cheek, then the right and again on the left.

Ella breathed in deeply. Owen smelled of cedar wood, sage, chlorine and a hint of lavender. Home. He smelled like a male version of home. Ella imagined what it would be like to fall into this man, her lips on his neck, his hands in her hair, whispering over her skin.

"You smell delicious," murmured Owen as he took a step back. "Ella?" Owen was standing before her with raised eyebrows. "Are you feeling alright?"

Heat spread out over her skin, and she opened her eyes. How long had she been standing there like that?

"It's a citrus lavender blend lotion. I make it myself," said Ella, lifting her wrist out to him.

Looking her in the eye, Owen took her outstretched hand and lifted her inner wrist slowly to his nose. There was the faintest caress of his lips against her skin as he inhaled deeply, holding her gaze as he did so.

Ella snatched her arm away as the restaurant door opened. Three men and two women walked into the entry. Ella busied herself with retying the black apron around her waist as she recomposed herself. Owen appeared to be unfazed.

"Owen! Sorry we are late. That last meeting of the day lasted an eternity. So, this place does look good. I'm starving, what do they have on the menu?" asked a short man with dark curly hair and brown eyes.

"I'm glad you made it, Lionel. I was ready to order a drink without you," said Owen, clapping Lionel on the back while shaking his hand.

Owen greeted the other two men with handshakes before turning his attention to the women. Ella smiled in satisfaction when she noticed he gave three air kisses to each woman, instead of kissing them directly on the cheek.

"I'm sorry, the restaurant isn't open for dinner tonight. The whole place has been rented out for a wedding starting in an hour. We are serving drinks, cocktails and appetizers on the terrace, though. Stay and I will bring you out a pitcher of our signature drink on the house," said Ella.

"Well then, what do you all think? Shall we enjoy a round of drinks and share some appetizers here and then head down to the pizzeria for dinner?" suggested Owen.

Ella waited for the round of agreement and then led them out onto the terrace. Pride welled up in Ella's chest at the exclamations of surprise from Owen and his colleagues as they walked out into the rose-scented summer night air.

In the middle of the patio, flames roared from a modern marble rectangular fireplace, while candlelight danced from the huge candelabras placed around the huge terrace. Large white oval containers overflowed with lavender, roses, daisies, hydrangea, peppermint and lemon grass.

Men and women lounged in groupings on black, eggshell shaped wicker chairs or in zero gravity lounge chairs. In the corner of the terrace, a couple cuddled together on a sleek white porch swing.

Ella led them to the end of the terrace and to the seating area directly next to the new clear-glassed infinity pool, the aquamarine of the water reflecting through the glass in the evening sunlight. Lionel was the first to sit down. As he relaxed back in a chair, his feet elevated up to the same level as his heart.

"Wow, you guys are going to love these. I feel weightless in this chair," said Lionel, placing his hands behind his hand and looking up at the sky. "I've never sat in a chair like this."

"It's called a zero gravity chair. They are supposed to make you feel weightless and relaxed. They are quite common in the United States, but I haven't seen a restaurant with them in Switzerland yet, and certainly not these high design versions," explained Ella. "Now, I'll leave you to look at the drink list while I attend to the other guests for a moment."

Ella quickly made the rounds, running for new drinks from the bar and ordering new appetizers from the cooks in the kitchen. Her heart was hammering in her throat as she set her empty platter on the bar.

"Thank goodness we have two extra servers and someone to help with the appetizers coming tomorrow night," said the chef Nick. "We are swarmed like bees to a honey hive, and it isn't even Friday night! The first few days of warm weather and everyone comes out of hibernation. How are you doing out there?"

"I'm literally running from table to table," said Ella.

"Well, shall we call it a day in thirty minutes and close the terrace to focus our energy on the wedding? You have been going nonstop since this afternoon, Ella."

"No way, this is great. We don't want to send away potential recurring customers," said Ella.

"I say it as I see, and I say you need to take a break, eat something and put your feet up for a moment," insisted the chef. "I need you in top form for the wedding. I will send out one of my cooks to cover for you for twenty minutes. There haven't been any new appetizer orders."

"Except ours," said a voice behind them. "If it wasn't for those relaxing chairs, my friends would have given up and headed for the pizzeria already. They're hungry."

"I'm so sorry, Owen. Owen, this is the chef, Nick Mueller. And you can't give up one of your cooks, Nick."

"It looks like you are a bit short if serving staff tonight," commented Owen with raised eyebrows.

"Too true, Ella here has been on her feet since early this morning. We decided to open the terrace today on the chance a few people would happen by for a drink. We just weren't expecting a crowd like this on a Thursday," said Nick.

"Well, let me help Ella, and she can have a bit of a break. Hand me your drink list and your appetizer menu, and I'll do my best to keep guests happy. I'll work for free appetizers and drinks for my friends and I."

"Do you even know how to mix drinks?" asked Ella.

"Sure. I worked in Florida at the Club Med All-Inclusive resort for a year as a bartender. I bet I am even better than you are," said Owen.

"Seriously? How is your English so terrible then?" blurted out Ella. "And what about your friends? What will they think about you abandoning them and serving drinks?"

"They won't care as long as they have food and drinks in front of them."

"Great, then come back in ten minutes, and I will have a large cheese platter with spinach and artichoke dip and another of coconut shrimp appetizers ready to go. You can give them this pitcher of Saffron Mojito cocktails on the house," said Nick. "They're made with saffron-infused gin, saffron syrup, lime, orange juice and Moroccan mint."

"I can't let you do my job," insisted Ella to Owen.

"What are friends for?" asked Owen as he grabbed a black apron off the counter and headed back out to the terrace without a backward glance.

"A friend of yours? Or a boyfriend?" asked Nick as Owen left the kitchen with a tray of drinks.

"I don't even know his last name. We have just bumped into each other a few times."

"I don't like the look of him," replied Nick. "Don't you get yourself any ideas about that one. You don't need an old man like that."

"It's not like that," insisted Ella. "He's married."

"Heaven help me, it gets even worse. Here is some dinner, Ella. Go put your feet up. The wedding will be a long night."

"I'll be back in thirty minutes," called Ella over her shoulder as she headed for the stairs.

She let out a sigh of relief. Halfway up the stairs, Ella realized she had forgotten her drink on the counter. She entered the hallway, but paused before rounding the corner to the kitchen when she heard Nick's voice.

"You listen to me, dude. You stay away from my Ella. Don't think I don't have eyes, because I do."

"Nick," came a deep baritone voice. "You have it all wrong. Ella was the one making a play for me. Ask Ella. I am a happily married man. You have nothing to worry about."

Nauseous hit Ella's stomach, bile rising in her throat. Shame flooded through her, prickling along her skin like tiny piranhas snatching bites from a submerged victim. She didn't know how she would go back downstairs and face him. She ate her dinner without tasting the grilled veal sausage from

St. Gallen with apple mustard and sautéed grated potatoes.

At the entrance to the terrace, Ella stood paralyzed for a moment, watching Owen carry a large tray of drinks over his head to a new gathering of six guests in the seating area under the climbing roses. Owen laughed, bantering with the guests. When he turned around, he caught her watching him and winked.

The piranhas were back. Her blood was seeping out into the inky water. She fought the urge to run her hands up and down along her arms, her legs, to fend off the unseen creatures nibbling at her skin.

Owen picked up two tables worth of empty glasses and made his way to Ella inside the doorway.

When he stepped inside the door to the restaurant, Ella smiled at him and reached out a hand for his apron. "You are now relieved from your servitude. Go in peace and enjoy your freedom," she said.

"I will toast my freedom with a large weizen. Care to join me?" he laughed.

"I wish I could," replied Ella. "But I have drinks to serve. Can I bring you a free round of drinks for your circle of friends instead?"

"My friends have headed down to the pizzeria, so I'll go join them. I can come back up after dinner, though, and help you with that wedding. You look really tired." Owen reached out a hand and gently pushed a loose strand of her hair behind her ear. "Are you okay Ella? Something seems…wrong."

Ella froze at the feel of his rough fingers on her skin. "Would your wife be okay with you coming home so late?" she asked.

Owen's eyes grew round. His shoulders hunched forward. "Yeah, I should get home after dinner to the wife. You're right. Good night, Ella."

Ella was shocked at the evaporation of Owen's good humor and confidence. It was as if he had withered up in front of her, all merriment gone from his eyes, the steel rod spine now rounded forward.

"Owen," she called. Without thinking, her hand shot out and grabbed his hand. "Thank you for your help. I hope I see you again. I mean, I hope you come again."

"It would be good to see you again too, Ella," said Owen, brushing his hand gently through her hair, then tracing a caress down the back of her long neck.

"You had some fluff from the cotton tree in your hair."

"Thanks," Ella smiled, her heart leaping in her chest like a flying fish. "Wait, what's that?" Reaching out, she pulled back the unbuttoned collar of his designer green dress shirt, revealing a purple bruise spreading down over his shoulder.

He grabbed her wrist in a vise-like grip, then froze when his eyes met hers.

"It was her, wasn't it Owen?" asked Ella. Her fingers were still on his neck, under his collar; his calloused fingers were still wrapped around her wrist. Anger seized Ella as she looked at the mark and could imagine all too well how he had received the blow that caused it.

"Was it the fruit bowl again?"

"What? No. It was a rowing accident."

"Liar," she breathed. She was close enough she could feel the warmth of his breath on her cheek, feel his body heat radiating toward her in the darkness. "You deserve someone who would shower you with kisses and adoration, Owen. Not abuse you."

"You wouldn't understand, Ella. Don't mention it to anyone. Promise me."

"Owen…"

"No," he pulled her by her wrist around the corner, down the steps into the tiny alcove one story below the terrace. Pulling her in close, he whispered in her ear, "You can't mention anything to anyone I work with, Ella."

"No, of course I wouldn't. Why would I? But you can't let her do this to you Owen," she reached her hand up, gently tracing the bruise on his chest again.

His eyes closed at her touch, his grip on her wrist loosening. He took a shuddering breath, shaking himself slightly before reopening his eyes just in time to see her place her other hand on his chest, lift up on her toes and press her lips against his. A moan rumbled in his chest as she wrapped her hands around his broad shoulders, pressing against him. His hands encircled her, drinking her in.

Ella's body began pulsing as the neighbor's hands traced along her neck, then caressed down her back. His tongue parted her lips. She drank him in, pressing her body to his.

Abruptly he pulled back, hiding his eyes with one hand. "Lord help me, I'm so sorry, Ella. I shouldn't have let that happen. You're gorgeous; I lost my head. It won't happen again." He leaned forward and kissed her on the left cheek, right cheek and again on the left.

Looking over Ella's shoulder, he stiffened. Ella looked behind her. Nick was glaring at Owen from above them on the terrace. He disappeared again, and Ella grabbed at Owen's arm as he turned away from her to leave.

"Owen, I want to tell you something."

"Oh Ella," said Owen, cradling her cheek with one hand. "The very best thing would be to forget this happened. It would be safer. You don't know what my wife's capable of. If she ever found out…"

"You should leave," breathed out Ella.

Owen smiled sadly, "Maybe I will see you tomorrow, yeah?"

Ella's eyes followed Owen as he strode down the hill toward the pizzeria. Owen glanced back and saw her still watching him. She stood up on her toes and blew him a kiss.

She saw him smile as he turned the corner and disappeared out of sight.

Ella walked back up the stairs and collected empty dishes on her way to the kitchen. Nick glared at her as she set the dishes next to the sink.

"What are you doing, Ella? That jerk is married."

"I just lost my head for a moment. It was stupid. It won't happen again. We'll just be friends, Nick."

"Yeah, well, hey, we all do stupid things some times right? I want you to meet my new sous chef, Adnan. His German isn't very good yet, but his cuisine makes up for his lack of language skills. Besides, I like it quiet in my kitchen. Hey, Adnan," called out Nick. "Meet my best waitress and now new manager of the front of the house, Ella."

"Pleased meeting you," said a handsome dark-haired man, nodding his head at her and smiling while continuing to stir a lime-green sauce.

"Wait, what? You are putting me in charge of the service team, Nick? It's a pleasure to meet you Adnan. Welcome."

"That's right Ella. It comes with a small pay raise too."

Adnan's smile grew even bigger. He nodded his head at her again in congratulations, and Ella returned his smile. Things were improving.

The move of his lips on hers, his fingers caressing her skin, the warmth of his body pressed against hers in the moonlight replayed in a constant loop. Before, he had been removed from her through glass. Now he was close enough to reach out and touch.

And he was ignoring her.

He was still pretending like the kiss hadn't happened.

"I'll have the fresh caught fish with truffle polenta and grilled vegetables Provençale, followed by a café crème. Actually, is it possible to have a second bottle of cucumber water? I'm parched after my swim in the lake."

Ella nodded, placing a hand on Owen's shoulder. "Sure. So how is your work coming along?"

"Could you get that order in to the kitchen, Ella? I don't have much of my lunch break left."

"Of course."

Ella spirits were dragging along behind her, a shadow grasping her heels. Today was more of the same, then. A tiny spark flared before her eyes. She turned on her heel to give Owen a piece of her mind, but when she saw him, her words caught in her throat.

A white bandage was peeking out of the collar of his blue dress shirt. She closed the distance between them and lightly traced her fingers on the back of his neck, just above the injury. It was as if an ice cube had been slipped down Owen's shirt. He sat up straight then spun around, catching her wrist in a steely grasp.

She raised her eyebrows. "Did she do this?"

He let go of her wrist and turned away, deflating before her eyes like a popped helium balloon.

"It's complicated."

Ella sighed and sat down in the chair next to him, leaning

forward. "It's abuse. You don't deserve this."

"Yeah, well, you don't really know me. I probably deserve it more than you think."

Ella reached out, covering his hand with her own. "I'm scared for you."

Owen barked out a laugh that turned the heads of guests at nearby tables. "It's a joke, isn't it? She's half my size."

Ella just continued to look at him, saying nothing, waiting.

He shook his head, running both hands through his hair.

He looked out of the window at the lake for a moment, before continuing. "No one would even believe me. She's so charismatic. I mean, her work colleagues, her friends and acquaintances, they all love her."

"Owen, I believe this is happening," said Ella, waiting for Owen to stop scanning the room. His eyes met hers, and her breath caught in her throat at the intensity of the anguish in his eyes. "You deserve a healthy, non-violent relationship, Owen. I'm here for you if you need me," she said, and then hurried back to her work.

CHAPTER 7

AT LAST, THE FINAL CUSTOMERS DEPARTED. Ella took out the dinner Adnan had left warming for her and walked to a table near the window. The twenty-four hour braised short rib melted in her mouth. Ella was just about to taste the glazed pearl onions and sweet mashed potatoes when she heard footsteps were echoing in the empty restaurant. Someone was walking toward the kitchen.

She had thought she was the last one in the restaurant. Her heart jumped into her mouth, pain searing through her elbow from knocking against the wall in her angst.

"Ella?"

Ella breathed a sigh of relief as she turned around.

"Adnan, what are you doing here? I thought everyone was gone. You gave me such a fright."

"Sorry, Ella. New idea for dish wanting to try," answered Adnan with a wide grin.

"Hey, Ella," said Nick, coming out from the terrace. "Do you want to lock up?" he said, pointing toward the front door. "I'm on my way out."

"You're still here too? What were you doing on the terrace, Nick?" asked Ella.

"After the last customer left, I headed out and kicked back in one of those zero gravity chairs with a ginger mojito," answered Nick, rubbing the curly beard on his face with his hand and then rolling his shoulders back.

"I must have fallen asleep for a few minutes."

"So who are you going to replace Holly with? She told me she's moving to Italy to be with her new boyfriend."

"We'll need a new server," said Nick. "Finding someone who will give that little extra charm every day is so hard to find in Switzerland."

Adnan brightened. "Aya!"

"Does she speak German?"

"She learning fast. Not like me. No problem. Hard working too," said Adnan, nodding his head while spreading out his hands in earnestness. "Like me."

"That's actually a good idea," answered Nick. "I'll figure out how to apply to have your wife join you here Adnan," said Nick, while starting to sear a steak at the same time.

"He had to leave her in Syria," he explained to Ella. "Isn't that terrible? You can't imagine how much he misses her. Tears run down his cheeks when he looks at her picture. He has it taped inside the spice cupboard and looks at it a few times a day."

Ella shook her head.

We know but a fragment of the truth that is a life story, she thought, even if we spend hours working with them every day, for months and years.

"Thousand thank you Nick," began Adnan.

Nick interrupted him. "Think nothing of it, man, you're an amazing sous chef." He yawned. "Now I'm heading home to the wife. See you all tomorrow."

"I'm going too," agreed Ella. "I'm exhausted."

"No, you trying dish. Come, come Ella," insisted Adnan, beckoning her.

With a sigh, Ella turned from the door and followed Adnan into the kitchen. She sat on the kitchen counter for the next hour, chatting with Adnan as he tried the dish one way, then another, tweaking some elements and offering Ella bite after bite for evaluation. Adnan's happiness was contagious.

He positively radiated joy as he told Ella the story of how he first met his wife, of their wedding, the funny little things she did that he found so annoying, yet endearing. Like the way she left only ever drank half of a coffee, leaving the half-empty cups everywhere. Oftentimes, the words failed Adnan and he turned to charades to communicate.

"I wake up, shirt all wet. What?" mimed Adnan, looking at the ceiling. "Is working?" he pointed at the roof. "No, no, is wife in sleep. Head here," he laughed, opening his mouth, tilting his head to the side as he faked a loud snore. "Is wife sleeping on me like so and water coming on shirt." He shook his head smiling.

"Drool, you mean she drools on you while she sleeps. Yuck," laughed Ella. "Why don't you just push her away?"

"Push?"

Ella pushed Adnan gently away from her.

"What? No, no. Never pushing. Maybe it's not a lake. Maybe just little bit," admitted Adnan, holding his thumb and finger a bit apart, his eyes twinkling.

Ella laughed, the sound echoing in the steel and white polished kitchen.

If she couldn't have love, it was good to witness someone else on the verge of happiness. She cherished the notion that someone would wait faithfully for years to be reunited with the love of his life against all odds.

"You're lucky Adnan," said Ella. "You sound very happily married." She sighed, relaxing back from her usual ramrod-straight spine onto the wall behind her.

"No, no, we fight," laughed Adnan. "Is so: 'Adnan, you no doing right!' Me saying, 'I doing right! You knowing nothing!' She saying, '*I* knowing everything, you blind."

"Oh no," said Ella, laughing at how Adnan impersonated his wife's voice.

"Yes, yes. But at night, she's here," said Adnan, pointing at his chest. "Two years, hard to sleep," explained Adnan, his eyes downcast, his shoulders slumping. "But I'm recognized refugee now. Mr. Vasiliev and Nick filling out papers for me. Wife is coming. Wife is coming: three days!"

Adnan pumped the sky with his fist.

"Wait, what? Mr. Vasiliev did that for you? The old man who eats here?"

Ella had taken an immediate liking to their most regular

guest, possibly due to the fact that he spoke with a Russian accent, which reminded her of her Grandmother. Even though she had left Russia at six, a part of her heart would always belong to her homeland. She was amused to watch the gruff old man hunched over the table, drinking coffee, reading and taking notes for hours after lunch.

"Yes, yes," said Adnan, his eyes still bright. "Good man."

"You mean grumpy man."

"Yes grumpy," repeated Adnan. "Grumpy good man."

Ella laughed as she jumped down off the counter.

"Whatever you say Adnan. This was fun. See you tomorrow, I mean, tonight. It is already a new day."

As she rode in the tram on the way home, Ella was still warmed from the inside out from laughing.

ELLA HAD JUST FALLEN into a deep sleep before the knock at the door. Counting to three, she forced herself out of bed.

"Hello, Babushka. Is something wrong?" Ella had already hugged Mrs. Annikov on her way home from the nursing home. Alarm bells began ringing in her head.

"Ah, my small sun. I am sorry to disturb you so late, but Sergey has fallen down and I can't help him up again on my own," whispered the woman, clearly rattled.

Ella immediately threw a silk robe around herself, drawing the belt tight as she slipped into her shoes.

"Here Babushka, let me help you down the stairs. I don't like you climbing these steep stairs on your own anymore," said Ella, taking the frail woman's arm in her own. "Not after your last fall."

Mrs. Annikov's door was ajar, and they walked through into a large apartment decorated in heavy antiques and sparkling chandeliers. How could it come to this in the six days since she last came to make lunch?

The flat had smelled pleasantly of lemons and bleach and a bouquet of fresh yellow flowers were set on the dining room table just last Saturday.

She had admired the rainbows dancing on the floor, thrown by the sparkling crystal chandelier. Their laughter had risen up and around them, cocooning her in warmth and a sense of belonging. Now the room was shuttered in darkness, musty and foul smelling.

Ella immediately spotted Sergey lying crumpled on the dining room floor and she rushed across the room. She knelt down next to the old man.

"How are you? Are you in pain? Should we call for help?"

Panting and struggling, she managed to pull Sergey to a sitting position and then unsteadily to his feet. They made their way, one foot shuffle at a time, to the bedroom, and she eased him onto the bed, lifting his feet up and removing his slippers from his feet.

"Now, what can I do for you?"asked Ella while pulling the blankets up around him.

"I'm hungry, I can tell you what, miss. Mighty hungry. But not hurt, no. Not hurt at all by that fall. Lucky this time, I was. Could you be an angel and make me some rye toast, with honey? There's a love," he said.

Ella looked over at Mrs. Annikov, noting her pale face and shaking hands.

"Didn't you tell me you have someone who comes in to cook and clean for you, Babushka?" she asked.

"Heidi didn't come in today," muttered Mr. Annikov. "She didn't come all week, for that matter."

"Is she on holiday?" asked Ella, looking first at Mr., and then at Mrs. Annikov.

"She's not coming back," grumbled Mr. Annikov.

Ella noticed the teacups stacked high on the bedside table. Turning, she took in the mustiness of the room and the clothes, which spilled like angry snakes from the laundry basket in the corner out of the bathroom. Without a word, she went to the kitchen. Moldy dishes were piled high in the sink, and food boxes and dishes were spread on every surface. The fridge was empty, save for some pickles and a jar of onions.

Ella was falling from a massive cliff into icy cold water, the weight of the water pushing down above her, her lungs screaming for air. Placing her face in her hands, she wept for these proud people, who were losing the capability to do what they used to, inch by compounding inch.

She ran out the front door, leaving it ajar, and up to her flat where she quickly grabbed some freshly baked black bread, butter, jam, tea and eggs. At the door, she paused, recalling the putrid smell of rotting food and the dirty counters of the kitchen below. Turning back to her clean kitchen, she efficiently pulled out a tray and quickly put together two plates of scrambled eggs, many thick slices of black bread with butter and jam and a pot of tea.

She descended the steep stairs and walked back into the Annikovs' apartment with the tray. She found the Annikovs in their bedroom. Mrs. Annikov was lying down next to her husband, their heads bent toward one another, hands entwined. Ella noticed the tears running silently down Mrs. Annikov's face. Mr. Annikov's reassuring whispers were a glow of love flickering in the dark and dirty room.

A smile twitched at her lips, a tenderness buoying her up to the surface of her previous despair, hope like a lungful of the purest sea air filling her with newfound energy. She knew what she could do, yes.

A strength was wakening from long hibernation, pulsing down from her heart, into her fingertips, waking her eyes from their dull sleep. Rhythm had always been her solace, her source of strength. She would need music tonight.

"Here I am again," she said smiling, while placing the tray down on the bed. "Let me help you both up so you can sit and eat and then I will see about cleaning the kitchen."

Mrs. Annikov's tears slid down her cheeks as she reached out and took Ella's hand, pressing it to her cheek and then kissing it. "I was so scared he was really hurt in the fall. I'm so relieved he doesn't need to go to the hospital."

Ella bent down and kissed her on the top of the her white hair. Without another word, she left the room as she looked at her watch. It was eleven thirty. How long would it take to scrub down the house?

Taking the stairs two at a time, she ran back to her studio flat. She changed into her ballet clothes and tennis shoes, tying a silk scarf around her neck to warm her, and grabbed her music. Placing her earphones in her ears, she snatched a pair of rubber gloves and her basket of cleaning supplies and ran back down stairs.

As she scrubbed the mold off the dishes, she made a plan. She would change their bedding, help them bathe and tuck them back into a sweet-smelling bed. She would clean the kitchen tonight. It smelled too bad to leave until morning.

Tomorrow, bright and early, she would return to pick up the apartment, air the rooms, dust, tackle the laundry, vacuum, mop and run to the store. She could make some sandwiches to leave in the fridge for them for lunch.

It was Friday night, but the lake front park was desolate of any evening strollers, the benches empty as she walked home. As she watched the swans glide over the dark water, she thought of the future. She had saved up enough money to travel to a new ballet audition in Paris. Yet she didn't know if she could handle another rejection. Her self-esteem was in shreds, as if her clothes had been ripped from her body, leaving her standing naked before a critical judging panel. Ella shook herself.

Sinking down on a bench on the water edge, she watched a sailboat traversing the pink-hued lake. Ella looked at the dark silhouette of the Alps in the gathering twilight, lost in thought. She knew pain, rejection and disappointment to be part of the package of training to be a professional dancer. Now that her mother and grandmother were gone, she needed to be her own support to move forward in the pursuit of perfection.

Okay, Ella, she told herself, you are doing this audition. You've spent six hours each day training. You have corrected your alignment issues, your turnout and extension. You have surpassed your previous level of conditioning. You are strong, long muscled, flexible and pliant. Your feet are fully arched, your lower and upper body lithe and light, your technique sound. At the bar you are pulled in and lifted, moving from a strong core and lower back while maintaining an ease in the shoulders, a long neck, beautiful, elongated body lines. You are ready for this audition.

Ella startled at the sound of feet crunching the gravel behind her. When had the dark descended? She jumped up off the bench and hurried to the tram stop. Zürich was a very safe city, but it still wasn't smart to sit out alone in the park in the dark. She quickened her pace, then broke into a run. The steps behind her churned the gravel.

Ella chanced a glance over her shoulder, slowly for a breath to seek out the person following her. There was a moving shadow in the darkness, nothing more.

Adrenaline shot through her, and her legs started pumping harder. The footsteps behind her were louder in her ears. The marina was eerily silent and still in the moonlight. She could see the tram stop lit up ahead of her and hear the laughter of guests spilling out of a waiting tram onto the street.

She was so close. A hand clutched her bare shoulder, and she threw an elbow back into the attacker's face, then turned to race the few remaining yards to the tram.

"Shit, Ella, that hurt like hell I'm bleeding everywhere. What are you bloody doing, hitting me like that?" yelled Owen.

Ella stopped, turned and walked slowly back.

"Owen? What are *you* bloody doing, chasing me like that? You terrified me."

"I called your name, and you just started running away from me. What the hell?"

Ella took a step closer. Owen was standing under an alcove of beech trees, holding a tissue to his nose. "What are you doing here? Why aren't you up there with your friends?" Ella gestured back toward Flavor.

"I was worried. Nick said Mary agreed to finish your shift because you aren't feeling well."

"I'm fine," said Ella, crossing her arms across her chest. "I just want to go to bed early. I have an audition tomorrow."

"Listen," said Owen, while closing the distance between them. "I wanted to get you on your own for moment. I'm sorry I have been so cold." Ella remained silent. Reaching out a hand, he smoothed her hair back from her face. "You dance beautifully. You'll do great tomorrow at your audition, I'm sure of it."

"You've mostly ignored me," said Ella, turning her head away from his touch.

"I've spent a lot of time thinking about what you would look like dancing. Maybe I've spent far too much time thinking about you in general. If I were a good man, I still would be. I would warn you to put as much space between you and me as possible."

Ella took a step forward, her heart roaring in her ears. He placed a hand on her cheek, and she looked up into his green eyes, searching for truth.

He took her hand and turned it to his lips, kissing the palm of her hand, her wrist and up along her arm. He pulled her into the shadows under a large tree, his lips caressing her neck, his hands smoothing down her dress and fluttering along the hemline of her dress.

His fingers danced a smooth soft line up her inner thigh. Ella pushed her hands through his blond hair, as his fingers inched higher, grazing lace.

She closed her eyes, her head falling back as his finger teased the trim of her underwear.

Suddenly a footstep crunched on the gravel. Someone was nearby on the path. Ella pulled away, her face burning, her skin tingling. She turned to look at Owen, whose face had turned ashen white in the darkness.

He pushed her behind the tree and jumped away from her. The footsteps on the path grew louder, stopping just next to the tree.

"Owen darling? Is that you? What on earth are you doing here, darling? I was down at the rowing club looking for you and started for home when they said you never showed up tonight."

Ella's heart hammered in her chest. What were the chances of Owen's wife just happening to walk past them in this park? Had she seen them together?

"I was feeling a bit depressed, so I skipped rowing tonight and went walking instead. Irma, the truth is, I'm moving out," Owen blurted out. "I want a d…"

"You're not depressed," interrupted Irma. "We're very happy together. You just have been exercising too much. You're tired. We'll pick up takeout and go to bed early tonight. You'll feel as good as new in the morning."

"Irma, I'm serious. This isn't working. I'm not happy."

"You are happy. You lack for nothing. Anything you want I

buy for you," corrected Irma, giving him a kiss on the cheek.

"I want to be a father, Irma."

"It's just never enough for you," hissed Irma. "You have a life most of the world would dream about, and it just isn't enough. Who says you would even make a good father? You would just end up making a mess of things, like your own father did with you. Why should I destroy my career and body because you suddenly decide you want a baby?"

Ella peeked out from behind the tree. She watched Irma grab Owen's hand and lead him like a child toward the tram stop. Their voices faded into the hum of the traffic on the street. Ella waited for a few minutes and headed for home.

She tried her best to shake herself free from the events of the bizarre evening as she walked. She needed to focus on her upcoming audition.

CHAPTER 8

FAILURE. IT LEFT A BITTER TASTE in her mouth. At least she had a day to enjoy the city before returning home. Ella sat outside the tiny charming Parisian patisserie Blé Surcré, and took a bite of her dessert, hoping it would make her feel better. The bottom layer of pastry crust was light and flaky. Above the crust lay a cream, followed by a decadently soft vanilla cake and then a subtle lemon crème as light as it was smooth. The top layer of lemon gelee was a decadent final touch. She took a sip of her espresso and thought about her audition.

Perhaps it was savoring the best pastry she had ever eaten in her life, or the thrill of a day in Paris ahead of her, but the bitterness seeped out into the cold morning air. Optimism permeated her being. So she hadn't won a place in the Paris Opera Ballet. At least she had received valuable feedback and learned from the experience. She hadn't fallen, like in her audition in Germany, or executed flawed technique, as she had in Amsterdam. So Paris was an improvement.

They had said that while her technique was impressive and she had beautiful feet, a sublimated anxiety had permeated her dancing. Ella had wanted to grab attention through eye-catching hyper extensions and six o'clock arabesques. Unfortunately, he was looking for a refinement she hadn't showcased. The last sentence of the director reverberated over and over in her head.

'We're looking for an ethereal fluidity, a musicality. The fine nuances of grace emanating from a unique authenticity.'

The ironic thing was Ella knew in her heart her strength as a dancer was not hyper extension, vigor and energy. Her strength was subtlety. She knew she had it in her to make each of her positions pliant and alive, living in beat with the music, her movement through space all perfect proportions and elongated elegance. She just needed to work harder. Keep going, Ella, she told herself. You can increase your lightness and speed, seamless liquid movements, emotional impact and harmony with the music.

Ella ate the last bite of her dessert and took a bite of the croissant. Slightly crispy on the outside, with warm flaky layers on the inside, it was buttery with a touch of sweet. The good news was she now knew what to work on for the next audition.

Ella wandered the streets of Paris. She was enraptured by the architecture as she made her way to the Eiffel Tower. On her way, she browsed through chic boutiques, eventually splurging on a new blue silk dress. After enjoying the view from the top of the Eiffel Tower, she planned on visiting the Louvre. But between the hours of ballet training and working on her feet for hours as a waitress, she was exhausted.

Spotting Bateaux Parisiens, she gave up her wish to admire the Winged Victory and made a rash decision to jump on a sightseeing cruise on the Seine River instead.

Relaxing back on the open air deck of the boat, Ella admired the Notre Dame, the Louvre, Pont Neuf and the Eiffel Tower as they floated past, the sun warm on her face.

After the boat cruise, Ella meandered toward the train station for her four-hour ride home.

On her way, she stumbled across a charming café. The moment she opened the door, the comforting smell of baking bread, aromatic coffee and melted chocolate engulfed her. There were fresh flowers on the tables, a rough stone wall, wooden floors and a metal winding staircase.

She ate a sandwich with buffalo mozzarella, roma tomatoes, pesto Genovese and grilled artichokes. The waitress brought her a small sampling of their chocolates, and Ella lost herself in the velvety richness of each bite.

The vanilla millefeuille was a perfect combination of light, crunchy layers alternating with a smooth vanilla cream.

Ella took the last sip of her coffee while conversing with the Parisian couple at the next table, warmed by the interaction. They had spotted her pointe shoes in her bag, and they had begun a conversation about ballet. Ella was proud her French was so flawless that they mistook her for a native Parisian.

All too soon, her day of indulgence was over. It was time to go home.

"**NICK TO ELLA.** Come in, Ella. Do you hear me?"

Ella turned to see Nick standing in the doorway. "Hey, Nick. How long have you been standing there?"

"I almost forgot, I had that call this afternoon… you know what you are going to do? You are going to try out for the junior ballet in Zürich. Here," said Nick waving a brochure in his hand. "I made an appointment and went up to Zürich this morning with Mr. Vasiliev. It was his idea. We talked to the ballet program director, and I showed him a DVD of your dancing. He is very interested. Great news yeah?"

"Excuse me, you did what? What dance DVD?"

"Well, I may have made a little video with my phone from the doorway. I couldn't have planned it better. You were doing your exercises next to the railing and then dancing on our restaurant terrace a few hours before the restaurant opened. I thought ballet was boring as hell. But watching you up close like that, well, it was awesome. The director agreed. By the way, how long have you been dancing, woman? And who is your teacher? I'm afraid I couldn't answer any of the director's questions."

Nick gave her a smile that reached his eyes while holding out the brochure.

"You videoed me dancing? Without me knowing?"

"Don't look at me like that, Ella. I know it's a bit sketchy. But you know me, I'm no creepy guy. The window from my kitchen looks right out over this terrace.

Did you think I wouldn't notice all the hours you've spent out there practicing?"

"Look, I'm sorry, Nick, about using the terrace. It's just that my studio is too small to properly train, and it feels so good to dance in the open air with a view out on the lake," stammered Ella, while waving a hand toward the view.

"Now, none of that. Like I care you if you use the terrace; you just should have asked."

Ella sighed, rolling her head on her shoulders.

"Listen Nick, I was just in Paris at an audition. I'm not ready for another dose of failure just yet."

"So you're just going to give up on this chance? Just like that? No way, Ella. Please go and try out for this director. He is expecting you Monday at nine am. You need to fill out the application here and bring it with you."

"I can't go. It's too soon. I'm not ready. I have some feedback from the last audition to work on first."

"It's your choice, Ella. I just have a good feeling about your chances. The director really loved your video. Look, I better get back to the kitchen."

"Why would you do this?" asked Ella while pushing her hands through her hair.

"You said you don't have any more money to travel to auditions. So Mr. V and I were talking and thought, why hasn't she tried out here? All it would cost is a tram ticket."

"I did try out for the junior ballet last year. I didn't make it."

"And you've done a lot of training since then. Even if you aren't any better, how many auditions have you gone to already? What's one more? What if you don't make it? Then you'll be no better and no worse off than where you are right now. If someone gives you a lotto ticket you got to scratch it, just in case you beat the odds. Am I right?"

"Oh alright, Nick. I'll go."

Nick smiled while retying his apron. He turned and strolled back to the kitchen.

"And Nick?" called out Ella after him. "Thank you."

SHE WAS WATCHING HIM from the doorway. Owen had come every Friday night the entire rest of the summer with friends or colleagues from work. Here he was again.

Regular as clockwork. Ella thought back over the past few

weeks. Owen was openly affectionate in a friendly, easygoing way now in public. He still kissed her warmly hello each time on both cheeks, and he even flirted with her in front of his colleagues as she took their orders and delivered their drinks and appetizers.

In private, his words were rich with adoration.

Sometimes Owen waited for her after work and pulled her into shadows of the park.

She'd let him, longing to feel the comfort of his touch. She'd savor the honey of his words, drink in his kisses. But when he pushed her against a tree, slowly inching up her dress, whispering, 'please Ella, my angel,' she would slip out of his arms and run back into the restaurant.

It wasn't healthy, her relationship with the neighbor. She felt shame pulsating through her entire being each time she kissed him. His hands left red hot prints on her skin.

Ella's face burned red when she recalled standing in his arms under the beech tree. She glanced back at Owen as she gathered the dishes from an empty table. He was always the center of any group he came with. Telling jokes, teasing and flirting, he was obviously admired and respected by the men and admired by the women.

She had noticed him flirting with his female friends and colleagues that accompanied him to the restaurant. More than once she had overheard Owen greeting a woman with, 'hey beautiful.' Was she the only one he was cheating with behind his wife's back? Was that what his wife's rages were about? Did she suspect, even know of her husband's philandering?

Watching the gregarious Owen slap the back of the man next to him as he laughed at a joke, a desire to prove the verity of Owen's façade burned within Ella. Was he really this happy? He didn't look like a man with a terrible home life. Ella wondered for the millionth time why Owen stayed with someone as abusive and unbalanced as his wife and if she should push him again to leave her.

"**MY LITTLE SUN.** You are such a dear. We know you have your job and your activities. We don't want to be a bother," replied Mrs. Annikov, shuffling into the kitchen.

"I am happy to help you, Mrs. Annikov," replied Ella. She realized with surprise that she had spoken the truth. Feeling needed, doing something of purpose was fortifying. There was a loosening in her chest as she took a large breath of the musty, foul air.

She would need to get done quickly, though. She wanted to practice for her audition on Monday, and she only had a few hours before her shift at Flavor started at four-thirty.

"Now. I am going to change your sheets and help you into the bath. When I am done, I will do a proper scrub cleaning and finish the lunch I started for us in the kitchen."

"We couldn't possibly let you do all that again," protested Mrs. Annikov while waving her hands at Ella.

"Of course you can. Just think of all those hugs. Remember all those times you left me baskets of freshly baked black bread, homemade jam, dried apricots, butter, milk, canned sardines and fresh flowers in front of my door? Now I can do something for you too."

"That was nothing."

"Nonsense. If it wasn't for you, I may not have eaten for weeks right after I lost grandma."

ELLA DIDN'T KNOW HOW LONG she stood in the entryway of Flavor, her apron in one hand. The grief of watching the Annikovs' health and strength deteriorate was still raw from the previous afternoon.

"Hello? Ella? Are you open?" called a voice from the front of the restaurant.

Ella took a deep breath and wiped the tears from her cheeks. She would need to go and inform this potential customer that they were closed for the evening. How did she forget to put out the sign and lock the door as Nick had requested? The restaurant had been rented out for a company party.

"Ella? What are you doing out here? Are you closed?"

"So that was weird, your wife showing up in the park like that," blurted out Ella, checking over her shoulder despite knowing they were alone in the restaurant. "I heard you say you want to leave your wife. Are you going to?"

"I didn't say that," he said, looking her in the eye.

Ella's stomach clenched, and she narrowed her eyes at Owen. He was a liar.

She had eavesdropped on that messed-up conversation. Her eyes roamed over Owen's lean, muscular body. Owen wore a red polo shirt, blue shorts and flip-flops. She hadn't ever seen him dressed so casual.

"Listen, we're closed for a private event tonight. The place is rented out. What are you doing here anyway? You never come on a Saturday," commented Ella as she picked up a tray of flower vases and began to distribute them on the tables throughout the room.

"Right, well, I'm on my own tonight actually. No one was in the mood to go out in this downpour. I'm starving, though. I guess I will eat a pizza by myself."

"I could come with you," suggested Ella, heat stinging her cheeks as soon as the words were out of her mouth. Did she have no pride? No sense? He had abandoned her in the park when his wife showed up, leaving her behind a tree.

"Yeah? You don't have to work?"

Ella paused internally. "I came early to dance on the terrace, but then the rain started. I have two hours to spare before I have to be back here."

"Well, then grab your coat and an umbrella, and we will make a dash for it."

Ella returned to the back room and grabbed her coat and an umbrella as Owen waited for her by the restaurant door.

Owen called out, "Hey Ella, what is this brochure?"

"What brochure?" she called back.

"This brochure on the Zürich junior ballet," he said.

"Oh," said Ella, returning to the restaurant while tying the belt of the red trench coat around her waist. "Nick procured that for me."

"Aren't you a bit old?" he asked.

"A bit old for what?"

"You know, to harbor unrealistic fantasies? You are wasting time on another audition? How many have you been to? Why would this one be any different? You know the Zürich ballet accepts applications from all over the world," he said, shaking his head and gesturing with his hand out the window.

Something about the intonation in Owen's voice set Ella's teeth on edge. Ella lifted her chin, her spine elongating as she took in a deep breath.

"You know, maybe I'm not that hungry after all." Who was he to know what she was capable of? And anyway, what business was it of his? She hadn't asked him for his opinion.

"Ella," laughed Owen. "Don't act childish. I'm just worried about you having lost touch with reality. Maybe you should see someone. It would be a shame if you ended up in a depression or turn to the bottle because you fail at audition after audition. I mean, you're a great waitress right? Why not stick to that?"

Ella lifted her chin, looking Owen in his blue eyes, and said, "You don't know what I'm capable of."

She wanted to add more: You don't know I started dancing at four under the tutelage of my mother, who danced as a principal in the renowned Bolshoi Theatre in Russia. You know nothing of the years I spent dancing with different ballet academies all over Europe, as we fled from one city to the next. I've never mentioned my daily barre practice, nor the hours I spend dancing. You don't know how much I sacrifice in order to pay for a private instructor each week and save money for the next audition's travel expenses.

"Hey, you're right," said Owen, shrugging his shoulders and smiling at her. "I'm sorry I jumped to conclusions. Who am I to say you can't gain a place in the junior ballet?" His laugh rang out in the empty room.

Ella crossed her arms across her chest and glared at him. He was mocking her, laughing at her. He was talking down to her like she was a naive child and he the knowing adult.

"Don't be angry Ella. In all seriousness, I know it isn't what you want to hear, but it's irrational to strive so passionately for something with such a small chance of success."

"Is it any different than athletes who aspire to compete in the Olympic games?" asked Ella with raised eyebrows. "What are their chances of success?"

The truth was, Ella knew her pursuit of ballet was beyond passionate. It was neurotic.

But Owen didn't need to know that her training had turned

into an obsession. It wasn't like that for many ballet dancers she knew. Then again, they hadn't lost all their loved ones, nor shared her traumatic childhood.

She could literally feel the anxiety, the fear, of what? She wasn't sure. It was there, though, the negative emotions building, twisting inside of her, tightening until she was trembling with the energy of their containment.

While strengthening her core and back, she could feel the negative energy within her warming, consolidating.

When her hand hovered on the barre and she began her exercises, her focus turned.

Time and space released as her concentration narrowed to each movement.

When she moved with controlled grace through the ballet movements, focusing on elongation, extension and long body lines, the ball of energy would release out from her center to the tips of her toes and fingers. At the end of her ballet training, she was wobbly from the exertion, warm and pliant, sometimes hurting. But always liberated.

The memory of that freedom compelled her each day back to the barre, the way it compelled some pregnant woman to obsessive cleaning in the dark hours of the night right before child birth. The way Ella saw it, there were worse coping mechanisms than ballet.

When she had quit dancing, she had turned to alcohol. Ella shook her head, watching the reflection of the city lights on the lake, fluid on the shifting water. It was more than an escape; when she danced, she was swallowed up by the music and uplifted. She found joy.

"Do you plan on answering me, Ella, or just standing there staring at me all night?"

Ella shook her head. How long had she been standing there staring into space, thinking?

"On second thought, I've lost my appetite. Have a good night, Owen."

Owen let out a huge sigh. "Listen, I was being a jerk. I just hate seeing you return from these auditions so devastated. Do you forgive me?"

Ella stared at him, considering. All her warning bells were

telling her to stay away from the man. He reached out and grabbed her hand, bringing her fingers to his lips.

"How about that pizza, Ella? I'm buying," he pleaded, while dropping her hand and giving her a charming smile.

Her pulse was thumping in her throat, her skin warm despite the chill. A part of her wanted to hold on to her anger. But she could still feel his lips on her fingers. She couldn't help but flash back to how they had whispered over her skin in the dark. She should tell this man to go to hell. What was she doing even standing here with him? She had promised herself after the last time to avoid the man.

Instead she smoothed down her dress, took a steadying breath and placed her hand in Owen's. He pulled her in to his chest and gave her a kiss on the forehead. The strength of his arms around her, the beating of his heart in her ear as she rested her head on his chest was like drinking a tall glass of icy raspberry mint tea after a hike through an arid dessert.

"I've missed you sweetheart. It's heavenly to have you to myself." He lifted her chin with his fingertips and kissed her lips gently.

"And yet all the times you've showed up since that night in the park and you haven't exchanged more than a few words with me. Like hell you've missed me," countered Ella, pushing him away from her.

Owen wrapped his arms around her again. "How could I do that with Nick and Mr. Vasiliev and everyone else we know buzzing around? Why do you think I always come to Flavor? I like to see you, Ella."

Ella pulled herself away from Owen's embrace and opened the door to the cold, rain-scented air. "Let's go eat."

Owen snapped the menu shut and took a sip of his wine. "Are you sure you don't want a glass of wine?" he asked.

"No thank you. How is your work going?"

Ella tried to concentrate on what Owen was saying to her, but her thoughts were flitting, like a butterfly, from one flower to the next. What should she wear to the audition? If she did gain a place in the Zürich junior ballet, would she make enough to stop waitressing? Was Mr. V right? Could she trust him? For that matter, could she trust the man sitting across from her?

"Ella? You seem a bit distracted," said Owen. "Did you hear anything I just explained about our new potential drug?"

"You mean homeopathic remedy?" asked Ella.

Owen's face reddened, and his lips flattened into a thin line, but within seconds, he gave a halfhearted laugh. "It will be just as effective, or more, as a 'real' drug in treating symptoms, and it will go through the same trials as a chemical solution."

"Sorry," said Ella.

"Nah, don't worry about it," said Owen with a grin. He winked at her. "Maybe I take my work too seriously. I get a bit caught up. Perhaps I feel a need to prove my work is on level with conventional drug manufacturers. My wife is one of the top managers in the pharmaceutical development at Novartis in Basel."

"Therefore she works all those long hours," said Ella.

"She's brilliant actually. She was the youngest woman ever to lead a research team at Novartis. It's really impressive. She teases me all the time about my job 'playing with plants.' She doesn't take my work seriously. And I make so little in comparison with her, she says I could just as well stay home and not work at all."

"What a lovely, supportive wife," offered Ella with raised eyebrows. "Has she always been so condescending?"

Owen shrugged. "Maybe she's right."

"One doesn't just work for a paycheck. One works to follow a passion, to contribute to society. To make a difference in the world for the better."

"Wow, idealistic much?"

"Tell me you don't feel like that?" demanded Ella, leaning forward and catching his eye.

"Okay, I admit, I feel like that," laughed Owen. "My wife feels like that too. She's just frustrated is all. Actually," Owen cleared his throat, looking around him before continuing. "I'd like to have some kids."

Ella waited for Owen to continue, eating her pizza in silence. Ella had found that silence was better than any question in extracting further information from someone.

"She doesn't want to have kids. I mean, she always said she

wanted children, but now she has such a promising career. She loves her work. She doesn't want to take time out to have a baby. She said she couldn't imagine having a little parasite growing inside her, stealing all her nutrients."

What Ella wanted to say was that an abusive woman like his wife had no business becoming a mother. Ella shivered at the mere thought. She didn't think she could say that, though.

He took his glasses off, rubbed the bridge of his nose and settled the frames back on his face. "Is it right to tell someone you want to have children before you get married and then go back on your promise? I mean, what am I to do? Just let go of my dream of a family?"

Irritation clenched at Ella's throat. The last thing she wanted was to agree with *her.* Giving into the emotion, the hand at her throat released.

"I can understand how she feels. A woman shouldn't have to get pregnant if she doesn't want it one hundred percent. She's worked really hard to get where she is and doesn't want to jeopardize everything by becoming pregnant. Kids require energy and time, both of which she must be in short supply of in her line of work. I mean, it's still a man's world out there."

Owen said nothing.

"You seem angry," remarked Ella.

"No, that's not it."

"Are you sure?" asked Ella. "You're laughing, but your hands are in fists."

"I think I sure as hell would know if I were angry. I said I'm not angry."

Ella noticed the other people in the restaurant had stopped their conversation and were staring at Owen.

The good-natured joviality Ella had witnessed every Friday night was gone. The veins in Owen's face stood out as he took a steadying breath and laughed.

"Sorry about that. I don't know what came over me," he said, noticing everyone staring at them.

"Hey, the only person who knows what you're feeling is you. But there's nothing wrong with admitting you're angry," commented Ella. "I don't understand what the big deal is. I mean, just say, I'm angry my wife doesn't want to have kids, when she insisted before we got married that she did."

"Anyway, it's not really any of your business."

"Oh yeah, then why did you tell me about it?" asked Ella with raised eyebrows.

Owen examined Ella for a minute in silence. She just smiled back at him. If he thought he could use the silence trick on her, he would be disappointed.

After another minute, he caved and muttered, "It's not like it would change anything. Admitting I'm angry."

"Maybe it would make you feel better?" offered Ella.

"No it wouldn't."

Ella took a sip of her water, paused, then shrugged her shoulders. "If you say so."

"God, you get under my skin like no one else can," answered Owen, running his hands through his hair and shaking his head. "Ella, just drop it okay? Letting anger overwhelm you is a dangerous thing."

"I didn't advise you to 'let your anger overwhelm you.' Just to admit to yourself when you're angry. It's weird how you laugh every time you're angry, to cover it up. I'm no psychologist, but I'm pretty sure that's not healthy," she said.

Owen took a deep breath and ran both hands through his blond hair yet again and loosened his tie, unbuttoning his collar. His hair was now standing straight up, which Ella found amusing.

She had never seen the man in a slightly wrinkled shirt, and now he looked a rumpled mess.

"You are exhausting me, woman. You are so irritating. I thought we would eat a pizza, maybe have a few laughs. You're miserable to have dinner with."

It was her turn to shrug. "Wow, that hurt."

She hadn't planned to fight with him either. His remark stung, and she struggled with her emotions. She took a sip of her sparkling water and looked out the window at the lights twinkling on the black water of the river.

"I'm sorry Ella. I didn't mean that."

"Okay," said Ella, still staring out the window.

"No, it's not. You're the only one I've ever been able to open up to about what's eating at me, and I shouldn't lash out at you. So, it's like this. I just, my father was abusive, Ella, okay? I don't ever want to be someone like him."

But you've married someone like him.

She wanted to ask Owen about his past. It was horrible that he had experienced fear and mistreatment instead of safety, trust, support, love and comfort in his childhood.

Instead she said, "I'm sorry you can't have the family you want, Owen. I think you would make a wonderful father."

"Thanks Ella. Could you do me a favor, though? Can we never talk about any of this ever again?"

Ella nodded, finishing the last sip of her espresso. "You have my word. Now I better get back to work."

"I'll walk you back to the restaurant."

Ella didn't argue. They stepped outside, opening their umbrellas against the rain.

"You don't have to stay with her, Owen. You can have the family you want," Ella said as they climbed the hill. "You are a smart, sexy man, and you deserve a wife who treats you well, who will treat your children well."

Owen sighed, taking her hand in his own. "Oh Ella, if only it were that easy."

At the door to Flavor, Ella paused, dropping her umbrella despite the rain pouring down around them, and slipped her arms up and around his neck. She pressed her lips to his, and he opened hungrily to her kiss, the rain falling soft on their faces as he kissed her. She drank in the smell of him, combined with the scent of rain.

Pulling back, the rain dripping down her bare legs, soaking the back of her dress, she shivered.

He pulled her back in, kissing her neck, the water running down his hair and dripping onto her face. She shivered, wrapping her arms around his neck, pulling herself closer to the heat of his body.

Her body was on fire, but something was tugging at the edges of Ella's awareness, telling her something was amiss. Her breath caught as he slipped a strap of her dress down, beneath her coat, kissing her bare shoulder.

She tore herself from his grasp, fumbling in her purse with

wet hands for her keys.

"We shouldn't be doing this. You're married."

"You're right." He smiled, his dimple showing as he flipped his wet hair out of his face. "Listen, let's just forget this happened, okay? I adore you, I really do. I could just avoid you from now on, if that is what you want. I want you to be happy. It's you who deserves someone better."

Ella tilted her head to the side, looking up at him. The downpour had given way to a light rain. Is that what she wanted? To never see him again? If she couldn't have him completely, did she want him to disappear from her life?

She shrugged. "Perhaps that would be best."

He nodded, and an instant later he was gone, walking away through the downpour. Shaking from cold and emotion, Ella walked into the restaurant and headed for the back room on wobbly legs. She spotted her reflection in the mirror. Her mascara was running down cheeks flushed with shame. Oh Ella, she thought. Why were you so naive?

Thankfully she had a spare dress to change into for evening service. Her dress was soaked through.

Chapter 9

Ella carefully smoothed her hair into a bun and ran her hands down her legs, feeling for a snag or tiny hole in her pink tights. She stood back up, admiring the diamond solitaire pendant Owen had slipped into her hand after his lunch at Flavor the day before.

She pulled the card out of her bag as she carefully tucked her necklace inside her makeup case.

To the gorgeous Ella, good luck at your ballet audition.
I am certain you will dance beautifully.

I am sorry for my misunderstanding and harsh words. You have my adoration and friendship forever. Love, your friend Owen.

Heat flashed through her cheeks. What had she been doing, carrying on with a married man? So his wife was abusive and she knew he should leave her. That didn't make what she was doing right or smart. She had told herself this a thousand times, but when he stood before her, it was as if someone had set a drink in front of an alcoholic or a triple layer cream chocolate cake in front of a binge eater. She couldn't seem to help herself. She took a deep shuddering breath.

She picked up her folder containing the application form and her audition photos and left the ladies room, making her way to the registration desk. She peered at all of the dancers pinning numbers onto their leotards and took a deep breath. How talented were these dancers? Ella shook herself inwardly. She needed to focus inwardly and let the world fall away to a dimension that lived and breathed within the music. The moment Ella set a foot into the studio her fear was washing off, like pollen in a cleansing spring storm. A thrill of excitement took its place at the prospect of dancing.

She would have someone analyzing her every movement, from her technique to her power to captivate the audience. A number of different dancers attempted to talk to her as she warmed up and began her stretches. She ignored their questions, too excited to talk, offering a bright smile before returning her attention to the mirror.

"Ella, what are you doing here?"

Ella snapped her head up. Marie and Anna were standing in front of her, dance slippers in hand.

"You can't seriously think you have a chance at making the junior ballet without continuing to attend a dance academy, can you?" asked Marie, smirking.

Ella didn't answer. Marie didn't know of her countless hours of independent training, nor of the private lessons she had paid for every Monday.

They didn't know of her two weeks in London at the Royal Ballet School's summer workshop. Above all, they would never understand the power of turning the energy of one's anxiety, obsessive compulsion and fear toward perpetually refining one's technique. Because while uncontrolled mental illness was repelling, there was something intrinsically awe inspiring when one pursued perfectionism in the mastery of an objective.

Ella believed above all else that beauty could bloom out of the refuse of death and decay. Within her rolled echoing depths of emotion these young women had never experienced, which she could bring forth in her dancing. She needn't tell them any of this, though. Her dancing would speak for itself.

"Are you sure you want to do this, Ella?" asked Anna. "I don't want you to hurt yourself if you haven't been training."

"Come on, Anna, what do we care? Just one less person in this room to compete against," interrupted Marie.

Ella stared at her own reflection in the mirror, slipping into the splits and then lowering her forehead down onto her shin.

The steely edge of competition was biting at her heels. She wasn't going to let these dancers get in her head. This was her chance at her dream.

She wouldn't let anything or anyone stand in the way.

Without thinking, she moved to the front of the line for the barre work. In the following stages of center work, allegro, pointe and choreography she moved as quickly as she could each time to gain a position in the front center. Each time the director criticized something, which was often, her heart jumped, and a bright smile flashed on her face. She soaked up the instruction and immediately incorporated it into her dancing. She was confident and poised.

In the final round, Ella was still dancing, feeling with each passing moment her movements take on a supple expression of emotion, an ease of movement and sensuality she hadn't experienced in Paris. There was an intensity of lightness, an effortless grace she hadn't radiated before. By the end of the audition, she was glowing. She knew it wasn't perfect: she still could work on her musicality, fluidity and refinement, but ballet was a constant journey toward perfection. She was happy with her performance.

After the audition, she paused in the entryway, pulled out a small flowered notebook and quickly jotted down the improvements the director had told her she should make to her dancing while walking into the corridor and slammed right into the director.

"I never see anyone with a pen and notebook anymore. Everyone always has an electronic gadget in their hands."

Ella turned to see the director walking toward her.

"I'm so sorry. I wasn't looking where I was going. I was just noting down your instructions, sir," she said, her voice quavering. Where had her studio persona gone? All the power, confidence and grace had evaporated. Awkwardness and anxiety flooded in, taking their place in Ella's heart.

"My instruction?" he repeated, lifting his dark eyebrows. "Good, I like that. So who is your current academy? You left the section blank in your application."

"I don't attend a school at the moment."

Ella looked down at her knee-high boots.

"But your resume said you've studied at the Bolshoi Ballet Academy, the London Royal Ballet School, at the Paris Opera Ballet School, the Royal Danish Ballet School and at schools in Dresden, Brussels, Amsterdam and Estonia. Now how is that even possible, Ella? Listen you were great in there, I'll be honest. I was impressed. But the fabrications on your resume, that gives us pause. We don't tolerate liars."

Ella looked up in shock into the eyes of the director.

"I'm not a liar. I did attend all of those academies. She changed ballet companies often, so we moved a lot."

"So if I call up these schools, then they will be able to tell me about Ella Chinchinian?"

Ella's heart fell. Of course they wouldn't. They had used new identities in each city. All at once, she couldn't stand the deception and lies. The unrelenting anxiety and fear swirling around her, threatening to suck her down beneath the surface. Ella decided tell this man the truth.

"No, because..."

The director interrupted her saying, "I thought as much. You should have let your dancing speak for itself..."

"Ella Chinchinian isn't my real name," blurted out Ella. "It's Karenina Mikhailov. We used new names in each city."

"Wait, what? We who?"

"My mother, my grandmother and myself," explained Ella, the truth buoying her. "We changed identities each time we ran, our names, our hair color, our back story and learned the new language. My mother danced in each of those cities on my list under different names. Here," Ella unfastened the rose gold diamond-encrusted locket from around her neck and snapped it open, revealing a tiny photo of her mother on one side, her grandmother on the other.

"This is my mother. If you were to look back through photos of past performances in those cities, you will see her face. She was often a principal. And you have my photograph. If you contacted the schools and sent them my photograph, then they would remember me."

"So your mother was a ballerina. And why were you running, may I ask?"

The director folded his arms over his chest, an indulgent smile replacing his frown.

"The Russian mafia."

Nothing is as burdensome as a secret, Ella's grandmother had always said. It felt good to admit the truth out loud.

"The Russian mafia," repeated the Director with raised eyebrows, and then began to laugh. "The Russian mafia was chasing a ballerina? For what purpose?"

"I don't know. We left Russia when I was six years old. My mother refused to tell me why we were running," said Ella, watching the director's smile widen.

"Well, why don't you give your mother a call, ask her as to why you have been on the run?"

"I can't, I've lost my mother. My grandmother too," Ella said, her gaze returning to the floor.

"Well that's rather convenient," commented the director. He crossed his arms over his chest, resting back on his heels. "The two people who could corroborate your story are dead."

Her heart hammering in her chest, she looked up into the director's eyes. "It's true."

"Come on, Ella. It's a good story, but you can't possibly expect me to believe it, can you?"

Ella shrugged her shoulders. Fatigue washed over her, a desolate loneliness weighing her back down. She held out her hand. "It was a pleasure dancing for you, Mr. Fischer. I wish you every success in your future work."

Mr. Fischer shook her hand. "The same to you."

Ella turned on her heel and walked to the front doors while putting on her hat and winding a scarf around her neck. Peering to the left and right before stepping out onto the pavement, she pulled her scarf up to her nose. A desolation washed over Ella as she walked out of the building, tying her red coat around her waist against the biting cold. It was still there when she walked into the restaurant for her shift a half-hour later.

"ELLA, THAT YOU? How is it? Audition," called out Adnan as Ella walked into the kitchen and leaned onto the counter.

"Depressing."

"Did you get job?" asked Adnan while continuing to chop vegetables at the counter.

"No," replied Ella, thinking with regret of her talk with the director. She berated herself for telling him so much. Why had she trusted him with her truth?

"You trying again?" asked Adnan.

"I don't know," sighed Ella.

"What mother think?"

"She's gone, Adnan. But she would want me to dance. She started training me when I was still a small child."

"Family?" asked Adnan. "Where are they?"

"I don't have any family," answered Ella, shrugging her shoulders.

"No good this. I not liking. I watch out for you, Aya watch too. She here tomorrow!"

"I'm happy for you Adnan. I can't wait to meet her."

Ella walked out of the kitchen, her eyes downcast, and crashed into Owen.

"Owen, what are you doing here?"

"I came to bring you these," said Owen, holding up three dozen yellow roses. "To celebrate your ballet audition."

Ella returned her gaze to the floor. "There is nothing to celebrate."

"It didn't go well then." Owen gently lifted her chin with his fingers so her eyes were looking into his. "Hey, I didn't say they are to celebrate you earning a place in the ballet. They are for being brave enough to go and attend the audition."

Tears began to sting her eyes, and the back of her throat began to itch. It was just one more ballet audition. She knew she needed to work to preserve herself in the face of rejection and try again someday.

"Hey, Ella, it wasn't possibly that bad was it?" asked Owen, wiping a tear off her cheek. "You didn't fall on your butt in front of everyone or something, did you?"

Ella laughed out loud.

"I've done that in an audition, actually. No, I'm proud of how I danced today."

"Well then, why the tears?"

Ella looked up at Owen from beneath wet lashes. Her

mascara was starting to run down her cheeks. She took the edge of her scarf and wiped under her eyes before letting out a huge sigh. Then she told him everything she had told the director.

"That is quite a story," muttered Owen, running a hand through his hair and peering at her as if examining her for the first time. "You've had quite a time of it, haven't you? Now you are all alone? I'm sorry, Ella, that's terrible. I know what it feels like to lose your family. But even then I had Irma and her parents. If it wasn't for her, I would be nothing now. I have to go, but I'll meet you here at the end of your shift."

"Your wife isn't suspicious that you leave so late at night for an hour to pick me up from work?" asked Ella.

Despite her better judgment, she yearned to feel his arms around her, to feel his lips traveling along her neck, as they had the night in the rain. In the week since the incident, Owen had kept to his word. He had made no move to kiss her in all the times he had walked her home from work, forgoing the tram ride to increase the time he could spend with her.

"Don't worry, Ella," said Owen, winking at her.

"You listen to me, you shameless jerk. You leave the girl alone. One can't build one's happiness on others' grief," came a gruff voice from the corner of the room.

"Mr. Vasiliev," said Ella in surprise. "I didn't notice you sitting there. This isn't your usual day. And I haven't seen you in a few weeks."

Mr. Vasiliev nodded while walking over to Ella. "That's right. I had something to attend to. I tell you, he who gains the rank like a fox, will be a wolf in the rank. I was a fool not to have seen it coming."

Owen looked first from Ella, then to Mr. Vasiliev and then back to Ella. "What is he talking about, Ella?"

Ella smiled, patting Mr. Vasiliev's arm affectionately. The other wait staff might detest the grumpy old man, but Ella and Nick had spent quite a few slow afternoons drinking coffee with Mr. Vasiliev as they designed the schedules and Nick created the weekly specials.

"Mr. Vasiliev is one of our most loyal customers."

"So she is not alone," said Mr. Vasiliev, while pointing a

finger into Owen's chest.

"You'd do well to know I'm watching you."

Owen took a step back in surprise at the old man's hostility, before quickly recovering himself. He let out a loud laugh. "There's nothing to watch. Ella and I are just good friends. Aren't we Ella?"

"A fisherman can tell another fisherman from afar. I can smell a fisherman too. I don't know what your game is, son, but I would move along," answered Mr. Vasiliev.

"It's okay, Mr. Vasiliev," said Ella, patting the old man on the arm of his designer dress shirt. She was touched by the old man's concern. "It's true. Owen is a friend. He doesn't mean me any harm."

Mr. Vasiliev turned to Ella, ignoring the handsome, blond-haired man in front of him. "I don't trust him. As twice times two is four. You need to be careful. I've known enough criminals in my time to smell one a mile away."

Ella laughed.

"And where have you met all these criminals?"

"Let's just say, where money speaks, there the conscience is silent," answered Mr. Vasiliev, shaking his head.

"Well, Ella," spoke up Owen. "This has been interesting. I'll see you tomorrow for dinner. I'm late for my rowing club. Congratulations again on your audition," he added, as he handed her the roses still clutched in his hand.

Ella lifted up on her tiptoes and kissed Owen on the cheek. "Thank you for the flowers, Owen. Have a good night."

Ella sat down at Mr. Vasiliev's table as Owen walked out the front door to the restaurant. "Mr. Vasiliev, what was that all about?"

"I told you, a fisherman knows a fisherman by his smell," repeated Mr. Vasiliev, shaking his head. "On his tongue there's honey, and on the heart there's ice."

"I also am not liking this man," came a voice from the entrance to the kitchen. "Why now, showing up, flowers? I not liking it. I not seeing, but I listening always listening," said Adnan, motioning a hand to the restaurant.

"Good, good," muttered Mr. Vasiliev. "A beautiful woman like you Ella, someone needs to be watching out.

"I can take care of myself," insisted Ella.

The restaurant phone gave a ring, and she went to answer it. "Flavor Restaurant and Bar, how may I help you?"

"I am looking for Ella Chinchinian?"

"This is Ella."

"This is Mr. Fischer from the Zürich Junior Ballet. Listen, I gave your story some thought and did a bit of research. It turns out I did find quite a few photographs of your mother in ballets in each of the cities you mentioned in your resume. I made some calls, and well, your story checks out. They remembered your mother."

"Yes," answered Ella, her breath catching in her throat.

"Your dancing was spectacular today. You had thrilling technique, and beautiful feet. I appreciate your ability to take correction and direction exceptionally well. I see great potential So I'm offering you a position with our junior ballet."

"When can I start?" asked Ella is disbelief.

"Well, we have some paperwork to fill out. Tomorrow. You are welcome to join technique class tomorrow at nine am if you are ready."

"Thank you Mr. Fischer. No one will work harder than I will. I give you my promise."

"I'm sure you will. Now get a good night's sleep, and I will see you in the morning. Come an hour early and I will have someone ready to go through the paperwork with you. Goodbye, Ella. Or do you prefer Karenina?"

"Ella. And thank you, Mr. Fischer."

Ella, still clutching the phone, did a pirouette and ended in an arabesque position with working leg à la hauteur. The triumph elevated her like bubbles bursting forth from a bottle of champagne. She was giddy with the knowledge that she would have a chance to dance on a stage.

She turned, turning a joyful smile to a clapping Mr. Vasiliev. "What's this? A restaurant with free entertainment?"

"I've been invited to join the Zürich junior ballet company!"

Ella turned to face Mr. Vasiliev, her face growing somber. "But I don't know if I can go, now that I face reality. I didn't ask how much I will earn."

"Ella, what's this about not going? Why ever not?" asked

Mr. Vasiliev, his mouth turned in a concerned frown.

"You can't forbid living beautifully."

"You're right," agreed Ella in defiance. "I don't know how much I will earn, but I will find the money somehow. I will sell my first edition books. Or I will sell some of the jewelry my grandmother left me."

"Settle down now, don't be selling of our family heirlooms. I will give you the money my dear Karenina," said Mr. Vasiliev.

"How do you know my name? Wait what do you mean 'our heirlooms'?"

"Better to be slapped with the truth than kissed with a lie," mumbled Mr. Vasiliev, while rubbing a hand over his face. Then he took a deep breath, straightened his spine and looked Ella directly in the eye. "I'm your grandfather, Ella."

She stared at him for a moment in astonishment before her face clouded over. "And I'm supposed to believe that?"

"I can prove it, Karenina. You left Russia as a little girl and fled with your mother and grandmother from city to city throughout Europe. Your mother told you it was to flee the Russia mafia. She acted as if you were always in danger, correct? But no one was chasing you. It was all paranoia, Karenina. There was no one hunting you down."

"You're lying."

"I wish I were, child," he said, shaking his head.

"But she was terrified when we fled to a new city. Each time we ran, I could see her terror with my own eyes. That was real."

"It was real, Ella. It was real for her. Every woman is a rebel, and usually in wild revolt against herself. Your mother experienced this to an extreme. She was the most exquisite creature on earth when she danced. It was impossible for anyone to ply their eyes away from her when she began to move even a single arm. I see that in you. She was so beautiful, so gifted. It broke our hearts when we discovered her mental illness, Ella."

"Grandma wouldn't let her move us from one city to the next without reason. What about the new identities? The women's shelters? Why would she go through all that? Why would she put me through all that?"

"Your Grandmother told you that if you wanted to stop the running from city to city, she would. She offered to take you someplace where you need never run again. She would have taken you home to Russia Karenina. You would have come home to me."

"Why didn't she?"

"What little girl wants to live without her mother? For that matter, what mother gives up on her ill child? Your grandmother would have left your mother to protect you, to give you a happy childhood. But she wanted to watch over her daughter, to serve as a steadying force in her life by holding her to a strict routine. Three healthy meals a day and critically, eight hours of sleep every night and regular hours of training kept your mother sane enough to pursue her ballet career. She found such joy in her dancing. We decided it was the right decision, your grandma and I."

Ella stood up and began pacing the floor. "Why didn't you come with us?"

"I couldn't just give up my job, Ella. Do you know how much a ballerina makes? Not enough. I was always adding money to your grandmother's account. Then a few years back, I found investments in a public Russian oil company my grandfather made. I sold some shares and deposited the money into accounts for your grandmother in Swiss bank accounts. You inherited that money from them when they died. Have you used it all already? How is that possible?"

"But they left me with nothing more than some cash in the flat, jewelry and first editions books."

"Your grandmother didn't give you her bank account when she died? But that's preposterous. Why wouldn't she? I talked to her about it the day she died. She said it was all taken care of."

Ella sat down in a chair. "She told me all her wealth could be found in her first edition of *The Lord of the Rings*. She handed it to me in the hospital."

"That's right. She'd already called the bank and put her money in your name. The account information is taped inside the back cover."

"I didn't notice it. I thought she was speaking metaphorically or delirious at that point from the pain." Ella paused in her pacing, flinging her arms wide. "You never visited. Why?"

"I watched every production your mother ever performed. I'm afraid I am the cause of a lot of your grief. Every time I tried to persuade her to come back home to Russia, she would collapse like a red star. You never saw me after the age of six because your grandmother and I wanted to protect you from the truth as much as possible."

Ella stood up, backing away from Mr. Vasiliev. "Why didn't you come after my mother died? And after my grandmother? You left me all alone," said Ella, a sob shaking her body. "I was completely alone."

Mr. Vasiliev brought his fingers to his eyes, looking down at the floor. Tears snuck out despite his holding his eyelids fiercely shut. He gulped a few times, took a deep breath and looked up at her.

"I didn't know how to approach you without telling you the truth, all of it. There are scandals even in the most noble families, but who wants to hear their mother was mentally ill? I didn't know if it was best to tarnish your memory of your mother. Your grandmother didn't know either. We agreed I would move to Switzerland and watch over you from a distance and wait to see if you would be better off without knowing me."

"Being all alone?" cried Ella. "You thought that would be preferable to knowing the truth? To knowing you? If you are telling the truth, it wasn't Mom's fault she was ill. So we were often on the run, apparently needlessly, and I suffered the trauma from that. It doesn't change how she loved me, nor what an exquisite dancer she was. I'm feel so lucky she shared her passion for ballet with me."

Mr. Vasiliev lifted up his palms to her, tears running silently down his face. "I didn't know, Ella. That's why I have been here from the moment you started working at Flavor. I was watching to see if you were mentally stable. I was waiting to see if you needed me, if it would serve you best to tell you the truth. But you always look so poised and happy."

"Impressions can be deceiving," said Ella. "Sometimes the brightest smile hides a broken heart."

Ella turned on her heel and walked to the kitchen, the doors swinging shut behind her. It was time to tell Nick the good news, and that she needed to reduce to working at Flavor to a few hours a week.

CHAPTER 10

WHEN ELLA OPENED THE DOOR after her first day in ballet rehearsal, she saw Owen waiting for her. He rushed up to her with a furrowed brow and a wrapped present in his hands.

"I'm sorry about what happened yesterday, Ella. Say you'll come to dinner with me so I can make it up to you."

Ella stood for a moment, a sensation traveling up her spine, as if a spider were slowly climbing up her back. Breathe, Ella. Just breathe.

"This is for you," he said, shifting from foot to foot. "I asked your boss your shoe size. I hope you don't mind."

Ella unwrapped the pale blue paper and opened the box. A new pair of pointe shoes lay nestled in the paper.

"I remember you saying the pointe shoes are so expensive. So I thought you could always use a spare pair. You know, for when yours wear out."

"Friends then?" she asked.

"Friends," he nodded.

"Thanks for the present Owen. Now I better get to work. My shift starts soon."

"Come," he said, holding out a hand with a bright smile on his face. "I'll walk you. I'm ready for some lunch."

ELLA HEARD KNOCKING on her door, expecting Mrs. Annikov.

"Owen! How do you know where I live?"

"Nick gave it to me. You weren't at the restaurant tonight." Owen held out three dozen yellow roses.

"What's this?" asked Ella. "It's not my birthday."

"Surprise! These are for winning a principal part in the junior ballet performance. They're to celebrate," he said. "They told me at the restaurant. Everyone is thrilled for you. I was hoping you had no plans and you could come over for dinner at my flat."

An uncomfortable feeling rattled around in Ella's empty stomach. She was surprised Nick would give out her home address. She didn't feel comfortable going to Owen's place for dinner. It sounded like a proposition she wasn't ready for.

"I'm exhausted, Owen. I don't think so. I was planning on making a sandwich, pouring myself a cup of rooibos vanilla tea and curling up afterward with a book. I need to go to bed early. I have my first ballet conditioning class early tomorrow morning, followed by six hours of rehearsals for the upcoming performance."

"Please Ella? Come over and let me cook for you."

"Where's your wife?" asked Ella, pulling her cashmere sweater tighter around her middle.

Owen took a step forward with a smile and slid his arms around her. He brushed his lips against hers in a gentle kiss. "She's on a work trip. I've missed you. Say you'll come."

Against her better judgment, Ella nodded.

"So, I'll just run down and pick up a bottle of champagne from the store and meet you back at my place in fifteen minutes," said Owen, holding out a card. His grin spread from ear to ear. He winked at her. "Here is my address"

"I don't drink, Owen."

"Tonight calls for champagne. It's a celebration, remember?"

A smile spread over Owen's face, and he gave a small wave on his way out the door.

As soon as he was out of sight, she turned the lock and began tearing off her lounge clothes and throwing them uncharacteristically on the floor as she ran to the shower, stepping under the warm water as her thoughts revolved back to Owen. Should she dress up, or would that send the wrong message? What message did she want to send?

She knew she was being naive and impossibly stupid, but part of her still hoped Owen would leave his wife for her. Ella grabbed a sky-blue sheath silk dress from Paris and pulled her blond hair out of a bun, letting it cascade down her back to her waist. She put on some mascara, added some moisturizer and liquid blush to her cheeks and a bit of gloss to her lips.

Thirty minutes later, Ella stood in front of Owen's flat. Owen opened the door to his apartment. His gaze traveled from her red satin high heels up her blue silk dress to her eyes. She blushed at his whistle.

"Did you put on that dress for my benefit?" Owen asked as he opened the door wider for her to walk in.

"No," smiled Ella.

"Of course not. She dressed up for me. Didn't you, Ella?" said a cool voice behind her.

The tiny hairs at the back of her neck stood on end. Ella turned. Owen's wife was just exiting the elevator. She wore satin heels, pearls, a perfectly tailored business suit and carried in one hand a pomegranate colored Hermes Birkin handbag worth at least six months of Ella's rent.

Her dark brown hair contrasted with her bright blue eyes and bright red lipstick. In the other hand, she held a plastic bag. Whereas Ella was tall, fair and lithe, with a long neck, small bust, slim hips and long arms and legs, this woman was short and curvy with smooth caramel skin.

Ella's heart sank. She could see why Owen fell in love with this woman. The wife was head turning beautiful.

Ella could understand why Owen was hesitant to tell anyone about the abuse. She wasn't sure she would believe this lovely woman was capable of what she had seen with her own two eyes from across the street.

"It's so nice to meet you, sweetheart. You're even more lovely than Owen described. I'm Irma."

Ella stood cemented to the floor, horrified.

"Don't just stand there with your mouth open, you idiot," she directed at Owen.

"Invite the lovely girl inside and fetch us some champagne

flutes so we can toast Ella."

Irma grabbed Ella's elbow and steered her through the open door, slamming it with her foot behind them. She set her bags down at the door and turned to Ella with a big grin, looking her up and down. A shiver ran down Ella's spine and her skin began to itch, as if a cloud of mosquitoes were swarming her, feasting on her blood.

Owen handed each woman a glass of champagne and then lifted his own. "To Ella," said Irma, smiling. "We are so proud of you. Aren't we, Owen?"

Owen stood like a limp flag on a breeze-less day, staring at his wife. Ella backed toward the door.

"Well, what are you waiting for *dear*? I'm hungry, and I'm sure Ella here is as well," said the wife through a broad smile.

Owen drained the glass in one gulp and went out onto the terrace. He came back in holding a handful of basil leaves off a plant from his terrace garden.

A few minutes later, a fresh pesto was whizzing in his food processor and whole grain ancient wheat pasta was boiling on the stove-top as he sliced roma tomatoes and grated fresh Parmesan cheese.

He tossed spinach leaves, raspberries, and walnuts, with pomegranate seeds in dressing and placed the wooden salad bowl on the table.

Ella stood on the other side of the counter, watching him cook as Irma chatted to her about her current drug research. She barely registered what Irma was saying. All she could think about were all the times Owen's body had been pressed to hers. Her face flushed hot. The wife must know, and she had shown up, catching them.

Ella needed to get out as quickly as possible. She was all too aware of the wife's violent tendencies.

"I hear my phone. I'll be right back," declared Irma, leaving the room.

Ella raised her eyebrows as Irma walked into the office.

"What is going on, Owen?" whispered Ella. "What is your wife doing here?"

"She's supposed to be on a business trip. She was offered a promotion, and I thought she was in Singapore to meet her new team. They want her to run their Institute for Tropical Diseases," Owen whispered back. "I don't know what she is doing here."

Ella's heart paused mid-beat. "Are you going with her?"

"What? No," he said. "I love Switzerland, this city, my job, my rowing club." He paused. "And you," he whispered.

Ella watched in stunned silence as Owen mixed the pesto with the noodles and added the fresh roma tomatoes and a sprinkle of Parmesan on top.

What kind of sick game was he playing inviting her here to eat dinner?

Had he been so certain his wife would be gone?

Had the wife really had a business trip, or had she said that to catch Owen?

Ella's nerves tingled to run to the front door and flee to the elevator as she watched Owen carry the plates of steaming pasta to the table. He took a platter of grilled vegetables out of the fridge, in addition to a plate of garlic-infused olives and prosciutto.

"Come sit down," said Owen while lighting the candle on the table. "She'll be in there for a while. We can start eating without her."

"How the hell does she know my name?" Ella hissed. "Forget it, I'm leaving." She hurried to the door.

Owen reached out and grabbed her, pulling her to him. "Don't go. Please. Just play along. I'm going to ask for a divorce," he whispered in her ear. "She doesn't know yet. I've told her about you. She just thinks you're a friend I met at Flavor."

Her thoughts were revolving faster than a pinwheel in the wind. Was he leaving his wife for Ella, or to escape the abuse at last? She wanted to ask him, but instead she whispered back, "so when are you going to tell her about the divorce?"

"I'm waiting to tell her until the day before she leaves for Singapore."

Owen put a finger to his lips and began talking loudly about his rowing club. A few minutes later, Irma joined them at the table.

"Sorry about that, Ella," said Irma, placing an arm around

Ella and steering her back to the table.

"They can't do anything at work without my insight. Really. Don't you like the champagne, Ella?" asked Irma. "It costs more than a hundred Swiss francs a bottle. You've almost eaten all of your food, and your glass is full."

"Actually, I have to go," answered Ella.

Irma placed the flute glass in Ella's hands. She raised her own glass in a toast while raising her eyebrows at Owen.

"To new beginnings."

Ella took a tiny sip and placed it back on the table.

"To Ella achieving your dream of becoming a ballerina," insisted Owen.

"I haven't made the ballet company. There's still a long way to go. Some mornings I wake up and think there is no way I can go on. Every fiber of my body aches and pain shoots through my left leg. Speaking of which, my body really is hurting. I'm going home to bed."

"And yet you keep dancing. It's inspirational. I know you'll have a place in the company if you want it," answered Owen.

"What do you mean if? Of course I want it. It's what gets me out of bed in the morning," said Ella while walking toward the front door.

"It is ballet, not brain surgery, Owen, honestly. So Ella," said Irma moving to block Ella's way. "Please stay and tell me a bit about yourself," Irma ordered as she took Ella's hand and led her to the sofa. "You are a dancer and you work as a waitress to pay your bills. What about family? Where do you come from?"

"I don't have any family. My mother died and then so did my grandmother a few years later."

"But how simply dreadful," sighed Irma. "You poor child. How did they die?"

"My grandmother died of cancer."

"Oh dear, that is something to think about," answered Irma, tapping her lips with her finger. "Does cancer run in your family, sweet girl? Is that how your mother died as well?"

"A car accident," mumbled Ella.

"But you have other family surely? Good family friends to look after you?"

Ella shook her head, slumping forward in her chair. "I'm tired, maybe it's best if I go," said Ella.

"Oh dear me no," answered Irma. "Tonight is a celebration. I bought a chocolate mousse cake as well as strawberry tarts from the famous Sprüngli especially for your visit.

"Zürich has some of the world's best chocolates, don't you agree? Even though there are bakery pleasures on every street in Zürich, I think Sprüngli is simply superior. You must stay for dessert."

Owen had just placed the desserts on plates and carried them to the table when Irma's iPhone began ringing.

"So sorry, just a moment. That will be work," called out Irma on her way back into her office. "Owen, hello? Where are the espressos?" she snapped her fingers in Owen's direction.

"Ella, look at me," said Owen, taking her fingers in his hand under the table once Irma was out of the room.

Owen brought her open hand to his lips, kissing the palm of her hand.

What the hell?

She suddenly had the sinking sensation that he was toying with her; she was transparent.

He could see she was in love with him, and he had been enjoying the attention of a younger woman. Now she was part of some sort of sick game that was getting more twisted by the moment. He was enjoying watching her squirm under the gaze of his wife.

Was Owen lying to her about leaving his wife? Did he have every intention of moving off to Singapore with Irma without a backward glance? Ella knew her loneliness had made her a fool desperate enough to ignore her intuition and good sense.

"You didn't comment on what I said before."

"What exactly?"

"That I love you," said Owen. "Please remember that. I really love you. No matter what happens in the future, I just want you to know that I mean it."

Ella wanted to believe him, but knew he must be playing with her. She was done with Owen.

"I'm leaving," she answered.

She yearned for real love, the evolving, mundane love of

waking up with ruffled hair and arguing over who should unload the dishwasher. A love that wouldn't take flight, leaving an empty vessel in an endless sea.

The kind of love that was thrilling and intense with passion and gave way to tenderness and comfort, a sense of security. This man belonged to someone else. Even if he had left her, the shadows would remain. She wanted someone who would belong only to her.

Ella shoved her last bite of cake in her mouth and stood up. It was time to just walk out, without explanation. This situation was just too weird. Ella opened the front door, when all of a sudden, a hand slammed the door shut. Ella gave a startled scream.

"Ella. Ella, stop that now," Irma soothed. "Sorry to startle you lovely. I just couldn't stand you leaving yet. You'll stay a bit longer wont you?"

She took her Ella's hand and led her away from the door. Irma handed Ella her champagne glass and pushed her into the chair next to the window.

"Now you sit down and rest that gorgeous body of yours and drink this expensive champagne. Then I'll have Owen walk you home. You too, Owen, get over here."

Irma waited for Owen to settle on the sofa and handed him a full glass of champagne as well. She looked at them expectantly, and Ella took a drink from her flute, gazing at the door. What should she do, make a run for the door? That would be awkward, wouldn't it? Ella hesitated, on the edge of her seat. She took a gulp of the champagne.

Owen pushed his glasses back up on his nose, then ran a wet hand through his hair. He drained his glass quickly as Irma talked about the latest tropical disease research.

Ella drank the last sip of her champagne. The fatigue was slowly spreading out over all her limbs, a drowsiness falling upon her. Within moments, Ella's anxiety and fear were drifting up and away, like so many iridescent bubbles blown by a small child in the warm sun of a summer day.

Ella eyes began to grow heavy. Through half-closed eyes, she watched Irma pick up a strawberry tart and take a huge bite. Irma asked if she would like one. Ella's speech slurred, and she fought her eyes from closing. She had only drank two glasses of champagne.

What was happening to her? Her eyes slid closed. The last thing she saw were Owen's eyes closing while Irma filled the void with what would happen if a virulent flu pandemic swept across the globe.

Chapter 11

Ella blinked her eyes open. The sun screeched into her head, sending vibrations of pain echoing through her skull. Her stomach turned over, and she crawled out of bed, hurrying as best she could on wobbling legs to the bathroom.

Oh God, she didn't know where she was. Where was she?

Ella tried to focus. Memories of the previous evening floated up. Owen had invited her over for dinner, and she had drunk a bit of champagne, which certainly wasn't enough to cause her to feel like this. Oh God, Ella looked around. She was in Owen's flat.

Bile rose in her throat, and Ella ran in search of a bathroom.

She hated throwing up. Only when her body stopped heaving did she notice she was completely naked and soaked in sweat. Drinking directly from the faucet, she suddenly panicked. She had been preparing for the performance today for months. This was her chance to make an impression, the potential to earn a place in the Zürich ballet company.

It was as if a bull had charged into her, tossing her like rag doll up into the air and trampling over her once she landed on the floor with a jaw-jarring thump.

Ella jumped up off the floor, her head pounding in protest, reaching out for the wall to steady her as a wave of dizziness washed over her body. Her fear was an acrid taste in her mouth as she threw a towel around herself and peeked out of the bathroom. No one. She looked in the bedroom. Empty. The office was empty as well. She took a deep breath and entered the open kitchen and living area. She was alone. What had happened? She couldn't remember anything after falling asleep in her chair.

Ella needed to flee this place.

Where were her clothes? She hurried back to the bedroom and saw her clothes carefully folded on a chair next to the bed. She went to pick them up when she spotted a framed photograph on the bedside table. She froze, then reached out with trembling fingers to pick it up.

It was a photograph of her training at the barre. In her flat. How did Owen have this? How would he take a photo of her in her flat?

"Ella?"

Ella startled, dropping the picture frame.

It shattered, flinging shards of glass all over the floor around her bare feet. Ella stood frozen, standing naked in Owen's bedroom, clutching a towel around herself, staring in shock. Owen stood before her, a pair of blue boxer shorts the only clothing on his tanned muscular body.

"Ella! Don't move," Owen called as he pulled his shoes on and walked over the glass. He swept her up in his arms, and she struggled against him.

"Let go of me, Owen."

"Calm down. What are you doing here? What happened? Dammit stop struggling."

He tightened his grip as he carried her toward the bed. Ella leaned into his neck, opened her mouth wide and bit hard, harder, until the metallic taste of blood was flooding into her mouth, and she was gagging. Still she continued sending her teeth deep into his flesh.

He cried out, dropping her on the bed in a heap.

Pulling the blanket around her nakedness, she never took her eyes off him. How could she get past him to the door? Desperately, she once again tried to remember the events of the previous evening. She was sitting watching Irma eat the tart, drinking a glass of champagne and then suddenly she had been so sleepy. What had happened next? The night was a complete blank.

"Owen, why am I here?" asked Ella.

"You tell me," said Owen as he tilted the dust pan in the rubbish bin. "I can't remember. I feel like hell though. How much did we drink last night?"

"Oh no," said Ella. "What happened? Where is Irma?"

Owen paused, pulling his hands through his tasseled blond hair, before running from the room. Ella heard retching from the bathroom.

The pounding in her head intensified to the thundering of a brass band. Could it be possible? Her face fell into her hands. She had been cheated.

Her first time and she remembered…nothing.

"Ella? Are you okay? Your face is very white." Owen crossed the space between them, crouching down beside her and peeled her hands from her tear-stained face.

"What? No," Ella pushed Owen away and attempted to stand, slumping back on the bed as a wave of dizziness hit her again.

"No, no of course not. Ella, you have nothing to worry about. You can trust me," smiled Owen. "We must have drunk too much and passed out. I am so hung over."

"I only drank two glasses."

Whatever happened last night, something was amiss. She most certainly couldn't trust this man, with eyes radiating calculating intelligence, his voice soft with tenderness.

"There you are, Angel," said Irma, walking into the room. "Is that you causing such a ruckus this morning? You really shouldn't have had so much to drink last night, you two. I hope you don't have a drinking problem, Ella, like my Owen. You don't, do you? As hard as you train, how would that even be possible?"

Ella sat motionless, shielding her eyes from the sunlight streaming in from the window. Ella's head was pounding, her stomach rolling.

"Now beautiful, you need to dance tonight," said Irma as she leaned in, gently brushing Ella's long hair over her shoulder and kissing her bare shoulder.

Nausea was somersaulting in her stomach, and her head

was spinning with dizziness, throbbing with pain. She was hurting and bewildered and wanted to push Irma away.

"What happened last night?"

"You passed out, I'm afraid. We didn't know what to do. So I had Owen carry you in here, and I undressed you and put you to bed. You must feel like hell this morning."

"And you, you slept…"

Irma laughed. "We slept on the pull-out in the office of course. Don't worry. If it came to sleeping on the sofa, you would have been there instead of here. I really need my sleep. Now I'm off to work. Get dressed, Ella, and I'll walk you home. I'm not leaving a pretty girl like you alone here with my husband. Ha. That's a joke. I trust him completely. But still, better safe than sorry, right, Ella?"

Ella grabbed her clothes and ran to the bathroom. She threw up again and rested her head on the cold porcelain of the floating toilet.

"Are you okay in there Ella? Come on, open the door, there's a good girl. You have us worried," said Irma.

Revulsion filled her gut, followed by shame, hot and seething, like worms squirming in freshly overturned soil, like maggots swarming over a kill.

Minutes fell scorching away, burning her as she sat on the floor, her knees huddled to her chest. At last the pounding came to an end.

"You can't stay in there forever, Ella," called out Owen. "You have a performance tonight, remember? You need to get ready. Come on, sweetheart, I'm sorry I let you drink so much last night. Let Irma walk you home."

CHAPTER 12

ELLA MADE HER WAY TO THE **bathroom**.

Turning on the shower, she stepped into the spray, feeling dirtier than she ever had before. She couldn't wait to scrub the creepiness of the past night off of her skin.

Five minutes later, she turned the handle to icy cold, the alpine iciness of the water stinging her skin, causing her feet to go numb. With hair dripping cold water down her back, she wrapped herself in an eggshell blue fluffy towel and padded to the closet, her head at last clearing. She took out her ballet clothes and pulled them on, followed by thick wool socks.

Feeling slightly better, she sat down on the edge of her bed, staring unseeing into in the distance. A brisk knock rang out into the silence. She wrapped her hair up in the towel and went to the front door.

"Ella? Ella, it's your babushka," called a voice.

Ella opened the door.

"What's wrong?" asked Mrs. Annikov. "I heard pounding. Are you ill? Should we get you to the doctor?"

"I didn't hear anything."

"Ella," said Mrs. Annikov, going and placing her hands gently on Ella's shoulders. "What's wrong?"

What should she say? Shame flooded through her. How could she explain what had just happened? She didn't even know what had happened.

"I was so sick this morning, and then there were footsteps. I thought someone had broken in," lied Ella. "I was terrified there was an intruder in the building."

"Oh dear. Should I call the police?"

"No, it must have been someone hanging a picture or something."

"Well, I'll go down and make you some porridge with fresh strawberries and raspberries, coffee and an omelet with toast," said Mrs. Annikov. "You pack your things together. You have your big performance tonight. You need to leave for rehearsal soon."

"Please, don't go to all that trouble on my account," pleaded Ella. "I'll be fine."

"I know you need to leave for rehearsal in a little over an hour," said Mrs. Annikov, a twinkle in her eye. "Don't take too long up here now."

Ella finished packing before going downstairs and knocking on the Annikovs' door. The door opened. Nick, Adnan, Aya and the Annikovs were standing in front of her, shouting, "surprise."

"What is this?" asked Ella, her hands pressed to her cheeks. Of all the mornings, she thought, it had to be this one.

Aya opened her arms wide to Ella and gathered into a hug. "It's to celebrate your opening performance as a principal tonight. We can't wait to see you dance."

"You're coming?" asked Ella, her jaw slack in disbelief. "The tickets are expensive."

"Well, it's not every day we can watch a friend dance in the opera house in Zürich, is it? Of course we're coming. We've been saving for three months for these tickets," answered Aya.

"I'm bringing my wife," said Nick. "She's a huge fan of ballet. She can't wait to watch you dance Ella."

"And you're not?" asked Ella.

"I'm open to changing my mind," answered Nick, grinning. "It's up to you to convince me tonight. No pressure."

"Nick is going to pick us up and take us as well, dear," added Mrs. Annikov. "I can hardly stand the excitement."

Ella was beaming.

"I can't believe you are all here for me," said Ella as Nick handed her a flute of fresh-squeezed orange juice.

"Yeah, well it was Adnan and Nick's idea," explained Mrs. Annikov graciously.

"Well we wanted to meet the Annikovs, after all you've talked about them," said Nick, taking a sip of his coffee. "Didn't we Adnan?"

After a bowel of porridge sweet with small, homegrown strawberries, many cups of coffee, and more omelet, bacon and toast than she thought she was capable of eating, Ella stood up, her nerves jangling like a pair of car keys.

"Ella, you look nervous," said Aya. "Let's go upstairs and I'll massage out those aching muscles for you." She tapped the chair in front of her.

Ella acquiesced. She felt numb, dissociated with her body. Her pulse was still screaming, but she sat immobile on the chair. Aya went to the bathroom, returning with a lavender almond oil and slowly began messaging it into Ella's legs, then her arms. At first the touch of Aya's hands sent fear spiking through her body. After ten minutes, the slow smooth strokes began to soothe her nervous system.

Something within her opened up, and hot tears stained her face as Aya took up Ella's battered feet and began massaging them with the oil. Ella felt the tension leaving her shoulders, her breathing began to smooth and soften.

"There, let's see about that hair," said Aya, placing Ella's foot gently back onto the floor. Taking out a hairbrush and a blow dryer from the bathroom, Aya unwound Ella's messy, still damp ponytail and began carefully untangling the long strands of Ella's blond hair.

"Thank you, Aya, I don't know how to thank you," Ella said, tears blurring her eyes. Aya's touch was so healing, their companionable silence so restful.

"There, done," declared Aya.

They descended back to the party. Ella hugged everyone goodbye before departing for the biggest day of her life

Ella leaned her forehead against the window of the tram, watching designer clothing shops, confiserie, banks, jewelry stores, café and restaurants roll past her window.

She desperately wanted someone to turn to, to confide in, but whom could she trust? Who did she want to admit the ugly truth that she was unsure as to what had happened last night? Anyone would think that she had drunk herself into oblivion and passed out on her neighbors' sofa.

No, decided Ella. I can't tell anyone.

Focus on the performance, Ella. Forget the past night, erase it from your memory.

Yet the morning's horrors kept spinning in her head, a shiny top twirling endlessly, impervious to the pull of gravity. As she entered the opera house, as she dressed, went to makeup and hair.

As she warmed up, stood behind the closed curtain, awaiting the start of music, it was still tormenting her. Until the first notes floated out from the symphony in the pit, pulling her thoughts up and away from her, leaving only movement and a mounting joy in her heart as she became a moving, three-dimensional vessel for the music, outside of normal space and time.

She took her first grand jeté and joy seared through her as she reached a full extension of the splits in the air. An energy directly channeled from the music propelled her through seven double and one triple fouetté en tournant of precision and grace. The light shined bright in her eyes, following her as she glided across the stage in eloquent elegance through the rest of the steps.

She inhabited a different dimension, until the curtain opened to applause and she lifted her head from a bow. Happiness bubbled up until she saw him. There, in the first row, rising to his feet to give her a standing ovation. Owen. He caught her glance, winked. The woman next to him leaned in, saying something over the roar of the audience. Ella's heart skipped a beat. He had come with his wife.

The moment the curtain closed she ran to her dressing room, shutting the door behind her, slumping to the floor out of breath. She didn't know if it was ten minutes or thirty when the knock came at her door.

The neighbors stood before her, wide grins on their face. *She* held out a bouquet of flowers.

"You were brilliant, Ella," Owen gushed.

Irma pushed past Ella into her dressing room and relaxed back onto the small sofa.

"It's a treat to meet you at last, Ella. Owen has talked so much about that restaurant you work at. I've been meaning for ages to find time to make it to Flavor for dinner. Work has been so demanding lately, I hardly find time out of the office to exercise and eat."

"I have met you, Irma."

"What are you talking about?" asked Irma. "I've never seen you before in my life."

"I had dinner with you last night in your apartment," insisted Ella. "You bought dessert from Sprüngli."

"Ella," said Irma, stepping in close and placing a hand on her cheek. "You're starting to scare me. That didn't happen. Owen and I were alone last night. We ate pizza and watched a movie. Are you okay?"

An ugliness entered Ella's stomach, wriggling in her belly like insects, like worms. Nausea rolled through her stomach. Ella's legs began to wobble, all at once giving out from under her, and she was falling. Owen caught her in the last moment.

"Looks like you danced your heart out, girl," he said. "You probably could do with a sit-down and a bit of sugar."

"I'll go fetch her a glass of orange juice from the lobby," offered the wife.

"She must be a bit delirious from exhaustion."

"I can go, love," answered Owen.

"No, you stay. I'm ready for a glass of wine myself. Be back in a blink."

Ella pulled herself out of Owen's arms and lowered herself onto the chair. "You brought your wife?"

"Of course," said Owen. "I told you we were coming tonight. Are you okay? Don't you remember?"

"What I remember is waking up naked in your flat this morning," answered Ella, her voice raising as her anger pumped through her veins.

"Shh, Ella," cautioned Owen, while closing the door to her dressing room. "What's wrong with you?"

"I'm talking about this morning in your flat. About last night, for that matter. What happened, Owen?"

Owen pushed his hands through his hair, straightened the glasses on his nose and shook his head. "What are you talking about?"

"I had dinner in your flat last night. With you. And your wife. You told me you love me, that you're leaving your wife," accused Ella. "I only drank two glasses of champagne. Why would I pass out from only two glasses of champagne, Owen? Did you drug me?"

"What? Please tell me you don't believe any of that actually happened. You can't possibly believe me capable of that, Ella." Owen threw his hands up in the air, his eyebrows raised. "I care about you. I'm your friend."

"Stop messing with me, Owen, this isn't funny."

"Ella, look at me. I came by the restaurant last night, brought you some flowers, and came home. The restaurant was closed last night, remember? My wife and I ate some pizza and I swam on the terrace. We watched a movie. Another perfectly boring Friday night. This morning Irma wanted to go to the farmers market, so we spent our morning wandering the stands and buying fresh produce so I could make Irma lunch today."

"That's not true. You were with me this morning. And then Irma walked me home and went into work."

"That didn't happen," insisted Owen, shaking his head. "I didn't see you last night, nor this morning. Are you feeling well?"

Ella sat in stunned silence. Her memories were real, weren't they? Hadn't it played out like she remembered? Or was she starting to suffer from some kind of delusional disorder, like her mother?

There was one way to find out. She jumped up and rushed to Owen, managing to unbutton two of the buttons of his shirt before he pushed her away. She strained against him to loosen his tie, to look at his neck. If she could just look at his neck, she would know for sure. There would be a wound. The bite marks would be visible.

The door opened and the wife entered the room. "Here is your orange juice, Ella," she began, then stood in shock to see

Owen holding Ella by her upper arms, attempting to hold her at arm's reach as Ella tore at the collar of Owen's shirt.

"What is going on?"

All the strain in Ella's body gave way at the sound of the wife's voice behind her. Owen released her.

"I think Ella is having a psychic break, Irma. She thinks she stayed the night with me last night. In our flat. With you there." Owen's laugh echoed in the room. "It's quite a story."

"Well, the strain of the performance must have gotten to her head," sighed Irma, taking a sip of her wine. She turned to Ella and said with exaggerated clarity, "Last night Owen was with me Ella, at home. Do you understand? This morning too, for that matter. We went to the farmers market. Found some lovely squash and a whole bunch of sunflowers for the table. Here, drink the orange juice, Ella. You'll feel better."

"I didn't even think she found me attractive," insisted Owen. "I'm almost twenty years older than she is."

"Oh love, you underestimate how sexy you are," said Irma, while walking over and giving her husband a kiss. Pulling back, she shook a finger at her husband, "I told you to be careful not to give her any ideas. You are the perpetual flirt." She walked back over to Ella, looking her over.

"You poor dear," said Irma, tracing a finger up the length of Ella's bare arm. "You have become quite infatuated with my husband. No, no, don't worry," she cooed to Ella, while taking her chin and lifting up to meet her gaze. "I'm not angry. A lonely young orphaned girl like you, of course Owen would appear as a sexy source of security. But you need to find a boyfriend your own age, do you understand, lovely?"

Irma let go of Ella's face and smiled. Ella didn't know what else to do but to drink the juice. She looked from Owen, to his wife, and back to Owen. The memories of the morning were so real. She couldn't possibly have imagined them, could she? Or had she? She had fantasized about Owen enough times; was it yet another of her mind's productions?

"Ella! We here! Hello?"

Ella recognized Adnan's voice at once. Relief flooded over her, like the feel of a hot shower after a day spent outside, chilled to the bone.

"Ah, Ella," exclaimed Adnan, taking her in his arms and kissing her directly on each of her cheeks before stepping aside for Aya to do the same.

"You were glorious up there, Ella," said Aya, her eyes ashine. "Tonight was truly a life experience I will always remember."

Adnan noticed Owen and his wife in the dressing room. "Owen, hello. So, you being wife of Owen. Maybe cooking time to time, man not needing come to me eating every day," said Adnan.

The wife laughed as if what Adnan said were a joke, instead of a slight. "It's so true! Just today I took Owen to the farmers market and told him to cook me something edible for a change. I keep telling him to take some classes. We could save a fortune in takeout bills. Say, do you give lessons Adnan?"

"No," said Adnan.

Aya held out her hand, "Hello, I'm Aya, Adnan's wife."

"Yes of course, Aya. Owen's talked about you too. The refugee. Where's your head-to-toe cover? Shouldn't only your eyes be peeking out at me?"

Aya took a step backward, her smile fading and her olive skin tone paling. Her dark eyes flashed. "First of all, I'm Christian. And second of all, not all Syrians of the Muslim faith cover themselves voluntarily. Terrorist groups have taken control of our beloved country and insist."

"Yeah, yeah, so tragic," yawned Irma, finishing her wine. "I'm ready for bed, as embarrassing as that is to admit. I'm afraid Ella here is feeling a bit crazy, out of her depth you could say, after the strain of her performance. Are you going to the tram together? I couldn't leave her in good conscience."

"Yes, we taking care," said Adnan.

"What do you mean, crazy?" asked Aya.

"Never mind," said Owen. "Once again, congratulations Ella, you were gorgeous up there. Wonderfully graceful. Get a good night's sleep, girl, and I'll see you on Monday for lunch."

Ella couldn't respond.

She stood dazed as first Owen, and then Irma kissed her goodbye, the perfume of the wife with its spicy scents of vanilla and cardamom overpowering her senses.

"Ella," asked Aya. "Are you okay? What was that woman

talking about?"

"Yes," answered Ella, shaking herself. "Yes, I'm…fine. I just don't like Owen's wife."

"Yeah," answered Aya, rubbing Ella's shoulder.

"We didn't like her either. She has a very peculiar energy, doesn't she, Adnan?"

Adnan nodded his head.

"I'm ready to get out of here," said Ella, already beginning to pack her bag and put away the makeup on the counter.

"Great, the Annikovs, Nick and his wife Julie and Mr. V are all waiting for us in the lobby. We are going back to Flavor for drinks and appetizers," said Aya, giving a little excited shake in her blue silk dress. "I haven't had this fun since… well, I haven't ever had this much fun."

"Wedding good night too," argued Adnan.

The couple began to bicker about which night of their lives had been the most fun as they headed to the lobby.

As Ella was pulling on her jacket and winding her scarf around her neck, Mr. Fischer walked into the dressing room.

"You were a dream, Ella. An absolute dream with your beautiful feet, sky high extensions and thrilling technique. But there was that special something missing. Tonight you radiated a magnetic grace that made it impossible to tear our eyes away. You were spell binding. Such, tragic sadness, such anger, such joy. I didn't get any of that emotional intensity in the rehearsals. Tonight I saw you weave jetés, arabesques and pirouettes into lithe, almost liquid musical phrases. You gave shape and movement to the music, revealing a musicality everyone keeps talking about. Everyone is raving. You've done it, Ella. You've done it. Few get there at all, let alone so quickly, but I'm here to tell you: you have your spot in the Zürich ballet."

"I can't believe it," whispered Ella.

"Congratulations. Now I'm off to shake hands and kiss cheeks. See you tomorrow."

Ella fell into the chair as soon as the director left the room, her forehead resting on the cool counter. Ella thought of all the hours she had spent daydreaming of hearing these exact words. She had always imagined elation streaming through her blood at the news. Instead, the events of the past twenty-four hours had sucked her dry of any emotion. She felt grey and hollowed out. Taking a deep breath, she looked up at her reflection in the mirror, carefully removing the tiara.

"Ella, I just heard the news. Congratulations! Guess who will be joining you? Me!" Ethan, a member of her junior ballet, was standing at the door, holding a single red rose. In the past week he had become a friend, her only friend in the world of ballet. His witty humor and playful nature made her laugh, and she savored such lighthearted moments in between the intense focus required in rehearsals.

"I'm not surprised, Ethan. Your leaps are jaw-dropping, not to mention your ability to bring any character to life."

"And you, beautiful, were sublime," replied Ethan. "You created an almost mystical connection between space and the music. Your arabesques were glorious, you made it look effortless from the audience."

Ella winced, all at once noticing the pain shooting through her knee and down her chin. "It didn't feel effortless, it hurt like hell tonight."

"The knee, right? Better have someone take a look at it as soon as possible. You don't want that getting worse and keeping you from dancing."

"Thank you, Ethan, you have no idea how much I appreciate you coming by to congratulate me," said Ella.

"Hey girl, that's what friends do," he smiled.

Tears were suddenly clouding her vision. "I'm sorry I'm so emotional. I almost don't trust that we made it, that it is real."

"I get it, girl. Our milieu is harsh. The competition is fierce, the expectations high and the long days of class and rehearsal take their toll. Listen, go home and get some sleep yeah? We start all over bright and early. You can do me a solid and bring me a pumpkin spice latte from Starbucks on the way here. Yeah?"

"You can count on it. Good night, Ethan."

She ran to the lobby, adrenaline pumping through her body, her cheeks flushed and her eyes bright. "Nick, everyone" she cried, running toward them. "I made it, I did it, I have a job in the Zürich ballet."

Aya, Adnan, Nick, Julie and the Annikovs gathered her into a group hug, their laughter and tears mixing together in the warmth of the embrace. At last they parted, breathless. When had they become such good friends? The bonds of their friendship had been laid so slowly working day in and out next to one another. Yet it was the generosity of spirit, one kindness after another, moment after moment of laughter and empathy that had built to this moment of connection.

"I knowing it. I saying to Aya, she going all the way, she dancing into very hearts of, of…" Adnan said, searching for the word in German.

"Audience," added Aya.

"I knowing word," insisted Adnan. "You having no time to wait."

"I'm not the impatient one," countered Aya, ruffling her husband's hair.

Adnan pushed his wife's hand away and glared at her. Aya stepped forward and kissed his cheek and slipped an arm around his waist, giving him a squeeze. Ella suppressed a giggle watching Adnan attempting to suppress a grin.

"It's time for those appetizers and drinks. Let's head to my restaurant, folks," spoke up Nick, already pulling his wife toward the door.

"My sentiments exactly," agreed Mr. Annikov.

They stepped out into the cold night and into a tram.

"Is that a hooded sweatshirt you're wearing under your suit jacket Nick?" laughed Ella. "I don't think I've ever seen someone wear a shirt, tie, hooded sweatshirt and a suit jacket to the ballet before."

"I'm setting a new trend," answered Nick. "And I lost my winter jacket in the tram last week."

After almost two hours of conversation and laughter over champagne, mock huckleberry martinis and appetizers, Ella was exhausted and glowing. She hugged and kissed everyone goodbye, and then walked with Mr. V, Adnan and Aya to the tram stop. By the time they entered the tram, their exhilaration had seeped out into the night and a fatigue had taken its place. They rode the train in silence. Aya fell asleep, her head resting on her husband's shoulder. She smiled to herself when they walked off the tram hand-in-hand a few minutes later.

"Is everything alright, Ella? Something is amiss. I sense it," Mr. V said, tapping his finger to his nose.

"Well," hesitated Ella. "It's Owen..."

"I knew it," interrupted Mr. V, pounding the seat in front of them with both fists. "I told you you shouldn't trust that man. Didn't I?"

"I'm afraid you were right. Or," sighed Ella, pausing.

"Or what? Speak it out girl, speak it out. I used up all my patience sixty years ago."

"Or I'm becoming delusional," mumbled Ella, gazing out the window at the deserted streets. "Like my mother."

"What's this? No, I don't think so," insisted Mr. V. "It's Owen, that slippery one with his designer clothes, that ridiculous long blond hair and the charm he spins out. I tell you, beware of the goat from its front side, of the horse - from its back side, and the evil man - from any side."

"I'm not sure he's an evil man," corrected Ella, massaging her temples with her fingertips. "He's been so kind to me."

This was a mistake, telling this cantankerous old man about something she was beginning to worry didn't, indeed, actually happen.

"Don't be afraid of the dog who barks, but be afraid of the one, who is silent and wags its tail. Whatever the story is, I have full faith," Mr. V shook his finger at her, "full faith that you own the truth and that Owen holds nothing but some slippery eels in his hands."

Ella sighed, slumping into a chair and resting her forehead on the tram window.

"Maybe I'm crazy and created everything in my head, like he insists. How can you be so certain I'm not becoming mentally ill like my mother? I am the one who looked like a fool, when his wife corroborated his story tonight."

"I really think you are of sound mind, Ella. I would tell you if I was worried. The truth is: one can't wash the black dog all the way to whiteness. I told you from the beginning: you can't trust that man, Ella. I have a bad feeling. He has a studied air of nonchalance, great style and charm, but underneath there's an undercurrent. You need to stay away from him."

Raising her head off the table, Ella wiped at the tears on her cheeks. "Thanks for believing me, Mr. V, even though you don't know the whole story."

"And how is it a show of faith to demand a recitation of what transpired and the various accusations involved? A man may lose everything, but he will still have faith and loyalty to give. And you have mine, child, forever."

Ella startled, staring open mouthed at the man sitting across from her. Those were the exact words her grandmother had recited to her over and over again, until the words invoked a sense of security and coziness, the belief that despite everything, she would be okay.

"My grandmother used to say those very words to me," breathed out Ella. "Only she added love."

"Yes, well," said Mr. V gruffly. "You have that too." He looked away from her out the window, then cleared his throat and took a deep breath before turning back to her. "You were a wonder tonight by the way," said Mr. V, his voice softening. "You wore your grandma's sapphire diamond earrings."

Ella paused inwardly, more closely scrutinizing the man sitting across from her. "I never told you those earnings were my grandmother's."

"You didn't need to. I gave her those earrings for our fifth wedding anniversary."

"I haven't ever worn them. I told myself that I would wear them for the first time if I ever danced in a ballet."

"I wish she could have seen you tonight. I wish both of them could have," he almost whispered.

"This is my stop. Thank you for coming tonight."

"I'll see you at your next one, Ella. Keep a look out for me."

Ella smiled as she walked off the tram. So he really was her grandfather. She didn't know if she was ready to welcome him into her life as her family, but Ella did know Mr. Vasiliev was right. She would avoid Owen and Irma at all costs. It would be quite easy, because from this point forward, she would no longer be working at Flavor, but in the Zürich ballet.

Chapter 13

THE NEXT MORNING ELLA AWOKE BUOYANT until the creepy events with Owen and his wife resurfaced to her consciousness. She checked her clock and realized she had slept late.

She only had an hour before rehearsal began. She would have to hurry. She flew through her cleaning routine at home and then raced downstairs to do a quick clean for the Annikovs. She threw some ingredients in the Crockpot so they would have a stew ready by lunch.

"I'm glad you have someone staying with you now," said Mrs. Annikov, as Ella diced onions and carrots to throw in the stew with the lamb joint. "A new boyfriend perhaps?"

"I don't have anyone staying with me," answered Ella, her knife paused in mid-air.

Mrs. Annikov reached out and took Ella's arm, patting it in reassurance. "It's alright, dear. I didn't mean to pry. Who you have visiting you is your business."

Ella stopped in her tracks. "Why do you think I had a visitor? Did you see someone?"

"No dear. I heard footsteps yesterday afternoon overhead. The day before that too, for that matter. I know you are usually at rehearsal then. Did you come home for a quick rest up?"

"No," she whispered. Her throat constricted, the tiny hairs on her neck standing up.

"I don't have any guests. Ever. Just you."

Mrs. Annikov's face drained of all color. She stood rooted to the spot, looking up at Ella with large eyes.

"Oh no, did someone break in? Do you need to go look if something has gone missing? We should call the police."

"Oh no!" yelled Ella, causing the delicate old woman next to her to startle backward, almost losing her balance.

"I have a lot of cash in my studio in the moment and my grandmother's jewelry. There are some expensive first edition books too, but a burglar wouldn't know a book's worth. I'll go up and take a look tonight after ballet conditioning and rehearsal. There isn't any time now. I didn't notice anything missing last night, but I came in so late."

"I hope nothing is missing, my little sun," murmured Mrs. Annikov as Ella put the top on the Crockpot.

Ella forced a bright smile to her face. "I'm sure it is nothing. This is an old building that creaks and groans. Now I'll see you tomorrow morning. The stew will be done at noon."

As Ella climbed the stairs to her studio in the evening, her heart was still pounding, roaring in her ears. She found it impossible to swallow. Her limbs were shaking.

When she opened the door, she was greeted by the smell of lavender, lemon and a hint of bleach. She searched her nightstand. The cash was still there. Her grandmother's jewelry still lay in the pale blue china dish on her side table. Ella surveyed her bookshelf. She stood up on a chair to reach her most beloved first edition books, running her hand gently over their spines. They were all here.

Then something caught her eye.

Behind a book weight on the top shelf, she could see a romance book. She didn't read romance novels. What was it doing up there? Stretching up on her tiptoes, she could barely reach it with her fingertips groping for purchase. At last she had it in the palm of her hand. She started to sway; the barstool was giving way beneath her feet.

Fortunately, years of dancing came to her aid. She landed on her feet as the stool crashed to the floor, the book tight in her hand. Had it been a book of her grandmother's, her mother's? No, she didn't remember it at all.

She turned it over, examining it. That's when she saw it. A small round hole in the spine. Ella turned the book over her chair and shook. A tiny camera fell out. She wanted to take the camera and throw it out the window into the street below. She took a deep breath, calming her impulse. She searched the camera and found a slot. She pushed the button and a memory card came out.

Someone had placed a camera in her flat. Someone had been watching her. Goosebumps broke out over her skin. Who? How did this camera work exactly? Was her every movement being transmitted somewhere, even now? She placed the lens toward her palm.

She needed answers and she needed them now. She was infuriated that all the stores were closed for the day. She would just have to get up extremely early the next day.

As soon as Ella opened her eyes in the morning, she threw on some clothes, applied some makeup, did a clean of her home and then flew down the stairs. She hurried through completing a quick clean of the Annikovs' flat, made a chicken noodle soup from scratch and put some sandwiches into the fridge for them lunch.

By eight thirty, she was down on the street. She was too stressed to take the tram into town. Instead she walked along the cobbled stone street, oblivious to the scent of freshly baked croissants and bread wafting out of the bakery on the corner. She walked over the bridge crossing the river, glancing up at the huge clock on the church tower.

Eight forty-five. The stores wouldn't open for another forty minutes. She slowed her pace, watching the tourists already strolling the Bahnhofstrasse, looking in the shop windows.

Ella walked into the electronic store and found a salesman. "Excuse me sir, can you tell me how this camera works?"

The balding man pulled his shirt down over his beer belly and straightened to his full height. "We don't sell these here. No idea. Hey Kevin, do you know what this is?"

An athletic-looking teenager with long blond hair and a tattoo of a bear on his forearm wandered over. He gave Ella a dazzling smile. "Good morning."

Ella smiled back and handed over the camera and the book housing a rectangular box.

"Wow, a wireless hidden camera with live high definition streaming. Awesome. Let me look up the specific specs of this model, just a second," said Kevin, pulling out his phone.

"I don't have any Internet connection. So that means the camera can't live stream, right?" asked Ella, crossing her fingers in hope.

"No," answered Kevin, still gazing at his phone.

"You can just see if someone in your building hasn't secured their connection and freeload their access. Wow. Here we go, I found the model. This one even has night vision to twenty-five feet. The footage streams to your smart phone for continuous monitoring wherever you go, day or night. And you can customize the recording options and playback from cloud storage. It even has motion detection so it only records when someone enters the room."

"Night vision? Are you serious?"

"Yeah, the camera can record in complete darkness."

"Which means I've been watched day and night by whoever put this in my flat."

"Savage," said Nathan. "Someone's been watching you? That's serious stuff right there. What's your plan? You going to the police or what?"

"I'm not sure if that will help," answered Ella, looking over her shoulder at the other shoppers. Even now, it was as if eyes were on her.

"If you're asking me? You know there aren't any anti-stalking laws here in Switzerland right? So what'd I'd do, is get myself a hidden camera detector. They're pretty cheap. Then you can sweep your rooms and find out if you have any more secret cameras in your place."

Ella brought a hand to her mouth. She hadn't thought of there being more hidden cameras in her apartment.

"Wait, what? You think there could be more of these?"

Kevin grimaced in response and Ella shivered. Oh god, she didn't want to go back there until she found one of these hidden camera detectors.

"Do you know where I can go buy a detector this morning?"

"Sorry, I think you have to order it online."

"I can't wait that long. What am I going to do?"

Kevin looked up at the ceiling, thinking.

"You know what? I might know someone who has one of those. Maybe they'd let you borrow it, or sell it to you or whatever. I'll give them a call. What's your name, Miss?"

"Ella."

Ella shifted from foot to foot, watching a few customers examining the merchandise.

A few minutes later, Kevin returned.

"So, good news. My colleague is willing to part with his detector. He grabbed it on his way out the door. He's on his way to work. You can pick it up from him at the Apple store. His name's Peter Odermatt."

Ella let out a huge sigh. "Thank you, Kevin."

"Know what else? I'd be checking your bathroom too. Prime spot for a creepy dude to want to have a view, you know what I'm saying? Miss? You okay?"

"Yeah," said Ella, clearing her throat. "I'm a bit scared. I can handle this though."

"Sure thing? You have an ex-boyfriend or something stalking you? You could go to the police if you suspect someone."

"No."

"So you have no idea who's doing this to you?"

Ella shook her head.

"Damn," replied Kevin, handing her back the hidden camera. "That's messed up. You watch yourself, you hear?"

"Wait, Kevin? Is there any way for me to view what footage was taken with this camera?" she said, holding up the camera in her hand.

"Sure, the camera has a 128GB SD card. Just pop it out here. Now you can view it on your laptop. Why you want to do that though? Won't you just be watching yourself?"

"I'm hoping I will see whoever put the camera in my flat."

"Creepy. Like I said, take care."

"Thank you," said Ella, already turning to the door. She now needed two things, a hidden camera detector and a new laptop. Her mother's paranoia had meant she had never owned any electronic devices that connected to the Internet.

That was about to change.

"HELLO, I'M LOOKING for Peter Odermatt?" Ella asked a petite plump young woman with curly dark hair and amber eyes.

Ella followed the pretty woman to the side of the store. A rail-thin man with jet-black hair and tattoos up and down both of his arms gave her a bright smile. "You must be Ella," he said, taking a small black box out of his pocket and handing it to her.

"How much do I owe you?" asked Ella. "And how do I work this?"

"Tell you what, you can have it in exchange for bringing me a vanilla latte and a tiramisu from the confiserie just down the street. I don't need the detector at the moment and I can always order another one."

"Really?" asked Ella. "Thanks."

"No problem. So what you want to do is just hold the camera finder to your eye, look through the lens, and activate the device's LEDs. Any camera lens in view will be visible."

"Thank you again, Mr. Odermatt. I'll be back with your latte and dessert in a few minutes," she said, smiling brightly.

Her fear was beginning to give way to determination. After returning to the Apple store and exchanging the treats for her detector, she wandered around. She wanted to buy a laptop, but she didn't want it registered in her name. She knew she was being paranoid. A childhood of listening to her mother's scare stories and warnings were hard to shake.

It only took a half-hour in the Apple store before Ella heard an American accent and made her approach. His cowboy hat and boots made her smile.

"Hey there. My name's Ella. In exchange for buying a Mac for me with your credit card and registering an account with iTunes with a gift card containing five hundred Swiss francs, I will buy you the latest iPad right now."

She smiled at the look of bewilderment on the ruggedly good-looking man's face. He took a step back, taking off his hat. His bright eyes widened and then narrowed.

"I wasn't born yesterday, you know. I don't want to get into any trouble."

"Listen, I'm hiding from a jealous former boyfriend. I need your help."

He examined her from head to toe, taking in her pale, blond, waist-long hair, her long, fake eyelashes, her shorts showing off long tanned legs, before agreeing.

"I shouldn't do this, but yeah. Yeah okay. I'll do it."

Ella discreetly handed him the cash for the purchase of all the items.

"I'll be right outside."

When he walked outside, he held up the bag and asked, "Now what darlin'?"

She hadn't noticed his startling green eyes in the store, nor just how attractive he was. She had been too wound up with fear and purpose before. Muscles rippled beneath his long sleeved t-shirt rolled up at the sleeves. He wore a pair of frayed jeans and cowboy boots. He was young, she decided. Not much more than twenty.

"If you help me set everything up, then I'll buy you lunch," she offered.

"Now is that right? Alright. Where we headed?"

He gave her a smile, and she liked the way it caused wrinkle lines around his eyes to appear. For such a young man, he had obviously spent a lot of time smiling and being out in the sun.

"How about the Bauschaenzli?"

"I'm not sure I eat that. I'm a meat-and-potatoes kind of man. And vegetables, Ma sure would hate for me not to get some of those."

"That's the name of the restaurant. It's a beer garden right on the river Limmat with a view of the old city, lake and mountains? Do you know it?"

"Nah, I'm a tourist here," he said.

"No kidding?" Ella tried to suppress a smile, looking down at his boots.

"Well, lead the way beautiful," he said, while holding out a hand. Ella hesitated for a moment before placing her hand in his and heading toward the river.

They walked along the narrow cobbled stone streets, pass the boutiques and shops, the café and a large church tower with a clock striking noon. After twenty minutes, they reached the Stadthausquai running along the river. They walked along the walk connecting the street to the island terrace jutting out into the river. They found a table free right next to the water. The waiter came and she ordered a salad, sparkling mineral water and Zürich Kalbsgeschnetzeltes.

"What are you ordering Mr.?"

"Joshua Harris. What did you order?"

"It's sliced veal in a champignon cream sauce with Rösti."

"Make that two. But with one of those large beers those two have over there," he said, pointing to two men with weizen beers at a neighboring table.

As they awaited their meals and then ate lunch, Ella couldn't help keeping a silly grin off her face at the stories Joshua told of misunderstandings he had experienced with the Swiss. She caught herself playing with her hair and giggling at his jokes. She never giggled. What was happening to her? When he stretched out his legs and they connected with hers under the table, she didn't move them. He smiled as much as she did. When she talked, he tilted his head and looked directly into her eyes, as if the rest of the world had ceased to exist for him.

After they finished lunch, she drank an espresso and he a coffee. Her fear over the hidden cameras had abated while sitting in the sun with Joshua, watching the river flow by and enjoying a delicious meal.

As he completed the registration of her Mac, he asked her if she was in trouble without looking up from the screen. She merely answered yes. As he helped her download her favorite music, movies and books to her Mac, she examined his brown hair, tanned skin and the lines around his eyes when he smiled.

She couldn't help but return his good-natured grin. He looked like someone who spent a lot of time laughing.

"Anything more I can do to help, darlin'? Beat up that schmuck boyfriend of yours?"

"I love your American accent," she answered.

"Now don't you try to go on and change the subject now. You sure you'll be alright?"

Ella tilted her head to the side, smiling. "Yes. Thank you."

"You sure? Cause if you are in any kind of big trouble, why you could come on home on home to Oklahoma with me. I think this sure may be love at first sight," he said.

"This is love at first sight?"

"Sure seems that way to me, doll."

Ella laughed, "Well when are we leaving for Oklahoma?"

"Serious now? Let's see, I'll be heading on back day after tomorrow," he said. "I was in town visiting my brother. He up and moved here to be with his Swedish girlfriend. Now what I don't understand is, why the two of them are living in Switzerland instead of Sweden. But she got herself a dream job working for Swarovski as a product designer in Zürich, so here they be. Ben found a job in marketing for a bank.

"He says he don't hate it, but between you and me, I know he misses the ranch and the family. I'm staying with them at their place. Lots of windows and furniture I'm afraid of sitting on because it's all white. Everything in steel, grey and white. A body can't feel at home in a place like that if you ask me. I like a real cozy place. Miss myself some comfortable furniture, the kind you can kick back in."

"So what is it that you do in Oklahoma Mr. Harris?" she asked, smiling up at him from under her eyelashes.

"Mr. Harris. I like that. Don't think anyone has ever called me Mr. Harris before. I'm a rancher. My family owns over nine hundred acres, cattle, fields, orchards. A right bit of heaven on earth, I tell you. Except the heat. Those hundred-degree days can be a hard take in middle summer," he said, leaning back in his chair and examining her with a grin.

"Oh what a shame. I can't tolerate the heat. And I can't really imagine myself a rancher's wife, but as cute as you are, I was almost ready to give it a go," she laughed.

"What? Hold up there now. Are you so pretty darlin', that I went on and proposed somewhere in the last few minutes without remembering it?"

"You strike me as an upstanding man, Mr. Harris. I can't imagine you inviting a young woman back to Oklahoma with you, without it indicating a proposal of marriage," she answered, smiling.

"In all serious now, how would you feel about going out to

dinner with me tonight?" he asked. "This city is expensive enough that a dinner would rob me of my entire bank account, but for a night with you, well, it would sure be worth it."

A lightness was washing over her. Could life be this light, so carefree and playful? It had been so long since she had experienced the emotion.

Perhaps it was the way he was smiling down at her with that good-natured smile, two dimples showing. A few hours ago, she had been scared beyond measure, and here she was reveling in flirting with a handsome stranger.

She was enjoying every breath of this moment, but as her Mama always told her, best to leave a party when you are still having a fabulous time. She almost wished she was older, experienced in life, one of those woman who could take up with a ruggedly sexy man like this and revel in the intoxication of an intense two-day affair.

"What a shame, I have previous engagement. But it was a delight meeting you, Mr. Harris," she said, standing up.

"Joshua," he interrupted, going to stand up as well.

She reached out a hand and gently pushed him back down in his chair. The spring air was fresh and cool on her face, and she could smell the chestnut blossoms of the tree above them and feel the sun warming the back of her legs as she stood over him. For a moment she was someone else, a character in a movie. Girl meets cowboy in Zürich, pan out to take in the church towers, the river flowing into a shimmering lake, the Swiss flags fluttering on the bridges, the alpine mountain range white dusted in the distance. Zoom in on a young woman looking into the eyes of a handsome man smiling up at her.

Her hand was still on his chest. Without thinking she leaned in, her other hand resting on his muscular arm, looking into his eyes.

"Hi there," he whispered.

His lips touched hers gently, a question. A kiss had never this sweet and carefree. Her heart was a hummingbird in her chest at the sensation of his lips on hers. He smelled clean and fresh with a touch of spice. He brought his hands up to her face, and she returned the kiss.

He stood up, just a breath taller than she was in her heels. Pulling her forward, he gently enfolded her in his arms, and she savored the strong line of him pressed against her. She pulled back dreamily, trying to remember all of it.

The blossom petals drifting down from the tree, the smell of espresso, the hum of a river boat cruising by, the toll of a church tower ringing the hour. But most of all, his eyes, the spicy smell of his aftershave, the feel of his lips on hers, his arms around her. He looked down into her eyes and she smiled up at him, heat flushing her cheeks.

"It was nice to meet you Mr. Harris. I wish you a most pleasant trip back home to Oklahoma. Inform me if you ever move someplace a little more temperate?" she almost whispered, his arms still strong around her.

"For sure," he said, pulling her closer. She pulled away, and he took up her Mac from the table, entering his information into the notes section. "Let me take you to dinner."

She shook her head, still smiling. "I already have plans."

Why did she feel the need to lie to this man? Ever since the bizarre events with her neighbors and finding the hidden camera, mistrust was branded into her very skin like a series of red hot iron marks.

"Well," he let out a huge sigh, shaking his head.

"You ever want to get in touch, you have my number and contact information. Don't be afraid of just showing up on my doorstep now. You'd be a sight for sore eyes any day or night."

She didn't answer. She lifted up on her tiptoes and kissed him on the cheek, then turned and headed up the street.

CHAPTER 14

ELLA EASED HER WAY ON SILENT FEET, her back pressed to the hallway wall, inching her way toward her studio while watching for any movement in the hallway. At the stairs to her flat, she paused again, listening.

Stair by creaking stair, she made her way to her door and tried the handle. Locked.

Ella opened up the door to her flat wide and surveyed the room. It was empty. She immediately went to the bathroom, searching in the wardrobe.

No one.

She took out the hidden camera detector. She held it to her eye to scan the room. She startled instantly backward.

That couldn't be right, could it? She turned off the light and carefully unwound a light bulb from above her mirror, examining it closely.

The hair on the base of her neck stood on end, her stomach churning. There was a camera hidden inside the light bulb. Fear crept along her skin, prickling and biting at the thought of someone watching her most intimate moments.

Sudden fury rushed in, a consuming fire raging and searing away her fear. She threw the bulb to the floor. She knelt down, picking up her scale.

She broke the light bulb on the first blow, but continuing to beat the fragments until the tightness of her jaw slackened, the red mist before her eyes thinning.

She stood up. She would clean up the mess later. First she needed to survey the rest of the small studio.

At the front door, there was one extra coat hook with a hidden camera inside. How had she not noticed it before? She tossed it outside onto the street below.

It was then she noticed the camera outside her window. She grabbed a chair and stood up to pull the last camera down from its place of concealment.

Were there any more? She obsessively went through every square inch of her home to find any cameras still lurking unseen. Although she couldn't find any more, she couldn't shake the feeling of still being watched.

Exhausted emotionally and physically she collapsed into a chair at her dining room table and opened her new Mac. She plugged in the memory card from the hidden camera, reviewing the footage.

Owen's face appeared huge was on the screen. She gasped, almost falling off her chair and began shaking uncontrollably. Owen's face diminished as he stepped down to the floor, replacing the chair he had been standing on to its exact position before walking out the front door, pulling it shut behind him.

How had he gotten past her four deadbolt locks?

Time skewed and became slippery in the backlash of seeing Owen's face on her screen.

At last Ella slammed the screen of her laptop shut, clicked off the lights and peered out the window at Owen's flat. She spotted him lurking in the shadows on his terrace, looking up at her window.

She froze, a moan escaping her throat. She clamped a hand over her mouth, as if he could hear her and sank to floor, wrapping her arms around her knees and rocking herself back and forth.

Breathe Ella. Just breathe.

She couldn't stay here. A compulsion to flee seared through her body. He had gotten in to place the cameras once with no sign of forced entry. How could she prevent him from doing it again?

No. She wouldn't live like this, feeling eyes creeping over her bare skin in the shower, following her every movement in her own home and even watching her sleep in the dark.

Quickly now, Ella. He could be contemplating walking across the street even now, while she sat here alone and vulnerable in the dark.

Ella sent a prayer of thanks up to her mother. She would benefit today from her mother's paranoia. She still had their two large, black, wheeled suitcases in their cellar storage unit, ready to go at a moment's notice to flee the Russian mafia.

She took the elevator to the dark cellar, undid the locks, pulled them out and upstairs with her. Once back in her flat, she opened one of them.

Almost everything she required was already neatly packed into a series of cloth bags and clear durable plastic bags with aluminum zips. One cloth bag held a photo album containing pictures of her mother, her grandmother and herself.

Another cloth bag held her clothes, a swimsuit and enough underwear for twenty days. Another held her own ballet shoes, as well as those of her mother.

A plastic bag contained her toiletries, a medicine bag, a curling iron and a hair dryer. Sheets, towels and a premium-quality, thin feather-down duvet were packed tightly in yet another bag.

A small pot, pan, set of dishes and basic cooking utensils filled a small box. A cloth bag contained a large quantity of high-protein Power Bars, nuts, crackers, dried fruit, peanut butter, jam and tea.

There was a small spray bottle of bleach, three microfiber cloths, citrus all-purpose soap, a small bottle of laundry detergent and multiple bottles of hand disinfectant in a double plastic bag. In the middle was a rolled yoga mat.

In the front zip of the suitcase, she had a solar-powered charging unit, which she could use to power her new Mac laptop. Adding the Mac laptop to her purse, she checked once again that the wireless card was indeed removed from the device as Mr. Harris insisted it was.

She had time to add a few more things to the bag. She quickly added the framed photograph of her mother, her grandmother's jewelry, her newest ballet slippers, some more of her clothes, thirty of her favorite books from her shelf, the duvet from her bed, the lavender spray from her nightstand and on last glance her favorite cashmere blanket.

She was ready. One trembling breath and she grabbed her coat, her purse and struggled with the two heavy bags down the stairs and back into the Annikovs' apartment.

Ella grabbed her jacket and locked the door behind her. She didn't know why she was bothering. The locks hadn't stopped him from getting in before. But they would slow him down, she guessed.

Ella decided to sleep on the Annikovs' couch for a few hours. Thank goodness she had them and a key to their flat, because it would be safer to leave in the day.

Or at least it would feel safer. Curling up on the couch, Ella stared at the chandelier until her thoughts fractured and she fell into a deep and dreamless sleep.

"**My little sun**, why are you sleeping on the sofa?"

Ella jolted up, bewildered for a moment as to why she was in the Annikovs' apartment. The events of the previous night came crashing back into her consciousness. An urge to flee from the flat into the early morning air overwhelmed her, but she took a deep breath and sat back down. She needed to follow her plan. But first she would follow through with her plans to help the Annikovs.

"I am sorry babushka," said Ella. "I can't live here anymore. There is someone stalking me."

"Stalking you, how can that be? Who? We'll call the police."

Ella shook her head. "I don't think the police can help. There aren't any anti-stalking laws in Switzerland. No. I don't want to leave you, but I need to move to a new town and start over, where he can't find me. It is so fortunate that we already arranged for someone from the Spitex to come for a visit and assess how they can assist you. Someone will need to come in once a week and clean and cook a few meals to put into the fridge. I want to make sure you will be well taken care of when I don't live here anymore."

"I just want you safe," said Mrs. Annikov.

"I'll call you as soon as I've found a new place to live," said Ella, tears stinging her eyes. It would be so hard not to see her regularly anymore.

Leaning over, Mrs. Annikov kissed Ella on the top of the head and then wrapped her arms around Ella, pulling her into a gentle hug.

The gesture brought tears to Ella's eyes. Taking a deep breath, Ella took Mrs. Annikov's hands in her own.

"Thank you," whispered Ella, rising and hugging the frail woman gently. "Now I will see about cleaning this flat and making you some meals for the week."

"You don't have to do that," said Mrs. Annikov.

"I want to. Please let me, babushka. I couldn't bear it if I didn't leave you in a clean, sweet smelling flat with food in the fridge."

Mrs. Annikov nodded and shuffled back into her room to dress. Ella stood up, stretching and put on her rubber clothes.

A few hours later, Ella smiled in satisfaction. The Annikovs' flat was sparkling clean, smelling of bleach and lemon. There were fresh flowers on the table, and she had filled the fridge with her homemade meals as well as lots of fresh fruit and vegetables, already cut up and placed into Tupperware.

It had taken backbone to force herself out onto the street and to the grocery store. Now she was happy she had braved the open street.

"Babushka, I need to go now. I love you."

Mrs. Annikov held out her arms, and Ella gathered the small woman into an embrace.

"I love you too, my granddaughter. You go and be safe. Don't worry about Sergey and I, we will be alright. You take care of yourself now."

Ella walked to the back bedroom and knocked on the door. No one answered. She opened the door.

Mr. Annikov lay asleep on the bed. Quietly she tiptoed over to the bed and kissed his cheek before soundlessly slipping out the door, down the hall and through their front door.

Ella made her way to the back entrance to their building and quickened her pace through the back alleys. Eventually she made her way to the Bahnhofstrasse.

If he was following her, then she needed to lose him. Her long pale blond hair was easy to recognize, her heels too loud, her makeup bold. She wove into the Prada store and out again. Pushing through crowds, slipping behind corners along the teeming street, she jumped onto a tram just as its doors were closing and jumped off again a few blocks later as soon as the doors swung open, dashing into the Grieder store, past the designer clothing and directly into the elevator.

The sweat was trickling down between her breasts, along her shoulder blades and beading on her forehead. It was a challenge dragging her luggage everywhere.

Not exactly discreet.

In the ladies room, she quickly freshened up and reapplied makeup. She sashayed from there straight to the reception desk of the salon, asking if they had an appointment free, immediately, while pulling out a one-hundred-franc bill from her pocket. The woman behind the counter nodded.

"In a half-hour there will be a spot I can squeeze you into."

Ella sighed, impatience flaring. She nodded and made her way to the Griederbar's elegant terrace overlooking Zürich's Paradeplatz. She settled back into a chair among the greenery, looking over her shoulder and ordered a cappuccino from the waitress.

She glanced repeatedly at her watch, circling her bracelet around and around her wrist. Tiny piranha fish were nibbling at her nerve endings. At last the thirty minutes were over.

"Would you care for a glass of champagne?" asked the receptionist as she led Ella to a salon chair.

"A sparkling mineral water please," she answered. She would have loved the glass of champagne, but she knew she mustn't drink. She needed all her senses acute.

A few moments later, a man with dark brown eyes and dark hair strode over to her chair.

Running his hands immediately through her long strands of blond, he smiled at her in the mirror.

"Beautiful, beautiful hair. What shall we be doing today? Just a little trim, hmm? Maybe a few lowlights?"

"I want it all cut off to my chin and dyed auburn brown."

"What? No, no, no, you will regret it, cutting off all this

beautiful hair. You don't want to cut it all off? From waist long to chin? Perhaps we take just a bit off today, go for the mid-back, then you come back next week and we see, hmm? Same price," he cooed at her, urging her to change her mind before it was too late.

"Yes. Yes, thank you. You are right. Just cut it to mid-back and dye it light brown."

"Would you be interested in some a deep conditioning treatment? Or some highlights?"

"Sure. But I am in a hurry to make a plane flight, so do what you can in the next hour. Let's get going," snapped Ella. She was instantly mortified. "I'm sorry for being so short, I'm just a bit stressed."

The stylist smiled, "Bad day?"

"You have no idea," she replied.

Thirty-two minutes later, Ella was starting to fume at how long the stylist was taking on her hair. She wanted to be out on the street again by three-thirty to take advantage of the throngs of shoppers on the Bahnhofstrasse and at the train station. She informed the stylist she didn't need her hair dried or styled, and a few minutes later she paid and was out the door.

While descending the stairs of the store, she noticed a white straw sun hat with a black band. She paid for it with cash.

Taking her bags in tow, she ventured forth back out onto the Bahnhofstrasse, swerving through the crowds, and hurried to her bank. In the lobby, she waited impatiently for a teller to become available. As soon as she reached the counter, she handed the grey suit behind the counter her withdrawal form.

"Excuse me, perhaps you have made a mistake with adding too many zeros?" asked the man behind the counter.

"No mistake. I would like it in one thousand dollar bills and small change," she responded, her chin lifted.

"One moment please, I do not have those funds available at the counter," he replied.

Ella tapped her foot impatiently as she waited. What is taking this dark suit so long? I will feel better as soon as I put some distance between myself and this city.

"Good afternoon, I am the bank floor manager. Is there a

problem?" asked a new suit. This one, she noticed, wore a red tie and a sour expression.

"I'm sorry for the inconvenience, but would it be possible to withdraw all my money from my account in cash?"

Her face flushed and sweat beaded on her forehead.

"Am I correctly informed that you are emptying your account with us? If you are switching to another bank, we are happy to assist you with a bank transfer and eliminate the danger of carrying such a large sum of money on your person. Just fill this out."

"No. As I stated before, I would like the sum in one thousand franc notes and smaller change please," repeated Ella. "I'm, um, going shopping," she improvised.

"Excuse me Madam, but may I ask if there is a problem with your Maestro card? We would be happy to give you a replacement so you can pay for purchases as you go."

Ella sighed. This man was relentless.

She was a bit surprised that it was proving so challenging to withdraw her money from the bank in cash in one lump sum. She would have to remember this when she accessed some of her other accounts at various other banks in the future. She would be better off taking out smaller sums over a period of time in cash.

Ella sighed. She had thought the blurry days of looking over their shoulders and running from one shelter to the next were behind her for good when they had landed in Zürich. She hadn't imagined standing in this bank, asking for over a fifty thousand francs in cash to be handed across the counter.

Ella knew she needed to hurry. Her grandmother had instilled in her both grace and politeness, as well as the necessity of responding to arrogance. She could almost hear her mother countering, 'Some people just don't respond to nice Mom. Don't turn Ella into a smiling victim.'

Ella lifted her chin and smiled with her lips pressed together. Raising her voice, she said, "Excuse me, sir, you are seriously trying my patience. Do I need to make a call to the police that this bank is refusing to return my funds into my possession?"

"What? No, of course not. One moment please."

The teller quickly returned, counted out the cash and placed it in an envelope, which he slid over the counter. She took the envelope and made her way to the restroom in the bank lobby. In a stall, she carefully transferred the majority of the cash from the envelope to a cloth zipped pocket sewn into her camisole.

Feeling relieved that the hardest task was completed, she made her way out of the bank and to the train station. On the fourth platform, she jumped on a train heading to the Zürich airport just before the doors closed shut for departure. She didn't know how anyone could have managed to jump on the train after her, even if they had managed to keep track of her to this point. They would have had to literally be on her heels, step for step. A few minutes later, the train arrived at the airport.

Ascending the escalator, Ella made her way to the Swiss airlines right in front of her. She went to desk and purchased a ticket for the next flight to Paris with her credit card. Ella had planned this all out years ago with her mother. Her next stop was to visit the Baggage Service. Until she knew where she was going to move to, she was too conspicuous with two large wheeled Samsonite bags. At the desk, she quickly paid for the maximum storage time of three months, just in case, and made her way to the security control line in the airport with one bag instead of two.

She browsed through the duty-free shops, bought a box of macaroons and a box of chocolates from the Sprüngli shop, a women's newsboy hat and a pair of large, rose-tinted Prada sunglasses before snatching up her carry-on bag and slipping into the restroom. In the restroom, she put on the wide brimmed hat she had purchased in the Grieder store, the sunglasses and a new dress before sauntering toward the exit doors and to the hair salon.

Fortunately, she only needed to wait a little over twenty minutes, her heart hammering in her chest, before a stylist was free. In forty-four minutes he was done. Ella examined her reflection in the mirror. Instead of straight brown hair, she now had a short auburn brown cut framing her face with pretty curls. She asked the stylist if she had any makeup remover on hand. She carefully removed her fake eyelashes, her layers of mascara and eyeliner, the bright red lipstick. She paid the stylist and made her way to the restroom where she changed out of her elegant dress and heels into jeans, a long-sleeved black t-shirt, a leather jacket, ballerina flats, and the newsboy hat. Surveying her reflection in the mirror with grim satisfaction, she looped a geometric patterned scarf around her neck. She looked radically different, scrubbed clean.

A little over ten minutes later, she leaped down the escalator stairs descending to track three and jumped through the closing doors of a train heading to Konstanz, Germany just as the doors shut.

Ella let out a sigh of relief. If someone was following her, they would have seen her purchasing a plane ticket and going through security into the main terminal. She had changed her appearance twice. Hopefully that would procure her some confusion. She didn't know how someone could have possibly followed her onto this train in time. But she still didn't feel safe.

She stood at the doors, waiting for the train to make its stop in Winterthur. In Winterthur, she exited the train and made her way slowly toward a coffee stand a few steps away. The train whistled and she pivoted, took up her bags in both hands and ran back to the train, stopping to look along the platform before jumping back into the train.

Taking deep breath to slow her racing heart, Ella made her way to the train restaurant compartment and sat down at a table for two. She wanted more than anything to order a glass of wine. Instead she ordered a mint tea and a piece of cake. A cup of tea was steaming, the cup warm in her hand as the rolling green hills rolled by outside her window, dotted with dairy cows, some with large bells around their necks. The knots in her neck and shoulders began to loosen as she took a deep breath and let it out.

She would need to start over once again, like so many times in the past. But this time was different. This time she was alone.

Ella knew her mother would run to a new country, contact a woman's shelter and work through official channels to obtain a new identity. Ella knew she wouldn't need to go through all of those energy-robbing steps. She would retain her own identity and she would return to Zürich to dance. He wasn't going to come between her and the dream she had worked so hard to achieve.

Ella had thought this all out after her Grandmother's death. In Switzerland, you could only rent a flat legally if you were registered with the town. Sure, plenty of people worked illegally in Switzerland. But with her mother's falsified Swiss citizenship, she had a right to apply to official jobs and a security net she wasn't yet ready to give up. She had applied to her job at Flavor with her mother's identity. She paid taxes under her mother's name and all the new bank accounts were under that name as well. Fortunately, her resemblance to her mother meant it wasn't even necessary to forge any documents with new photographs.

So the question was, where in Switzerland should she live? It would need to be within an hour of Zürich. Ella knew she would need to spend a few days moving from one town to the next. But then she could settle down somewhere. Ella envied the man at the table across from her with his iPhone. He could search the Internet at a whim. She would need to find a public computer in order to research her options. Her laptop didn't have the capability of connecting to the Internet anymore, even if she wanted it to.

Ella noticed her table had access to a power outlet. She took her Mac out of her purse and plugged it in to charge. She had the solar power charger, but she wasn't sure what the weather forecast would be in the next few days. Ella smiled, the memory of how she had procured her laptop briefly surfacing. She already missed Joshua Harris.

Ella thought of their first kiss and considered emailing the cowboy. She'd memorized his contact information. She shook her head.

The memory of her afternoon, the kiss, was already one of her most beloved possessions. Especially after all she had just been through, she didn't want to sacrifice the perfection of that moment to the mundane exchange of words spewed across cyberspace. She had been so wrong about Owen. She didn't want to be wrong about Joshua too.

Chapter 15

In Konstance, Ella jumped on a series of buses, cruising the town looking for a hotel. When she spied a hotel on the banks of the river, she jumped off at the next stop. Ella checked into a hotel suite with floor-to-ceiling windows looking out over the river. The first day, she passed some cash to the front desk for accessibility to the ballroom so she could continue her ballet training sessions.

Using the computer in the business office, she ordered a Kindle to be shipped to her, care of the hotel. A longing to be with the Annikovs, or with Adnan, Aya, Nick or even grumpy Mr. Vasiliev manifested itself as an ache radiating down her back. She wanted to call them, but what would she say? She wasn't ready to explain why she had fled Zürich. Loneliness was biting at her heels. After hesitating for a moment, she changed her mind about the cowboy. She opened a new Gmail account and sent Joshua an email.

Dear Joshua,

You have not been far from my thoughts. Are you enjoying your work on the ranch? I didn't tell you this when we met, but I was a ballet dancer. I sometimes felt silly, spending so many hours by myself, training. I wasn't sure I would ever dance again on a stage. Yet it gave me a joy and inner strength I can't explain, so I continued and just recently was offered a job in a ballet. What gives you joy? I hope this email finds you healthy and happy.

With warmest wishes, Ella

Ella pressed send and then cringed. Was that a stupid email? Then again, did it matter? She wouldn't ever see Joshua again. He probably wouldn't answer. She was about to close Internet Explorer when an email popped into her box.

Ella, darlin',

What took you so long to write? I have thought of you literally every day since I last saw you. I feel a fool I didn't chase after you; lett'n you walk away from me like that. A ballet dancer huh? I sure can see it. Hey if it gives you joy, then keep dancing! The luckiest know what makes us happy and seize it with both hands. For me it is sitting on my horse at twilight, a coolness seeping up out of the fields, the first stars coming out as I ride towards a home cooked meal. Hope you don't think less of me; I still live with my Mama. But it sure does seem awful silly, to get my own place in the small town, only to commute out here each day more than half an hour to the ranch to work.

Miss'n you. Joshua PS. Have yourself a new fella?

Ella grinned from ear to ear. Her mother and grandmother would have been horrified by the rough edges and lack of refinement of Joshua. She, in contrast, found him a breath of fresh air after spending a life around the type of people who lived for classical ballet. Without hesitating, she wrote him back.

Dear Joshua, No, I don't have a new boyfriend. You?

She waited breathless for a response. But none came. She waited ten more minutes and then logged out of her account.

As she left the hotel business center, a voice called out, "Hey beautiful, can I interest you in a drink?"

Ella glanced over her shoulder, thinking how harsh German

sounded after years of listening to the melodic Swiss German dialect. The German man was dressed in a full suit, briefcase in hand. He stood waiting for her answer, obviously on his way to the bar after a day of work.

"I'm pregnant and madly in love with my husband," she answered in Swiss German. She pressed the button for the elevator. She found it amusing that while the Swiss Germans could understand German, the majority of Germans couldn't understand the Swiss German dialect.

"Excuse me?" he answered.

Ella waved goodbye to the German as she stepped into the elevator.

It had been painful to leave her bookshelves full of books behind, and she hoped to someday build her own personal library again. She thought of her empty hotel room and wished she had something to read. When her Kindle arrived, she could use the hotel Internet to download as many books as would fit on her new device. Until then she would have to find something else to do. Seeing the bathrobe laid out on her bed, she made up her mind.

Relaxing a few minutes later in the sauna, she felt her muscles releasing tension in the heat. She started thinking about where she should live next. After a jump into an icy pool, she showered and changed, before walking across the street and bringing takeout back to her room. She refused to think about the Annikovs.

Just the mere whisper of the thought of the life lost to her, her friends at Flavor, her volunteer work and above all the love and comfort of her self-appointed grandparents left her close to melting to the floor, like a popsicle in the sun on a hot day. It was then that her thoughts turned to Joshua's email, which made her smile.

The next day Ella returned to Zürich for ballet class and rehearsal wearing sunglasses and a hat pulled down over her hair. She called a taxi and dashed into it to make the long commute back to a different hotel in Constance.

On the third day, Ella didn't have ballet rehearsal. She sat at the hotel computer looking through flat listings. Her ears were ringing, and she couldn't focus enough to make any decision on where to look for a new flat. Instead, she checked out of the hotel and jumped on a series of buses, which landed her in Kreuzlingen, Switzerland where she made her way down to the harbor.

She made sure she was the last one to jump on the ship, scanning the park for anyone who might have been stalking her to the lake front. Yet again her resolve to start a new life began wobbling. The memory of finding the surveillance camera on her bookshelf floated into her consciousness. There was no going back, only forward into the abyss of chance and circumstance.

"Is this seat taken?"

Ella flinched, looked up with bloodshot eyes, startled from her reverie. Mr. Vasiliev stood before her with his broad shoulders, twinkling blue eyes behind round spectacles, bushy white eyebrows and white hair. She shook her head.

"What are you doing here?"

"Everything alright? You look rather lost."

"Fine. Actually, can I use your phone?"

"What? Why?"

"I'm looking for a new flat."

The old man shook his head. "No Internet connection I'm afraid. However, I do know of a beautiful flat for rent in the small castle in Romanshorn. If you are interested, I will tell my real estate friend to meet you there sometime this week for a viewing. Why are you moving from Zürich?"

Ella tilted her head, considering his offer. "Why are you on a boat on the Bodensee, Mr. Vasiliev?"

"Call me dedushka."

Ella shook her head.

"A good grandfather wouldn't leave her granddaughter to grieve for her mother and grandmother alone."

"I'm here now, aren't I? I followed you all the way from Zürich. Are you okay?"

Ella whipped her head around. "How is that possible?"

"I dropped a GPS tracker in the inner lining of your purse a long time ago, when I thought you might get your mother's illness. I didn't want to loose you."

"No," inhaled Ella. "It was you. You hid those cameras in

my flat. How could you? Get away from me!"

Mr. Vasiliev took a step back. "Hidden cameras? No!"

"You followed me here," stammered Ella.

"Why are you stalking me?"

"Ella, this is serious. I didn't hide any cameras in your flat," insisted Mr. Vasiliev.

"I find that hard to believe. Because someone is stalking me, and here you are, on the same boat as I am."

Mr. Vasiliev collapsed onto a chair, tears streaming down his cheeks. He placed his face in his hands. "You've inherited your mother's illness. Good god, not again. I can't bear it."

"I'm not delusional, Mr. Vasiliev," said Ella, turning back around to face him. "I have proof." She pulled out her laptop and the smashed hidden camera from her bag. She opened the screen and pressed play. "See for yourself."

Mr. Vasiliev raised his face from his hands. He stared in disbelief at the screen and then at the tiny smashed camera on the table. "Who?"

"Owen. I think, or, I don't know what to think. Who else could it be?"

"I'll kill him with my bare hands."

"Perfect. Just perfect. You do that," muttered Ella.

"I'm your grandfather. I will help you however I can. I'll figure out a way to do it."

"What? Stop talking like that. You know what, I'll have a look at that flat of yours. Call your friend."

"Done."

"And stop following me."

Ella looked out at the waves and the rolling green hills of Switzerland. She was just admiring an orchard and a vineyard passing by on the hills rolling down toward the lake shore when Mr. Vasiliev turned toward her.

"What about looking at the flat today at four?"

"Sure," said Ella. "Now leave me alone Mr. Vasiliev."

"Not on your life. I already made the mistake of staying away from you since you were six. I plan on staying close the rest of your life, especially after all this," he said, gesturing at the broken hidden camera. "Don't tell me you remember nothing of me from when you were little."

The trouble was, Ella did have happy memories of a man with dark hair and strong hands. That was part of the reason she had taken to him so instantly in the restaurant in Zürich. He had reminded her of the grandfather who had held her little fluttering hand on walks through fields of wildflowers as a child. Who had gone berry picking with her, and taught her how to swim in the lake they visited each summer at their Dacha.

"Where is my father, Mr. Vasiliev?"

"If you won't call me grandfather, at least call me Mr. V."

"Fine, Mr. V, about my father?"

"I'm sorry child. Your grandma and I were never certain who he was. Your mother refused to tell us."

Ella walked to the window, her heels echoing in the empty room against the hardwood floors. She tapped her sunglasses against her hand, thinking.

She liked the view. A small vineyard lay nestled at the foot of the castle.

The rolling town gardens along the lake stretched out green to the left, while straight ahead the turquoise blue of the lake sparkled in the morning sun as the ferry made its way into the harbor.

"Generally one can see the Säntis as well, but the clouds are blocking your view today."

Ella turned to the short, dark-haired man standing behind her. He shifted from one foot to the other, waiting for her to respond. She turned back to the window, lost in thought. The hardwood floors were gorgeous, perfect for dancing. The ceiling moldings were elegant and intricate. The kitchen was remodeled all in modern elegant white. But the bathrooms were ugly and out of date. It didn't matter.

The flat was far too large. She only wanted to finance a small flat. She wanted to make what money she had inherited from her grandmother last. Who knew what the future would bring? Money meant a certain degree of security. What would the rent be on such a flat? Ella looked around. It was such a pity she couldn't afford a home like this.

Looking back out the window, she surveyed the view. There were no neighbors to watch. There were no neighbors to watch her.

Clearing his throat, the real estate agent behind her walked to stand next to her at the window.

"There is another party quite interested in this property. In fact, if you deliberate much longer you could miss this once-in-a-lifetime opportunity to live in a castle."

"It's probably for the best. I probably couldn't afford the rent anyway...."

"Don't be so certain," came a voice at the door.

Ella swung her head around. A woman in her early sixties entered the room. Her silver hair was cut in a stylish A-line cut that came to her chin. She wore perfectly tailored black jeans and a black blouse with ballerina flats. A diamond necklace glittered at her throat.

"My name is Mrs. Frieden," she said, offering her small hand to Ella.

Ella shook her hand and gave a tight smile.

"And you are?" asked Mrs. Frieden.

"Ms. Chinchinian," answered Ella.

"Aha. So not Swiss then. Pity that, I had a proposition for a resident interested in renting this flat. But I don't know about taking up a partnership with a foreigner."

"Well, I was raised in Switzerland. I am a citizen, if that changes anything."

"Hmm, well, it helps a bit I expect. That and the fact you speak Swiss German. Yes," continued Mrs. Frieden, looking her over. "And you look lovely. So. I will be purchasing the castle. I will take the top floor of course, it has the best views of the lake and the Alps.

"You can rent this floor, and the second will be designated for common use when we don't rent it out for seminars or weddings. I plan on opening the restaurant up again. I expect it can be a success if I can find a great chef, a good team and add some ingenuity to the customer experience. I have some great ideas on how to differentiate from the competition."

Ella sneaked a peak at the real estate agent to see if he had secretly planned this meeting.

She watched him wink at Mrs. Frieden. "My seller has sold the castle to,"started the real estate agent.

"Me," interrupted Mrs. Frieden.

The real estate agent paused and turned toward Mrs. Frieden with raised eyebrows. He cleared his throat before continuing. "I must reiterate that the castle must retain its historical appearance.

The government will insist upon preservation regulations being respected in full."

"Of course, of course," answered Mrs. Frieden. "That we will do. Now, shall we go out for a bite to eat and talk things through Ms. Chinchinian? We won't be needing your help Peter, just accompany us down and lock up and you can be on your way. We'll get in touch."

"Well, you have captured my curiosity," said Ella. "But I'm not sure I can afford the rent."

"We'll discuss all that over lunch. I know a cute pizzeria just around the corner. Goodbye Peter, as I said, we will get in touch," said Mrs. Frieden, offering a firm handshake to the real estate agent. Without a backward glance, Mrs. Frieden started walking briskly down the hill. Ella hesitated a moment, then hurried to catch up.

"It's lovely down here on the lake, don't you agree? It will be a dream to live in that small castle and run a restaurant."

"What exactly is your plan?" Ella was a bit out of breath at the sudden emergence of this woman of curt forthrightness.

"Hello, Antonio, are you well? Do you have a table next to the window for two for lunch?"

"Mrs. Frieden, what a pleasure to see you. Yes of course. It is a bit early for lunch. We have yet to turn on the pizza oven. Would you like to enjoy an aperitif while you wait?"

"In that case, we will return in an hour. We will go and enjoy a drink near the water."

"I will reserve your table."

"Now," said Mrs. Frieden, turning to Ella. "We'll just settle in at the beach bar across the way there with a drink and discuss everything in detail. It's probably for the best we are too early for lunch. Antonio is a dear, but he is known to have rather large ears."

"What a brilliant idea," said Ella. Nestled at the edge of the walkway overlooking the lake harbor, the beach bar had a great view of the ships, the water and the Alps in the distance. Pure white sand was spread smooth, held in place by wooden rimming. Cloth lounge chairs were spread out over the man-made beach, while elegant modern couches and lounges sat under sun shades on the wooden deck. Ella began to make her way to the sand. Cool fingers grabbed her on the arm, steering her to the deck.

"Shall we sit at a table?" asked Mrs. Frieden. "The view is excellent, but I do hate getting sand in my shoes. What would you like to drink? It is self-service, I'm afraid."

"Whatever you are having is fine," answered Ella, reaching in her purse for some money.

"I invite you," called Mrs. Frieden over her shoulder, already on her way to the bar.

Ella surveyed the entire lounge, twisting backward to see the entire walkway along the harbor as well as the street behind them. She didn't see Owen, or anyone suspicious. Relief didn't wash over her as she had hopped. She still felt watched. Ella wondered how long it would take for the feeling to go away.

Mrs. Frieden returned with two glasses, setting them down on the table and turning her face up to the sun. "Here we are, two Hugo cocktails. There is nothing quite so refreshing as Prosecco with a dash of elderflower syrup and plenty of mint and lime."

"Thank you," said Ella, "How much do I owe you?"

"Nonsense dear, I said I invite you."

"Invite me where?"

"For the drink. Though I am happy to pay for lunch too. I am really too thrilled at the prospect of finding a partner. Even if you are a foreigner, not to mention far too young. But you look like a girl with a good head on her shoulders. You don't seem as silly as most of the young women your age, the way they flit about in tight clothing and tasseled hair, traveling all over the world at the drop of a hat. You put yourself together very nicely. You seem, serious. Yes. Are you serious Ella?"

"Yes. I suppose I am."

"And, if you don't mind my asking, how is it that a girl

as young as you look is living on her own? You look all of sixteen. Perhaps we should be sitting together with your parents as well?"

"No," Ella took a sip of her drink, trying to swallow the lump that had formed in her throat. It never came easily, saying the words out loud. "I don't have any family. And I'm seventeen."

"No family at all? Grandparents, aunts, cousins…" began Mrs. Frieden.

"No," interrupted Ella.

Mrs. Frieden regarded the young woman sitting with a ramrod-straight back across from her, with her short auburn hair and sad eyes.

"Never mind dear, never you mind now," said Mrs. Frieden, while reaching out and patting Ella's hand. "I'm sure you have plenty of friends. And someday you will fall in love and start a family of your own."

Ella just smiled at the older woman and then glanced down at the table. In the following silence, a bird trilled a song in a tree overhead. The splash and hum of a ship entering the harbor drew Ella's attention.

A ferry was docking on the other side of the small harbor, passengers flowing off the ferry from Friedrichshafen, a few running along the harbor and down the ramp to the train station. Ella wondered absentmindedly if they would manage to make their tight train connections. She looked over her shoulder again.

Mrs. Frieden patted Ella's arm and sighed. "I know what it is like you know. I lost my husband Hans to a heart attack nearly seven years ago. My two children are living in the United States, in Idaho of all places. Anna has four children and a handsome American husband. They visit here once every year or two. It is difficult for them to get away, you see, they own a working ranch in the middle of nowhere and need to hire someone to tend to it while they are gone. It is gorgeous, absolutely gorgeous, the panorama where they live: purple mountains in the distance, fields of rolling wheat and pastures of steers grazing along a crystal clear river.

"About ten years ago my son Gabriel, his wife and their

two babies went to join my Anna and her husband when the ranch next to theirs came up for sale. They combined their acreage and work the land together now.

"I wish I could go visit their ranch again, but I had open heart surgery last year and now I am terrified to get on a plane. My doctor assured me it would be safe, but I am just too scared to fly alone."

Ella squeezed Mrs. Frieden's hand and let go. "Don't you have someone who could fly with you?

Mrs. Frieden's face flushed. "No. I'm alone, just like you. I was an only child. My parents both passed away years ago, and Hans broke off contact with his parents when we married. I had my Hans, Anna and Gabriel, and that was more than enough for me. I didn't feel the need to develop new friendships when I moved here from Geneva, and I lost contact with my childhood friends over the decades. Every available moment, I wanted to spend it with the children or Hans. We were so happy. He died at least twenty years too soon. I miss him beyond measure."

"And now you want to purchase a castle? Why don't you move to Idaho and live near your family?" Ella leaned forward in her chair, resting her arms on the table and waited for an answer. Silence fell over the table again, but Ella didn't gaze away this time. She looked squarely at Mrs. Frieden.

"For the simple reason, that, well, I'm scared," Mrs. Frieden stammered. "And I don't speak any English."

"Well, you could learn," answered Ella. "You could move to Idaho if you really wanted to."

Mrs. Frieden startled in her chair and looked at Ella with a frown on her face before breaking into a grin.

"How so very true, my dear. I like you more with every minute. Sympathy can be the sweetest arsenic known to mankind. More often than not, we need someone to order us to stand up straight, take responsibility and work to change the future in front of us.

"I have always dreamed of opening a restaurant. I'm not getting any younger, you know. This is my last chance. So about this castle. I have worked with my lawyer already to draw up a full contract. Shall we take a look?"

Ella read through the document carefully, including all the fine print. Still gazing at the document, she shook her head. "So you would own the castle and give me the permanent right to live rent-free in the third floor residence, with use of the second and first floor? In exchange I would pay a one-time payment."

"Exactly so," nodded Mrs. Frieden.

"But I don't understand. Why wouldn't you just rent out the third floor? Why the twenty thousand-dollar investment?"

"Now you've come to the central point my dear. I do not want a succession of renters. I want someone who has an investment in the place, who will work with me to make the business on the first and second floors a success. Here, I'm getting hungry. Let's wander over for some pizza."

"Mrs. Frieden, I am part of the Zürich ballet company. I can't help you run a restaurant too."

"Think of it as your hobby dear. You're young. I'm sure you have the energy. And of course I would pay you."

Ella was quiet on the walk across the street to the pizzeria and while they waited to order. She liked Mrs. Frieden and the castle was gorgeous, but would it be wise to invest so much money up front to live there? What if Owen followed her home from the ballet and started stalking her here too? She would need to run again.

Then again, she would have a hard time finding any flat with three rooms for less than a thousand dollars a month, even if it was an older apartment with no view. Mrs. Frieden was offering her a fantastic deal. After just eighteen months, Ella would be living rent free for the rest of her life. That couldn't be right. What was the catch?

Only when a steaming thin-crust pizza covered in ham, fresh mushrooms, artichokes, olives and red peppers was set before her was Ella ready to talk.

"What I would like to know is, why are you doing this? It would be more profitable for you to charge rent each month. And what happens if you sell in a few months? Am I out of the twenty thousand dollars?"

"Look at page four," said Mrs. Frieden. "But watch that you don't get pizza on the contract."

"If you sell the castle, or if your children sell the castle upon your death, then I will receive my twenty thousand dollars back in full, as well as first right to purchase the castle if it is put up for sale." Ella laughed.

"Like I would ever have the money to buy a castle."

"Now, said Mrs. Frieden, taking a sip of her sparkling mineral water, "are you interested?"

Ella took a bite of her pizza, savoring the taste while looking out the windows at the harbor and the snow-covered Alps in the distance.

"I don't trust this. Honestly, it sounds too good to be true."

Mrs. Frieden frowned and then threw up her hands. "You leave me no other choice but to tell you. Your grandfather is behind all of this. He's a friend of mine and he put me up to this. He is worried about your safety. He plans on installing the latest security system in the castle."

Ella shook her head and placed her face in her hands. "Why didn't he just tell me?"

"He wanted it to be your own decision, dear."

"Thank you for being honest with me, Mrs. Frieden." Ella kissed the older woman on the cheek and stood back, smiling. "I'll take the deal. When can I move in?"

Chapter 16

She knew she should be content. The moment she moved in, she went through not only her flat, but the entire castle looking for hidden cameras. There were none. Mr. V installed a security door at the bottom of the stairway up to the flats with a security camera. Ella hired a car to take her to and from Zürich each day. She at last began to feel safe.

She enjoyed planning the restaurant with Mrs. Frieden, and its opening was a smashing success.

In addition to numerous repeat customers, they had a flood of day tourists, in particular on the weekends.

Ella knew it was the little touches that enabled her and Mrs. Frieden to enjoy such success. Whenever possible guests were greeted by name. A free bottle of ice-cold cucumber or lemon-infused tap water was always brought to the table, as was a basket of house-made rosemary mint crackers. When the bill was paid, homemade chocolate mint truffles were offered.

Every Thursday, they brought out the popcorn trolley and served baskets of free hot buttery popcorn. Every day there was a new specialty martini, which could be ordered by the glass, or at a huge price reduction, by the pitcher.

Each week they created a new conversation game and placed a copy on each table. In addition, there was a basket next to each table on the terrace with adult coloring books, colored pencils and crayons. She had been rather shocked at the hours her adult guests would spend peacefully coloring. Every Friday they had a themed evening with decorations and live music.

Their first themed evening had been a Hawaiian luau, which the Swiss had enjoyed so much, they had repeated the same evening again a month later.

The first step had been hiring the staff.

Ella had called Adnan at once. She felt guilty about trying to steal him away from Nick, but she missed him and Aya so much, and it was an opportunity for Adnan to be an executive chef.

Mrs. Frieden, who professed to abhor so many foreigners moving into Switzerland, thus hired a chef who knew only a handful of German words. At each interview Mrs. Frieden requested every cook to prepare an appetizer and a main course. Adnan's food was going away the most delicious and inspired. Both Ella and Mrs. Frieden had never had anything quite like the meal Adnan had prepared. Only after they had tasted all the meals did Mrs. Frieden review the resumes of her applicants.

"Adnan is a refugee with permanent residency approval pending," sighed Mrs. Frieden. "He has completed some sort of refugee cooking apprenticeship program and worked as a sous chef at Flavor in Zürich. The other applicants are all Swiss or German. It would be a lot less paperwork to hire one of them. Not to mention easier to communicate with our cook. Ella? Are you listening? It would be unwise to hire Adnan, surely. You know how I feel about foreigners. We can't have all these bloody people pouring into Switzerland non-stop. It is a small country! We're up to almost twenty-five percent of the population being foreigners."

"I'm telling you Mrs. Frieden, I worked with him at Flavor in Zürich. He is a fantastic cook and a good man," insisted Ella. "You won't regret hiring him."

"The man's food was spectacular. Shouldn't the job go to the most talented cook, irrelevant of other circumstances? I don't care if this woman worked in the five-star hotel in St. Moritz. Her food was a fraction as good as Adnan's."

"You're going to hire him, aren't you Mrs. Frieden?"

"I suppose I am. But you see here, I want a cook I can talk to. You call him up and tell him: no German course, no job. Do you hear me? There is an excellent German class in town, and he is to report there for class once a week. I know most of the teachers."

"And the servers? Who shall we choose?"

"I told you Ella, I choose the cook, you choose the servers."

"I want Adnan's wife Aya. And I liked the young Swedish sisters Elin and Malin," decided Ella.

Mrs. Frieden shook her head. "No. I'll take one refugee but not two. Elin and Malin are fine, though those girls are studying up in St. Gallen. They will work the summer and quit once school starts up again."

"Yes, I know," admitted Ella. "I think that's a good thing. I am sure things will slow down considerably in the fall and winter. We won't need additional servers in the cold months."

So it was that Elin, Malin and Adnan joined their team. Ella complained bitterly about Aya not being hired to the team, to no avail.

To Mrs. Frieden's chagrin, she had hired a staff full of foreigners. On their first day, Mrs. Frieden lined the new staff up in the restaurant, like a drill sergeant.

"I don't care where you came from before, you are all in Switzerland. I insist on perfect punctuality. You show up for work late and you are fired. There will be no excuses around here. Second of all, you will be polite and discreet. You will greet the recurring customers, whenever possible, by their last name. There will be none of this, 'my name is Jenny, how are you today?' nonsense like in the United States. It isn't that we don't care how are customers are doing, the point is, it is none of our business," instructed Mrs. Frieden.

Ella raised her hand.

"Yes Ella," asked Mrs. Frieden.

"Wouldn't it be a good idea to be friendly? I mean, isn't it kind to want to know how their day is going?" asked Ella.

"Dear lord and then what? What if their dog was run over, or they lost their job, or they are going through a divorce? What then, child? What are you going to answer? It isn't as if you can sit down at the table and discuss their problems with them. We are serving food and drinks and a delightful atmosphere, not therapy sessions."

"Oh Mrs. Frieden. I don't think people will actually answer those things. They'll just answer fine, even if they aren't. And if they are having a great day, they'll mention it's their birthday, or they aced a test, or got a promotion at work. Things like that."

"Now why ask if you don't want a real answer? No, I don't want any of these superficial shenanigans going on. We are a Swiss establishment, even if you lot aren't, and we will be polite, discreet and attentive. Not all Swiss restaurants have good service, but we will have the best."

One of their first regular customers was the white-haired Mr. Vasiliev. He was the only customer on the terrace on Wednesday afternoons the first two weeks after opening. Ella tolerated his presence on the condition he not tell anyone he was her grandfather.

The old curmudgeon actually insisted on going back to the kitchen and showing Mrs. Frieden and Ella how to make a Raf coffee his first visit to the castle terrace. Mrs. Frieden led him tight-lipped to the kitchen's espresso machine. Mr. Vasiliev made a shot of espresso, added it to the silver milk jar, added cream, one tablespoon of plain sugar and then one tablespoon of vanilla sugar. He steamed everything together and poured it from a height into his coffee cup.

"That is how you make a Raf," exclaimed Mr. V. "Put it on the menu please. It will be a hit."

Mrs. Frieden put her hands on both hips and glared back at the man in front of her. "This is my restaurant, not yours. Do you know how unhealthy that drink is? Two tablespoons of sugar and a bunch of cream? You are asking for health problems. I'll tell you that right now."

"Helen has a face of a beauty, but only hell likes her temper," laughed Mr. V to Ella. "Give it a try, woman, don't be so stubborn. If it doesn't sell well in a fortnight, then I'll take you out to dinner every Friday night."

Mrs. Frieden tried her best to suppress a smile. She shot Mr. Vasiliev a look that was hard for Ella to read.

"Who says I want to go out to dinner with the likes of you?"

asked Mrs. Frieden, her hands still on her hips.

"I'll be ordering a few every Wednesday, so you best learn how to make it properly," laughed Mr. Vasiliev. He winked at Mrs. Frieden as he shuffled by her back to the terrace, where he settled into his place in the corner next to the red climbing roses and began to color.

"What a character," laughed Ella, her feelings toward the old man softening. She noticed Mrs. Frieden smiling to herself and watching Mr. V while folding napkins.

"Is there something going on with you and Mr. V, Mrs. Frieden?" asked Ella. "I sense a chemistry?"

"What? What would give you that idea?" scoffed Mrs. Frieden and disappeared into the kitchen.

Mrs. Frieden and Ella fell into a routine. Mrs. Frieden knocked at her door at six-thirty every morning, carrying fresh croissants, dark rolls, fresh berries and a French press filled with aromatic coffee. They ate together on Ella's terrace. Sometimes they discussed the restaurant and their guests. Other times they sat in companionable silence, watching the sailboats exiting and entering the harbor, the smell of roses and lavender wafting to them and mixing with the aromatic smell of the fresh coffee.

Mrs. Frieden was able to snatch the free daily newspaper, *20 Minuten*, and they would take turns leafing through the pages, the only sound a cooing of a morning dove on a tree branch in the lake front park.

Ella was driven into Zürich each day for class and rehearsal, sometimes only returning late at night after a performance. She knew she would never be able to return to the street where she had lived in Zürich. She sent a private car to pick up the Annikovs and bring them to every performance she danced in. Her heart warmed every time she could wrap her arms around them in the lobby of the Opernhaus. A few times she sent Nick and his wife free tickets to the ballet and they came. They took her to Flavor after the ballet, and she relaxed into their company, filled up with the warmth of their laughter and stories.

On her free evenings, Ella returned to the castle and chatted with Adnan in the kitchen before eating dinner with Mr. V and Mrs. Frieden on the restaurant terrace. After dinner, she did a half-hour of yoga on her terrace to strengthen her core and back and stretch out before bed beneath the stars.

She liked the murmuring of conversation and laughter wafting up to her from the restaurant terrace, the cool night air fresh on her face after an entire day spent inside.

Her life was filled with friends she loved and the job she had always dreamed of achieving. Beneath the surface of her smile and graceful movements, fear was creeping up Ella's spine each moment she stood in the open in Zürich.

She was on high alert and felt dangerously exposed if she ventured out of rehearsal with Ethan to grab a coffee and something to eat in a café. Before each new performance, she shook with anxiety. Would Owen and Irma show up again to watch her from the audience? Would they surprise her in her dressing room, or try to follow her driver back to Romanshorn?

After a little more than a month, something surprising happened. The more time she spent on stage, the more the fear evaporated up off of her, like steam.

To begin with, her smile was a mask she placed on her face with each performance in the corps de ballet. Yet with time, her smile softened and came naturally to her lips. Perhaps Owen and Irma had disappeared out of her life for good.

ELLA ENTERED THE HOTEl lobby after a later performance. She had decided to stay the night in Zürich, since her body ached with fatigue and she was experiencing shooting pains in her knee. The director was insisting on new refinements to make to her technique and style. She would need to wake up early and go in to practice on her own, before classes started for the company.

Ella made her way to the free computer set up on a desk in the lobby and logged into her email account. She had promised to write Mrs. Frieden an email. She sat staring at the Gmail account login. What was her password? She hadn't checked her email in weeks, since before she moved to Romanshorn. She shrugged. She could just open a new account. Suddenly the words and numbers of her password flashed into her head, and she logged in to her account. Her mouth dropped open. She had thirty-two emails from Joshua. With growing fascination, she read through each and every email, then started from the beginning again. Some of the emails were only a sentence long.

Others detailed his entire day on the ranch, his hopes and insecurities, even his dream of owning his own ranch someday. The last few emails had a hollow and desperate tone. The last said he wouldn't write her anymore, because she obviously wasn't interested in continuing the relationship, or had found a new fella. He wished her the best of everything in life. With a pounding heart, Ella dashed off a new email.

Dear Joshua,

I haven't checked my email in so long because I moved. I was delighted to see my mailbox filled with your emails! I enjoyed reading each and every one, except the last, which said you won't write to me anymore. Please do! If I had known you would write me back, I would have checked my email every day. I am currently in Zürich, training as part of the corps de ballet. I am getting used to criticism and corrections thrown at me every few minutes. I know I should be grateful to learn and improve my art.

Sometimes I feel naked dancing again with the group, under scrutinizing eyes. Now that I made the Zürich ballet company, I yearn with all my heart to be a soloist someday, or even a principal. Every day I work towards that goal, trying to perfect my art in motion. I hope I can see your countryside someday. You paint an enticing landscape with your words.

With love, Ella

Ella thought for a moment, then took out her USB stick and attached some of her professional ballet photos to the email. Ella pressed send, and a few moments later the computer gave a ping. She already had a reply.

Hello gorgeous! Those were some photos. Goodness, you're even prettier than I remember. Don't you go thrown' around those 'with loves' unless you mean them. You may just break this poor cowboy's heart.

Love, Joshua.

PS. Give the word and I will be saving myself up some money to fly over to see you. I just need to wait until I can sell some of my steer.

Ella smiled. Did she want that?

Dear Joshua,

Schlossbergstrasse 26, Romanshorn, 8590 Switzerland.

Sending kisses on the wind, Ella

THE HEAT WAS STILL radiating up off the parking lot as Ella crossed to the gravel path leading along the lake with Mr. V. They walked in silence. There had been no sign of Owen in Romanshorn nor at the Zürich Opernhaus, but she still didn't feel up to wandering alone in twilight. She wished she had an email from Joshua to look forward to, but he hadn't written in weeks.

She took a deep breath, savoring the cool breeze traveling to her from the lake, caressing her bare legs and arms, swirling her sea foam green dress as she walked. The waves were breaking on the rocky shore, the rhythmic sound soothing her, if not loosening her sorrow. She sat down on a bench, watching a warm gold moon rising over the lake as the first stars broke through the pink and grey twilight.

The last email from Joshua had said that he wouldn't be able to come and visit. Ella had written him back, asking him why. That was three weeks ago, and he hadn't ever replied. Ella felt stupid for feeling so crushed.

After all, he was just a man she had met once. They had exchanged emails for a while. So why did she feel like her heart was breaking? Could you really fall in love with someone at first sight, deepening it through letters? Ella brushed the wetness on her cheeks away with her fingertips. Mr. V reached out and patted her on the shoulder and she gave him a weak smile. She was so thankful he didn't ask her why she was upset. Her thoughts circled back to Joshua. Obviously he wasn't interested in a relationship. She had been a pen pal of sorts, and now it was over. Ella asked herself if it was really Joshua that was causing her sadness.

Ballet training and rehearsal were a grueling tax on her body and mental concentration. On top of her exhaustion, she had the strain of constantly looking over her shoulder. She didn't rise from the bench until the sky was unfurled velvet overhead, the moon high in the night sky. Mr. V still didn't say anything. He looked at her damp cheeks and held out a rough wrinkled hand. She took it, saying, "thank you for not asking me what is wrong."

He nodded his head, looking forward at the trees swaying in the wind and the castle lit up above the gardens. "You can't expect perfection every time. Patience and work will fray through anything."

"It isn't the ballet. I met an American in Zürich and we have been exchanging emails. He's stopped writing me."

He stopped, looking at her in the gathering darkness. "Ah. Love. It will either rain or snow; it either will or will not. Give him time."

CHAPTER 17

"ELLA, WHAT IS WRONG CHILD?"

Ella turned to see Mrs. Frieden walking to her from the kitchen. There was nothing so burdensome as a secret, and she wanted to tell Mrs. Frieden everything. About Joshua and Owen and her entire troubled past. Yet what would Mrs. Frieden think of her? Where would she even start? Then there was the Annikovs' declining health.

"It's nothing," replied Ella, brushing the tears away with her fingertips.

"Nonsense child, we're a team. You tell me all about it," insisted Mrs. Frieden. "Come sit here next to me. We have time. All the customers are taken care of for the moment."

"Well," began Ella, taking a heaving breath.

"It's the Annikovs. Mrs. Annikov thinks they need to go into a nursing home. They aren't doing well enough to continue to live on their own. Even with the traveling nurses from the Spitex and the cleaning lady. Mrs. Annikov just can't get the washing and cooking done anymore."

"Oh dear. Nursing homes aren't very happy places, are they? Who wants to wake up to four walls of the same tiny room, cut off from society like that? And nursing homes in Switzerland are very expensive," added Mrs. Frieden, shaking her head sadly.

"I know. I don't want that for them at all," whispered Ella, tears gathering in her eyes again. "They are lovely people."

A silence fell over the two women. Ella closed her eyes, leaning back in her chair, feeling the sun's warmth on her tear-stained cheeks. A dove was cooing in the distance.

"You just leave this to me, Ella. I have the perfect solution. I will help them book a cruise."

"You, wait what?" asked Ella, sitting up and examining Mrs. Frieden. "This isn't a joke, Mrs. Frieden."

"No of course it isn't. I'm perfectly serious. Why shouldn't this couple have a bit of fun before kicking the bucket? Why should they be put in a prison of a place when they can watch the scenery change before their eyes every day?"

"I don't know how much money they have," replied Ella. "Do they have enough for a cruise? And what if they need a doctor. What then?"

"That's just the thing, Ella. They have a doctor on board. And a cruise is much less expensive per day then being in a nursing home. Didn't you know that? I thought everyone knew that. Anyway, their room will be cleaned every day, they will receive free linens and they can go up and enjoy meals in the dining hall, or even have room service delivered. They can even attend the evening shows, if they feel up to it, or swim in the pool. Or just sit in a lounge chair on the deck and watch the world go by while holding hands and drinking a lemonade. It was always my plan with my dear husband, that we would go onto a cruise ship instead of a nursing home."

"Yes, but I don't know if they have the money for a cruise," answered Ella, but she wanted to say, 'I don't want to lose them.' It was selfish, and yet Ella would prefer to have the Annikovs move into a nursing home near her in Romanshorn where she could visit them every day.

"Oh dear, there is that point I suppose."

"Well, there is no use speculating and prattling on when there's work to do. You give me their address, and I will go and pick them up and bring them here. Then we can have a nice long chat together over coffee and cake."

"I don't know what to say. It's so kind of you to bring them to me, Mrs. Frieden," began Ella.

"Well, that's settled then," said Mrs. Frieden, pounding her armrests with a smile.

"ELLA! MY LITTLE SUN, how we've missed you," called out Mrs. Annikov as she walked out on to the castle terrace, her arms outstretched.

Wordlessly, Ella set down her tray and wrapped her arms around the small woman, before turning to Mr. Annikov and hugging him as well.

"This is a fine new home you have yourself here. Mighty beautiful," offered Mr. Annikov while examining the castle and the terrace.

"It *is* lovely. It does my heart good to think of you living here in all this light and space. I hated you shut up in that small studio on your own," added Mrs. Annikov.

A flashback of the small tower studio and the weighted hours of loneliness hit her. Shaking the memory from her head she smiled. "It is a good change. But I miss living near you, Babushka."

"Look at you all brown and fit. You positively radiate health and well-being," replied Mrs. Annikov, smiling up at her. "You are much better off here."

"Well, these two are sure to be thirsty after hour car ride. Show them to some chairs and bring them something to drink," directed Mrs. Frieden.

Ella brought back a pitcher of strawberry lemonade and some glasses. Mrs. Frieden insisted Ella sit down and enjoy a glass of lemonade while she went to the kitchen to prepare the cakes and coffees. A half-hour later she returned to the terrace and set down a tray filled with strawberry tarts and coffees.

"So, there are few things better in life than enjoying a fresh strawberry tart and a delicious coffee on a terrace in the sun with good company," remarked Mrs. Frieden.

"I'll second that," agreed Mr. Annikov. "Except I don't take milk in my coffee."

"Sergio, don't be rude," whispered Mrs. Annikov, before turning to Mrs. Frieden "Thank you Mrs. Frieden, I can't believe you drove all the way to Zürich to pick us up."

"My dear Mr. Annikov, that is a flat white coffee. You will like it, give it a try. It's deliciously smooth and creamy and really lets the espresso sing the lead."

Mr. Annikov looked dubiously at his coffee cup before taking a sip. "Say, not bad this. Not bad at all."

"A flat white?" came a gruff voice from behind them. "What are you doing serving these fine Russian patriots a flat white? Why not a Raf?" asked Mr. Vasiliev.

"It is no business of yours," retorted Mrs. Frieden. "And people of any proper upbringing know not to eavesdrop on other's conversations."

Mr. Vasiliev pushed away his colored pencils and stood up, walking over. "Can a homesick old man help it if his ears prick up at the sound of a Russian accent? The name's Vasiliev," he said, while stretching out a hand to Mr. Annikov.

"Annikov," responded Mr. Annikov, standing to shake hands with the gruff old man standing across from him. "And this is my wife. We are Ella's grandparents," explained Mr. Annikov in Russian.

"Now how is that?" responded Mr. Vasiliev in Russian, raising his bushy eyebrows in surprise. "Her grandparents you say?"

"Yes, she let us adopt her as our granddaughter," chimed in Mrs. Annikov in German as she shook Mr. Vaseline's hand.

Mr. Vasiliev looked at Ella. Ella nodded her head, "I don't know what would have happened to me after my Grandma died if the Annikovs didn't bring me baskets of fresh food and welcomed me into their lives."

"She's been a bright ray of sunlight in our lives, I'll tell you that," said Mrs. Annikov.

Mrs. Frieden cleared her throat, glaring at Mr. Vasiliev, who glared back, then gave Mrs. Frieden a wink and an impish grin. Mrs. Frieden pinched his arm.

"Every thing is under control Helen," muttered Mr. Vasiliev to Mrs. Frieden, patting her hand.

"What's under control?" asked Ella bewildered.

Sighing a deep sigh Mrs. Frieden said, "Never you mind Ella. Now, Annikovs, Ella told me you feel you need to enter a nursing home, but looking at you two it doesn't make any sense to me at all. Is one of you ill?"

Mrs. Annikov looked down at her wrinkly hands, clutching her coffee cup. "No, no we are in the great health. Yet I have difficulty keeping up with the cooking and cleaning these days. Going out for a shop is exhausting. And well," Mrs. Annikov hesitated, looking over at Mr. Annikov, who nodded his head at her. "I don't want to give up our autonomy, but it's all getting to be too much for us. I know a young woman like you can't imagine giving up her independence."

Ella could see the dishes piled in the sink, smell the musty scent of sweat and mold. She saw them lying on the bed together, their hands entwined, their heads leaned toward one another, hungry. She didn't want the Annikovs living like that.

"A young woman like me? No one has called me young for longer than I can remember," laughed Mrs. Frieden.

"Well, you look like a young chicken to us," agreed Mr. Annikov. "We're going on eight-five years old. How old are you then, no more than fifty I would guess?"

"More like sixty-two," answered Mrs. Frieden.

"Always did like a younger woman," declared Mr. Vasiliev. "I'm seventy-one myself."

Ella gave a belly laugh. Was Mr. Vasiliev flirting with Mrs. Frieden? They were so…old. She didn't think the grumpy Mr. Vasiliev had it in him.

"You started all over at sixty-two with a new restaurant? Lord bless you love, aren't you brave," exclaimed Mrs. Annikov while fluttering a hand at Mrs. Frieden.

"I couldn't do it without Ella. She has marvelous idea and found our truly talented executive chef. She could do with a little more fun in her life to be honest. She should spend more time with young people her own age instead of oldies like us," said Mrs. Frieden, shaking her head.

"I'm sitting right here," piped up Ella.

"I say it as I see it," parried Mrs. Frieden.

"What if I enjoy your company more than the young people I've met?" asked Ella

"Well that is understandable," said Mr. Annikov.

"Exactly right Sergio," agreed Mrs. Frieden. "These young

people are quite self-addicted. I call it the cult of self. Always on the move, taking a million photos of themselves, posting every trivial thought that flutters through their heads and every activity they undertake. It makes me wonder how they have time to focus on really loving someone else, noticing if anyone around them needs a helping hand."

"A bird may be known by its song," observed Mr. Vasiliev.

Everyone paused and looked at the gruff Mr. Vasiliev for a moment in silence.

"They think about what the world can offer them, instead of what they can offer the world, more's the pity," sighed Mrs. Annikov. "Poor darlings. It won't make them happy, living with that mentality."

"I couldn't have said it better myself love,"said Mr. Annikov.

"I agree," said Mrs. Frieden, violently nodding her head.

"Come now, it can't be as bad as all that," offered Ella.

"I don't know about that," grumbled Mr. Annikov. "Aren't these young people running around with phones in their hands all the time? One can't even sit in peace at a beautiful café without a ding here and buzz there and a revolting melody suddenly destroying the reverie of a man who likes his peace. They only converse through their gadgets anymore, instead of sitting down and giving their undivided attention to a real conversation without interruption."

"Well," spoke up Mrs. Frieden. "Shall we talk about your future Mr. Annikov? I propose that, instead of a nursing home, you consider buying a cabin on a world cruise ship. Then you can retain your independence while having services provided that will take away the struggle and fear."

"Are you mad woman? How would that work?" asked Mr. Annikov. "What if we need a doctor?"

"And there's the falls dear," added Mrs. Annikov. "Wouldn't they happen more often on a ship?"

"There's a doctor on permanent residence on the ship and staff always present in case Mr. Annikov should have a fall. Your linens are changed and washed for you, your cabin cleaned daily. All your meals are available in the dining rooms and they will even do your laundry for a small fee per bag. All you have to do is enjoy the pool, the fitness center, the evening shows and dancing or just lying in a lounge chairs side by side, watching the world go by. You get to stop off in different ports and visit new destinations all over the world."

"It sounds lovely dear, just lovely. But we aren't millionaires, you know," replied Mrs. Annikov.

"That is a point. It costs one hundred and fifty thousand dollars to purchase the cabin and sixty-five thousand dollars a year in service fees. Also, any alcoholic beverages, travel expenses you incur while off the ship enjoying the port visits are also not included. But everything else is. How does it look financially? Do you own your flat?"

"Yes, actually we do," answered Mrs. Annikov. "We paid it off years ago. And we have a bit of retirement savings, but not a lot."

"That won't matter a bit," interrupted Mr. V. "Do you know how much you can sell that flat for in Zürich? The prices have gone through the roof in recent years. Your flat is huge and in a beautiful, quiet, central location. I bet you could get a million for it easily. I can assure you Annikovs, if this is what you want, I can help you make it a reality."

"I agree," said Mrs. Frieden. "That would mean you will have enough for ten years on the cruise ship, at which point, you will have used up all your money and you can return to Switzerland and live in a nursing home. When your money is all gone Switzerland will pay for your stay in a nursing home for you if you're Swiss."

"Yes we are Swiss citizens. But that doesn't seem right," said Mr. Annikov. "Why should they pay for us when we have used up all our money living it up all over the world on a cruise ship?"

"Oh dear Sergio, that would mean we would be over ninety-five years old. What are the chances we live that long? And at which point, I don't think the state would need to pay for us for very long," said Mrs. Annikov.

"Actually, the cruise ship is less expensive than a nursing home in Switzerland. We will be saving ourselves a lot of money by living on a cruise ship instead. Not to mention I think they will treat us like a customers instead of like patients, which I think is a major plus," declared Mrs. Annikov.

"I might just join you in ten years' time. It sounds like a good deal and a lot of fun to me," spoke up Mr. Vasiliev. "Who wouldn't rather live on a cruise ship instead of in a nursing home?"

"Someone who hates change and wants to die someday in his own home?" replied Mr. Annikov.

"Oh dear, please let's do this. I am going out of my mind with boredom. Think of all the new interesting people we could meet on the ship and all of the new places we could visit. I'll make our cabin our new home. I actually feel a thrill of excitement at the thought," said Mrs. Annikov with twinkling eyes. "I never thought we could set off on a new adventure at our age."

"Yes, well, we have to get our affairs in order first love," said Mr. Annikov while taking his wife's hand in his own. "But once we sell our flat, then I will follow you anywhere you want to go. Mind you don't get your hopes up; in case this is all some kind of hoax. Sounds too good to be true to me. No use going and having some hooligan steal our hard earned money only to live in abject poverty the rest of our lives."

"What was written by a pen, cannot be taken out with the axe," stated Mr. Vasiliev.

Mr. Annikov looked at Mr. Vasiliev for a moment and then nodded his head.

"I am in full agreement with you Mr. Annikov," said Mrs. Frieden, ignoring Mr. Vasiliev. "We will research the options very carefully and then may I suggest my lawyer take a look at the contract and research the authenticity of the business before you sign?"

"You're a sensible woman Mrs. Frieden," said Mr. Annikov. "And until everything is sorted out, I will come and pay a visit Monday morning and do some meal preparation for the week."

Ella sat in silence, listening. A squid's tentacles wrapping around her midsection, slowly squeezing. She didn't want to lose the Annikovs, but it did sound wonderful for them. Ella forced a smile, rising and kissing Mrs. Frieden's cheek, followed by Mrs. Annikov's and Mr. Annikov's.

Hesitating a moment, she turned to Mr. Vasiliev and kissed

him on the cheek as well.

"You are lovely people and I'm so lucky I found you. I will miss you so very much, but it sounds like a brilliant plan."

"Oh my little sun," answered Mrs. Annikov. "We love you more than thirsty fields love the rain."

Chapter 18

Ella continued to write to Joshua, despite his lack of reply. It soothed her, like writing in a daily journal. Every once in a while she felt foolish. He probably wasn't reading her emails. Or he thought she was pathetic, the way she continued to write to him despite his ghosting her. He was most likely out there right now, kissing some cowgirl. She told herself she didn't care. Writing her daily emails had a healing effect.

Watching the raindrops splash against the windowpanes, Ella sighed.

They didn't have a customer in the restaurant, despite it being Friday night.

"Well, I told Adnan he can go home for the night. He may as well take the evening off, seeing as no guests are turning up for dinner. It's already eight thirty at night. Turn the sign to closed, Ella."

Ella turned from the window and smiled at Mrs. Frieden as Adnan came out of the kitchen.

"So I go home now, pleasing you?" asked Adnan, his white teeth flashing in a bright smile as he shook his dark hair out of his face.

"Yes Adnan, please take the evening off. No one has arrived, so there's no sense keeping you here twiddling your thumbs in the kitchen when you could enjoy your evening with your wife," answered Mrs. Frieden.

"Good night Adnan," said Ella. "See you tomorrow."

Mrs. Frieden turned to Ella once Adnan had opened an umbrella and stepped out into the downpour. "First for the good news Ella. A postcard came in the mail today from the Annikovs. They're in Iceland and sound very happy."

She held out a postcard with a photo of the Northern Lights on it to Ella.

Ella smiled as she read Mrs. Annikov's beautiful script.

Mr. Annikov had fallen in love with Iceland. He deemed it the most beautiful place on the planet. The whale watching was awe-inspiring. Mrs. Annikov wrote she had already made a friend and loved her morning Zumba class. They were both already counting the days until Ella would join them on the ship to celebrate Christmas.

"I've had a call today, Ella," spoke up Mrs. Frieden. "From my daughter. She," Mrs. Frieden gasped, her usual ramrod-straight spine rounding forward as she placed her face in her hands. "She has cancer. I told her I would be on the first plane over there. She's never asked me for anything since she moved to Idaho, and now she is. I need to take care of her and my grandkids. Will you be alright on your own?"

Ella felt the bee sting, sharp and unexpected, of yet another person walking out of her life, leaving her alone in these beautiful echoing rooms.

She wanted to cry, 'No I won't be fine on my own,', but instead she placed a hand on Mrs. Frieden's shoulder as she said, "How silly, of course I will be fine on my own. The restaurant is dead, and it isn't even October. We will hire Aya to come and take your place waiting tables."

"What a brilliant idea," said Mrs. Frieden, looking up with red-rimmed eyes. "I should have hired her from the start. She is a charming and hard-working young woman. Ella… I'm terrified to get on that plane," admitted Mrs. Frieden.

"Do you want me to go with you?"

"Yes. I'm selfish enough that I wish you would not only fly with me, but stay with me in Idaho too, but you have your ballet and someone needs to be here. We don't want to shut up the restaurant entirely, do we? What would Adnan do for work? He needs the job, especially right now. They are still debating his and Aya's permanent residence request," insisted Mrs. Frieden.

"I thought you wanted refugees to go back to where they came from?" teased Ella.

"Well, yes, there is no bloody debating that. All these people can't just come and stay and live off the government. Our Adnan is different though. He is an upstanding, hardworking and good man. He's not some freeloader."

"When are you leaving, Mrs. Frieden?" asked Ella.

"Right now, child. Mr. V is driving me to the airport. He's coming with me, Ella."

Ella's heart fractured, a house leaking its warmth into through unseen cracks. She managed to keep a smile on her face despite the cold seeping through her. It would be very lonely without Mrs. Frieden in the castle. No one would stop in with breakfast and the newspaper each morning. She would no longer take walks with Mr. V, nor eat dinner with the two of them in the evenings. First she had lost the Annikovs, and now Mrs. Frieden and Mr. V. Why was her family always torn away from her?

"How long will you be gone?" asked Ella.

"At the moment it is difficult to know how things will progress," answered Mrs. Frieden while wiping the tears from her eyes.

"How silly of me. Yes, of course you can't know. I wish your daughter a fast return to good health."

Ella looked into the red-shot eyes of this impetuous woman with a heart of gold. Tears were welling up in her throat, threatening to choke her. She nodded her head and wrapped her arms around the strong, slim-waisted woman. A loud knock vibrated through the front hall.

Wordlessly Ella opened the front door. Mr. V gave her a kiss on the cheek and gathered up Mrs. Frieden's bag. He handed her a card.

"Here is my number, Ella. Call me anytime, day or night, and I will be on a plane back to you," said Mr. V, his voice tight with emotion.

Ella didn't trust herself to answer, so she just nodded. She was afraid she would start crying at any moment.

"Goodbye. Good luck with your upcoming performances dear. I'll ring you often," called Mrs. Frieden as she followed Mr. V out the door.

Ella forced a smile on her face, and then shut the large door with a loud click.

ELLA SAT IN HER ARMCHAIR, wrapped in her favorite sea-foam-green cashmere blanket, breathing in the smell of peppermint from the steaming hot teacup in her hand. She watched the snowflakes falling outside and worried. She couldn't understand the nausea tormenting her all day, the debilitating fatigue. She was concerned about the extra pounds she had piled on in the past few months. Adnan's food and Aya's cakes were so good that she reasoned she had probably been eating too much lately.

Ella was proud that Adnan's cooking had achieved rave reviews in the newspaper and their restaurant now drew patronage from customers throughout the region.

The surprise had been Aya. She now spoke fluently and without accent, much to the pride and amusement of Adnan, who still struggled along with his disjointed speech and grammar errors. Customers loved Aya and her baking almost as much as Adnan's cooking.

Aya cultivated a personal relationship with each customer, never forgetting a face or a name.

She treated return customers with extra care, which went over extremely well. And her cakes were simply delicious.

In the winter, they had changed to offering just two four-course menu options. This had been much more popular than they could have ever predicted.

Apparently people were overwhelmed with choices in their lives. It was a relief to only need to choose between two meal options at the same flat rate, including tip. It was very profitable for the restaurant because they only needed to carry a very limited stock of groceries.

The food was extremely fresh as everything was always sourced from local farmers the same day it was cooked.

Ella snuggled down deeper in her blanket, took a drink of tea and smiled. It was a great comfort to walk into the kitchen every evening to the happy faces of Adnan and Aya. Her body may be heavy with fatigue and aching from ballet rehearsal, but the soul-feeding scents of the kitchen always raised her spirits: cinnamon and cardamom, nutmeg and vanilla or the savory smell of slow-cooked meat, roasting vegetables, garlic and onion. Seeing the smiling faces of Adnan and Aya working together to make the restaurant a success gave her joy.

Ella was worried something was seriously wrong with her health to feel like this. She had an appointment in two days. It was moments like these that she missed her grandmother the most. In a snap decision, she dialed the number Mr. V had given her.

"WELL, ELLA, I HAVE some good news," said the doctor as he walked into the room. "You are in perfect health. The symptoms you are feeling are very real, but they are nothing to fear. They are perfectly normal in pregnancy."

Ella sat on the examination table, her skin breaking out in goose bumps. "Excuse me? I can't be pregnant."

"What? Didn't you know?" asked the doctor, registering surprise and alarm. "You should be taking prenatal vitamins, going in for regular checks. Didn't you notice missing your past few cycles?"

She had noticed missing her period for a few months, but her cycle had always been irregular.

"Yes, but I didn't think much about it," admitted Ella. "My cycle has never been regular. You must have made a mistake."

"You're on birth control then," he said. "That is generally ninety-nine percent effective, but you have to remember to take each and every pill. If you missed even one, then pregnancy can occur."

"No, I'm no on any birth control," admitted Ella, shaking her head. She didn't add that she wasn't on birth control because she wasn't having sex. She had never had sex.

"Well then..." trailed off the doctor, shifting the folder from one hand to the other. He cleared his throat. "In any case, you should visit your gynecologist immediately. You're pregnant."

"Actually," said Ella, her face flaming red, "I've never been to one before."

"Here, I'll call up a good colleague of mine and ask for an appointment for you this very day. She could have a cancellation. You'll like her."

"Hey Katie, this is Ryan How are you? Listen, do you have any free appointments? I have a patient here who is four months along and didn't realize it. She's never been to a gynecologist before and I want to get her right in and make sure everything looks great with the baby. You do? In an hour and a half? Great Katie, I'll send her over."

"So," said the doctor, turning back to Ella. "That's great. You can go over to Dr. Brown in an hour and a half. That gives you time to go and eat some lunch and then head over. Her office is just across the street."

"Thank you doctor," said Ella.

She walked out of the office, along the corridor and down the stairs to the cobbled stone street in a haze. It was as if she had been loosened from her body and was floating up above, watching herself meandering down the street filled with pedestrians and find a table in the sun at the café. She looked out at the St. Gallen monastery vis-a-vis the café, founded in 718 and now a World Heritage Site containing the famous medieval library. Ella watched a large group of Chinese tourists snapping photos of the monastery grounds and the cathedral. The huge clock tower began tolling twelve o'clock, and Ella gave a small shudder. Only thirty more minutes until her appointment.

She didn't taste the dark green arugula and strawberry salad she ate, nor notice the strawberry infused green tea was scalding her mouth. All her senses were muted; grey-tinted glasses were balanced on the bridge of her nose, stealing the world of its color.

She stood shivering on the street, fifteen minutes too early for her appointment. She bought a bag of roasted chestnuts from the street vendor in hopes that the hot, meaty nuts would warm her. She stood munching and watching the firefighters hanging Christmas lights over the streets and an array of workers building the small wooden huts for the Christmas market. Ella loved Christmas and waited for joyful anticipation to wash through her. There was nothing.

It wasn't until she was lying on the gynecologist's table, a wand rolling over the cold gel on her still-flat belly, that she was sucked back into her body.

It was the heartbeat, thumping loud into the white sterile room that pulled her back into reality. She stared at the black screen. How was this possible? All at once the memory of waking up naked in Owen's flat flooded back. She cried out in anguish, throwing an arm over her eyes as tears fell down her cheeks.

"There," said the doctor, pointing at a white blur on the black screen. "Do you see that there?"

Ella peered out from tear-soaked lashes. The blur seemed to give a jump, then settle back into stillness.

"That's your baby," said the doctor. "You are about five months along. Shall I print you a photo?"

Ella shrugged. She hadn't said a word since entering the room. She was frozen.

"You look like you're suffering from a bit of a shock. I take it from my colleague that this is a surprise pregnancy?

Ella found she couldn't answer. She merely nodded, while wiping the gel off her stomach and pulling her red wool dress back down over her hips.

"There's nothing I can do?" asked Ella almost in a whisper, hesitant, her eyes searching out the doctor's before returning her gaze to her knee-high leather boots.

"No, you've waited too long. Abortions need to occur before three months. You're at the end of your fourth."

A deep, soul-crushing despair caused Ella to sink back down onto the examination table. Ella sighed, gave a shrug. Did it matter one way or another? Did anything matter, now that she could see her ballet career floating up and away from her, a bright red balloon in a darkening sky?

The doctor walked over to Ella and took her hands in her own. "How old are you, Ella?" asked the doctor.

"Almost eighteen."

"Are you studying? Working?"

"Working."

"What is it you do?"

"I dance with the Zürich ballet company. It's clear that will soon be over."

The doctor tilted her head in consideration, tapping her pen on the desk. "Not necessarily. If you kept up low-impact training all the way up to the birth, I don't see why you couldn't regain your form and fitness level again after the pregnancy. The health of the baby comes first of course, but if you want to return to dance, you could plan it. I recommend doing some research. I am almost certain you wouldn't be the first one returning to the stage after a pregnancy."

A gentle breeze of hope lifted Ella's spirits. Perhaps it wasn't the end of everything. But what would she do with the baby?

"MIND YOUR HEAD getting into the car there, Ella," said Mr. V.

"Thank you so much for coming to pick me up," said Ella, sliding into the red car. "I can't believe you immediately flew all the way back from United States for me because I told you I was feeling ill yesterday."

"I meant it when I said I would come the moment you needed me."

"This is a nice car," commented Ella. "Is this a Ferrari? What are you doing driving a Ferrari?"

"Why shouldn't I drive a Ferrari? Just because a man is getting wiser doesn't mean he is losing his appreciation of beautiful things. And enough of changing the subject. What happened? Why didn't you have me go to the appointments with you?"

"I needed to do this on my own. I would have been fine getting home too, only the doctor wouldn't let me leave on my own," mumbled Ella, smoothing her skirt over her lap and clasping her knees with both hands.

"What kind of country is this? That's crazy. Why?"

"I received some shocking news. She was just worried I might leave and do something stupid."

"What news Ella? It's not cancer, is it?" Mr. V's voice shook. "You're not dying?"

"I'm pregnant."

Ella looked out the window as the car rolled over the top of the hill and the Bodensee came into view below them, the sails of the boats white dashes against the turquoise blue of the lake. She gave a sigh. Next would come the loud lecture and endless stream of sayings and recriminations. She braced herself.

"Is that all? We can handle that."

Ella sat in silence, wondering over his answer.

"What do you mean 'we'?"

"I mean thank the heavens you're not dying. It will be a short break from your dancing, but you can go back again. And I know how to take care of a baby."

"You?" laughed Ella.

"Everything genius is simple. I'm telling you I'm great with babies. And anyway, I'm sure I won't be the only one helping. You will have Mrs. Frieden."

"I don't think Mrs. Frieden is coming back."

"She sure is," said Mr. Vasiliev, while passing yet another car. "I talked to her just yesterday. Her daughter has been a few months in remission and Mrs. Frieden will come home in a few months, after the calf branding. She adores being with her daughter and grandchildren, but she is really homesick. And let's be honest, Mrs. Frieden is used to living alone and doing things her own way. Her daughter probably wants her household back," laughed Mr. Vasiliev.

Mr. Vasiliev was a silent for a moment. "I miss her already."

Ella looked over at him. "What is that supposed to mean, Mr. Vasiliev?"

"Oh all right, I'll tell you. Mrs. Frieden is my gal."

"I suspected as much when you went with her to America," Ella wondered.

"We're in love, Ella. Helen didn't want anyone to know until it was a sure thing. That's why I've spent the entire time in Idaho, instead of with you, where I belong. New lovers are selfish. Spectacular, the raw beauty of that Idaho landscape. I want you to see it someday."

"So will you move in with Mrs. Frieden when she returns?" Ella realized she liked the idea of Mr. V wandering around the place. It would be reassuring.

"Two bears don't live in one lair. We're too used to doing things our own way after so many years."

"But I'll stay over from time to time, I expect. Now, about this baby. Who the hell is the father? Did you go and fall in love while I was gone?"

Her chest was tightening. She couldn't get enough air into her constricting lungs, and her breath grew shallow and frantic. She was hyperventilating.

"Ella? Ella, what's wrong?" Mr. Vasiliev pulled the car to the side of the road and ran around the car, opening the door. "Come, step out here. Take a deep breath now, child."

"It was Owen."

"That son of a bitch. Forget having him killed, I'll kill him myself with my bare hands."

Straightening up Ella hugged Mr. V, tears still streaming down her cheeks. "Thank you for believing me Mr. V. And for not lecturing me about being pregnant."

"I would have been a mean fool if I had. One shouldn't beat the one who fell, you know," said Mr. V, patting Ella on the back. "Now, let's get you home and make a plan. The sun will shine on our street too. You'll see."

Chapter 19

Mr. V walked with Ella into the castle through the restaurant. "What you need is a fortifying lunch and a nice soothing cup of tea, Ella."

Both Ella and Mr. V stopped abruptly, staring at the back of Owen's head as he sipped a coffee and turned the page of his newspaper. At the sight of him, Ella had a frantic need to run away and a concurrent lust to pick up the steak knife on his table and hurt him for what he had done to her. Fear and rage collided, leaving her shaking with indecision.

Mr. V marched up to Owen and tore the newspaper out of his hands.

"You old bastard, how dare you show your face here. I'll kill you for getting my Ella pregnant," he raged, pushing a finger into Owen's chest. "I'll kill you I tell you."

The other restaurant guests paused in their conversation, forks half-raised to open mouths, water glasses held in mid-air. Adnan had come out of the kitchen at the sound of the yelling. Aya moved to Ella's side, wrapping an arm around her waist.

Owen calmly pushed Mr. V's finger away from his chest and stood up, towering over the white haired man. "I have no idea what you are talking about. Ella, sweetheart, you really need to stop telling these lies. Why are you doing this?

Mr. V, come now, Ella and I are friends."

"Don't be afraid of the dog who barks, but be afraid of the one who is silent and wags its tail," yelled Mr. V. "I believe my Ella."

"Yes well, I adore Ella too, Mr. V. I don't know why she is lying about my paternity. Who knows? Perhaps she's had an affair with her ballet director or something, and can't admit that he's the father. But it certainly isn't me, really. Actually, I wish it were true. I'd love to be a father."

"We can get a paternity test done, you know," said Mr. V as he shook his fist. "The scythe has hit a stone. I won't let you run away from your responsibility to provide for Ella, even if I'll be damned if you have anything to do with her child."

Ella found her voice at last. "I don't want his money."

"Of course you don't, child, but that's not the point. He has to own up to what he's done. Tell the truth, man. Admit it, tell the truth, you dog," said Mr. V, taking hold of Owen's tie, yanking Owen's face down to his own.

It was uplifting to see Mr. V accost Owen. She hadn't thought Mr. V was capable of more than bluff and bluster.

"Poor Ella, she's delusional," said Owen, trying to pull his head free from Mr. V's grasp. "Nothing has ever happened between us. I'd never leave my wife. Now let me go. I don't want to hurt an old man."

He appeared completely calm, but Ella noticed a twitch at his eye, his hands shaking at his sides. Owen tore himself out of Mr. V's grasp, straightened his tie and walked with languid strides out of the restaurant.

"Well there you have it, Ella. The dog will never man up and admit what he did, nor tell his wife. Far better to be slapped with the truth than kissed with a lie though. Good riddance to him, I say."

"Yes, yes," agreed Adnan from the doorway while retying his white apron. "Bad man."

"Come into the kitchen, Ella," said Aya, taking Ella's hand and leading her through the maze of still-staring guests. "And we'll get you something to eat."

"Mr. V," said Ella, her body trembling like a leaf in the wind, "how did he find me? How does he know I live here?"

THAT NIGHT ELLA SAT NUMB in front of the restaurant computer as Adnan and Aya cleaned the kitchen. Joshua still hadn't written to her. It didn't matter. She wanted a confidant, and he was perfect. She would never see him again. She wrote him about everything that had happened. It was healing to write the story down in a way she hadn't expected.

Voicing her rawest vulnerabilities and insecurities in words had anchored her back down to the ground. Steadied, she read through the long email, realizing what an idiot she had been in so many ways. Now she was pregnant. Did she really want Joshua to read this? Ella decided it didn't matter. She pressed send.

BY THE END OF HER PERFORMANCE Ella was exhausted. She had told the director that she was pregnant.

Disbelief flashed over his face when he heard the news, followed by a grim determination.

"I have to be honest, Ella. I don't know if you will be able to make a comeback. But I'll never say never, okay? The important thing is you take care of yourself and this baby."

Ella had hugged herself, an icy chill thrown over her at his words, like a bucket of arctic water being thrown over her head. She knew that was what he would say. Yet some small piece of her had hoped she would hear, 'just have that baby and come right on back.'

Ella smiled, tight lipped. "Thank you. See you tomorrow."

"Is that a good idea, Ella? Perhaps you would like to step out now?" The Director shook his head, assessing her body. "Your body is already starting to change. I'll have to pull you from performances anyway."

"I'd like to attend morning class as long as I can," asked Ella. "Please."

"Sure, sure, don't cry. We're not trying to get rid of you, Ella. If you think this is the first time I have encountered this, then you're wrong. It's just never so young…and just months after joining us."

Ella's face was red with shame and stained with tears when she left the Opernhaus. She almost fell over Nick, who was sitting on the steps waiting for her.

"Nick, what are you two doing here?"

"Mr. V gave me a call and told me about what you've been through. Hey, I'm sorry, girl. Come on, I'm going to take you back to Flavor for some dinner and then take you to a hotel. Mr. V will pick you after ballet class tomorrow morning. He's in Bern renewing his Swiss residence permit. Tomorrow Mr. V will move into Mrs. Frieden's flat so you won't be in the castle alone."

Ella threw her arms around Nick's neck and buried her face on his shoulder, breaking into tears.

"Thank you for coming, Nick."

"What are friends for?"

After dinner with Nick, he dropped her off at a hotel near to the Opernhaus and agreed to wait for her while she checked her email in the business center. Her pulse quickened when she saw an email from Joshua in her in-box. She knew Nick needed to get home to his wife and kids so she printed the letter to read later.

Nick insisted on walking her up to her room before saying good night, to make sure she was safe, despite Ella's protest. After he left, Ella settled herself into bed with a mint tea with the email, then changed her mind. She would keep it, like saving a present.

It would be something to look forward to in the morning. She turned off the light, but she tossed and turned. Thoughts were terrorizing her and pulling her away from the sweet oblivion of sleep.

Her face was hot with tears. She tried to take a steadying breath, to still the sobs wracking her body. She was pregnant, and she had no memory of ever having sex before. In her mind, she was a virgin.

Why hadn't she gone to the doctor when she started feeling nauseous? Ella sighed. What was done was done. She just didn't know how she would love this baby when it came. There was a fear that if she kept the baby, it would remind her of Owen every time she looked at it.

Should she give it up for adoption? She reasoned that it would be better to give it to adoptive parents capable of showering the baby with love and good parenting. Yes, she decided. I won't keep the baby. Ella turned back on the light and snatched up Joshua's letter.

She couldn't wait until morning. She needed something uplifting right now.

Dear Ella,

It made my heart ache, reading what happened to you darlin'. I'm so sorry for the pain you've suffered due to abuse from that jerk. If I could plant a fist in that man's face I sure would find me some satisfaction, I tell you what. And please keep your guard up in the future Ella. Some men out there, they're no good through and through.

True enough, it wasn't right, you taking up with a married man. Acknowledge it was wrong and forgive yourself.

You need to believe the truth, that you are not responsible for the bad thing that happened to you. Let go of the shame Ella.

I'm not one to talk though. I'm real ashamed to admit I've drank myself far too much since I lost everything. Got me into some brawls outside bars. Found comfort in the arms of too many gals to count. I'm not proud.

I've cleaned up now, forty-two days now and steady going.

I'm a changed man, Ella. Being an eternal optimist is gone. It sure has been a spirit breaking time for me this past year. I couldn't bring myself to tell you of the fury, tears, worry, accusations and grief. We lost the farm Ella.

I won't ever again sit myself on a tractor in the twilight, admiring the green of new crops peeking out, the crickets beginning their song as I drive my tractor home. I'll never sit at my Ma's table and enjoy her food again. The drought hit our crops. The feed prices for our cattle skyrocketed. The bank came in and took everything. It went that fast, 'cause last year was a poor crop too and a huge corporation wanted our farm.

My father couldn't face leaving our land. The day they hauled our cattle away, evicting us from the farm, he threw himself in the river. My Mama got real sick after his death. They said she died of pancreatic cancer. I know the real reason she died.

It sounds real childish I know, but it ain't fair. We were a hard working people, a happy family, real content with working the land from dawn to dusk.

I can't find work Ella. I sure do wish I had myself a university degree. It seems it's what you need to get yourself a job these days. I've been hitchhiking my way across the country, working as a ranch hand or doing dishes for a night in exchange for a meal. I've gotten as far as Utah.

You won't hear from me for awhile I reckon. I found a job cleaning hotel rooms and they have a free computer here in the lobby. But I'm not made to spend the entire day indoors. I'm near losing my mind. Tomorrow I hit the road again. I need me the freedom of working under a bright blue sky.

Your emails sure have saved me more than once from doing something real stupid. I sure do wish I could fly over to you, but I probably won't ever see the kind of cash a ticket would take. It don't matter much. A cultivated woman like you wouldn't go for a guy like me anyway, even if I could make us a living. I sure am hoping your pregnancy goes well and you have yourself a real pretty, healthy baby Ella.

Love, Joshua

ELLA IMMEDIATELY PICKED UP the phone after reading the email.

"Hi Mrs. Frieden. How are you? Listen, does your son-in-law, or someone else out there in Idaho need a farm hand? I have a friend who has lost his farm. He's looking for work."

"Ella, tell me about the baby."

"Is that a no?"

"I want to talk to you about your future, Ella."

"He's a really kind man, Mrs. Frieden. Extremely hard-working. He lost the family farm and both his parents all in the last year."

"Lord save me, hold on," said Mrs. Frieden.

Ella could hear Mrs. Frieden's voice in the background and then footsteps echoing on wood floor. "Ella child, are you there? Yes, actually, we do need some help. Meals and lodging, no pay until the crop comes in. Happy now? So, what's this about you being pregnant? When were you going to call and tell me?"

"So you are in love with Mr. V," said Ella, snuggling under the feather duvet, her body weary with fatigue. She didn't know if she could wake up the next morning and go to class. What whispers and snickering would she face?

"Well who do you think told me about the baby, dear? A messenger angel?"

"I'm going to give it up for adoption and return to the ballet." Ella brought her hands down to her belly, feeling the tiny mound. Her heart constricted.

"You don't need to decide that now, Ella. Or I could take the baby."

Ella smiled. "You're too old to adopt a baby. And you aren't even here. You're in Idaho."

"Now, when is the baby going to be born?"

"The end of April or the beginning of May."

Ella pushed back the duvet and started pacing the hotel room. Mrs. Frieden couldn't be serious about adopting her baby. How would she bring up a baby at her age? No, Ella would need to go through with finding adoptive parents.

"I am giving up my baby."

"How about this, you wait until you have the baby and then you decide? I'll be home in March. Mr. V will live in my flat until I get home. He promised me he will take good care of you. Now Ella, you make sure you are eating enough. That baby needs food. And get plenty of rest. No upsetting yourself. Stress is bad for the baby."

"How's your daughter?"

"She's getting stronger every day. I am beyond grateful, you can just imagine our gratitude. I miss you and Mr. V. I can't wait to come home, despite how much I will miss my grandkids. Uh oh, a child's crying. I better go. I love you, Ella.

Give your friend this number. He can call for an interview."

"I love you too, Mrs. Frieden," said Ella.

Ella tuned off the lamp and snuggled down under the feather duvet. Her eyes slid closed just as her door crashed forward into the chain with a loud clang. Ella bolted upright in bed and threw herself toward her bag. She stood shivering in the middle of the room watching the hand reaching to unleash the chain.

With a cry, she threw herself against the door with her full body weight. She heard a muffled shout from behind the door and voices in the corridor. She stepped back from the door and the hand disappeared. Ella slammed the door shut, leaning against it, sucking in big drinks of air.

A knock at the door. The telephone was ringing. She lifted the receiver. "Is everything okay, Miss? Room service saw a woman attempting to gain access to your room."

"A woman? How did she get a key to my room?"

"Excuse me?"

"Whoever it was had a key to my room. I put the chain on. That was the only thing stopping her from getting in."

"I have no idea. I'm very sorry."

In the morning, Ella was still shaken and exhausted. It had been difficult to sleep, despite the visit from the staff and their assurances they would ensure her every safety. She dashed off an email to Joshua before her morning class from the lobby business center. She had trouble not looking over her shoulder every other minute.

Dear Joshua,

I am so sorry for the loss of your family, your home and your ranch. You have suffered such pain all alone. I of all people can understand why you have acted out in unhealthy ways to try and find relief.

Please stop blaming yourself for what happened. You radiate an inner goodness and I wish with all my heart for you to rediscover an inner peace and the joy you told me you experience while out in nature.

A friend of mine will hire you to work in exchange for meals and lodging until the crop comes in and then they can offer a small compensation.

The the contact information is attached to this email. Call for a phone interview and I know you'll get the job.

Sending my love to a good man, Ella

Chapter 20

For the next few months, Ella persisted with attending morning class in Zürich, despite the side looks and muffled laughter at her expense. She was certain they would have been supportive and warm to her if she had a loving partner. It was the simple fact that she had answered, in a moment of extreme nausea, that she didn't know who the father was.

Now everyone thought she was a slut. The ironic thing was that in her mind, she was a virgin. She didn't know whether to be horrified or thankful that she couldn't remember the night she had been impregnated. Joshua had written her countless times that she shouldn't feel shame over what had happened, but she did, a raw pulsating ickiness that hit her every morning. Deep down, she was desperate for no one to find out what had happened.

She thought there would always be those who thought she had somehow been 'asking for it' or had put herself in the wrong situation. She couldn't face them. She hadn't even had the heart to tell her grandfather that she had been raped. Mr. V was angry enough at the thought that an older man had seduced his teenage granddaughter.

Ella just couldn't explain the sordid details of that night, and the next morning, to anyone but Joshua. A single tear slid down Ella's cheek as they stretched before class.

"Don't let them get to you, Ella. Just focus on how good

it will feel to come back here and steal a coveted principal position out from under them," whispered Ethan as he slid into the splits.

"I'm not even sure I will be able to make it back into the corps de ballet," answered Ella.

"With that attitude you won't. No one achieves anything without belief that it is possible."

Ella stood up and hugged Ethan, "You're a good man."

"You bet I am," he said, raising his voice, "too bad there aren't more good-hearted people around."

After class, Ella asked Ethan if she could borrow their iPhone. She checked her email. Had he written?

Dear Ella,

I have fallen in love Ella. Her name is Lucy. She is a sweet tempered chestnut quarter horse. I was never much of a horseman back in Oklahoma but it is a necessity on this ranch to be able to herd the cattle. So they were good enough to lend me a horse and teach me to ride.

I love stepping out into the pink tinged dawn, taking a breath of the fresh pine scented air and going to saddle Lucy up for a ride along the rolling fields of wheat to move the cattle to a new pasture. Tomorrow I'm going salmon fishing for the first time. Thanks again for setting me up with this gig out west darlin'.

You are never far from my thoughts. Love, Joshua

ELLA HUGGED ETHAN goodbye and headed outside, where Mr. V was waiting curbside to drive her home.

A tiny foot was kicking her out of sleep. Good morning to you too, she thought, as she blinked her eyes open and gazed out at the tulips starting to open on her terrace. She rolled to her side and pushed herself up, her hands coming reflexively to her distended belly.

She threw on some leggings and a loose t-shirt and went into the kitchen for some toast and a tea. A few minutes later, she opened the door and walked out onto the terrace, turning on her music, and placed a hand on the barre. Happily, the nausea had disappeared after the fifth month.

Frowning, Ella continued flowing through the familiar movements. Why was it so effortless today? For the past few months, she had felt her body growing bigger and the movements more difficult to execute with her growing belly getting in her way and throwing off her balance. But today it was suddenly easy, despite her large stomach. She felt looser, more powerful. She shrugged her shoulders. That extra hour of sleep must have paid off.

After a beautiful lunch with Aya and Adnan at eleven, before the lunch service began, Mr. V was ready to drive her to Zürich. A smile spread over her face as she hugged the old man hello. Why did she feel so happy today? Her stride felt looser, smoother. She looked forward to an afternoon of wandering the cobbled stone streets of Zürich, shopping in bookstores. In the evening, she would attend the ballet to watch Ethan and bring him by some flowers and a bottle of champagne. It would be his first night dancing as a soloist.

As Ella exited a book boutique with a coveted first edition of *The Great Gatsby*, she realized she hadn't looked over her shoulder once the entire day. Mr. V had hired a bodyguard to trail her at a distance, just in case. He said it was worth the price. She was thankful. The protection was healing in that the stimulus of constant alertness, the feeling of needing to evade, run and hide had been seeping away for some time.

There had been no sign of Owen or his wife for months. Ella had never noticed anyone following her. The security company had found no hidden cameras or anything amiss in their yearly inspection. She realized she had unconsciously decided it was over.

"Excuse me, miss. You dropped your wallet."

Ella spun around, her heart in the throat. In front of her stood a handsome man in his fifties in a perfectly tailored designer suit, leather shoes and a Patek Philippe watch on his wrist. He smiled at her and the lines creased around his eyes. Ella felt her shoulders relax. She motioned to the bodyguard with a hand gesture. She was fine.

"Thank you so much. I don't know how it fell out of my

purse." Strange, thought Ella. I remember pushing it to the bottom of my handbag.

"It is a lovely purse, but perhaps you should acquire one that zips closed?" asked the gentleman with raised eyebrows. "It is really such a hassle to lose a wallet."

"Yes, you're right. Thank you again," said Ella. She gave a smile and continued walking.

She breathed a sigh of relief.

It would have been complicated indeed to lose her wallet. Ahead she saw her flower boutique and ducked inside the small store.

"Why hello there again. This is a coincidence." The man who had returned her wallet stood in front of her, paying for a dozen long-stem roses.

"I have an order to pick up. It's a good thing I have my wallet so I can pay for it."

"Think nothing of it my dear," said the gentleman. "You know, you look familiar. Have we met before?"

"No, I don't think so," said Ella as she handed cash to the florist behind the counter.

"Are you in the theater perhaps?"

"Ballet."

Ella saw the man look at her stomach, clearly puzzled. He cleared his throat.

"I mean; I'm not performing at the moment."

"Well, I am on my way there now to watch Ethan Mueller dance his first solo performance."

"You know Ethan?"

"We are close. I'm assuming you danced with him?"

"Yes. He is a good friend actually. Shall we walk up together?"

"By all means," responded the man, holding out his hand, "my name is Alan Schmidt. A pleasure to meet you."

"Ella."

"We better hurry," said Alan, offering an arm to Ella as they walked back out onto the cobbled stone street. "Or we shall be late."

What a gentleman, thought Ella, as she interlaced her arm with his and they began the walk up to the Opernhaus. At the steps of the Opernhaus, she told Alan to go inside without her. She wanted to catch her breath in the fresh air. She turned to her bodyguard when the doors shut behind Alan as he approached.

"You can come back when the ballet is finished at eleven. I'll wait for you to pick me up inside the front lobby," she said.

"Are you sure, Miss? I could wait inside the lobby through the entire performance, just to be sure."

"No," answered Ella, smiling and patting the giant of a man in front of her on his arm. "It's okay, Mike. Go ahead and go out to dinner."

Ella took a deep breath and entered the lobby. Alan waved her over and introduced her to his friends.

"Ella!" shouted the director, making his way through the crowd in the lobby.

"Excuse me, I need to steal Ella from you for a moment." He took Ella gently by the elbow and steered her away from Alan and a bit apart from the crowd, near the front doors.

"Ella," said the director, his tone hushed. "You wouldn't believe how many calls we've gotten asking when you will be returning to the stage. International press too. They want to know about your journey from pregnancy back onto the stage. Hell, we've even had someone calling about you making a barre fitness video for pregnancy."

"Wait, what?"

"The office doesn't have your number. Give me your contact information, and we can discuss exactly when and how you will return to the Zürich Ballet in detail. And then I'll schedule the interviews with the media for next week. Though," he looked at her, surveying her stomach, "perhaps we should arrange the interviews for later this week. If we want pregnant photos of you, we better take them soon!"

"I have a month until my due date, Director," replied Ella. "We have time."

A light flashed. Suddenly cameras were flashing all around her, and calls of 'look this way Ella' took her by surprise. She looked around, bewildered by the attention.

"Did you arrange this?" she asked.

"No, but what luck!" said the director. "They will get some great photos of you tonight." He looked over at her shocked expression and ordered, "Smile, Ella, this is great publicity for the Zürich ballet. And for you of course. You *do* want to return to dancing, don't you?"

Ella's thoughts were racing. She smiled, hope arriving cool and sweet, like a summer rain on parched, dry earth. She turned toward the cameras, lifting up on her toes in a beautiful arabesque, her distended belly obvious in her clinging dress. Pulling up and in, she briefly closed her eyes, finding her balance.

The hope was rushing through now, washing her clean of fear, opening her up. Joy radiated down her fingertips and the extension of her leg. A flurry of flashes lit up around her. Alan started cheering near the front doors and the entire lobby broke into applause.

The reporters started firing off questions, but the director held up a hand, warding off the inquiries.

"You can give me your cards, and Ella will be pleased to call each and every one of you tomorrow for a personal interview. Right now she is looking forward to watching the ballet from the audience for a change," said the director, while placing a protective arm around Ella's shoulders. "Which starts in three minutes."

The bright glow on her cheeks warmed her as Ella entered the gilded opera hall and lowered herself into a plush red seat in the center of the second floor balcony.

Despite everything and anything that was whirling around her in her life, dancing had been her refuge, her source of meaning and chance at pure joy.

She thought the door to her dreams had slammed shut in her face when the baby began growing in her belly. Now a window had been opened a crack, the light seeping out into the night. Slip through if you dare, Ella. She would fight to be a prima ballerina.

It wasn't just a matter of natural gift, or luck, or political connections. Ella knew what few would accept, that genius took spark within those that offered up everything as kindling until there was nothing left but pain and the tedium of continually throwing all one's energy at striking rock to rock in the hope of that flash of light.

AS SOON AS THE CURTAIN closed, before the applause came to an end, she was on her feet, making her way to the dressing rooms. Ignoring the stares and whispers, the appraising eyes on her belly, Ella walked past her fellow dancers until she found Ethan. She held out the flowers and the bottle of champagne, saying, "you were amazing, Ethan."

"Ella, you came to see me?" He threw his arms around her, pulling her in for a careful hug. "How are you feeling?"

"Excited for this to be over so I can return to the stage," said Ella, motioning to her stomach.

Alan strode up with open arms. "Awe inspiring, Ethan!" Alan gave Ethan a soft kiss and then turned to Ella asking, "Wasn't he amazing?"

Ella smiled, nodding. "See you two in the lobby."

She hurried to the restroom. Her underwear was wet. She was humiliated. Could she no longer control her body functions, now that the baby was a constant pressure on her bladder? There was no other choice.

She pulled off her underwear and threw them in the trash. She surveyed her powder blue silk dress from every angle in the mirror, looking for wet marks. There weren't any. She gave a sigh of relief. Taking out her purse, she reapplied bright red lipstick, running her hands through her waist-length blond hair. Fortified to walk through the scrutiny of the crowd in the lobby, she took a deep breath and left the ladies' room.

As she made her way toward the lobby, she heard footsteps behind her. She had thought she was alone on the landing. She heard a long whistle.

A hand caught her, preventing her escape, pulling her backwards through a door and into the empty opera hall. Ella looked down at the fingers wrapped around her upper arm and up into the blue eyes of Owen.

He stood broad-shouldered before her with a two-day stubble, looking handsome in his blue Armani suit.

"I've been watching you all night, waiting to talk to you alone. I love you, Ella. I want to take care of you and our baby. I've left my wife. You don't have to do this alone. We can be a family. Don't you want that? To be taken care of?

To be loved?"

She moved to walk past him, but he blocked her path. Placing both hands on her bare shoulders, he turned her gently to face him, his eyes traveling down the length of her body and back up to her eyes.

"You do realize that dress leaves nothing to the imagination?"

Heat tingling across her cheeks, Ella struggled to break free of his grasp.

"Let me go Owen," she yelled.

"Calm down Ella or I'll walk out those doors and make a grand announcement to the media. That would hinder your ballet career, no? I only want my baby. I'm so sorry you've gone through this pregnancy alone. It was just such a shock finding out about the baby. I got scared, I'll admit it. But for months I have been getting more and more excited about our baby. I want to be with you, Ella, with you and our baby."

Leaning in, he kissed her lips, her throat, her neck.

Frozen, Ella's every nerve twitched to run, to hide, to flee. She told herself she was safe. They were in the Opernhaus. He wouldn't dare hurt her here.

His hands slipped down her sides, whispering past the fullness of her breasts, to rest on her stomach. Bile rose in Ella's throat, heat spreading out along her skin as he caressed her belly.

Sweat glistening on her cheeks, her arms, the back of her neck. Owen glanced up from her belly, his smile widening, causing his dimples to show.

"You're glowing, Ella. Hello baby," he said, while bending down and kissing her belly. His hands continued to caress her stomach through the thin fabric of her dress. He straightened up, taking her chin in his fingers, lifting her face upward.

"So naughty of you, enlisting the help of that cantankerous old man and his bloody bodyguards. But they're not here tonight, are they angel?" he asked, while one hand slid up from her belly to cup a supple breast.

"So, let's discuss what will happen when my baby is born."

He gave her breast another squeeze, and she shut her eyes. There was a fear, burrowing up through her feet like parasites, insidious and silent. She pushed Owen's hand away.

"Stay away from me. I don't want anything to do with you."

Ella ran toward the door, only realizing at the last second that she was too late.

He was spinning her around, clutching her in a viselike bear hug from behind as he pulled her into a dark corner. He began grinding himself into her back.

"Let go, Owen."

She fought to free herself from his bruising grasp as his calloused fingers whispered along the hemline of the back of her dress. She heard a buckle snapping open and a hand was thrust over her mouth, another pushing up her dress, searching fingers slipping between her legs.

"You dirty slut. You're not wearing any panties. Fuck me, I've never been this hard in my life," he breathed into her ear. "You're even more fucking beautiful pregnant than you were before."

She struggled against him, and he pushed her forward, slamming her head against the pillar, dazing and disorienting her. She could feel his skin against her buttocks, poised.

"You've missed my huge dick inside you, haven't you love?" he whispered.

His knee forced her legs apart, and he shuddered with pleasure as he rubbed along her inner thigh, seeking entry. Tears were slipping down her cheeks from under her closed eyelids, the hand over her mouth suffocating her as she disengaged from what was happening, floating away.

Her stomach cramped, pain shooting through her body, bringing her back into the gilded opera hall. She screamed through the hand pressing against her lips, her eyes widening. Water was sloshing down her legs. Her water had broken.

The baby shouldn't come for another four weeks.

The pain from the contraction filled her with a primal anger, a raw strength she had never felt before. Reaching up, she clutched a handful of Owen's long, blond hair and threw her head back into his face. She dropped down into a wide plié, bringing a hammer fist back into his groin.

His hands fell away from her mouth, his grip on her loosening. She drove an elbow back into his stomach as hard as she could. He doubled over, and she spun around, taking another handful of hair, pulling his head up before slamming it down into her knee.

She took a shuddering gasp as she stumbled backward, and then turned, running for the door. Her stomach was soft, the pain gone. She pushed open the door and stumbled as she reentered the lobby while smoothing down her dress.

"Ella, look at you! Your stomach is huge! Such a lithe woman and then this huge bulge. I don't know how you don't topple right over onto your face," laughed Irma, while grabbing Ella's elbow. "God, it's terrible isn't it? I don't know how you can stand it really: the pregnancy I mean. Knowing that you are losing your career must be devastating for you." Irma paused, waiting for a reaction from Ella.

Ella stood rooted by shock to the floor, speechless.

"You thought you would be dancing in this performance, didn't you? But then," Irma waved a hand at Ella's belly, "we had him give you a little surprise, now, didn't we?"

"No," said Ella, bringing a hand to her mouth, her mind reeling. "You knew." Her belly was starting to harden again, causing Ella to gasp, her hands holding her stomach.

"Don't be silly, Ella. I'm the one who sent Owen in there with you." She waved a hand at the opera hall door. "I was watching you."

Irma stepped forward, tracing a single finger down Ella's cheek before leaning in and licking Ella's ear. She whispered, "I have always been watching. Windows work two ways, Ella. All those evenings you spent drinking alone in the dark at your window: I could see you. We both could."

Irma took a step back. She placed her hands on Ella's belly, caressing it. Ella was too stunned to walk away.

"All the times I threw things around? That was for your benefit. I'm quite the actress, don't you think? What fun that was. It's been a sexy game, stalking you. Do you think it was chance Owen ran into you on the train? You didn't recognize me sitting two tables back, did you? You didn't notice me following you to Constance and staying in the same hotel either. What was leaving the city all about anyway? Anyway, I'm tiring of the game."

Irma ran her fingers through Ella's hair. "Once you have the baby, you will give it to us. After all, you don't want it ruining your ballet career, now do you? And every time you looked at it, you would remember the night it was conceived. Oh wait," said Irma, stepping in so close Ella could feel her breath on her cheek, "you don't remember that night, do you?"

She kissed Ella on the cheek.

"Irma," said Owen, stepping out of the Opera Hall. He grabbed his wife's elbow and pulled her away from Ella to face him. "Why didn't you help me?"

Blood dripped from his nose. Irma reached nonchalantly into her purse and handed Owen a tissue.

"I rather enjoyed watching you be trounced by a pregnant woman a fraction of your body weight," laughed Irma.

Ella at last regained her senses as her stomach hardened again. Still shocked, she ran through the crowded lobby toward Ethan, searching the crowd for her bodyguard. Where was he? Ethan was holding a champagne flute, laughing together with a woman in her eighties in a bright red gown.

"Ella, are you okay?" asked Ethan, looking with concern at her tear streaked face.

Ella paused, catching her breath. Her stomach tightened and she bent over, resting her hands on her knees. She couldn't face telling anyone.

"I think the baby is coming," she said, sitting down on a chair. She still didn't see her bodyguard. She couldn't wait any longer for him to drive her.

"Could you call a taxi, Ethan? And don't leave my side."

She felt her stomach muscles cramp up again. This should hurt, shouldn't it? If it didn't hurt, then perhaps this was normal. Perhaps her water hadn't broken. Her face flooded with heat, and she stood up. Should she tell Ethan what had just happened? She could call the police. No. She couldn't bear it. And the baby was on its way. She just needed to get away from Irma and Owen as fast as possible.

"Are you crazy? I'm not letting you go to the hospital alone in a taxi! I'll go with you."

"What's this about a hospital?" asked a deep voice behind her. She turned to see Alan.

"Ella's having the baby."

"It may be a false alarm," insisted Ella.

"Well then, I will drive you to the hospital. Where are you registered?" asked Alan.

"Munsterlingen."

"Well that's a bit of a drive. Think the baby can hold on that long?"

"Did you hear that?" called a man near them with a camera. "Ella's just gone into labor!"

The flurry of flashes began as her stomach began tightening. Breathless, she held her pose. As a ballet dancer, she knew how to work through pain. She could hold a smile or serene look on her face during a performance, despite a piercing injury. Yet the next wave of stomach tightening made her smile falter, and she cringed. Ethan and Alan saw the change in her expression. They ran to her side, helping her out of the building and down the street to Alan's car.

"Let's get you to the car, Ella. Imagine, stopping to pose for photos while in labor," laughed Ethan. "You really are a diva."

Chapter 21

Ella climbed into the back of the blue BMW sedan and Ethan into the passenger seat next to Alan. The cramps in her belly came and went, but she felt comfortable now.

She was happy that Alan and Ethan were involved in their own conversation about the night's performance and the politics of the ballet. She rested her head back, her arms on her tightening stomach and took calming breaths.

"Could I use your phone, Ethan? I've lost mine."

"Sure thing. How are you doing back there, Ella? You're so quiet. Aren't you suppose to be screaming?"

"We dancers have a high pain tolerance. Thank you for driving me. It's really sweet of you, of both of you."

Ella dialed Mr. V's number. "Mr. V? This is Ella? Some friends are driving me to the hospital because the baby might be coming."

"The baby's coming! Why didn't you say so? I'll be there in ten minutes."

"What? No Mr. V, we won't even be there for forty more minutes. Take your time."

"Are you scared Ella? Don't worry, child, everything will be fine with you and the baby. See you soon."

Ella returned the phone to Ethan. No, she wasn't scared. She was excited. She wanted this baby out and her body back. The pain didn't intimidate her either. Aya had insisted childbirth needn't be agony; this was a mental construct that had been superimposed by men onto women and reinforced by the media. Aya had told her to think of it more like a marathon.

Grueling, sure, but something one could train for and that had a beginning, middle and end.

It wasn't something that happened to you, child birth, but something you could execute, like a perfect pirouette. Ella had never run a marathon like Aya, but she decided it must be like going to morning class, followed by six hours of rehearsal and then a three-hour long ballet performance such as *Sleeping Beauty*. Could it be tougher than that?

Aya had given Ella a hypnosis-for-pregnancy book with accompanying audio guide. She had been listening to it every night for an hour for months. She wasn't quite sure if she believed in hypnobirthing, but then again, she couldn't see how it hurt. On the contrary, she had found it incredibly soothing to curl up under her duvet each evening and float away to the sound of the woman's voice.

Ella took out her ten-year-old turquoise iPod and placed the ear buds in her ears, closing her eyes. Within minutes of listening to the hypnosis audio, she fell asleep.

HE COULDN'T KEEP the grin off his face. Everything had played out just as he had strategically planned it out. All the phone calls and directives had worked. There were advantages to being in a position of power, and he had used them all.

Patience and attention to detail, those were the keys to unlocking success. Now Ella would regain her career, despite the pregnancy.

She thought him the bane of her existence. If only she knew! It had torn him apart to watch her destroying herself after the death of her grandmother. So he had sent her the Annikovs, followed by Mrs. Frieden.

The letter from her Grandmother had been pure gold. It had ensured that the Annikovs and Mrs. Frieden had known just the right things to say.

He wished she knew that her entry into the ballet was because of him. He was so proud of how she had progressed once she was admitted, with no interference on his part. To see her gain a place in the ensemble of the Zürich Ballet on her own merit, well, that had repaid his effort in spades. To see her flourishing due to his intervention had been priceless.

The pregnancy had thrown her career into jeopardy. It had taken him a long time to develop a plan on how to support her returning to the stage. It had finally dawned on him, and almost too late. He, of all people, knew of the power of the media, the power of cash. Where the money speaks, the conscience is silent.

It took quite a bit of work. Now her photo would be splashed all over the Internet, newspapers and magazines. He was proud of Ella's grit. Without her continued commitment to her training, he would have been left with nothing. Now he would build a brand around her that would push her into celebrity status.

Everyone loved a story of redemption. She wouldn't like the story he leaked of her being raped on the street outside the Opernhaus, nor the gossip that was how she became pregnant. It couldn't be helped. People liked to be titillated, as revolting as it was. Still, the ends would justify the means, and he knew the truth wasn't far off from the story he had given.

Now the baby might be coming. Earlier than was planned, but then again that was the way with babies, wasn't it? They came when they wanted to.

The soft indirect lighting and the wooden cabinets gave the birthing room a cozy feel. Ella let out a sigh of relief and relaxed into an armchair. She found the overpowering smell of bleach and disinfectant reassuring.

Ella was thankful the room didn't have the harsh lighting, white walls and squeaky floors of a normal hospital room. Ella smiled when the nurse came into the birthing suite.

"You can go home. This is a false alarm. It's normal to have some light contractions in the last month of pregnancy. This doesn't mean you are going into labor."

Ella looked at the woman. In the past hour, the surges of her stomach tightening had been intensifying and getting closer together.

"The baby is coming," smiled Ella. "I can feel it."

"Yes well, when labor really starts, you won't be smiling anymore," insisted the nurse.

Ella felt the blood pounding in her ears. "I'm not leaving," she answered, gripping the armchair.

The nurse looked at Ella in surprise.

Ella knew the Swiss to be a rule-following people, who readily adhered to regulations and the directives of doctors, nurses, teachers and so forth. But she wasn't Swiss. The nurse's look of surprise turned to one of irritation.

"There are women coming in who are in labor, and you will be needlessly keeping the nicest suite from them," chastised the nurse.

"I'm not leaving," shrugged Ella. Adrenaline was surging through her veins.

Once the nurse was gone, Ella peeked out into the hallway, where Alan and Ethan were waiting. "You two go home. Ethan, you have a long day ahead of you tomorrow. I can't thank you enough for driving me all the way here."

"Good luck, Ella. Call me tomorrow with the good news, gorgeous," said Ethan, coming forward and planting a kiss on her forehead.

Alan gave her shoulder a soft squeeze. "All the best to you Ella. I look forward to seeing you on the stage again sometime soon."

Ella smiled and waved as the two men turned the corner and disappeared from view, hand in hand. Moments after shutting the door and examining the large, free-standing bathtub in the room, she heard a grumpy voice yelling in the hallway.

"I tell you, she's family. Where is she?"

Ella opened the door. Mr. V was standing in the hallway, feet planted wide apart, his hands on his hips, arguing with a nurse. When he saw Ella, his face broke into a grin and he brushed past the nurse. He marched into Ella's room with his arms spread wide and she walked into his embrace. Only once Mr. V had let go did Ella notice tiny Aya walking behind him.

"Ella, how are you?"

"You'll never guess what happened, Mr. V. The director says people are requesting me to return to the ballet. The media are fascinated by the story of a pregnant ballerina making the journey back to the stage again. You can't imagine how thrilled I am. I thought my dream was lost forever and now my chances of dancing again are very good," said Ella. "Only who put the media on to my story?"

"Don't you worry about that now, you have a baby coming," answered Mr. V. "I will be waiting right out here for you. I want everything to go exactly how you want it to. If you need anything at all, you come and get me. I'll straighten up these nurses."

"Ella, how exciting," said Aya, pulling Ella into a hug. "Do you have your audio with you?"

Ella nodded, and Aya led the excited Mr. V to a chair in the hallway before shutting the door with a soft click.

"So, the best thing will be for you to sit on this exercise ball," said Aya softly, while rolling the large green ball next to the bed.

Ella squatted down on the ball, bouncing up and down a bit. "Like this?"

"If that's what feels good to you. I would recommend rolling your pelvis back and forth, which will help with moving the baby down. As the surges get more intense, you can place your forehead down on the table, which will soothe your nervous system. My role will be to ensure you aren't disturbed once you go under the hypnosis and rub your back during the surges."

Elle began to nod. Her eyes suddenly widened, and she sucked in a breath, going rigid at the pain. "Ouch!"

"You're holding your breath, Ella. Remember the breathing. Take a deep breath in, and let it out through pursed lips as slowly as you possibly can. Don't tighten into the surges, relax into the wave each time your stomach tightens. Okay? This isn't any different than running a marathon or dancing a ballet. You need to focus, relax and work through to the end."

Ella nodded and placed her ear buds back into her ears. She listened once again to the soothing words of the hypnobirthing track from the beginning. Only this time, she didn't fall asleep within minutes. She had always wondered what the woman said while she was hypnotized, as she could never recall hearing her say anything but the first two minutes of the track before falling asleep. Now she savored the words of encouragement and reassurance. Her stomach was surging together again.

She rolled forward and back on the ball, breathing slow in and out twice as slowly while her stomach surged together. Aya perceived the change and came behind her, massaging Ella's lower back.

A nurse came into the room, requesting Ella to climb on top of the table so she could strap on a fetal monitor. Ella ignored her and heard Aya whispering. A strap was tightened around her middle, and the room returned to quiet. Ella lost track of all space and time, concentrating on each breath. Had hours gone by? Minutes? Ella wasn't sure.

Someone came into the room. Ella felt a rush of fury, cold in its heat, to be pulled from her focus, to have the words of the woman in her ear overwhelmed by the grating voice of the nurse insisting Ella get up onto the bed. At first, Ella pretended not to hear the nurse.

The nurse shook her shoulder, demanding she climb onto the table for examination.

"I'm sorry, Ella, you have to do what she says," said Aya.

Ella climbed slowly onto the table, with closed eyes, trying to retain her focus.

"Good grief, she's crowning," cried the nurse, and ran from the room to find the midwife.

The door opened, then slammed shut. Ella struggled to maintain her focus despite the flurry of activity in the room.

"You need to push, Ella," said a voice. A hand was running up her inner thigh, opening her legs for a view of the baby.

Something in Ella snapped. Cold fury turned to fear, a rabid anger, "Get away from me. Get them all away from me," yelled Ella, struggling to get off the table.

She was awake. The hypnosis was broken, and Ella fell back onto the table, stunned by the pain as her stomach tightened.

"Let me go, let me go, leave me alone." Hot tears were

stinging her cheeks as she fought against the arms restraining her gently to the table.

Aya was at her side, placing a calming hand gently on Ella's heart. "You are safe, Ella. If you run, you take the baby with you. Breathe and push when you feel a surge, okay? You're almost done, Ella. Just a bit farther to go."

Ella looked into Aya's eyes, grounded by the quiet calm of her speech and the reassuring hand placed on her heart.

"Push on my count," said the midwife.

"Leave her alone," said Aya quietly. "Let her push in her own way, in her own time."

The midwife started to argue, and Aya held up a hand, a finger to her lips.

"We want a peaceful, soothing birth for Ella."

"Fine," agreed the midwife doubtfully. "But if she doesn't progress, I intervene."

The room descended into silence. As her stomach surged together, she pushed; as her stomach relaxed, she lay back, breathing deeply. Less than ten minutes later, the baby was held up by the midwife, wiped quickly clean.

"How long have we been here, Aya?"

"I arrived four hours and thirty-two minutes ago. You did marvelously, Ella."

The nurse placed the infant in Ella's arms.

"It's a girl."

Ella looked down on the tiny face, the fists waving in the air, waiting for emotion to flow into her. There was nothing. She was empty.

"Aya, please take it away from me," cried Ella, the tears still streaming down her cheeks. "I don't want it."

Tears slipped down Aya's face as she opened the buttons of her shirt, gathering the baby to her bare skin. "Shh, Ella, you are exhausted. You can take a shower and have something to eat. Sleep. You will feel different in the morning."

Chapter 22

Ella gazed out the window, the unending tears wetting her pillow. The baby was in the nursery. Yesterday the nurse had rolled the baby into her private room, the wheels of the bassinet squeaking on the floor. The nurse unwrapped the baby from her blanket before placing her gently in Ella's arms. Ella waited for joy and love to fill her.

There was only emptiness and fatigue.

Every time she looked at the baby, she remembered that morning with Owen, saw his face above her, felt the fear and anxiety burrowing into her skin, as if she had been pushed into a putrid pond and emerged covered from head to toe in green slime with bloodsucking leeches leaching at her skin.

The baby had remained the rest of the day in the nursery. Ella was dreading its return.

A knock came at the door before it swung open. The nurse rolled the wailing baby into the room in its bassinet. She unwrapped the baby and held it out to Ella, insisting that Ella must nurse her child. Ella shook her head no. The nurse raised her voice over the frantic crying of the infant. Ella rolled over onto her side, pulling the duvet up over her head.

She couldn't bring herself to do it, despite the pain of her enlarged breasts. How could she, when every time she looked at the child such strong negative emotions rolled through her mind, convulsing in her body? The nurse left in disgust with the baby in its bassinet, unable to convince Ella of the health benefits for her baby, if she would just nurse for even the first few days. Relief flooded through Ella once the door closed, shutting out the piercing cries of the hungry infant.

Aya had visited the day before, bewildered by Ella's response to her baby. Ella hated to disappoint Aya. She knew what Aya must think of her, what they all thought of her. There was nothing she could do. There was no energy within her to pretend.

"Ella, how are you today?"

Ella didn't turn her head to the sound of Aya's voice. Aya sat down on the bed, placing a hand on Ella's side.

"I don't want the baby," Ella spoke to the grass waving in the wind outside the window. "I'm going to give her up. I don't love her."

"You don't mean that, Ella."

"I'm sorry Aya. It's true. I don't want her," said Ella, turning her gaze back to the field outside the window, waving grass dotted with yellow dandelions under a perfect blue sky.

"I've talked it over with Adnan, Ella. We want to take care of your baby for a few months. I can see that you need some help. We'll have your baby in the castle with us when we work and take her home with us at night. You will see her every day. And after a few months, you can decide what you want to do. This could be postpartum depression Ella. I talked to the doctor, he's signed you up for treatment.

Ella continued to stare out the window, the duvet pulled up to her chin. Aya reached out and smoothed her tangled blond hair away from her feverish face.

"We are happy to adopt her permanently, if that's the best thing for both of you. But we want to give you time to heal, to fall in love with your child. Above all we want what is best for you, and if that means giving the baby to another couple, then we support you completely."

Ella at last looked up at Aya.

"Why would you do this for me?"

"We love you. So we love your baby. It's as simple as that."

Ella broke into sobs, her body shaking with emotion. She wasn't overwhelmed by love when she held her infant, but she was scared to death to give it up for adoption.

The thought of not knowing for certain if the baby would be happy and loved filled her with trepidation. With Aya and Adnan, Ella was certain she would be well cared for.

"Does your baby have a name?"

Ella turned with tear-stained cheeks to Aya. She spotted her reflection in the mirror across the room. Her blond hair was in a tangled mess, and dark circles under her eyes stood out against the ghostly white of her skin. Her pajama top even had a large coffee stain down the front. She had never looked this terrible: not after her she lost her mother, nor after her grandmother's death. She didn't even look close to this awful during her drinking phase, when she had skipped dinner in favor of a good portion of a vodka bottle. She shuddered, noticing for the first time the stickiness of her skin, the pungent smell of her sweat.

"Who am I to name her?"

"You're her mother, Ella. You'll get through this. The first step is to take a shower. I'll go check on the baby while you do that and grab a cup of coffee. See you in an hour," said Aya, taking Ella's hand and leading her from the bed to the shower.

"Anneli Alessandra."

Aya stopped walking.

"That's what I want you to call her. Anneli Alessandra. After my two favorite ballerinas."

CHAPTER 23

HE LOOKED THROUGH THE GLASS of the nursery window at the tiny, blond infant. He longed to reach out and pick her up, admiring the tiny hands and bright blue eyes, smelling the newborn scent.

He was shocked by Ella's reaction to the child. Love for this tiny being already coursed through his veins, and he hadn't even held her.

He had learned of Ella's plans to put the baby up for adoption. Fear had given way to an intense rage. An adoption would throw his patient planning into disarray.

"She's agreed," said Aya, stepping up next to him and looking through the glass. "We have at least six months."

"I knew I could count on you, Aya. In six months, if I am satisfied with your care of her, then the restaurant is yours to run independently and rent free," he said. "We'll give it to you in writing. Right, Mrs. Frieden?"

"Yes, of course."

"It's a gorgeous baby," answered Aya, pausing before the words tumbled out of her mouth. "I don't understand. Why are you doing this?"

"Don't worry, Aya. This will be the best for everyone. Ella can't be a single Mom and pursue a dancing career. She knows it. That's why she's rejecting the child."

"She's rejecting the child because…"

"None of that, Aya. We will never talk about any of that ever again. Do you understand me? Aya?"

Straightening to her full height, Aya turned from admiring the infant and met his gaze.

"The baby's name is Anneli Alessandra. Ella at last gave her a name today."

"Anneli Alessandra," he murmured, turning to admire the baby. "I like it."

CHAPTER 24

ELLA LOOKED OUT AT THE SNOW falling outside the private car window. A smile touched Ella's lips at the memory of the morning she walked back into ballet rehearsal. The look of surprise on everyone's faces had been satisfying.

No one had expected the director to announce that Ella would be rejoining the chorus in the next performance. It was a beginning. She still puzzled over how she had gained the attention of the reporters.

The media frenzy surrounding her pregnancy and return to the stage had opened the door wide for her return to the ballet. She didn't understand their questions about a rape on a street near the Opernhaus being the cause of her pregnancy. Had someone witnessed Owen grabbing her in the Opernhaus that night? But she had already been pregnant then. So that didn't make sense of the rumors, even if someone had seen them behind the pillar in that gilded hall. She just offered a "no comment" to questions of this sort, which offered more fuel to the rumors, much to her chagrin.

Experts had been enlisted to offer up advice on how she could most quickly make a comeback. She had shot a ballet fitness DVD for postpartum women. A leading women's magazine was charting her step-by-step progression back to her previous fitness level and back into dancing in the ballet again.

Ella rolled her shoulders back as she stepped out of the car. Her body ached and pulsed with pain from a gut-wrenching day of ballet conditioning and rehearsal. It was infuriating to be thrown backward by her postpartum body. Every day of her pregnancy, all the way to the day she gave birth, she had trained. Yet she still needed to claw her way back to her pre-pregnancy form and fitness. Her body felt different, looser in her hips in a way that helped with her extension, even if her core was still lacking in strength. Ella sighed, thinking of the hours of training expanding out into her future.

She walked into the restaurant, taking off her jacket as she joined Aya and Mr. V at the table by the window. Aya kissed her, and Mr. V poured her a cup of tea. Ella took a sip of her rooibos tea and watched Aya over the rim of her cup. It was close to midnight, and the restaurant was closed for the night. Mr. V sat drinking a whiskey next to her as Aya finished giving the baby a bottle.

Silence wrapped over them: a blanket worn soft by years of use, warm out of the dryer. The day's anxieties and fear unhooked within Ella, places of tension unbinding in the cozy presence of her friends. The only sound was the clatter of dishes in the kitchen as Adnan experimented with a new dish. Aya's nose was pressed gently to Anneli's, her dark brown hair contrasting with the bright blond curls of the two-month-old baby. Aya kissed Anneli's forehead and tucked the baby-blue blanket tighter around the baby. Aya looked across the table at Ella and broke into a smile filled with such raw, vibrating joy that it took Ella's breath away. She found she couldn't help but beam back. It was like the joy Ella felt on stage. Why didn't she feel that, when she first held her baby in the hospital?

Ella shook off the guilt and confusion like a horse shaking away a fly. It wasn't important. The baby couldn't be more loved or better cared for. She watched as Aya handed the baby to Mr. V.

"Hello there, angel. How's the prettiest little baby in the whole world?"

He held her gently against his chest, gently patting her back so any bubbles in her tummy would rise to the surface.

A smile spread out over his gruff features. The baby gave a burp and milk flooded out over Mr. V's carefully pressed designer shirt. Aya rose to take the baby, and Mr. V waved her back into her seat, shifting the baby to his other dry shoulder. Still smiling, Aya took a drink of her cooling tea. Mr. V had proven he did indeed know how to take care of a baby. He showed up every day to take care of Anneli while Aya served lunch and again during the dinner service. If she needed a nap or a break, Aya knew she could call up Mr. V to come over to help her.

Who knew a baby would turn the gruff Mr. V into a smiling socialite? He showed off the baby to anyone who came in the restaurant. If Aya and Adnan were in a state of pure bliss, then so was Mr. V. Only, unlike Aya and Adnan, he didn't have to deal with the sleep deprivation of caring for the baby at night and the fatigue of running a restaurant. Some people broadcast loud their longing for a baby, for a grandchild, and some held it secret.

Three weeks after Aya went home with the baby, she rang Ella's bell, and ascended the stairs in tears to Ella's flat. She couldn't take care of the baby, she said.

Aya was falling in love. If she kept Anneli any longer, it would be too painful to give her back. Like cutting off her own arm. Tears streamed down her cheeks. The baby slept peacefully on, wrapped tightly to her chest in a front pack. Ella didn't have to consider. She gathered Aya into her arms, the baby between them.

"And Adnan, how does he feel?"

"He wants a child so much. We have tried for years, but, we can't..."

"She's yours, Aya. She's yours forever. We'll sign the papers. We'll make you and Adnan her official parents."

Aya's tears turned into sobs. "How can you bear to give her up?" She wrapped her arms around the baby, kissing the top of Anneli's head, drinking her in. She lifted her gaze back up to Ella.

Ella looked down into Aya's tear-stained face, twisted with fear and pain and hope.

"I've seen the way you hold Anneli, the way you care for

her," she whispered, and kissed Aya's forehead. "It is clear you love Anneli."

Aya kissed Anneli's blond tufts of hair and nodded.

"I will never take her away from you," promised Aya. "You will always have a place in her life. What do you want to tell her?"

"I'll be Auntie Ella."

"Are you sure?"

Ella nodded, pain searing her heart. It was harder this way, bittersweet. But perhaps, one day, the shame and fear would heal. The memory of Owen and Irma might fade, and she would be left with nothing more than the echo of this child's laughter. In the meantime, she would be able to see Anneli grow and know she was well cared for and loved.

ELLA WALKED IN the door, the aroma of freshly baking bread engulfing her as she shook the snow off her jacket and hung it by the door. Hunger rumbled through her stomach at the smell as she walked into the kitchen.

"Ella, you're here! I need you to take Anneli tonight. Aya has the stomach flu. Mr. V is gone. I cooking, and not easy with baby. Malin's coming. She's serving," said Adnan, as he transferred fresh baked rolls into breadbaskets.

Ella stood frozen by the counter, unable to speak. She hadn't touched the baby since the hospital. She was afraid to hold it in her arms, even for a moment. What was she going to do? Could she refuse to help?

Adnan finished placing the last of the thyme and sea salt rolls into the baskets and kissed the top of Anneli's head, who was beginning to fuss in the front pack strapped to his chest.

"She is hungry. You can watch: I make up a bottle. Then you take Anneli upstairs with you and feed her. You hungry?"

Ella shook her head. Hunger had been rattling through her a moment before, but now her stomach had cramped up.

She didn't think she could force down a bite of anything. She watched as Adnan prepared the bottle and set it on the counter. Unstrapping the front pack, he reached in and held Anneli out to Ella.

Ella just stood there, staring at the fussing baby. Shaking

her head, she said, "I don't know how to take care of a baby."

Adnan gave a sigh.

Pulling the baby to his chest, he nuzzled the top of her head with his cheek while rocking her back and forth.

"You cooking tonight instead, Ella?"

"Could I?"

Adnan gave a chuckle. "Sit here," he motioned at the chair. "I start on citrus curry lentils."

No sooner had Ella lowered herself onto the chair than she was being handed the baby and the bottle. She sat rigid, her muscles taut, her lips pressed together into a thin line. She didn't look down, instead focusing on Adnan as he whipped around the kitchen, trying to make up for lost time.

Anneli reached up and patted Ella's face. Ella glanced down, righting the bottle so the milk flowed again, before refocusing on Adnan. She tried to ignore the presence of the baby. But the warmth of the soft bundle in her arms was seeping through her shirt. The smell of the baby was wafting up to her, despite the competing smells of the kitchen.

"Look, she sleeping," said Adnan. He planted a quick kiss on the baby's cheek and smiled as he returned to the stove. Ella lowered her gaze to the sleeping baby in her arms. She leaned in, drinking in the sweet baby smell. Contentment washed over her, as if she had spent a lifetime in the bitter cold of a subzero landscape, only now to settle down by the warmth of a roaring fire. A warmth was spreading through her body, making her feel languid and at peace. She let out large sigh.

"You going upstairs with Anneli? I come tomorrow morning."

"You want her to stay with me for the entire night? I can't. I won't. I don't know how to all on my own."

"You learning it. I here until midnight. Tomorrow, Aya maybe not sick," replied Adnan while removing pomegranate seeds from its rind. "Go. Maybe you lucky. She sleeping few hours. You sleep too." He rinsed his hands in the sink and packed the baby formula and extra bottles into the diaper bag, slinging it over Ella's head. He took Anneli out of Ella's arms and placed her gently in the baby carrier, picking it up with one hand and a dish of food in the other.

"Fast, fast, I carry up."

Ella followed Adnan into the foyer of the castle, dread and worry churning together with the fatigue of a long day of ballet rehearsal. She was so preoccupied with her thoughts, that she didn't notice they weren't alone.

"Adnan, Ella, it's so good to see you again."

A chill passed down Ella's spine. She knew that voice. A hand touched her arm, and she leapt back as if the tentacle of a jellyfish had made contact with her bare skin.

"What are you doing here?"

"I am looking forward to trying your delicious food the newspapers have been raving about. And this must be your baby. Isn't she gorgeous? Oh Ella, she's absolutely precious. What did you name her?"

She was here. Standing inches away, her dark eyes trained on the baby. Ella's heart jumped, and her breath caught in her throat as if a stampede of bulls were barreling down upon her, threatening to trample her in their wake.

"How do you know it's a girl?"

"Oh, well, it's just clear. Isn't it? Oh I really must hold her. She's just so cute." Irma took a step toward the baby.

Adnan pushed the plate of food into Ella's hands and held the baby carrier away from Irma's outstretched arms. "Not holding my baby."

Irma paused, frowning. Then her face broke out into a smile. "Ah, so you're the father. So you two are together now?" she asked, waving a hand between Adnan and Ella. "What happened to your wife after you left her behind for all this?" Irma gestured to the castle walls and back toward the restaurant. She gave a laugh that echoed against the stone floors.

"You know who the father is, Irma," said Ella, her voice cold.

Adnan's face turned bright red. "Out, no eating here. You go out," he yelled, pointing a finger at the door.

Irma reached out and patted Adnan on the shoulder as if he had made a hilarious joke.

"Dear Adnan, don't be sour with me. Such a pretty young woman is hard to resist, I'm sure. These things happen. Now, show me to a table by the window."

Adnan closed his eyes, his hand clenching into a fist. He let out a deep breath and met her gaze. "No."

A bemused grin settled onto Irma's face. She took a step closer to Adnan, her focus still locked on the baby. Lowering her voice, she said, "Now, Adnan. You don't really want to turn me away, now do you? You wouldn't want a rumor about cockroaches in the kitchen and cases of food poisoning to start going around. Think over what that would do to your business."

Adnan set down the baby carrier and rushed toward Irma. Ella threw out a restraining arm in front of Adnan, while balancing her dish of food in the other.

"Get out, Irma," she said.

They waited until Irma left, then headed to the hallway. Ella took out her keys and opened the door. Adnan rushed ahead of her up the stairs, taking two at a time until he stood on her landing, and slipped off his shoes. Ella opened the door to her flat. Adnan pushed gently past her, depositing the baby carrier on the floor next to the eggshell-blue sofa. Ella set the dish of food on the table.

"Good night angel," he cooed, a hand resting gently on the sleeping baby. "Good night Ella. You eat. It's good," he insisted, shaking a finger at her.

She gave a small smile, nodded and he reached out, patting her cheek, his scowl turning into a grin. "Good, good, you too thin. Now, we see us tomorrow. By then Mr. V's here. Any trouble you find me."

The door shut behind her, and she automatically went to the door, sliding all the deadbolts into place. Leaning against her door, she stared at the room, her attention landing on the plate of food. She stole a peek at the sleeping baby before going to the table, devouring Adnan's citrus curry-infused lentils, pomegranates, green beans and fresh caught fish baked with thyme, rosemary, roasted tomatoes and sesame seeds. It was now cold, but still delicious. As she was carrying her empty plate to the sink, the baby let out a cry.

She went to the baby carrier, the intensifying cries at last forcing her attention to the tiny being wrapped in a pale-blue blanket, its tiny, five-month-old fists waving around in front of its face. Hands shaking, heart thundering in her mouth, she picked the baby up out of its carrier. The baby continued to cry.

Ella mimicked Adnan's earlier rocking movements. The baby cried harder. In desperation, Ella brought her lips to the baby's cheek, kissing her as Adnan had, the silky softness of the baby's skin and her sweet scent overwhelming her with an unexpected emotion. The baby was quiet in her arms. Ella stole a peek. As she looked into the bright blue eyes looking up at her, a fierce desire to protect the tiny being welled up within her, a hot spring melting her frozen resistance. Anneli was gorgeous. She ran her fingers tenderly through the silk-soft blond hair that grew in tufts all over the baby's head.

"Hello there, Anneli," she whispered.

Anneli kicked her feet and gurgled, waving her little arms. Ella kissed her head. She snuggled her cheek against the soft, rosy cheek of the baby.

"Do you want to play?"

Ella pulled the cashmere blanket from her favorite armchair and laid it out on the floor. She placed the baby down on its stomach. The baby gave a small cry. Ella looked in the diaper bag and found some toys, which she placed in front of the baby. Anneli grabbed one and immediately brought it to her mouth, rolling around on the floor. In the kitchen she made a Nespresso coffee, the aroma filling the room as she took her first sip.

Ella sat down on the floor, leaning back against the sofa, her legs stretched out in front of her. She sipped her coffee, the baby content next to her, as she watched the snowflakes falling outside in the darkness. Halfway through her coffee, the baby began to fuss. Ella picked her up, placing her on her chest, then holding her to a sitting position on her legs. The baby laughed, and Ella gave a sigh of relief. But only a few minutes later, the baby began to fuss again. Ella tried playing patty-cake. She tried singing.

"Good grief, how does Aya do this all day?" asked Ella aloud as she picked the crying baby up and rocked her.

She wandered around the room. The baby cried louder. She made up a bottle and tried to give it to the baby. Anneli took a few gulps and resumed her piercing wail. Ella handed her a piece of bread. Anneli threw it on the floor.

Ella changed Anneli's diaper, but she continued crying. Ella's heart was revving up, adrenaline pulsating through her veins. She didn't know what to do. Ella placed the screaming baby in the baby carrier and rocked her back and forth. She picked Anneli back up, cuddling her. She tried singing again. Nothing helped. She picked up the phone.

"Adnan? There is something is wrong with Anneli! I've tried everything, and she keeps crying! What if she's sick?"

"I coming."

Within one minute, Adnan was buzzing to be let upstairs. Ella checked the monitor. She released the lock and opened her door, watching Adnan take the stairs two at a time as he raced toward her. He took the crying baby from her arms and looked her over. He pressed his lips to her head and then his ear to her stomach.

"No fever. Tummy. You dress her warm, you go walking, okay? Stroller's in front. If she crying, then walking good plan," he explained as he led the way to the stairway. "Now I go down. Good."

Ella nodded, and Adnan kissed Anneli twice before handing her back to Ella.

Ella slipped into her boots and then pulled a warm jacket on over her thick sweater and wound a scarf around her throat. She didn't want to risk seeing Irma again, but the crying was screeching on her nerves like nails on a chalkboard. Adnan said to take the baby walking if she cried. So walking they would go, despite the dark and the snow swirling in the fog outside her window.

Ella descended the stairs, holding the banister tightly, afraid of falling and dropping the baby down the stone stairs. She carefully laid the baby into the stroller, zipped the sheepskin sack up around the baby to her chin and tucked the fighting fists inside. She placed the fleece hat carefully on Anneli's head and over her tiny ears.

Opening the front door wide, Ella pushed the stroller out into the snow. She walked out into the icy mist and pulled the sun shade down to protect Anneli from the falling snow. The path down to the lake was illuminated by the street lamps, light holding the snapping jaws of darkness at bay.

Her footsteps were swallowed up by the soft layer of snow beneath her feet. Within moments, the baby's cries stilled. Ella peered down. Anneli was quiet, watching the snowflakes drifting down. Ella turned at the bottom of the hill, making her way along the harbor. It was only seven thirty, but the lake front was desolate of life.

The only sound was the crunching of her feet on the snow and the waves splashing against the pier, the rocky shore.

Ella was alone. A chill went down her spine, and the tiny hairs at the base of her neck tingled. Someone was watching her. She whirled around, looking in every direction. But there was no one, just swirling fog and the sound of the waves splashing against the pier. She let out her pent-up breath and continued walking.

She passed the lake hotel, its windows bright aquariums swimming with light and the faces of the few dining in the restaurant. She continued on into the darkness. She made the loop around the playground and returned back toward the castle. The street lamps glowed, round halos of light floating in the fog. The baby's eyes were beginning to close. Ella stood at the base of the small hill heading back up to the castle.

She decided to walk a final stretch along the harbor before going home.

Chapter 25

Ella blinked open her eyes. She lay in a Russian four-post mahogany bed. She stared up at the intricate molding on the ceiling before shifting onto her side. The silk of the sea-foam sheets glided over her bare legs. The terrace door was open, and Ella heard the horn of a ferry sounding its imminent departure.

A grey dove swooped down, landing on an apple-tree branch just past the terrace railing. Listening to the cooing of the dove, she closed her eyes. The fresh smell of spring drifted in from the outside and the aromatic smell of coffee filled her apartment. She heard voices in her kitchen. Who was in her apartment?

"Better to be slapped with the truth than kissed with a lie. We have to tell her what we know. It isn't right."

"She's not ready yet, Serge. I won't let you."

A memory rushed in, crowding out the spring morning. Ella sat up straight in bed, her heart leaping into her throat. For one torturous moment, the remnants of the past hung suspended in a mist before her eyes.

Shadowy images, ethereal in their rejection of all gravity, twisted and spun in the icy chill of a winter night. She took short, rapid breaths as her heart clenched in her chest. She clutched the sheets, twisting them in her hand. Where was Anneli? What happened? How did she get in her bed?

"Anneli! Anneli!!" Ella fell out of bed and fell on her way to the door with a loud crash. She heard feet thundering down the stairs from above. The door burst open.

"What's wrong, Ella?"

Ella looked up. She lay sprawled on the floor in her negligee, staring up at Mr. V and Mrs. Frieden.

"Mr. V? Mrs. Frieden?"

Mr. V helped her to her feet and guided her into the living room. Mrs. Frieden picked up Ella's cashmere blanket off the couch and wrapped it around Ella. She pulled her gently down onto the couch, her arms around her shoulders.

"Where's Anneli?" asked Ella, her heart still racing.

Mr. V and Mrs. Frieden looked down at the floor. Mr. V mumbled something under his breath.

"I thought she was improving this past week," said Mr. V to Mrs. Frieden.

"Where is Anneli?"

"She's gone," answered Mr. V, while patting her shoulder. "She's gone." He shook his head.

"What are you doing here?" asked Ella.

"I've been home for months now, dear. Do you know what day it is?" asked Mrs. Frieden.

Ella's brain fought for purchase. It found only slippery memories, slick with uncertainty.

"January?"

"It's May twenty-seventh Ella. Try to remember yesterday. What did you do?"

Ella's mind began its search. Nothing. She could remember nothing of yesterday, nor the day before that.

"Ella?"

"Shut up! I don't know, okay? I don't remember a thing from yesterday. Get out of my face."

Ella felt heat spread across her chest. What was happening? She began to cry, her fury turning to depression. She was a terrible person. She had lost Anneli. Where was she? What had happened?

She looked from Mr. V to Mrs. Frieden and then back again. "Why aren't you in Idaho helping your daughter?"

"Don't you worry, Ella; my daughter is in remission. She's

doing just fine in Idaho. It's you we need to take care of now. You had a terrible head injury a few months back, Ella. You're still suffering from amnesia."

"And a head injury," interrupted Mr. V.

Ella looked from one face to the other.

"Since your brain injury, you've been having a hard time remembering anything since you went out for that walk with Anneli on the night of the accident," explained Mrs. Frieden. "We've explained this all to you every morning since you woke up in the hospital. The police found you naked, bleeding profusely from a head wound in a sailboat cabin. You had severe hypothermia. A few more hours and you would have died."

"Where is Anneli?"

Mrs. Frieden walked into the kitchen and took out eggs and vegetables from the fridge and placed them on the white marble counter top.

Ella looked up at the molding around her living room ceiling, trying to recollect anything. A disconnected memory arose. Her cheek was resting on a lifesaver ring, the cold piercing her, and her entire body was shaking from the onset of hypothermia.

"Oh, Ella. We don't know where Anneli is. The police, well, the police think she drowned when you two slipped and fell in the lake."

Ella sat up straight. "Anneli didn't drown! We didn't slip and fall in the lake. I was pushed. But Anneli wasn't with me.... She didn't fall into the water." Ella looked outside the window at the apple blossoms waving in the breeze.

Mrs. Frieden paused in the kitchen, the whisk still in her hand above the bowl. "Wait, what do you mean? Serge, come out here."

Ella's eyes widened when Mr. V walked out of her guest room while buttoning up his shirt. "Are you staying here? With me?"

"He sleeps in your guest room, honey," answered Mrs. Frieden. "We wanted someone in the flat to make sure you're safe. Sometimes you wake up in the night in a real fright," continued Mrs. Frieden.

"Ella remembers the night of the accident. She says she was pushed into the lake. Anneli didn't fall in with her. Who pushed you, Ella?"

"I don't remember," stammered Ella, closing her eyes in pursuit of the memory.

"They found the stroller at the bottom of the harbor Ella. We lost our Anneli. She died," said Mr. V, clearing his throat and looking down at his shoes. "Enough of this, we're all wasting time. To fall is allowed, Ella. To stand up is a must. No one blames you for what happened. It was an accident. You hear me? An accident," said Mr. V, turning and shaking his finger at Ella. He pulled his tie around his neck and knotted it while looking in the mirror next to the front door.

"You need to eat some breakfast, and we need to be on our way to ballet rehearsal. Without effort, you can't even pull a fish out of the pond. We'll watch a video of yesterday's rehearsal in the car on the way to Zürich so you remember what happened in yesterday's practice, Ella. Be downstairs in thirty minutes please. You keep an eye on the child, Helen. I don't need to have her forget and head off to the bakery again."

Mrs. Frieden poured the eggs into the pan and added ham and fresh chopped veggies to the omelet. "You're the one who forgot to put away her ballet bag in the closet. Last time she put it in the refrigerator instead of the milk, and we searched for it for an hour."

Ella hated the smiles they shared at her expense. She was a joke to them. She sat motionless as Mr. V kissed her on the top of the head on their way out the door. She tried to recall anything about the past week or month. Her mind was blank. She sat motionless, gazing at the birds fluttering between the tree blossoms and a sailboat heading out of the harbor. The last she remembered was snow. Now it was spring.

"I'm going outside."

"No," insisted Mrs. Frieden, pushing her with soft force back down onto the sofa. "You go on and drink this and then get dressed for work. Everything is going to be okay."

As Ella drank her espresso in the sunshine, a flashback hit her. She was clutching the lifesaver, her body shaking uncontrollably with cold and a pain piercing her skull. She was certain she was going to die. But here she was, with the velvety feel of the cashmere against her skin, the smell of the coffee in her hand, the rose-filled vase vibrant in front of her, the twitter of birds on her terrace. Mrs. Frieden was humming in her kitchen while she cooked them breakfast. Ella was overwhelmed by a sudden gratitude to be alive.

Mrs. Frieden took the empty cup from her and held out a hand. "Time to go on and get dressed while I put breakfast on the table."

Ella placed her hand in Mrs. Frieden's. The feel of the small hand beneath her fingertips was familiar in its frailty. How did such a small woman radiate such force and fortitude?

"You've held my hand a lot," she said, more to herself than to Mrs. Frieden. "In the past few months. Haven't you?"

"Do you remember?" asked Mrs. Frieden, her eyes widening in hope.

Ella sighed. "No. It's just that your hand feels so familiar in mine. I remember this," Ella said, lifting their interlocked fingers upward. She examined the blue veins of the elder woman's hand.

"Oh, well then," said Mrs. Frieden, and she gave Ella a soft pat on the cheek.

"That's something, isn't it? Your ballet rehearsal clothes are already laid out next to your bed. Then come and eat some breakfast. You have a long day ahead of you."

Ella dressed in her pink tights and red leotard, pulling warm booties on over her feet and tying a blue wrap dress around her midsection. She reentered the living room and sat down at the table in front of the omelet.

"We don't eat eggs for breakfast. We eat yogurt and rolls and croissants."

"Well, now we eat omelets, seeing as you don't like eating more than a yogurt for lunch during rehearsal," replied Mrs. Frieden. "Eat up. You have to leave in twelve minutes."

Ella walked down the stairs and into the restaurant. Aya was already folding napkins for lunch service. Adnan was carrying in a box full of fresh fruit, vegetables and herbs from the farmers market.

"Good morning, Aya," said Ella, as she walked over and attempted to give her a hug.

Aya took a step backward, out of Ella's reach. Ella's eyes brimmed with tears, threatening to spill over. Aya fled to the kitchen, the door swinging shut behind her. Ella placed her face in her hands.

"Space. Give her space," said Adnan, while patting Ella on the shoulder.

ELLA WATCHED THE rolling green fields and small Swiss villages with their church clock towers pass by outside her window. She turned over the memory of the accident. Every smell, sensation, and emotion of falling into the icy water whipped through her with startling force.

She knew she hadn't slipped and fallen into the lake. But what had happened? Ella punched the car seat in frustration at her malfunctioning memory.

She couldn't accept that Anneli had drowned. She could remember walking with the stroller through the fog, her feet crunching on the newly fallen snow. The lake front was completely deserted. The next thing she remembered was falling into the lake. What happened next?

"Did they find Anneli's body?"

"Ella," sighed Mr. V while rubbing his eyes. "Do we have to go through this interrogation every morning? You need to be watching the video I filmed of you yesterday so you are prepared."

"I asked that yesterday?"

"And the day before that, and the day before that." Mr. V massaged his forehead.

"Well?"

"No. They never found her body."

"Wouldn't it float to the surface?"

"Ella! Enough. Watch the video."

Ella couldn't bear the look of grief and resignation on Mr. V's face, or on Aya's, Adnan's and Mrs. Frieden's. She had been entrusted with the baby for one night, and now she was gone. They would never forgive her for losing Anneli. She would need to move away and start all over again.

She would be alone.

There would be no more wandering into the spicy smells of the kitchen to chat with Adnan and Aya, nor the soul-steadying Sunday mornings of sitting in silence next to Mr. V, drinking coffee and reading the newspaper together.

No more swimming laps in the summer with Aya and lying under the cotton trees afterward, listening to the waves and watching the soft puffs of white float out over the turquoise lake. She would lose her long talks with Mrs. Frieden on the castle terrace, a cold drink in their hands, the sun warm on their skin. No more meals eaten all together on a winter evening, Anneli cooing and laughing while being bounced on a knee.

What was life without love but a never-ending cascade of time, hollow of meaning and happiness?

The car was pulling up in front of the white-columned Zürich Opernhaus. Ella looked up at the winged angels on top of the building. She would take solace in the knowledge that the tormented were multidimensional in their artistic performance. There was a cultivation of empathy for the pain throbbing through the world that added dimension and nuance to the work of an artist.

Ella turned her attention to the video. She watched herself and the other dancers rehearsing. Remnants of memory snapped in her brain. The day before began to come back to her. She remembered dancing these steps. The movements vibrated within her body. She watched the video all the way into Zürich. The car pulled up at the front curb.

"It is essential you let on to no one that you are confused or that anything is wrong with you at all. Do you understand?"

"Why? Don't they know about my accident?"

"No. They don't know. No one knows."

Ella looked at Mr. V, her eyes round, her hand on the door handle. "But how is that possible?"

"Extinguish the spark before the fire, deflect the trouble before the strike. We didn't want it interfering with your ballet career, not after how hard you were working to return to the stage. So we requested the police keep the incident private. Now, have a good time."

"I was in the hospital, right? Didn't I miss conditioning and rehearsal? What did you tell the director?"

"You were ill. Now let's go, you'll be late."

"You're coming with me?"

Mr. V nodded as the climbed the steps. "I told him I'm making a documentary of the Zürich Ballet."

"You are?"

"Well, I am now. It was the only way I could think of to gain access to rehearsal so you could remember the rehearsal from the day before via my videos."

Ella pulled open the front door. Her head was throbbing. She muddled through the information she had gained that morning. The last thing she remembered was heading out into the snow on a foggy night with Anneli in the stroller. This morning she woke up to Spring. She had some sort of amnesia. What kind had they said? Anyway, she couldn't remember anything since that night. Anneli was gone. She had suffered a brain injury. They thought she had slipped and fell into the lake, the stroller falling into the lake with her. Why would they want to keep her accident secret?

A thought occurred to her as she walked down the corridor. Maybe they didn't think she slipped and fell into the lake. Maybe they thought she jumped. Maybe they wondered if she pulled Anneli in with her, on purpose. Bile rose in her throat, and she dashed into the women's room, retching into a toilette. Sweaty and pale, Ella splashed cold water on her face and then leaned against the cool wall. But she didn't attempt suicide. She would never harm any baby and certainly not her Anneli. They must know that. They knew that, didn't they?

"Ella, is that you?" A dancer peeked into the restroom. "Are you okay? We're waiting for you.

"Yes, yes I'm fine. I'm coming."

Ella took a deep breath and headed toward a future of seemingly perpetual uncertainty.

Ella was relieved when the car at last pulled up the road to home. She opened the car door and stepped out into the heat of an abnormally warm spring day.

"I'm going for a swim in the lake," she announced to Mr. V.

"Not alone, you're not."

Ella spun around, surprised. Did he seriously just forbid her from going swimming? Who was Mr. V to say what she did and when? Amnesia or no amnesia. She wanted to go for a swim in the lake. She could already imagine the cool water gliding over her sticky skin and her fatigued muscles relaxing in the gentle waves of the lake.

"Yes I am."

"You haven't gone swimming since the accident. I'm worried what could happen to you Ella."

"Today's the day, Mr. V. Don't worry."

She turned and walked away from him to the terrace. It was filled with guests enjoying dinner alfresco. She smiled at Aya as she hurried past with a large tray of meals. She glanced up at the sound of hammering. There was a man up on her private terrace. How did he get in? What was he doing up there?

On her way into the restaurant, Ella nearly collided with Mrs. Frieden, who was carrying a tray of drinks to the patio.

"There's a man on my terrace."

"Don't be alarmed dear. It's Joshua," replied Mrs. Frieden as she continued out the door. "I told you this morning. He's installing a new sunscreen."

Joshua. Ella stood motionless, her pulse racing. Joshua was here? How many hours had she relived their kiss and wished she hadn't left him standing in that café in Zürich? She had printed out all his emails, bound them with a silk ribbon and kept them in her bedside table. She hadn't dared to let herself fall into his words, sticky with declarations of adoration and love. Owen taught her that kindness and friendship were often used by men to seduce and control. It was a lesson her mother tried to impart, but sometimes the only way to learn a lesson is through experiencing it for yourself.

A single tear fell down her cheek as the memory of her mother danced before her eyes. Ella walked into the entryway of the castle and leaned against the wall, resting her cheek on the cold stone wall, thinking of Owen. Why was it that so many men couldn't just admire beauty, but were possessed by a desire to possess and dominate? Why hadn't she been able to see Owen for what he was? What if she was wrong about Joshua, too? Would Joshua's charm and devotion give way to control and abuse?

How could she know with certainty any new relationship wouldn't play out as it had with Owen? Ella's mother had told her that her father's abuse and control began after Ella was born. Before that, her mother said her father was the most charming of men and certainly one of the most powerful in Russia.

Ella wondered for the millionth time who her father was. Ella stood up straight, squaring her shoulders. She wouldn't be like her mother and abdicate all romantic relationships with men. Whereas her mother suffered from mental illness, Ella did not. And she had to believe there were good men in the world and Joshua could be one of them.

She unlocked the door and raced up the stairs to her flat. She ran through her front door and out onto her terrace.

"Joshua," she cried, her face lit up with a bright smile. He stepped down from the ladder, a screwdriver still in his hand, and she threw herself into his arms, knocking the cowboy hat off his head. She pressed her cheek to his neck, her lips to his bare shoulder. He gathered her tighter to him, picking her up off the ground and kissing her cheek before he released her.

"It's so good to see you," she said, and she lifted up onto her toes, pressing her lips softly to his in a quick kiss.

"So is that a yes?" he asked, his face serious.

"A yes to what?"

"We had ourselves a real heart-to-heart last night. Do you remember that?"

She looked into his green eyes. She took a step back and wandered over to a container of lavender, trailing her fingers through the purple flowers. She couldn't remember last night.

"I don't remember," she admitted, turning to face Joshua.

"You remember anything from the past week?"

Ella shook her head.

"The past few months?"

Ella looked down at her shoes.

He shook his head, rubbed the two-day stubble on his chin

and picked up his t-shirt from a chair, pulling it down over his sweaty muscular torso. He ran a hand through his short brown hair and placed his cowboy hat on his head.

"I'd be lying if I didn't say I'm disappointed. For a week there, you were making real progress. Oh Ella, I love you, but I don't know how much more of this I can take."

"You love me."

"It damn well may break my heart, but yeah. I sure do. Every once in a while, on a good day, you are throwing yourself into my arms, like today. But then other days, you'll be real suspicious and cold. It's a real roller coaster ride. You're a slot machine in a casino. There's always that chance there that I could win big. You toss me a few dollars out every once in a while, and I'm hooked by hope."

She walked back to him, placing a hand on the soft worn fabric of his t-shirt. "Yes to what Joshua?"

He let out a big sigh, trying to turn away from her. She grabbed the frayed front pocket of his jeans, forcing him to stay. "Tell me."

"I'm damn exhausted, Ella, by all the talking, every day explaining anew, questioning. I don't know if I want to ask that again. No, I just can't do it."

Ella nodded, reaching up and gently turning his chin so he would meet her gaze. "Fine. Then I'm going swimming in the lake."

"That sounds mighty refreshing, but I should get on home. I have a train in twenty-two minutes. And I don't think you should go swimming on your own. You haven't been in the lake since your accident."

"Yeah, well, I don't answer to you."

Joshua laughed out loud, his eyes merry with amusement. "Well that's for damn sure. Okay, you win. I'll come with you."

Ella didn't answer. She went inside and found a bag and threw in two towels and placed it on the sofa. Then she went to her room to change. As she pulled on a turquoise two-piece suit, she heard Joshua come in from the terrace. When she re-entered the living area, she found Joshua in her kitchen, leaning back on her white-marble counter top, drinking a beer.

She wanted to ask him when he had come to Switzerland. She was curious about all the days since the accident she couldn't remember. But she pushed the questions down with impatience. He didn't want to rehash everything again. How many days had he done just that for her? Once? Twice? For weeks? She would ask Mr. V or Mrs. Frieden in the morning if they knew.

"Well tarnation. You're a sight for sore eyes."

"Thanks," said Ella. "If you're lucky, I will curl up with you on the sofa after our swim and we can read together.

"I'm not much for reading."

"Then we'll just canoodle instead," she said, while throwing a dress over her head.

"What the heck you talking about, woman?"

"You know," she answered, while grabbing the bag. "We'll cuddle up on the sofa and kiss. Okay, I'm ready."

"With Mr. V here? And you still waking up most mornings not remembering the day before?"

"I didn't say sex. Or has that already happened?"

She watched Joshua's cheeks turn crimson. "No. I'm not that kind of guy Ella," he said, grabbing the bag out of her hand and slinging it over his shoulder.

"You sure about that? You wrote me that you ran through a great number of women for a while. How is this any different?"

"Because I was happy to leave my whole life and fly here as soon as I heard you were hurt? I love you, but I don't know… maybe that's not enough."

"What are you trying to say?" asked Ella.

She sat down on the kitchen stool and began rearranging the flower arrangement on the granite counter top.

"What I want to say is, I feel lost here. This country doesn't fit me and it doesn't feel like home. When Mrs. Frieden got that call that you were unconscious in the hospital, well I bashed my pride to pieces and begged her for a ticket so I could come see you. You had us all scared. Now I'm working on restoring this beauty of a castle but I'm real homesick for the joy and freedom I feel out on a ranch and for the US of A in general. My brother bought me a ticket," he said, running a hand through his hair, shifting from foot to foot, causing the old, wooden floor to creak beneath his feet. "I fly back to Idaho in five days."

She walked to the door and looked over her shoulder. "Are you coming or what?"

Ella was surprised. Instead of sadness at the news that Joshua was leaving in five days, she found relief. He wasn't on a vendetta to win her and control her. This was nothing more than a brief and mutually agreeable love affair. True, she couldn't remember it, but Mr. V and Mrs. Frieden had been watching over her. Joshua laced his fingers through hers and she smiled, and when he pulled her into an embrace, it felt like coming home.

Their footsteps crunched on the gravel path as they walked along a pink and purple lake, the crickets beginning to chirp as the sun set over the mountains. Ella had written Joshua that she loved him, but now she knew she meant it. She didn't want to imagine her life without him sharing it with her.

It should have been the most romantic walk of her life, but she couldn't get Anneli out of her head. They climbed down the stone steps toward the lake. Joshua took out candles and lit them before handing Ella a sparkling lemonade and taking out a beer for himself. He took her hand and pulled her against his chest, resting his chin against her hair.

"When did you pack all this?"

"While you were changing."

"Ella?"

"Yes?"

Ella's heart began to flutter in her chest and skin tingled, looking up into his startling green eyes. Was he going to change his mind about leaving and ask her to marry him?

"You've had a real tough go of it, Ella, what with your grandma dying and being all alone in the world after that. No wonder you took up drinking and stalking your neighbors."

"Wait, what?" asked Ella. She pushed Joshua away and sat down hard on the steps. "How do you know that? And I didn't stalk my neighbors. I watched them. It was a long time ago."

"Yeah, well, it's over, and that's a good thing. I'm proud of you for taking control of your life and turning it around. And what Owen and Irma did to you was in no way your fault. If I could get my hands on that bastard...."

Ella stretched out her legs, watching the stars start to fade into view and feeling the cool breeze coming over the lake caress her bare legs. She couldn't remember telling Joshua any of this. She looked over at him. How could she not remember revealing all her secrets?

"I believe you that you didn't jump into the lake with Anneli on purpose. You fell. It was an accident. You have to know that before I go home. That's not why I'm leaving. I don't blame you for Anneli's death. I believe you."

"I didn't kill Anneli, Joshua."

Panic rose in her belly. She threw off her dress and jumped into the water, swimming hard out into the dark water, trying to wash off the panic and ugliness of her past, to out swim the residue of fear and shame. Her lungs burning, she broke the surface of the water. Ella turned back toward shore. Joshua wasn't there.

"Ella!"

He was beside her.

"You scared the hell out of me, Ella. Don't do that again. This water is near pitch black. How could I find you if you went under?"

Ella looked down. He was right. The last rays of sun had faded from the sky and the water was no longer cast in pinks and purple. It was dark. It was ink black and cold. She began to shake. It was so cold. She gave a startled cry and began clawing at the water, splashing and churning it around her. Joshua was immediately by her side, an arm around her chest, dragging her to shore. That's when the night of the accident flooded back into her awareness.

Chapter 26

JUST UNTIL ANNELI IS SOUND ASLEEP, she reassured herself, and then I'll head back. Ella reached the end of the peninsula and turned the stroller around. The pathway was deserted as far as her eyes could see through the swirling fog and falling snow.

She was safe.

Her shoulders relaxed, and her breathing smoothed its ragged edges. The baby was sleeping soundly. It was time to go home for a hot chocolate, with whipped cream and chocolate sprinkles. Ella could already feel the heat of the cup in her hands and taste the sweet creamy drink. She pulled the visor down lower, protecting the sleeping baby from the falling snow, and looked up again.

She screamed in surprise as a dark shape jumped off a sailboat anchored beside her and ran up the slope toward her. She took a step backward, instantly realizing that there were only the waves splashing against the stone pier behind her. She was trapped.

Ella started to run forward, before coming to a screeching halt a few yards away. She had left the sleeping baby in the stroller behind her, alone on the path. Guilt crushed down on her shoulders, a giant machete splintering her sense of self with its bloodied blade. How could she leave the baby? What was wrong with her? She turned, expecting the dark figure to be right behind her. He wasn't. He was running toward the stroller. Ella's heart leapt into her throat.

My baby! Aya, Adnan, Mr. V… oh God no. If anything happened to Anneli…

Ella gave a leap, crashing into the dark-clothed man as his gloved hand reached into the stroller. They crashed together to the snow, Ella partially falling onto the man. The fall had knocked the hat from his head. Ella knew the wavy blond hair, the intense blue of his eyes. Owen was already struggling to jump up. She beat him to his feet, dancing just out of his reach and grabbing the stroller handle. She began to run forward, knowing with a sickening jolt that she couldn't outrun him with the stroller. She stopped, turning.

"Leave us alone," she screamed, slipping on a patch of ice as Owen nearly collided into her.

"Calm down, Ella. I'm here to help you. You don't have to give her up. You don't have to struggle alone anymore. I'm here now. I'll take care of you. I'll take care of you both."

Owen grabbed the handle of the stroller around Ella, trapping her in his arms.

He brought his face within inches of hers. She could smell the mint on his breath as she struggled to free herself from his grasp, but her arms were pinned to her sides. The snowflakes were catching on his dark eyelashes. He smiled, his dimples showing, although his eyes remained cold and steadfast.

"Listen," he said, while bringing a gloved hand up to Ella's cheek. "I love you. We can be a family. Wouldn't you like that? To be surrounded by warmth and affection? To be protected?"

Owen's lips brushed against hers, warm and searching. Her stomach turned over. The scene in the opera house flung itself before her closed eyes. She pulled her head back, nausea rolling in her belly.

"Get away from us, Owen. Let me go."

"I love this baby, Ella: our baby. I want her more than anything in life. She's my daughter, and I'm taking her home. She deserves a father. She deserves a family."

Ella remembered all the nights she had walked into the castle, the cold still clinging to her clothes. Stress, fatigue and hunger were usually aching through her body as she unwound her scarf at the door.

But then she would hear Mr. V's deep gravelly voice cooing to Anneli in the corner as he bounced her gently on his knee. Aya's lips were soft on her cheek, welcoming her home and placing a hot tea in her cold hands. As she sat down next to Mr. V, Aya and Mrs. Frieden, Adnan would appear, setting down a plate of dinner for her, patting her on the shoulder, telling her she should eat more before planting a kiss on the top of Anneli's head. She had a family. Anneli had a family.

"Anneli has a family."

"Ella," cautioned Owen, his face grimacing as he took her chin in his fingers and brought her face within inches of his own. "You are a terrible mother."

Ella flinched as if hit. It was true. How did he know?

"What the hell, Ella? I have never seen you hold our child. Not once. I've been watching. I know Aya and Adnan watch her all day and take her home with them at night. It's time for Anneli to come home with her Daddy. It's time for her to be properly taken care of instead of hoisted around all day in a front pack by working immigrants or held by that insane old man."

"No," said Ella, bringing her head back and then throwing it forward as hard as she could against Owen's nose. This wasn't about her anymore. A primal scream rose out of her, and a power she'd never known before shot through her muscles. She had to protect Anneli.

Blood gushed through Owen's nose and he bent forward, winded. Ella turned to grab the baby and run.

The stroller was gone.

Oh my God! The baby, where was the baby?

Adrenaline rocketed through her veins as she searched the path behind her for the baby buggy. Ella ran down the slope to the very edge of the pier, looking into the inky water. Had the stroller rolled into the lake? Was the baby even now drowning in that icy water?

That's when she heard it. The wail of a baby. She turned her head and saw a dark-haired woman step out from behind the shadow of a tree. She gave the stroller a push and sent it careening down the slope. It was rolling straight toward the water. How long could a baby survive in icy water?

Ella jumped up and raced after it, reaching out. Her fingers grasped the handle. But the stroller had gained too much momentum. Her feet fought for purchase on the icy concrete, the stroller teetering on the edge, pulling her forward. Her feet slipped out from under her, and a fraction of a second later, she fell into the water with the stroller with a splash.

She swam sideways, out from under the weight of the stroller and struggled to the surface. Her boots and clothes sucked to her skin, a dead weight pulling her down. She kicked her boots free, struggled out of her coat, churning the icy water around her. She fought her primal instinct to save herself, to swim immediately back to the pier, and dove down, searching for the stroller. She broke the surface of the water once again, spluttering. Anneli!

She dove under into the darkness. The stroller was gone. She floated onto her back, trying to conserve some energy, pulling air into her heaving lungs. The drumbeat crashing in her skull throbbed as she looked up and saw the fog had lifted, the clouds shifted.

A star-studded sky was starting to appear. Her body was already beginning to shake uncontrollably. Ella took a deep breath, mentally preparing herself to swim to the nearest sailboat moored in the harbor.

That's when she heard him.

"What the hell did you do? I told you to wait in the castle restaurant. Why do you insist on being so stupid?"

"Yeah well, you've botched up taking back the baby enough times already. If I hadn't shown up, she would have gotten away and alerted the police. Then you would have never gotten your baby back."

"I don't see her in the water. Are you freaking out of your mind? Her death will attract all sorts of attention. It wasn't the plan. They'll come looking for Anneli even faster now."

"It doesn't matter love. We're taking the plane to Singapore, tonight. And you can't possibly plan on calling her Anneli."

"How about Ella after her dead mother, then?"

A wave of pain seared through her head, and Ella slipped beneath the surface. She fought frantically upward, sucking the freezing night air into her heaving lungs. Ella couldn't make sense of what Owen was saying.

Lies. Abuse. Love. Honesty.

She began kicking her way toward a sailboat. The ladder was up. She looked at the next sailboat, but its ladder was out of reach too. There! A wrought-iron ladder built into the concrete wall of the pier. She just needed to climb up. She began kicking furiously toward the rungs.

She placed her face in the water to swim freestyle, but it was like putting her face in a bowl of ice cubes and she came up spluttering.

As she swam forward, she could see Owen arguing on the pathway. She couldn't hear him over the splashing of her swimming, nor see any signs of the baby stroller. She reached the ladder, pulling herself out of the water.

That's when she heard the cry of a baby. Anneli! Ella's heart leaped, tears coming to her eyes, blurring her vision. She hadn't been in the stroller. She was alive. Ella stifled a sob while relief flooded through her heart.

"Wait, what was that? Did you hear something? Damn, this baby's screaming. Let's give her a sleeping pill already to shut her up and get out of here before someone sees us."

"Irma, what the hell? You can't give a baby sleeping pills."

"To hell I can't. How else do you think we will get it out of here and all the way to Singapore without attracting the attention of the authorities?"

"Just give me my baby, Irma."

Ella pulled herself up to the last rung and peered over the rim of the harbor. Owen and Irma were standing just a few feet away in the shadows of a tree. She watched as Irma handed Anneli to Owen, who immediately opened his jacket, revealing a front pack, which he slid the crying baby into. He zipped his jacket up over the baby, rocking her back and forth as he pulled out a pacifier and slipped it into her mouth.

"Damn it, Irma, she is freezing. What the hell are you doing, carrying her around in the night air like that? She'll get sick."

"You selfish, egoistical bastard," said Irma, pushing Owen hard with both hands. "Don't you start with me. I had to take her out of the stroller before pushing it into the lake. I'm the intelligent one in this relationship, and don't you forget it. Now everyone will think the baby drowned. It will buy us time to get away undetected. We wouldn't even be in any of this mess if you hadn't insisted on your own biological baby. We could adopt instead."

"What? You were the one who refused adoption. You were the one who insisted we needed my own biological baby. This game was your idea. We could have even found a surrogate! Fuck Irma, this is all so convoluted and messed up! The cameras in Ella's flat, the slow seduction. All of it. I've done everything you wanted so we could have our own baby. But now you're going to hold it over my head for the rest of my life, aren't you? Now I can't even come home to Switzerland someday. You've killed Ella! What the fuck? You're a monster. Get away from me!"

Owen turned and began walking away, his shoes crunching on the snow and ice.

Ella's hands were becoming too cold to retain her grip on the rung. She had to pull herself up onto the path. Could she do it without attracting notice? She didn't want them to leave with Anneli, but if they didn't walk away, she wasn't sure she could hold herself to the ladder any longer.

"Owen, stop! Don't tell me you didn't enjoy our game as much as I did. And the baby was as much your idea as mine."

Ella willed Owen to keep walking. She had lost all feeling in her fingers. If she didn't climb up now, she wouldn't be able to. Ella's hands were slipping from the ladder rung. She slowly placed a hand on the snowy concrete walkway. She pushed herself up as a foot slipped off the railing. She inched herself forward on her elbows. She watched as Irma ran after Owen, grabbing his hand and bringing it to her heart, tears streaming down her face.

"After all I've done for you, after all we've been through, how could you say those things to Ella? I'll go to the police. Who will they believe?"

"Stop, Irma, stop!" said Owen, while grabbing his wife by the shoulders and giving her a rough shake. "Of course I was lying. It was still just part of the game. She's our plaything. I love you. I have my baby now, our baby, that's all I ever wanted from Ella. But I didn't want to kill her! How can I live with you now? You're a fucking murderer."

"Owen, calm down. We are both just out of our minds with stress and terror from what just happened. It was a mistake. A horrifying accident took place. We didn't want any harm to come to Ella. But they won't believe that, don't you see? We have to go before they notice Ella and the baby are missing, or someone sees us out here!"

Ella continued to inch forward, praying Owen and Irma wouldn't notice her below them.

She lay perfectly still, willing them to start walking away from her. She could feel her clothes stiffening as they froze in the frigid night air.

"Come now, Owen. We've been together for sixteen years. We have our baby. It's all over now, sweetheart. I'll get you a great new research job in Singapore. I'll have my new promotion as Director of Research. We'll be happy now. No more stalking games. Just us. Now let's go." She placed an arm around Owen, and they began walking away.

Ella brought her knees to her chest, sitting up on her heels. She pushed her hands into the snow in an effort to struggle onto her wobbling legs. There was no more time to waste. She had to get Anneli away from them, or run for help. She placed one foot quietly in front of the next. She didn't see the black ice until she was falling sideways onto her hip.

Owen stopped walking. He turned, searching for the source of the noise. As soon as he spotted her, he began running.

Adrenaline flooded Ella's system, but she was moving through Jell-O and her every motion was delayed. Ella cringed as Owen reached out, taking her under the elbows and lifting her to her feet.

"Ella my angel, you're alive. Oh thank God." Owen began to cry. "I thought you were dead." He took a deep shuddering breath. "Let's get you back to the castle quickly. You'll freeze." He placed an arm around Ella, supporting her as they began to walk toward the castle. She fought against him, but his grip was too strong.

"Calm down dear. You poor thing, you must be freezing. We'll get you straight up to the castle and take care of you.

Everything is going to be beautiful for you and Anneli. I'll make sure of it."

All at once, dazed from her struggling, Ella began shaking uncontrollably, her last strength evaporating into the frigid night air. She slumped against Owen, moving forward as if in a dream, her eyelashes frozen wings in the biting cold, her clothes hardening to icy burdens. She could no longer think straight.

"Owen," roared a voice behind them. "Get out of the way." Owen turned as Irma stepped forward under the pool of light from a lamppost. Irma hurtled herself toward Ella as Owen sidestepped off the path and beside a tree. Irma punched Ella in the face. Ella brought her hands to her bleeding nose, doubled over.

Irma stepped forward and pushed as hard as she could. Ella fell backward, her head cracking into something, a pain piercing into her skull.

The water rushed up to grab her, pulling her under, holding her captive beneath its fluid weight. Her lungs heaved.

Kicking widely, she fought to reach air. Just as tiny stars broke out in front of her eyes, she broke the surface. She tasted blood in her mouth. All her strength was gone. Panic welled within her as her body grew heavy and cumbersome with fatigue and cold within seconds.

Just then, she saw a buoy hanging down from the sailboat next to her. With her last ounce of strength, she grabbed for it, holding on with her whole body weight. The rope loosened and tore free. Kicking frantically, she pulled her head and body up out of the water, resting her face on the smooth surface of the red and white ring. Everything went black.

CHAPTER 27

"ELLA, STOP STRUGGLING! Let me pull you in," yelled Joshua while attempting to grab hold of Ella without being pulled under the water himself.

She laid her head back and lay still, taking huge gasps of air. At last she was being pulled up onto the stone steps. She lay still as Joshua pulled both towels around her and rubbed her hands and feet to warm her up. The winter night was still before her eyes. The crying of Anneli reverberated inside her skull.

"What happened out there Ella? Did you get a cramp?"

"Anneli is in Singapore."

"Say what?"

"Anneli is in Singapore. I remember that night, Josh. We have to notify the police. We need to tell Aya, Adnan, Mr. V, Mrs. Frieden. Hurry, Josh," she said, while jumping to her feet and beginning to run back to the castle in her swimsuit.

Adrenaline rushed through her system and lent flight to her bare feet.

She heard Joshua swearing behind her, trying to pull on his trousers and cowboy boots. She ran into the castle and into the kitchen, her hair dripping down her back and onto the spotless clean floor.

"Anneli is in Singapore."

Adnan stood stock still at the counter, his knife held aloft over a mango. After a moment, he slowly turned to face Ella. "What?"

"Anneli is in Singapore. I remember now. I remember the night of the accident."

Aya walked into the kitchen. "What is going on here? Ella, why are you in a swimsuit? Have you completely lost your mind?"

Joshua came lumbering into the kitchen, shirtless and holding the bag and dripping wet towels under his arm. "Damn it, Ella, what the hell is going on?"

Mr. V crashed through the door to the kitchen, followed by Mrs. Frieden. "What happened?"

Suddenly Aya was talking to Adnan, Mrs. Frieden was commiserating with Joshua and calling him a hero and Mr. V was shouting out into the room in general.

"Everyone quiet," yelled Ella.

Everyone stopped and stared. Ella began to shake again and Mr. V reached out and put his jacket around her shoulders.

"Listen to me, I remember the night of the accident. Anneli is in Singapore. Owen and Irma kidnapped her to Singapore. We have to get her back. Now. Tonight."

Everyone continued to stare at her. Adnan's mouth had fallen open.

"I knowing he is a bad man," declared Adnan.

"Beware of the goat from its front side, of the horse - from its back side, and the evil man - from any side," agreed Mr. V. "This is my fault. I should have gotten rid of him a long time ago."

"But what happened?" asked Aya impatiently.

"First," insisted Mrs. Frieden. "Ella is going upstairs and taking a hot shower and getting dressed. You have guests to serve. When the service is done, we will all sit down and listen to what happened with a lovely cup of hot tea."

"You drink hot tea, woman, I need a whiskey," declared Mr. V.

"That makes two of us," agreed Joshua.

JOSHUA TOOK ELLA'S HAND as they stepped out of the train at the Zürich airport. They ascended the escalator in silence. Ella tried to let go of his hand as they walked toward the airport security check. He held on tighter.

"I don't want to leave you," he said, while pulling her into a bear hug and resting his cheek against hers.

"Then why are you?"

"You know the Swiss only let an American stay three months before they have to leave the country unless they have a working permit."

He pulled her to him and she smelled the fresh scent of his clean white t-shirt and spicy notes of his aftershave. She put her head on his chest and listened to the rhythmic beat of his heart. Silent tears slipped down her cheeks. Joshua pulled back just enough to see her tear-stained face.

"I hate seeing you like this. It breaks my heart. I have no idea how, but I'll get your daughter back."

"You will?" She looked up at him, her heart fluttering in her chest. "How?"

"Well I don't rightly know how, but I'll think of something. We'll go to Singapore together and find Anneli."

Ella rested her head once again against Joshua's chest, drinking in the feeling of his strong arms around her, the feel of fingers running up and down the muscles of his back through his worn t-shirt. No, she decided. She couldn't have this good man risk potential imprisonment in an international kidnapping attempt.

Ella had immediately notified the police once her memory returned, but international parental kidnapping was a long and difficult crime to resolve.

They had found out that Singapore was not a party to The Hague Convention on the Civil Aspects of International Child Abduction. The Swiss authorities said they could do little but attempt negotiation, which could take a very long time.

Adnan had also offered to fly to Singapore and hunt Owen and Irma down himself, but Mrs. Frieden warned that if he did that, he could end up in a Singapore jail. Custody orders and judgments of foreign courts, like Switzerland's, were not enforceable in Singapore.

Yet Ella couldn't accept a future in which they just resigned to perpetual grief at the loss of Anneli. How would they all overcome such a loss, such an injustice? The worry over Anneli's well-being was insufferable. Her only consolation was the knowledge that Adnan, Aya, Mrs. Frieden, Mr. V and even Joshua shared her sorrow and outrage.

"No," she took a deep breath and stepped back, squaring her shoulders. "It has to be me. I'm her mother. The courts might understand a mother stealing her own child back, if I'm caught. They will charge anyone else for attempted kidnapping. I'll bring her back on my own."

"Ella," began Joshua, taking her hand and bending down on one knee. "I fell in love with you the first time I looked into your eyes. I realized right then and there that you were the woman I'm met to share my life with. It scared me stupid, I'll admit. I knew this wouldn't be some fairytale happy ever after story, or that you will make me happy the rest of my life, in some marital bliss bull they sell in movies and such."

"Wait what?" asked Ella, taking a small step back. "You don't think marrying me will make you happy?"

"Yes, I mean no. Ah shit, I'm messing this up," he muttered, shaking his head and looking down at his boot. "I mean you're my soul mate, Ella. We're meant to be a testament to each other's lives, to push each other to grow and become stronger and better people. I know I am the one to push you and support you as you grow. So that when we take our last few breaths we can say, well we sure did give it all we got."

"Who says I'm not giving it all I have now? Or that I need some man to push me? I push myself harder every day I show up to dance then you will ever understand. I pulled myself together after the death of my mother and grandmother. I found a job waitressing. I eventually made it into the junior ballet after countless failed auditions."

"Well, there sure was quite a bit of drinking, isolation and depression somewhere in the middle of that story," said Joshua, standing up.

Ella gasped, crossing her arms and looking around to see if anyone had heard.

"I don't want that to happen again, Ella. I want to be your source of strength, your step so you have a bit of help getting back up in the saddle when you fall off the horse. Move to

Idaho with me, Ella. You would love it there. I'll save up. In a few years I will have enough to pay a down payment and mortgage on our own ranch."

"So you take all the times I confided in you about my worst vulnerabilities and mistakes and throw them in my face? As part of a marriage proposal? What the hell Joshua?"

"I'm sorry Ella, I..."

"Do you know how hard I had to work, am still working, to be a part of the ballet in Zürich? Why would I give that up to be some uneducated ranch hand's wife in the middle of nowhere?"

"I'll take that as a no then." Joshua put the ring back in his pocket and picked up his bag.

Ella covered her face with her hands. Why had she been so cruel? She looked up to see Joshua turning to walk through the security doors. She ran after him, grabbing his back jeans pocket and pulling. She couldn't have it end, at least not like this. The regret would tear into her, a constant drip of recrimination.

"Joshua wait, please."

He turned, and she grabbed his hand, pulling him out of the line. She slid her arms around his waist and hugged him. He stood stock still, not moving a muscle. Ella took a step back.

"I'm in love with you, Joshua. But it sounds like you want to push me to grow into whatever projection you have in your mind of what a dream ranch wife should be, and I'm not interested in living like that. I want a marriage at eye level and to come home to an oasis of calm and acceptance. I don't want a man trying to control me, to fit into his dream. I have dreams of my own."

"It isn't like that, Ella," answered Joshua. "You already are my dream woman. I don't need to change one thing. I meant I would only support you in growing how you want to so all your dreams can come true. I want you to do that for me too."

Ella shook her head, "If that were true, you wouldn't ask me to move to the middle of nowhere in Idaho. The Zürich ballet is here. My family is here."

Joshua sighed, brought his hand to cover his eyes. A moment

later, he cleared his throat and lowered his hand. "If you ever change your mind, I would walk on air."

She offered a weak smile and shook her head. "I'm not giving up my ballet career. You could move here."

"Stay here?" he laughed, but then his face grew grim. "What would I do here? A man needs a job, Ella. I need wide-open spaces and the sun and rain on my face while I work. I don't see any cowboys in these parts. I feel like a fish out of water. Not to mention I don't understand the language."

She shrugged her shoulders and looked down at her red shoes. "I love you, Joshua. Sometimes that's not enough." There was nothing else to say. His arms were around her, and he buried his face in her hair.

He pulled her even tighter to him.

"You ever need me, you go on and pick up that phone straight away and call, you hear? I will be here straight away. Will you write me?"

She nodded, and he kissed her while a family pushed past them with luggage and crying children. The world dissolved, and it was just the two of them, suspended in time, free of the past clutching at them and the future whisking them forward.

She pulled back and, without a word, walked away.

"You'll always have a place in my heart darlin'," he called after her, but she didn't turn her head.

Chapter 28

Ella climbed the small hill to the castle and walked onto the terrace. Mr. V was sitting with his coffee and a whiskey, staring into the distance. She walked up to him and placed a hand on his shoulder. "I'm going after my baby, Mr. V. I fly to Singapore tomorrow."

He reached up and grabbed her hand in a viselike grip. "How, Ella? Even if you do find them, how could you get Anneli home? If you attempted to take her back to Switzerland and the Singapore authorities caught you, you could end up imprisoned for kidnapping."

Ella pulled her hand away, placing both fists on her hips. "I know where she is. Narcissism can be the downfall of the evil. Irma is on every social media platform available and posts her every twitch. She received a promotion in Singapore. I already knew the company she worked for. It wasn't difficult to find out where she lives with some hours of Internet research."

"You're not going. Those two monsters are too dangerous. I already lost your mother, grandmother and my great-granddaughter. I couldn't bear to lose you too."

Ella sat down and grabbed Mr. V's glass. She threw back the whiskey, the alcohol burning on its way down.

She wanted another.

"What is she going to do, Mr. V? Try to drown me in a

lake again? My eyes are wider, my innocence drowned. I'm stronger for it. This time I know who I am facing. I'm going, and I want you to come with me."

"Why would you want an old man to come with you?"

Ella sat down in the chair opposite Mr. V and looked him in the eye. "Because, old man, you are a part of the Russian mafia organization."

"Preposterous. And give me that glass. You told me you don't drink."

"Don't lie to your granddaughter anymore, dedushka. I know the truth. My mother was running from the Russia mafia. It wasn't paranoia, it was the truth. She was running from you. She didn't want to have anything to do with you. That is why Grandma never touched the money in those bank accounts, isn't it? My mother wouldn't let her, because that dirty money came from you. Well she may have feared you, but I don't. You're going to help me."

Mr. V sighed. "For the first time in my life, I actually wish I were in the mafia. No, my little sun, I was a professor of business at Lomonosov Moscow State University. I am still a guest lecturer and I am working on my fifth book. You've watched me read and take notes by the hour, seen me typing on my laptop, first at Flavor and now here in Romanshorn.

"Your mother insisted that we were in fear of our lives, that someone was coming to kill us at any moment because of things I had done. It wasn't true, Ella. She told me we would never be safe as long as I was a part of the organization. I tried repeatedly to convince her of the truth, to no avail. The money in your accounts isn't mafia money. It comes from selling off part of the shares my grandfather purchased in the Lukoil company."

"So you've never killed a man?"

Mr. V ran a hand over his face. "No."

Ella rested her face in her hands and then stood up and went inside, where she poured herself a glass of vodka. A retired professor was going to be of minimal help in getting her Anneli back.

"Ella," said Mr. V, grabbing the glass out of Ella's hand. "Do you really want to drink that? Is that what you want? You told me you don't drink anymore."

Ella glared at him, then shook her head, tears blurring her vision as she handed him her glass. "I can't bear it anymore. I have to get her back. I never thought I would feel like this. I didn't realize how much I loved her. There was too much shock, shame and fear, like a thick fog keeping me from feeling the warmth of my love for my baby."

Mr. V patted her shoulder and then took her hands in his own. "The beautiful thing is you feel that love now. No one can take that knowledge away from you. Listen, I may not be in the mafia, but I can help you. I want to go with you. Anneli is my baby too."

"Then it's time to make a plan, Mr. V."

Chapter 29

Ella followed Mr. V through Changi Airport, past an orchid garden and a pond with brightly colored orange fish. Mr. V headed for a pay-phone and lifted the receiver. Ella stepped up next to him and held her breath. She hoped this worked.

"Am I speaking to Irma Meier? This is Mr. Tay from blue deep scuba diving. Wait, no, I'm not selling anything. Don't hang up. You are one of the lucky winners of the inspirational women in science award. You were nominated anonymously by multiple people at your workplace. I am so pleased to welcome you on our two-night scuba dive getaway," said Mr. V. "Your winning package is a scuba diving trip to Pulau Tioman in Malaysia this upcoming weekend. You are invited to bring one guest. Excuse me?"

Mr. V paused, listening.

"No, it is for this weekend only. Your dive trip includes two-way transport from Singapore, two nights of accommodation at our four-star resort, full board meals at our resort, up to six boat dives, full equipment rental and dive guide services. If you have never gone diving before, you can attend the dive preparation classes in our hotel pool. Can you attend?"

Ella held her breath, awaiting a response.

"Wonderful," replied Mr. V. "Then just come to our office this Friday and we will send you on an unforgettable holiday."

Mr. V hung up the phone and turned to Ella.

"Thank God. The first step is complete."

ELLA AT LAST STEPPED through the front doors and took a deep breath of Singapore's humid air. Mr. V came out behind her, shielding his eyes from the bright morning sunlight. Ella hailed a taxi, and they settled into the backseat. She hadn't slept the entire flight.

Ella only had a few days before she needed to return to perform in a ballet that weekend. She was chancing her career just by pretending severe illness. It would be all too easy for someone to find out her lie. Ella grimaced and turned her attention to at the inspired architecture of the Singapore skyline, thinking.

When she went swimming in the lake with Joshua, she had regained more than her memory of her terror-filled night when Anneli had been kidnapped. Standing in front of the people she loved that night and recounting her struggle with Owen and Irma, Ella had a startling revelation. She had a victim mentality.

Being pulled from one town to the next by a paranoid mother her entire childhood had made her feel that others were responsible for her circumstances. Her entire life, she had surrendered her power to others.

The control and responsibility always lay outside herself. Losing Anneli had made her wake up. A new fire burned within Ella. She wouldn't be manipulated anymore.

Mr. V reached out and patted her shoulder. She dropped her hands to her lap, giving him a small smile. All that was in the past, there was no use wallowing in shame. She no longer saw herself as a victim, which meant she had to deal with the feelings of guilt over what she had done and forgive herself someday. Now that her victim mentality had passed, she also understood that she had the ability to change her circumstances. Whatever life threw at her, she could act to improve her situation, if only it was by changing her attitude.

The love for her daughter was changing her from the inside out. There was an inner resolve, a strengthening. She was reclaiming her power. It was time to put her resolve to the test. As the taxi pulled up outside the Chinatown complex food centre, she took a deep breath and tugged at her red wig. She put on her oversized sunglasses and turned to Mr. V.

"I'll see you back at the hotel, Mr. V."

"I'm coming with you. I don't like this."

"No, you're not. We're sticking to the plan. Just wait for me as discussed. Here, take this," she insisted, holding out a smart phone.

Mr. V took the phone and held it out in front of him at arm's distance, peering at the screen with suspicion. "I thought you didn't own one of these."

"Like I said in the plane, we need to be able to contact each other at all times. We don't know how the plan is going to play out."

Mr. V grunted, frowning up at her from under his reading glasses. "Like I said. Be careful."

Ella stepped out of the taxi and looked up at the building's façade. Now she would wait. Fortunately for Ella, Irma's need for attention was insatiable. She had already created her own You Tube channel about her life as a Swiss expat in Singapore. Ella pulled out her phone and re-watched the video, which had already attracted thousands of views.

Irma talked about what life in Singapore for an expat was like, her superior work ethic at her important job and how she allowed herself the treat of going out to eat each lunch at a hawker center, whose food stalls had some of the most delicious food in the world. Ella cringed when Irma talked about how her adoring and devoted husband met her for lunch and brought their beautiful baby daughter so they could enjoy some quality time together. At this point, the video faded out and in on a smiling Owen holding Anneli.

Ella had checked Irma's other social media sites repeatedly in the airport. Today Irma had plans to meet Owen and Anneli to check out the only hawker food stand to achieve a Michelin star. Ella wandered up to level two of the food centre and found the Hong Kong Soya Sauce Chicken Rice and Noodle stand. Her stomach growled. She looked around and decided to wait in the long line for a plate of food.

After forty minutes, Ella was beginning to wonder if she

would ever get to the front of the line and if Irma and Owen were ever going to show up. At last she reached the front of the line, paid for her chicken and noodles and sat down at a table with her food. Ella discreetly scanned the line of people waiting for food at the stand while she took a bite of the succulent caramelized chicken and spice-infused noodles. It was then that she spotted Irma in the line.

Irma was telling a joke and watched as her colleagues laughed in response.

Ella's heart squeezed in her chest. Maybe he wouldn't come with her. Maybe Irma posted lies on her social media, and Owen never met her for lunch. Ella continued to eat her food, trying not to stare at the vile woman who had tried to kill her. From here, she looked like a curvy, beautiful, charming woman with adoring work friends. Amazing how deceptive appearances could be.

Ella was about to leave when she heard his voice. Owen was kissing Irma hello and Anneli was in his arms, crying. Ella fought the instinct to run across the space and snatch her baby away. She took a deep breath, shaking her arms. She needed to wait. She watched Owen greet the three men and one woman standing in line with Irma.

After getting their food, the group eventually settled at a table a stone's throw away, and Owen struggled to eat his meal while holding Anneli and spooning food into her mouth. After twenty minutes, Anneli began to cry. Irma glared at Owen, and he immediately stood up to walk around with the baby. Irma continued eating and conversing with the four colleagues at her table. After ten minutes, Anneli was still crying hysterically. Ella's heart clutched in her chest. Every fiber of her being wanted to take the baby and soothe her.

Ella thought of the months she had missed when Anneli was an infant because she was battling with shame, depression and fear. Fear, always the fear that she had nothing to offer her baby, indeed that she could act as an impediment to her baby's development and happiness. She didn't feel that way anymore. She didn't think she could be a perfect mother, but Ella knew she could enable this child to feel unconditionally loved and cherished for the rest of her life. And she realized she no longer saw carrying for Anneli as a burden she need carry alone.

She had a net of friends to turn to for help and support. Tears stung her eyes and her body, rigid with anticipation and nervousness, relaxed.

Ella watched Irma continue to chat and laugh with her colleagues as Owen paced around the complex. Owen gave Irma a kiss on the cheek and grabbed the diaper bag as Anneli continued crying in his arms. Irma didn't even look up. She waved sideways at him and took a sip of her drink.

Owen headed toward the exit. Ella forced herself to count to twenty before she stood up and threw away her plate. She followed Owen out onto the busy street. Owen walked up to a young Asian woman who was waiting at the bus stop with an empty stroller. Owen held out the crying Anneli, and the woman scooped her up in her arms, cooing and kissing her.

Anneli immediately stopped crying. Ella breathed a sigh of relief as Owen turned and walked in the opposite direction.

A bus pulled up, and Ella sprinted forward to jump in after Anneli. A few minutes later, the maid maneuvered the stroller out of the bus, and Ella followed. At the entrance to Alanet Residences, the girl entered the lobby, and Ella followed directly on her heels through the door. The young woman looked back at her suspiciously.

"Hi," said Ella cheerfully, holding up her keys. "I'm new in the building. I moved here with my husband last month. I'm Anna." Ella held out her hand.

The small young woman paused, looking down at Ella's outstretched hand.

At last she shook it gently, adding, "I'm Nan Thiri."

"Pleasure to meet you, Nan Thiri. Would you like to join me for a cup of coffee?"

The young woman didn't hesitate for a second. "No, I can't."

"Oh, too bad. Listen, I hate to push, but do you think you could come for just fifteen minutes? I'm really lonely. My husband says everyone in Singapore works at least ten-hour days. I hardly see him and I haven't made any friends yet."

Nan Thiri stood silent in front of her. Ella began to panic. This wasn't going to work. She would tell Owen or Irma about meeting a strange woman in the lobby. They would get suspicious. They'd keep Anneli under lock and key. It would be impossible to ever get Anneli away from them.

"Listen, it's fine, I'll just go walk along the sky bridge and lay by the pool a bit," she said, turning to go up the stairs.

"I'll come with you," spoke up a voice from behind her.

Ella grinned. "Great."

Nan Thiri pushed the button for the elevator, looking down at her feet for a moment.

"You have a beautiful baby," said Ella.

"She's not my baby. I'm the maid," replied Nan Thiri.

"So did you grow up here?" asked Ella, hoping to ease the young woman into a comfortable conversation with her.

"No, I'm from Myanmar," she answered.

"So you know how I feel," exclaimed Ella. "I miss my family and friends from home so much." Ella waited for Nan Thiri to answer. An awkward silence fell over them as the elevator doors opened, and they walked out onto the sky bridge connecting the two resident buildings three stories up.

"I'm sorry, I was projecting. I'm sure you love your job, your new friends and this city. 'Singapore is a clean, safe city with inspired architecture, delicious food, beautiful gardens and a thriving multi-ethnic culture.' Those are the reasons by husband keeps saying he loves living here, anyway." She sighed. "But I hate it here."

Nan Thiri stopped in the shade of a tree. "I hate it here too. I miss my friends and family in Myanmar. And I haven't seen anything of the city because I must stay within the residence except for bringing Anneli to lunch once a day. I live for lunchtime."

"At least you can enjoy the amazing food then," offered Ella.

"No," she answered bitterly. "I am not allowed to eat with them. I have to wait at the bus stop for them to bring Anneli back to me. But at least I am out in the city."

Anneli began to fuss, and Nan Thiri handed her a toy and patted her cheek before pushing the stroller forward again. Ella paused at the fifty-meter pool and reclined on a lounge chair. Nan Thiri hesitated and then did the same.

Ella extracted some Swiss crackers and a Swiss chocolate

bar she had thrown into her purse for the plane ride. "Would you like to try some?" she asked. "I brought these here with me from Switzerland."

Nan Thiri nodded, and Ella handed her both packages. She watched as Nan Thiri stuffed down the snacks.

"You look really hungry. I should let you go home so you can eat some lunch. Thanks for chatting with me."

"No food in the flat," answered Nan Thiri between bites. "Just a bit of white rice, baby food and baby formula."

"Great, I needed to go shopping too. I have nothing in the house but cereal. We can go together."

"I don't have any money," replied Nan Thiri. "My boss does all the shopping."

Ella sat still, considering. She didn't want to leave Anneli. There was a chance Nan Thiri could disappear while she was gone, and she would have to wait until tomorrow for a new opportunity. On the other hand, this was her chance to slip the drug in the woman's drink.

"Listen, I'm going to run down the street and bring you back something to eat. Wait here for me?"

Without waiting for a response, Ella leapt up and headed for the elevator. She ran down the street and purchased a meal of chicken and noodles and a drink from a street vendor and hurried back to the residence. In the elevator, her heart was beating so quickly she was short of breath. Would Nan Thiri still be by the pool?

Ella's shoulders relaxed when she spotted tiny Nan Thiri walking along the deserted pool holding Anneli. Ella smiled, holding up the bag of food and two cold sodas. She crossed to the lounge chairs next to the stroller and set down the food and a soda.

The other she took a long drink of before lounging back in the chair. Nan Thiri attempted to put Anneli in the stroller, but she began to cry each time, she tried to set her down. Ella forced herself to appear nonchalant.

"Would you like me to hold her so you can eat?"

Ella opened her arms, and Nan Thiri placed Anneli into them. Ella was overcome by buoyancy as she looked into the blue eyes of her baby girl. It was as if she had been living under the earth, to suddenly float up and into the light. It wasn't just an end to darkness. Not only could she see the light, feel it on her skin, but she could taste it, hear its echoes of timelessness, the potential for transformation. She had her baby back.

"I hate it here," said Nan Thiri, her mouth full of food. "I want to go home."

"Then why don't you go?" asked Ella, her face cuddling Anneli's soft cheek.

Nan Thiri shrugged, looking around the still-empty pool area. "Impossible to get away."

Ella tightened her grasp, fear already colliding with her relief to have her child in her arms. She wouldn't feel safe until Anneli was in her arms in her flat in Switzerland again. "Why can't you leave?"

"They still haven't paid me," she answered. "Everything I've made in the past few months has gone directly to pay the company who brought me here. I haven't had a day off yet. I can't even afford food, so there is no way I could pay a ticket home to Inle Lake."

Nan Thiri shook her head, wincing at the memories, as if they could scald her. "In the beginning, there were many good days, even weeks at a time, when she would bring me home delicious meals from the hawker market and luxury beauty products for me to try. Once a silk scarf. She gave me all her paperback novels when she was done reading them. With time, it changed. I never knew what was coming."

"That's terrible Nan Thiri. I'm so sorry. They are terrible people. They shouldn't leave you all day with no food."

"I work from morning until I go to bed in the closet," admitted Nan Thiri, lowering her voice to a whisper. "If she finds anything not perfectly clean, or if the baby is crying when she gets home, she throws things at me. She doesn't buy any food for me the next day. I've lost fifteen pounds since I moved here. Once she accidentally poured boiling water from the tea kettle on my legs." Nan Thiri pulled up her dress to reveal burn marks.

"Does he try to stop her?"

"No, he just requests her permission to come here to swim

as soon as he gets home. He never sees it. I don't think he wants to. She's warned me against talking to him. We don't have any contact, except to pass the baby back and forth."

"Why haven't you gone to the authorities?" asked Ella. "You should file a case against her for abuse."

"I just want to get away and go home and forget it ever happened. I need to save money first to send home for my little sister. She is mortally ill. Then I'll save money for a ticket and leave."

Ella paused. "She hasn't hurt the baby, has she?"

"No. She adores the baby for how it makes her look: a successful woman with a beautiful family. Owen is the one who plays with Anneli."

Nan Thiri picked up the soda, and Ella knocked it from her hands. She couldn't drug this girl, knowing what Irma would do to her once she found Anneli gone. Ella shuddered.

"Listen to me, Nan Thiri. I will pay for your ticket home and six months' worth of salary if you come with me right now," said Ella, while shifting Anneli onto her hip and pulling an envelope out of her purse.

She showed Nan Thiri the money inside.

"Why would you do this?"

"Because this is my baby, and I came to get her back. I want you to help me."

"What do you mean?" asked Nan Thiri in disbelief.

"They kidnapped Anneli from Switzerland. She is my baby. I was just going to put some drugs into your soda and take her with me. But now I know I can't leave you here with them, knowing what Irma is capable of. I need to buy you a ticket home so you'll be safe."

Nan Thiri stared at Ella in silence. Her gaze switched from Anneli, to Ella and then back again. Ella's muscles tightened to run. Adrenaline began pumping through Ella's veins. She was poised at any moment to flee.

"She looks like you," offered Nan Thiri. "I love her, you know. Anneli. Yes, I'll come with you. She won a two-night scuba diving trip. They won't be home until Sunday. They took their luggage with them to work."

Ella forced a smile, her legs suddenly weak. Every inch of

her being itched to run from the building. She forced herself to say, "I can wait for you to pack your things."

"I can't. They have cameras videoing every inch of the flat. Even the bathroom. They watch me all day from work." Nan Thiri picked up the rest of her lunch and placed it in the bag to take with her. Ella wanted to shout at her to leave it, but then remembered how hungry the young woman was and clamped her lips together.

"Hidden cameras? Let's get out of here as fast as we can and to a safe place." Ella set Anneli down into the stroller and practically ran toward the elevator.

As they hurried toward the elevator, Nan Thiri explained, "The cameras aren't hidden. They said they have to be there so they can be sure their baby is safe at all times."

They stood waiting for the doors of the elevator to slide open. At last the elevator dinged that it had arrived on their floor. Ella recognized Irma just in time to jump behind a bush as the doors opened.

"What are you doing here, you worthless slut? I forgot to pack my swimsuit, go get it for me. You should have been home with Anneli over an hour ago. I don't pay you to lounge in the sky park. Wait, what's that?" exclaimed Irma, grabbing the plastic sack of food from Nan Thiri's hand. "Where did you get this? Did you steal from me?"

Ella crouched lower as Irma slapped Nan Thiri across the face. Irma took a step outside the elevator and threw the remains of Nan Thiri's lunch into the trash.

"If you want to eat, then you better work," said Irma as the doors of the elevator slid shut. "And if I find you stealing again, you'll be out on the street."

Ella slid to the floor and burst into tears. She had had her baby in her arms. All she had to do was drug that young woman and run. Why didn't she? Why did things always go wrong for her? Why did Irma forget her swimsuit? Why was Ella always so unlucky?

Stop it Ella. You're not a victim, she told herself, shaking her head. She had made the right decision. Drugging an innocent and abused young woman was not the way to get her daughter back, knowing what Irma could do to Nan Thiri once she discovered Anneli was missing.

Ella took the stairs to the lobby and hailed a taxi to the hotel. She just needed to be patient. Either they would take the bait and go on the scuba diving trip, or they wouldn't. Either way she would find out in a few short hours. If this plan didn't work, she would need to make a new one.

CHAPTER 30

ELLA INSPECTED MR. V'S NEW LOOK in the hotel room. He had jet-black hair, a matching black mustache, trimmed dark eyebrows and tanned skin via a bottle. Instead of his usual button-down designer shirt and slacks, he had on jean shorts, a t-shirt, a baseball cap and flip-flops. Would they recognize him? The anxiety vibrated down her nerve endings. She wanted a drink so bad that she could almost taste the alcohol on her tongue.

"So, let's review the plan one last time," insisted Ella.

"Just breathe Ella. We've gone over it enough. It will work," grumbled Mr. V.

Ella ignored him, saying, "You greet Irma and Owen and hand them their tickets. You make sure they depart with the bus and then you call me. I'll be waiting outside their apartment building. As soon as you send them on their way to Malaysia I'll buzz their flat and collect Anneli and Nan Thiri. I'll take Nan Thiri to the airport and stop to get passport photographs taken of Anneli. We'll meet you at my room in the Fullerton Bay hotel. The flight to Russia is tomorrow at seven twenty."

"Don't worry Ella," smiled Mr. V. "Everything is going to go as smooth as glass. Now we have five hours until we switch from the Marina Bay Sands to the Fullerton Bay hotel. Why don't you go for a swim? Maybe it will calm your nerves."

Ella nodded and returned to her room. If she didn't swim, she would be tempted to have a drink. The anticipation and anxiety were almost unbearable. She pulled on a swimsuit and ascended the elevator to the sky park. The first thing Ella noticed were people sipping expensive looking cocktails from the sky bar. Every part of her longed to relax in a lounge chair with a drink.

Swallowing hard, Ella slipped into the largest rooftop infinity pool and swam to where it looked like the water fell off the side of the fifty-seventh floor of the Marina Bay Sands hotel. Unlike the other guests, she didn't stand in the pool posing in front of the Singapore Skyline. She was the only one swimming laps, the breathtaking view forgotten as soon as she began her strong, smooth strokes across the pool.

A FEW HOURS LATER, Ella stood shifting from foot to foot in agitation. Within minutes of waiting in front of Irma and Owen's building, Mr. V called Ella with the all clear. It had felt like hours. Ella rang the intercom, and when Nan Thiri answered the speaker she said, "It's Anna, Nan Thiri. Grab Anneli and meet me on the street."

This time Ella didn't take an extra second at the building. As soon as she saw Nan Thiri, she took Anneli out of the stroller and hurried with her to a taxi waiting up the street. She was thankful that Nan Thiri followed her into the cab without asking any questions.

Anneli fell asleep in the taxi, her breathing soft and sweet against Ella's cheek. They remained silent the entire ride. When the taxi pulled up in front of the airport, Nan Thiri's eyes widened.

"You're really sending me home?"

"If that's what you want."

Nan Thiri was already opening the car door. Ella followed her into the airport, and they walked to an airline desk where Ella conversed with the representative to discover the next flight to get Nan Thiri home to Myanmar.

"So, I can book you a flight home tonight to Heho airport," said Ella. "There's a flight which leaves in a few hours. Can you find your way to Inle Lake from the airport?"

"Yes. Of course."

"Perfect. Now, will you be okay waiting for your flight? There is a free movie theater, a rooftop pool, a sunflower garden, a butterfly garden and plenty of restaurants and shopping in the airport. Wait, you don't have a purse?"

Ella moved to a chair beside security and struggled to unload the contents of her purse into her bag while holding the still-sleeping Anneli. There was no way she was going to set her baby down again until they were safe at home in Switzerland with the door locked firmly behind her. After checking twice more that the purse was empty, she carefully put in the airline ticket and the cash she had promised Nan Thiri. She zipped the turquoise Kate Spade purse closed and took a deep breath.

"Here you go, Nan Thiri. Do not lose this purse. It has a thousand Swiss francs and your plane ticket inside. You can exchange the money into Burmese kyat in the airport. I wish you every happiness and safe travels home to your family."

Ella looked up, expecting joy, excitement or at least relief. Instead Nan Thiri stood in front of her, her face buried in her hands, weeping. Ella didn't know what to do. Every inch of her was feeling the fatigue of continual anxiety, desperation and sleepless nights. She was ready to take her baby back to the hotel, eat some dinner and crawl into a decadent bubble bath with her daughter before snuggling up beneath the feather duvet together. Instead she asked, "What's wrong?"

"I'm just so relieved it's over," sobbed Nan Thiri. "Thank you."

Ella gathered the small young woman into a hug. "It could have happened to me, if I was born into a different life," she murmured.

Nan Thiri, tears still streaming down her cheeks, kissed Anneli on the cheek and whispered, "I won't forget you."

At the Fullerton Bay hotel, Ella hurried across the spotless floor to the elevators. She was too tired to gawk at the high-design chandeliers and décor of the lobby. By the time she reached the hotel room, she was sweating from carrying Anneli and her suitcase.

She placed Anneli in the middle of the bed and turned to look out of the floor-to-ceiling windows looking out on the floor to ceiling windows at the bay. After a bath with Anneli, she would order some room service and wait for Mr. V. Then there was a week of hiding out in this hotel while Mr. V returned to Russia to obtain a passport for Anneli. Ella sighed.

She wouldn't feel safe until they arrived back on Swiss soil. Even then, she couldn't eliminate the possibility of Irma and Owen trying to steal Anneli back again.

Chapter 31

Mr. V hoped his disguise was good enough to fool Owen and Irma. His entire plan depended upon it. He had been waiting in front of the scuba diving office for over an hour. If Irma and Owen were to slip past him into the scuba diving business, the front desk assistant would know nothing about their award trip. His phone began vibrating. He took it out, held it out far from his face and punched at the screen.

"Mr. V? Mr. V?"

"Ella."

"I have her, Mr. V. I have Anneli. We are safe and waiting for you."

"Thank God. I'll be there as soon as I can."

He ran a hand over his face, then rubbed the back of his neck, rolling his shoulders. At last he saw Irma walking toward him, her head held high. Owen followed, carrying their bags.

"You must be Mr. and Mrs. Meier," he greeted them, forcing his voice to sound cheerful and welcoming despite the fury pounding in his heart at the sight of them.

"The other guests left hours ago for early check-in and are already at the destination. You'll meet them all at the hotel later this evening."

"I wasn't told about an early check-in option," said Irma. "Why do the other guests get early check-in?"

"Your award entitles you to exclusivity, Mrs. Meier. Instead of traveling by bus and high-speed ferry, you will be traveling to our destination via a chartered yacht. Now, if you'll just show me your tickets and identification, then I will drive you down to the launch point."

Irma waved a hand at Owen, and he fumbled forward, looking through a bag for the documents. He held them out to Mr. V. Mr. V peered at the documents, his heart continuing to pound in his ears.

"You look familiar," spoke up Owen, his face puzzled.

"I get that a lot," Mr. V improvised. "Here, I can carry those," he added, taking the bags and turning to Irma with a smile. "You must be a very smart lady, winning such an award."

Irma smiled as she climbed into the rental car. "I am passionate about finding new cures to tropical diseases. It is important work."

"Ah, so impressive. And you?" asked Mr. V, turning to Owen. "What do you do? How old are you?"

Irma waved her hand in Owen's direction. "He is creating new all natural cough drops," she said, raising her eyebrows. Irma chuckled as she climbed into the car.

As they climbed aboard the luxurious white yacht, Mr. V said, "Welcome to the Isaiah. You can enjoy your cocktail hour on the upper deck while taking in the views of the Singapore skyline as we leave the bay. If you would like to relax in the upper-deck Jacuzzi with your drinks, you can change into your suits in the master suite straight ahead."

"The Jacuzzi sounds great," answered Irma.

"We leave in about ten minutes," answered Mr. V. "I'll take your bags to your suite and meet you on the upper deck."

"What are you waiting for, Owen? Let's go change."

Mr. V ascended the stairs to the upper deck and waited for the couple. Everything was ready. He had loaded the yacht with everything he would need for this trip hours ago.

Irma and Owen climbed the stairs to the upper deck in their swimsuits. Owen immediately sprawled out on the white seat looking at the view as of the Singapore Flyer lit up against the dark sky, the skyscrapers of the central business district and the Marina Bay Sands Hotel. Irma slid into the hot water and turned on the jets of the Jacuzzi.

"Come in, Owen, this is heavenly."

"What would you like to drink? I have champagne, beer, soda, and an assortment of juices," asked Mr. V.

"We'll take a glass of champagne," said Irma.

"I'll take a beer," said Owen.

"What? You don't want a beer. All those calories. You aren't getting any younger, and I don't want to be married to a man with a beer belly. He'll have a glass of champagne. And get in here with me. The water feels delicious."

Mr. V went down to the kitchen, brought up a chilled bottle of bubbly and took out two crystal glasses. He covertly slipped in a powerful dose of sleep medication and topped the glasses with champagne while Owen climbed into the Jacuzzi next to his wife.

"So, I'll just set the bottle here in the ice bucket next to the tub so you can refill when you are ready," he said.

"Wait, what do you mean self-service? Where are the other crew members?" asked Irma. "Yachts are always staffed by more than one member, aren't they?"

"Not when there are only two guests," answered Mr. V.

Mr. V started the engine and thought of the ordeal he had had to go through in order to rent the yacht without a crew member from the yacht rental company.

He smiled in triumph as he looked out at the futuristic oval Esplanade Theatres on the Bay. His international yacht training certificate convinced the owner his yacht was in trained hands and in no danger. The couple clinked their refilled champagne glasses in the Jacuzzi as they passed the white, flower-shaped Art Science Museum. Mr. V turned around and announced, "We're just passing the Gardens by the Bay on our right."

"Look, Owen, the Super trees are beginning their light show," said Irma, rolling onto her stomach to gaze out at the grove of twenty-five to fifty-foot vertical tree gardens flashing in different colors behind the huge Flower Dome, the largest glass greenhouse in the world.

"I'll just stop the yacht here for a moment so you can enjoy the view and head downstairs and bring up some snacks," announced Mr. V. The couple ignored him, spellbound by the flashing trees.

Mr. V had spent hours thinking about what to do with Owen and Irma. He had always thought of himself as a gruff, but gentle soul with a passion for learning. He prided himself on being a learned man, a professor of the highest echelon of cultivation.

He had never had the urge to hurt anyone or anything in his life. That was before he found out how Owen and Irma had stolen Anneli and tried to kill Ella. He didn't care if it cost him his freedom, or his life, but he had to bring Anneli home to Switzerland and ensure his two girls need never fear another attack by Irma and Owen.

Mr. V walked downstairs and pulled the two small ice chests out of the cabinet. He carried one up the stairs and stood shivering next to the Jacuzzi. Owen and Irma had already fallen asleep in the Jacuzzi, their heads leaned back against the edge of the tub. Mr. V took a deep breath and set down the ice chests. His mouth was dry and pain was radiating through his chest. It was horrifying what one could purchase from China via the Internet.

He pulled on bite-proof handling gloves, just in case, and carefully tipped the contents of the first ice chest onto Irma's brilliant yellow string bikini top. The tiny golden octopus with luminous tentacles was no longer than the length of a pencil. It rested on Irma's chest. Mr. V took out a pole and prodded the octopus, until the blue rings covering its body darkened and began to flash, glowing iridescent blue.

Mr. V took the second ice chest and tipped it out onto the chest of Owen.

This blue-ringed octopus needed no provocation. Its blue rings were already glowing iridescent blue. Mr. V watched, spellbound in sickening fascination, as the tiny octopus bit Owen's chest with its beak.

Mr. V knew that the bite was painless, but the venom injected by the blue-ringed octopus was more than a thousand times more potent than cyanide and strong enough to kill twenty-six adults.

Irma's eyes popped open, her mouth opening in a soundless

scream as she struggled in agony for breath. The blue-ringed octopus's tetrodotoxin was coursing through her body already, causing paralysis.

Owen's eyes opened next, his breathing labored. Both pairs of eyes stared up at him. Although their bodies were almost completely paralyzed, the venom had no impairment on consciousness. Their eyes followed his movements. Mr. V stood frozen, riveted by the horrifying spectacle of the toxic blue-ringed octopi creeping along the frozen bodies of Owen and Irma.

Mr. V ran down the steps and grabbed the five long-handled nets he had brought with him. He ran back up the stairs to the Jacuzzi. Terror-filled eyes stared up at him from cadaver-like bodies. Mr. V looked away. He couldn't bear to hear their breathing becoming increasingly labored.

He reached out with a net, trying to scoop an octopus up just as the yacht rocked to the left as a huge boat glided past. Mr. V teetered forward, almost falling into the Jacuzzi. At the last moment, he reached out a hand, bracing himself from falling into the water with some of the world's most venomous creatures.

His hands were shaking as at last he captured the first octopus in the net. He hurried to the railing and threw the entire net into the ocean with the octopus inside. He picked up another net and returned to the tub.

Sweat rolled down his cheeks as he fought to scoop up the other octopus, which kept hiding under Irma's paralyzed legs. Mr. V swallowed hard.

At last he had the pulsing creature in its net, its blue rings luminous in the dark. He threw the net over the railing, sucking in large breaths of air as if he had just surfaced from the ocean after a deep dive. He returned to the wheel and drove the yacht along the dark, deserted beaches of East Coast Park.

He went to the Jacuzzi, averting his gaze from the terror-filled eyes of Irma as he hurried around the Jacuzzi to her back. He slid his hands under her arms until her wet hair pressed against his cheek. He bent his knees and pulled with all his might.

Irma slid out of the Jacuzzi, her legs hitting the floor with a sickening thud. Step by step, he pulled her toward the railing. He turned around, lifting her up and then let go. She fell head first, her stomach landing hard against the railing. He squatted down and lifted up her legs up until she unhooked from the railing and fell into the ocean headfirst. She barely made a sound as she hit the water.

Panting, Mr. V returned to face Owen. He had one more body to throw overboard, and this horrific reckoning would be over. He walked behind Owen, sliding his hands under his armpits and pulled with all his might.

Inch by painstaking inch, Mr. V pulled Owen out of the pool. Owen was taller and heavier than he was, and it made this part of his plan risky. Mr. V prayed he would be able to get the man over the railing without suffering a heart attack or collapsing on the deck.

He decided to force himself to go slowly, pacing himself as a marathon runner would. He had time. It was all about using his knees to lift and dragging more than carrying him.

In a flash of revelation, Mr. V realized that the sight of these corpse like, conscious victims would haunt him for the rest of his life. All at once, nausea rolled through his stomach, and he threw up, his sickness landing on Owen's face and torso.

Mr. V took the last two steps to the railing and turned. He pushed Owen forward as hard as he could. This time the body didn't catch, but tipped forward, teetering a moment on the railing before falling forward into the dark water with a loud splash.

Mr. V collapsed to the floor, seeing stars. Utterly exhausted, he couldn't find the strength to stand. Instead he crawled to the steering wheel. There was no time to lose. He had to get away from this nightmarish scene, the two white bodies floating in the dark water.

Any moment another yacht could drive by and see the bodies. Mr. V looked around in panic. Was anyone watching? Had anyone seen him throw the bodies overboard? No, his yacht was alone.

As he turned the yacht and accelerated away from the bodies lurking face down on the water's surface, a much larger yacht drifted by. Laughter and conversation rang out from a party on board. Mr. V could see guests swaying to music on the upper deck, drinks in hand. He hoped they were too busy partying to look down at the dark water. He increased his speed. No mess, he told himself. No mess.

If all went according to plan, then Irma and Owen would either sink or wash up on the beach. If the cadavers were ever found, the authorities would think the couple had been wading through tidal pools and stepped on or stupidly picked up the small, beautiful blue-ringed octopus.

Three hours later, Mr. V walked into the Fullerton Bay hotel lobby. He went immediately up to the rooftop lantern bar and pool. He ordered a scotch with ice, the cubes clinking as his trembling hand brought the glass to his lips. His gaze was caught by the light and water show of the Marina Bay sands. For a few minutes, he was transfixed by the multicolored lights echoing off the mist of water spraying up from the bay into the night sky.

He was startled from his reverie by the loud laughter of a provocatively clad American woman sitting two bar stools away. He looked around the rooftop. A few minutes later, he was satisfied that no one had followed him to the hotel from the marina and he made his way to Ella's room.

He knocked gently. No one answered. He knocked harder, with still no response. His mouth turned dry with fear. He took out the extra key, opened the door and stepped inside. Ella and Anneli lay curled up together under a feather duvet in blissful sleep, a small smile on Anneli's face. Her tiny fingers were curled around the strap of Ella's nightgown, their foreheads resting together. Mr. V slid soundlessly out of the room and to his own next door. He fell onto the bed fully clothed. It was time to get his angels home.

It took him five days and some palm-greasing in Russia to obtain the passport for Anneli. As soon as he landed in the Singapore airport, he called Ella from a pay phone and told her it was time.

He paced in front of the airport, his hands clutched behind his back. Every time he looked at his watch, only two or three minutes had passed. An insidious voice in his head kept whispering that they wouldn't get out of Singapore. Perhaps someone from the party yacht had seen him driving away from the floating corpses. He knew cameras were everywhere now, watching, always watching.

Exactly thirty-six minutes later, Ella climbed out of the taxi holding Anneli and carrying her bag. Relief, adrenaline and delight coursed through his veins.

After purchasing the tickets to Friedrichshafen, Germany, they had four hours before their flight. He was sure he was having a heart attack when they went through the security check. Would they notice that his and Ella's passports had incoming stamps, but Anneli's passport was brand new? Would they pull them out of the line?

He almost couldn't believe it when the grim faced security waved them through and they stood inside the airport, wondering how to pass the next four hours until their flight.

They decided to take Anneli to the butterfly gardens. His heartbeat slowed when he saw Anneli's eyes light up with delight, heard the sound of her laughter effervescent as she watched the butterflies. More powerful still was seeing the wide smile on Ella's face, the way she held her baby close, nuzzling her neck, kissing her cheeks.

He didn't even mind the thirteen-hour flight to Germany with a baby. Even when she cried, a warmth rolled through him. He took turns with Ella walking up and down the aisle, holding her, playing with her.

It was only on the ferry from Friedrichshafen, Germany to Romanshorn that his body began to throb with pain. The trip had taken a toll on him, but the constant flow of adrenaline had kept him wired. Despite the pain screaming in his back and radiating down his legs, he only let himself relax onto his bed in Ella's guest room when Anneli and Ella were happily eating in the restaurant with Helen, Aya and Adnan.

He closed his eyes and slept the night through for the first time in days.

Chapter 32

He watched Ella playing in the pool with Anneli, cherishing the sound of Anneli's laughter and the warm smile that stretched over her face.

He would do it all over again, to keep his girls safe, despite the sickening feeling of revulsion that seized him every time he remembered his night on that yacht in Singapore.

"You cannot throw a word out of a song," he murmured to himself.

"What was that, dear?"

"Nothing," he answered, kissing the back of the hand of the love of his life.

"I still don't understand how you found her so fast, after just a few weeks, and brought her back without involving the police."

He sighed, considering.

"I want to know," she insisted.

"The less you know, the more soundly you sleep."

"I don't sleep well anymore anyway. Tell me."

The truth was such a weight on his soul. He looked over. He could trust her. He knew it instinctively.

"I killed Irma and Owen Helen. They won't ever hurt my girls again."

He watched Helen drop her glass of strawberry lemonade on the pavement. Luckily the glass was plastic.

He didn't feel up to a scene.

"You're not serious?"

"There are scandals even in the most noble families, my love," he sighed, shifting his gaze from Ella and Anneli out to the sailboats gliding on the sparkling lake and the Alps rising grey blue in the distance.

"Well, that explains your shell-shocked demeanor since you returned."

"Promise me you won't ask me for details," he answered, the words heavy in his mouth. If they had taken Anneli back to Switzerland, would Irma and Owen have left them in peace? Had he murdered them without necessity? He closed his eyes, rubbing the bridge of his nose. Now they would never find out.

"You had both of them killed? Good God, did Ella see it?"

"Helen, calm down. Ella knows they are dead, but she doesn't know the details."

"Which are? What if the Singapore authorities find out it was you?"

"There's no way they can link me to the deaths. I left no trace at all."

"How did they die?"

Anneli came running to them, and he swung her up onto his lap, despite her wet swimsuit and dripping hair. His heart was lighter just having her in his arms. It had all been worth it. He had been able to make things right at last.

"Dedushka! I found a rock? See? So pretty."

"Beautiful. Just like you," he said and kissed her blond curls. She slipped down and ran back to her mother, who gathered her into a large fluffy towel.

He constantly fought a desire to keep Ella and Anneli within a stone's throw at all times, even though he knew Irma and Owen would never return to hunt them down again. There was a saying that one can't build one's happiness on another's grief. He wasn't sure if that was true.

Ella was safe and happy, and so was her little girl. He gave himself a mental shake. He had done what was necessary to keep his family safe.

"Well? Are you ever going to tell Ella?"

"Tell her what?"

"About you killing Irma and Owen? About sending the Annikovs to her doorstep to help her? About having the real estate agent bring her to the castle property and having me lie in wait with a proposal that she live there with me? That it's you who really owns the castle? Of your agreements with Adnan and Aya? That all the money in her accounts came from you?"

"Ah, dear one. A liar should be a man of good memory, and my memory is already starting to falter. The full truth may come out one day. But for now? I told her the truth about her mother and that she is my granddaughter. She knows that the money in her accounts came from me. The rest?" Mr. V shook his head, taking Mrs. Frieden's hand in his own and giving it a squeeze. "I will tell her someday."

He looked over at Mrs. Frieden. She nodded.

He let out a sigh of relief.

Just then Ella ran up the rocks with Anneli in her arms and sat down on a lounge chair beside them, ringing the water out of her wet blond hair.

"So Josh told me last night that someone bought him a ticket to visit Switzerland for Christmas. It arrived in the mail yesterday. I wonder who that someone can be?" asked Ella, looking from Mrs. Frieden to Mr. V.

Mrs. Frieden pointed to Mr. V with a large smile. Ella kissed his cheek.

"Thanks, Mr. V. You're my hero. First helping me get back Anneli, and now this. You really love us, don't you?"

"Go on and buy yourself and my little angel an ice cream and leave a poor old man in peace," he grumbled, waving them off.

Aya ran up, the water still glistening on her distended belly. She slipped on and Adnan lounged forward from behind her, steadying her so she wouldn't fall.

"Careful, Aya!" he warned, his brows knitted together in a scowl. "Pregnant woman: no running."

He shook his finger at her.

Aya pushed Adnan playfully. "Don't worry."

"Aya, you look more beautiful than ever, dear," said Mrs.

Frieden. "Two more weeks to go."

"Thank you again for the beautiful new flat, Mr. V," said Aya.

"Debt is beautiful only after it is repaid. You earned that," he answered. "I know it wasn't easy to give Anneli up. Ella promised you adoption."

"I have Anneli with me a lot. Ella is gone dancing a good deal of the week."

"It's not the same, Aya," he answered, shaking his head.

"I'm happy Ella wants to be her mother," she answered, placing a hand on Mr. V's arm. "Really. And if it wasn't for your help paying for the IVF, we wouldn't be pregnant. We're all happy, Mr. V. Just try to enjoy it."

"Yeah, sure."

He could do that, he decided. Just as soon as he found a good man for his Ella. He wouldn't be around forever to watch out for her. He sighed again. There was time for that. First, he was going for a swim in the cold water of the turquoise lake.

He jumped into the water and gazed at the rolling green hills, the Alp chain and the ferry gliding over the water toward Germany. He attempted to immerse himself in the beauty and to rid himself of the sight of Owen and Irma's eyes following him from lifeless bodies.

He stopped at the group's large blanket spread out by the lake, dripping water. He just stood there for a moment, catching his breath, looking at Ella and Anneli, Aya and Adnan and his lovely Helen.

"I'm heading home," he said.

"You have an hour to shower and rest," replied Aya. "Then we're going out on a dinner cruise."

"We who?"

"The family. Be at the harbor at seven," grumbled Aya, impersonating him and shaking a finger. "Punctuality is important. And don't bring one of those damn phones with you."

He shook his head, smiling as he walked toward the castle. 'The family'. He liked that. After all these years of being without a home and loved ones, he had one. A family. And more importantly, so did Ella.

Chapter 33

Two and a half Years Later Ella walked out into the lobby of the Opernhaus.

Her muscles were Jell-O after two back-to-back performances Friday and Saturday night of *The Nutcracker*. She immediately spotted Joshua. He was holding Anneli over his head as she giggled with glee.

"Over here, Mommy! Look Mommy, I'm the Sugar Plum Fairy, just like you."

Ella smiled. It was amazing how quickly children grew and changed. She was thankful for the inner resiliency of her daughter. She was certain there would be psychological repercussions from the kidnapping, but she prayed everyday she could mitigate them with love, structure and a sense of safety. It was a huge responsibility. Ella was so grateful she had Aya, Adnan, Mrs. Frieden and Mr. V to help her with the burden and the joys of raising a child.

Joshua set Anneli down, and she ran in her sparkling dress and matching red patent shoes toward Ella. Ella scooped her up and held her close as she walked toward Joshua, Aya, Adnan, Nick, Julie, Mrs. Frieden and Mr. V. As she drew near, they all broke out into applause.

"You danced beautifully, dear," said Mrs. Frieden.

"We're proud of you, Ella," said Mr. V as he handed her a huge bouquet of long-stemmed white roses.

Ella beamed at her adopted patchwork family.

"This is such a surprise. Why didn't you tell me you were all coming tonight? I was just expecting Joshua."

"It was Mr. V's idea to surprise you," answered Aya. "He bought all our tickets and had a limousine drive us all here. What a treat. And now he is taking us all out to dinner at the restaurant in the Dolder Grand, and we're all staying the night."

"And then we're flying tomorrow morning to England to celebrate Christmas with the Annikovs on their cruise ship. We'll sail from Southampton to Hamburg and visit its Christmas market. The ship then goes on to Amsterdam and Antwerp before returning to the UK. We'll be gone seven days," added Mrs. Frieden.

"What do you mean 'we'?" asked Ella, setting her squirming daughter back down.

"Adnan, Aya, Helen, you, Anneli and even the cowboy here. The ballet has no performances for the next week and a half. And myself of course. I'm taking everyone on a holiday. We deserve one, after what we have been through in the past year. Especially you and Anneli," explained Mr. V. "I offered to take Nick, Julie and their kids, but Nick can't get away from his restaurant."

"We are, however, looking forward to dinner and a night in the Dolder," spoke up Julie. "What a treat. I'm so happy my mom could take the kids for the night."

"But I haven't packed. Anneli, come back here," she called. "Stay close to me."

"I packed for you both," said Mrs. Frieden. "I hope you don't mind. We wanted it to be a surprise. Will you come?"

"I'm thrilled. Thank you," she answered, kissing both Mrs. Frieden and Mr. V.

"Let's go everyone, the limousine is waiting and I don't want to be late for our dinner reservations," ordered Mr. V.

Ella caught the giggling Anneli and picked her up. She followed everyone outside and waited in the frigid night air as everyone climbed into the limousine one by one.

Ella caught Mr. V's sleeve as he was about to climb into the limousine.

"I have to come late to dinner. Can you all watch Anneli for me and order for Joshua and I? We'll follow you in thirty minutes."

"What's this?"

"Mr. V? Please? Promise me you won't let Anneli out of your sight even for a second."

Mr. V nodded his head, grumbling to himself about 'kids these days.'

"Hey there," said Joshua. "We're not going with them? I've been running all over hell's half acre helping the folks all pack for our Christmas cruise. I'm plum tuckered out and mighty hungry."

"I had a surprise planned for *you* tonight. I had no idea what Mr. V and you all had in store for me. Come on," she grabbed his hand and pulled him into the car waiting for her on the curb.

Her stomach was twisted in knots. Was she doing the right thing? Ella took a deep breath. Could she trust this man? Down the road, everything could change. He could change.

After all, her mother always said her father was the most charming man in Moscow until after Ella was born.

What would she do if Joshua started controlling her, or manipulating her as Owen had?

Ella shook her head. She was strong. She would leave, just like her mother had. If it happened.

The car stopped in the middle of the Quaibrücke. She opened the door and stepped out onto the bridge. Joshua climbed out of the car and looked out over the water of the lake. He turned to take in the lights flickering on the black water of the river on the other side of the bridge. Ella grabbed his hand and knelt down on one knee, taking out a box.

"What in tarnation are you doing down there? It's cold woman, get up."

"Joshua," said Ella, opening the box to reveal a Bremont Terra Nova watch.

"Will you marry me?"

"Will I what? What kind of watch is this?"

"It's the same watch that polar explorer Ben Saunders wore when he made his record-breaking, 1,795-mile trek to the

South Pole in 2013," answered Ella.

"Ain't I supposed to be the one doing the proposing?"

"No man should have to propose twice," answered Ella. "Or at least not to the same woman, anyway."

Scowling, Joshua pulled Ella to her feet.

"You know I respect you as an equal darlin', but you got to let a man do the chasing. And the proposing. Some traditions are still important."

"But you flew all the way here. And you already proposed. Forget it, I'll return the watch."

"Hold steady there, hold steady. I love that watch. Looks real rugged, like it could take a beating and keep on ticking. Like you, Ella." He sighed, pulling her into his arms for a hug before turning away and staring out at the Christmas lights strung up over the streets. He turned, leaned his arms on the railing of the bridge, staring out at the lake while kicking the snow with his cowboy boots.

"Well? Is it Anneli?"

"What? Now don't pitch a duck fit, let a man think it over. You know it isn't that I don't love you and Anneli both."

Ella watched the snowflakes drift into the inky darkness of the lake. She couldn't help but take a step back away from the railing, images of almost drowning clouding her thoughts. Perhaps this hadn't been such a good spot to propose.

She said, "I know you love us. You've proven it."

"Yeah?"

"I remember the months after the accident now, leading up to the day I went swimming in the lake and the night of the accident came back to me. Thank you for all the hours you spent at my bedside in the hospital and all the days you spent helping Mr. V and Mrs. Frieden take care of me.

"Mrs. Frieden told me how you worked for her daughter and his husband from dawn to dusk for only room and board when you found out their farm was near foreclosure after the bad harvest. They have you to thank for being able to keep their farm. Your idea of starting a side business hosting working tourists was brilliant. They didn't think there was a chance in hell people would actually pay them to train and work as a ranch hand for two weeks. Now they're booked solid for the next six months.

Ella reached out and took Joshua's hand. "I've watched you play with Anneli. You are a good man with a tender heart. I trust you. I would be very lucky to have you as my husband. I want to share my life with you."

Joshua took out a small box and knelt down on the icy, snow-covered pavement.

"I was going to do this at the restaurant, but you sure did beat me to it. I thought a good deal about what you said when I proposed that first time. Ella, I promise to see you for who you are and not to try and change you or model you into some idea I have in my head. But I want you to promise me the same thing.

"You have to know I don't fit here with you in these classy joints. I'm no opera man. I love watching you dance but feel as uncomfortable as all get out in a suit. I'll have to show up in jeans, boots and a sports jacket in the future. As lovely as you are, you can't make me happy. Every man has to create that for himself. I have a passion for farming. Nothing makes me happier than working in the dirt and being out on the land under an open sky. And that's what I plan on doing the rest of my life. It doesn't pay much, and that's right fine with me."

"I love you, Joshua, just as you are. Yes."

"Hell yeah," shouted Joshua, struggling to open the box as he stood up. At last it sprung open and Ella gasped.

A huge oval sapphire lay nestled in a ring of diamonds.

"How could you afford this?"

"I told Mr. V I was going to propose, and he gave me this. It was his mother's wedding ring. Turn it over, do you see the Russian inscription on the inside band? He said it says, 'you have my heart forever.' Do you like it?"

She nodded with a grin from ear to ear. He slid the ring over her finger before pulling her in, looking into her eyes. She could feel the warmth of his breath on her lips.

Her body began to shiver from the freezing temperature and exhaustion. Joshua leaned in and kissed her neck and along her collarbone before finding her lips. Ella melted against the warmth of him, an inner heat radiating a need to pull him in even closer. He felt like home.

"Hey," called Ella's driver through the open car window. "Hurry up and jump in before someone back there runs into the back of me. This bridge is icy."

As soon as they were in the car, Joshua reached for her, pulling her close, his hands running through her long hair. Ella gently pushed him away. She took out a ring of keys from her pocket and shook them.

"These are for you."

"What are they for?"

"A new tractor. And a farm of your own up the road on rolling hills overlooking the Bodensee. Looks like you'll need to learn real fast a whole lot about dairy cows and tending a vineyard and apple orchards."

"Don't tease me now."

"I'm serious. The only catch is that we need to stay part of the week in our flat in the castle so Anneli can be taken care of by Mrs. Frieden, Mr. V, Adnan and Aya while I'm in Zürich working. You'll have to commute. But some of the nights we can spend in our house on the farm. What do you say?"

"Damn woman. I say that sounds too good to be true. How could you buy a whole farm?"

"I couldn't, but Mr. V gave me some money," said Ella, resting her head on Joshua's shoulder. "It was enough for a down payment. But we, my love, will have a large mortgage. I hope you are good at farming."

AS ELLA WALKED WITH JOSHUA hand-in-hand into the restaurant, her heart warmed at the sight of her family.

"Guess who is getting married y'all," shouted out Joshua, holding up Ella's left hand.

The entire table gave a cheer and surrounded Ella and Joshua, hugging and congratulating them both.

Anneli bounded up to Ella and reached out her arms. Ella picked her up and held her close as Joshua wrapped his arms around both of them.

Mr. V was always saying that when something is obtained cheap, it is easily lost. Ella looked around. Some Russians, a few Swiss, two Syrians and an American.

They might not look like a family, but they had grown together. They had supported one another through hardship and obstacles, rejoiced in each other's joy. She was willing to fight for each and every one of them.

AUTHOR'S NOTE

THANK YOU for reading CONFESSIONS OF A NEIGHBOR. I hope you enjoyed it and I would love to hear your feedback.

Please write a review on Amazon or Good Reads, or write to me directly with any thoughts you have:

heather.n.lenz@gmail.com.

I value each and every review and each one influences my future writing.

Thank you again for reading!

Warm wishes to you, Heather Nadine

ACKNOWLEDGMENTS

THANK YOU to my husband, who continues to bring me cups of coffee and spends hours listening to discussions of potential plot lines. I love you.

To my parents, thank you for giving your children a magical childhood and for all your support and love. To Holly, Nathan and Nick, thank you for being a constant source of inspiration and love.

Thank you, Dr. Harry and Mary Chinchinian, for being the most loving and generous grandparents on earth.

I'd also like to thank David Yost for his brilliant editing work and for motivating me to make the book better than I could have without his insight.

To everyone who has helped along the way, I would also like to say, thank you.

AUTHOR BIO

I BELIEVE IN LOVE at first sight, second chances and the power of kindness. As a child growing up in Boisé Idaho I loved the beautiful landscape and friendly people. I adore my family. I never planned on leaving.

But sometimes life takes us where it wants to, especially if we follow our hearts. Mine took me all the way to Switzerland, where I have lived for over twelve years now with my Swiss husband.

When I'm not enjoying time with my three children and husband, you can find me writing, reading, or doing yoga. My first book, Beneath the Surface was published in 2015.

Also by Heather Nadine Lenz...

Natalia has a secret. She thinks she's going crazy. When she awakes one morning she doesn't remember marrying the man standing in her bedroom. She doesn't recognize the children calling her mom. Why can't she remember the past few months of her life? The high concept plot of this psychological thriller keeps you riveted from the very beginning. Beneath the Surface is a gripping mystery that keeps you in suspense, turning the pages to discover the truth.

Beneath the Surface

A LIGHT PIERCED NATALIA'S EYES. She closed them against the brightness.

"Wake up, Natalia! Your children are here," called a voice.

Natalia tried to open her eyes; she tried to answer, but she was just so tired. Her entire body heavy with exhaustion, she felt herself drifting away, slipping back into sleep, until she heard her children. They were all crying. She needed to go to them. In a panic she tried to sit up, but someone was holding her back.

"Let me go," she screamed, but no one answered.

The brilliant light was gone and she was in darkness. She couldn't see anything, nor could she hear her children any longer. All at once she felt pain flash through her entire body and explode in her head. She he felt her limbs go weak and she fell, slipping and falling, as her scream was swallowed up in the void around her.

With a sharp intake of breath Natalia opened her eyes, sitting straight up in bed, all her senses heightened. She could hear children playing downstairs. She felt the silkiness of her duvet cover. Surveying the way the light hit the blue vase of pink roses next to her bed, Natalia smiled at the smell of freshly baked bread wafting up from the kitchen.

"Good morning, love," said a ruggedly attractive man with tousled dirty-blond hair, green eyes, and an extremely muscular physique while walking into the room.

"I thought I heard you scream, are you okay?" Sitting down next to her on the bed, he placed a cup of coffee on her nightstand and smoothed the hair back from her face. "Were you having a nightmare?" he asked.

"Evan," said Natalia. "What are you doing here so early?"

"It's time for you to get up, love, the kids and I have been awake for hours and we are ready to start the day's agenda. Here's a cup of coffee to get you going," he said, motioning toward the cup. "Drink it while it's hot."

Falling back against the pillows, Natalia asked again, "What are you doing here so early?"

Evan frowned. "It isn't early. We've all been awake for hours. It's time for you to get up too. See you downstairs, dressed and ready to go in fifteen minutes, yeah?" he said on his way out of the room.

Natalia felt she would give anything to fall back asleep, even for a few more minutes.

Her entire body ached with exhaustion. But what was Evan doing at her house? Concentrating didn't help. She couldn't remember why he would be at her house so early in the morning and where they were going together.

In fact, she couldn't remember what day it was. Or what she had done yesterday, or the day before that. In fact, she was having trouble recollecting the entire past week. Natalia shook her head.

Coffee will help, she reasoned. I'm just not awake yet, and sleep deprivation can cause havoc with memory.

Natalia counted to three and jumped out of bed all at once, quickly dressing in an aquamarine dress. Twisting her red hair up and pinning it expertly on autopilot, she took three more minutes to efficiently add some makeup to her face, grimacing at the sight of her normally bright blue eyes, now bloodshot. Why did she look and feel so terrible this morning? Where had she been the night before?

Natalia, frowning, realized she still couldn't remember.

Wandering barefoot down the stairs and toward the kitchen, Natalia paused when she heard children playing. She didn't recognize the voices. With a knitted brow, she walked into the family room. Three little faces looked up at her.

"Who are you?" she asked. "Where are my kids?"

"What do you mean, Mommy?" asked the little girl, pausing in her play and tilting her head to one side.

"We're right here."

"Very funny, sweetheart," Natalia replied while admiring the pretty little girl's curly blond hair and bright blue eyes.

"Where are my children? Do I know you? Are you new neighbor kids?

One of the boys stood up. "Mom, tell Nathan it's my turn to play the game."

"No!" screamed a boy identical to the first, pushing his brother. "Mom, Nick played the game the entire morning. It's my turn!"

Natalia turned and looked behind her. Was their mother here? What were these strangers doing in her house?

"What's going on?" Natalia wondered out loud. "Where are Anna, Allan, and Ben?"

"Who are they, Mom?" asked the girl on the floor, without looking up from the Lego tower she was building.

The breath caught in Natalia's throat. Her heart began hammering louder and louder as the room began to spin faster and faster.

Grabbing onto the nearby cheery wood desk to keep from falling, Natalia asked, "Why are you calling me Mom?"

The two boys, whom she could now see were identical twins, had bright blue eyes and pale blond hair just like their sister. Both came and hugged her around the waist.

"Mom, I don't want to go swimming, I want to go to the zoo," declared one of the twins.

The little girl jumped up from the floor.

"The zoo? Me! Me too!"

"I want to go swimming. Dad promised we could go! Don't listen to them, Mom. Mom! Mom?"

"Are you okay, Mom?"

Natalia's hand was still clutching the desk, and looking down, she noticed her fingers turning white from her grip.

She was swaying a bit from side to side; the room was beginning to spin.

She heard a voice down the hall say, "Hey, honey, I thought we should go swimming with the kids this morning at La Meer. I know you love that warm salt-water pool and perhaps I could go to the sauna while you take the kids down the slides? We could eat lunch in the café. Natalia? Natalia, where are you?"

Evan entered the room and examined Natalia closely before

kissing her lightly on the lips.

"Are you okay, Natalia? Your face looks a little white."

Natalia could hardly believe Evan had just walked into the room and kissed her in front of these kids. What on earth was he doing? And who were these children in her house anyway? Natalia inspected the children more carefully. She noticed the boys had blond hair exactly like the little girl. Three pairs of bright blue eyes looked up at her.

"I need to talk to you alone," said Natalia.

"What, why?" asked Evan.

Natalia didn't answer.

She had already gone into the kitchen and was looking out the floor-length windows into the garden.

"Okay, my little bunnies," said Evan, "you are allowed to watch one cartoon and then we are leaving for swimming. No, we are not going to the zoo today, but after the swimming we can go out to lunch in the cafeteria."

As the boys and little girl happily cuddled together onto the couch to watch a DVD, Natalia began searching the entire ground floor, then made her way upstairs and was glancing in each bedroom in search of her children. Evan found her looking into the children's bathroom. Wordlessly he took her by the hand and led her down the hall to the master suite. She felt so bone tired. All she wanted was to find her children and have them climb back into bed with her. They could cuddle up and she would read books to them for the next hour. But where were they?

Suddenly, thoughts of her children swept out of her mind. She stood there, suddenly frozen, watching as Evan relaxed back onto her bed. What was he doing? She could hear the children's voices rise in argument from downstairs, debating which episode to select, and then an irritated boy's voice admonishing his younger sister for taking up too much space on the couch. Then silence fell over the house.

"I can take our kids up swimming alone if you're not feeling well," Evan offered, relaxing back on his elbows and splaying out his legs in front of him.

"Oh. Well, that is really sweet, Evan. But I don't even know where my children are. Let's go find them," answered Natalia as she turned to leave the room.

"What are you talking about?" asked Evan. "We just left our kids watching cartoons downstairs."

Natalia recoiled in surprise. Did he say our kids?

No, Natalia decided she must have misheard him. And yes, she did think it inappropriate of Evan to be so at ease in her room, lying back on her and James' bed. Even if she did adore Evan and he was her best friend, he was still Eva's husband. She knew James would be less than thrilled to come home and find Evan in their bedroom.

Then again, what was Evan thinking leading her into the master suite instead of back downstairs into the living room in the first place? Natalia imagined James leading Eva into her bedroom. She didn't like that thought at all.

"Did you hear me, Evan?" asked Natalia.

"Let's go back downstairs. Where is Eva anyway?" she asked. "Where are my kids? Where are your kids, while we're at it?"

"I have no idea where Eva is. Why would I know where Eva is? And our kids are happily engaged for a few moments, so..."

Evan reached forward and pulled Natalia onto his lap. Natalia gave a shout of surprise and clumsily freed herself from Evan's embrace.

"What are you doing, Evan? What are you thinking?"

"What do mean? Oh."

Something seemed to occur to him. He stripped off his shirt, revealing a sharply defined stomach and muscular arms. Taking off his jeans, Evan went to the bedroom door, firmly shutting and locking it behind him. Natalia watched, mouth open in shock.

This is a dream, Natalia, she told herself, just like the one before. Any moment you are going to wake up and snuggle up next to your husband, feeling just a bit guilty for dreaming about your best friend.

Evan walked back to her and leaned in again for a kiss. Natalia took at step back, knocking over her vase of flowers.

"Evan, no. What, are you crazy? What has gotten into you?"

Natalia turned and began gathering the flowers back into

the vase. "Can you hand me a towel to mop up this mess?" Natalia asked.

"Leave that for now," whispered Evan, reaching out and pulling her to him. "And don't worry about our kids; they are watching something educational for a few minutes."

"Our kids? Are your children and my children down there watching now too? Who are those other children in my family room anyway? When did they get here? Oh, I'm going to go call James," sighed Natalia, heading toward the door.

Evan blocked her way. Reaching out, he took hold of Natalia by the shoulders and considered her a moment, head cocked to the side. Then, giving a forced laugh, he released Natalia and sat on her bed once again.

"What is this? Are you trying to make me jealous or something? I know you have always had a crush on the almighty James," said Evan. "I didn't think you were in regular contact with each other."

"Of course I am in regular contact with him, and I certainly think we are beyond the crush stage. And why would I try to make you jealous of James? That is ridiculous. Listen, Evan," said Natalia, "let me use your phone, okay?"

Not taking his eyes off her, Evan handed Natalia his cell phone and Natalia dialed James' number.

"Hello?"

Natalia felt her entire body relax at the sound of James' voice. Of course she had been overreacting, she thought. Her children were off somewhere with James. Evan, the eternal prankster, was playing a practical joke on her. He would probably be telling this story at every cocktail party they all went to for the next ten years.

"Hi, love, listen, where are you, Anna, Allan, and Ben?" asked Natalia, smiling. Natalia glanced at Evan while sitting down on the bed beside him. He was glaring at her. Smiling back at him, Natalia punched him playfully on the shoulder.

"Natalia, is that you?" asked James, sounding bewildered.

"Yes. Hello, James. I am here with Evan. Where are you? Are the kids with you?"

"The kids are all out shopping with Eva. Listen, can I talk to you tomorrow? I've got to go. I am meeting Eva, the kids, and my parents for brunch downtown in ten minutes and I still need to jump in the shower; I'm going to be so late. But I am looking forward to seeing you at your office tomorrow. Until then, darling!"

Natalia's heart was racing again. She felt cold, as if she had been standing for hours in a freezing wind. Without thinking she climbed under her duvet and pulled the covers up to her chin. She just couldn't make sense of what was going on. Why were her children shopping with Eva? Why was James meeting Eva, the children, and his parents for brunch? If this was some kind of practical joke James and her friends were playing on her, well, it was going to end now.

"Okay. This isn't funny anymore, Evan. I want to know what is going on," said Natalia.

"Natalia, listen. I agree it isn't funny anymore. Our kids are downstairs. You just saw them. And don't even think about it; Eva's kids are not coming over. I am not up for six kids in my house this weekend," sighed Evan. He started fidgeting with his watch, and then he looked into her eyes as he continued to speak.

"And what is the deal with you calling James 'love'? Are you just trying to start a fight with me this morning or what? That's what we call one another; it's our thing. How would you feel if I called Eva 'love'? I know James has always called you darling. That guy better watch himself. He is continually overstepping."

Evan pressed his lips into a thin line, and Natalia could see the muscles in his shoulders and neck tensing.

"Evan, you are not making any sense," began Natalia.

"I got up with the kids early this morning, baked bread, fed them breakfast, cleaned the kitchen, and played three rounds of a racing rabbit board game with them while my wife slept peacefully on in our bed," interrupted Evan.

Frowning, he glanced at his watch.

"Look," he said, motioning at his watch, "it's almost nine thirty. I have been up with the kids for over three hours while you lay sleeping. And here you are now, calling James 'love.' It is too much, Natalia. Every day, five days a week, you leave before the kids wake up in the morning and come home after they are in bed. I do all the housework, all the parenting, and spend my evenings preparing for school and correcting tests and homework. But I make an effort to find time to organize romantic nights together on top of everything else. Only, you almost always cancel on me. Why do I keep trying so hard? Nice guys come in last, even after they get married. You don't deserve me as your husband," said Evan, crossing his arms over his chest.

But then he saw Natalia's expression out of the corner of his eye. Turning to really look at her, Evan saw that Natalia's entire body was shaking, ever so slightly, and her eyes were wide while her hands continued to clutch and unclench the top of the duvet.

"You are not my husband Evan."

Evan stood up abruptly and stared at her open-mouthed.

"What?"

"You heard me," said Natalia. "

"Well, I mean, I know we have been fighting quite a bit lately," said Evan, running his fingers through his hair and beginning to pace back and forth.

"Really for years now, and all right, yes, I have been very bitter and even mean to you in the past few months," he admitted with a sigh.

"What are you talking about?" Natalia interrupted. "No, you haven't. You are so good to me, Evan. Really, I couldn't ask for a better friend. I appreciate you so much. I just don't think this joke is funny anymore. Game over. You have totally confounded me; you win."

Evan stared at her. "Natalia, you can't just say 'this isn't funny anymore' and walk away from your husband and children. That isn't what you are really saying, is it? Natalia?"

Evan paused, looking at her intently. "You, you are not really asking for a, for a divorce?" he stammered.

"What?" asked Natalia, sitting up in bed.

"No," breathed out Evan, reaching out and taking her hand. "No, of course not. I know I may sometimes be unhappy and unload all of my stress and bitterness on you and sometimes I have been downright mean. I am sorry. I never want to lose you. Can you forgive me?"

Natalia took Evan by the other hand, looking into his eyes.

"Oh, Evan, you have never been mean to me. On the contrary, you have been a brilliant friend. And I understand that you need to vent sometimes, really. I vent to you too. That is part of being a good friend: listening when someone you love is upset, acknowledging their feelings, telling them they have a right to feel whatever they are feeling, and telling them the truth, no matter how hard it is to hear. You are so good at that, Evan, which is really so rare, I'm telling you. And we also always share our good news and happiness with one another. It isn't all just bitterness and complaining."

Running his arms slowly up and down her bare arms, Evan said, "You must be exhausted from working ten-, twelve-hour days all week. Hey, there have been times when I myself have wanted to disown you and our kids out of sheer exhaustion. Life can get overwhelming. I don't want you burning out, or falling into a depression or something. I'm taking the kids swimming. You can go back to sleep and take a bath, or do some kick boxing to vent. Whatever you want. Even if it would be nice for you to do some of the gardening or housework for a change, though we both know you won't end up doing that."

"What do you mean, our kids? Evan, I mean it. Knock it off. You're going to take my kids swimming?" asked Natalia.

Sighing, Evan nodded and went to reach for his clothes, but then turned back, reached out, and gathered her in his arms and held her for several long moments.

"I spend too much time angry. I would never want to lose you, do you hear? We have shared so much together. I love you," he said softly and kissed her on the forehead.

"What?" asked Natalia. "You love me?"

Natalia felt breathless; her heart was racing. Evan was close enough that she could smell the fresh scent of his shampoo, the clean fragrance of his aftershave. She had hugged Evan more times than she could count. This was different. They weren't giving each other a quick squeeze and letting go. Evan was holding her in his arms, smiling down at her, his strong arms still wrapped around her. I

t felt electrifying. It felt wrong. Her friend's husband was holding her close to his bare chest. Evan brought his hands to her face, gently tracing his fingers along her jaw line. He had let her go. She could have taken a step back. But she didn't.

His eyes shining, softening, he smiled. She lifted her chin, gazing up at him, parting her lips. Evan leaned in and kissed her. His lips were so soft, and then his arms were once again encircling her, pulling her even closer to him. Running her fingertips slowly up and down, Natalia felt the muscles in Evan's back. Warmth flooding through her body, Natalia returned his kiss, her anger and confusion at the strangeness of the morning fading away.

Evan's kiss turned angry, searching, devouring. She felt lightheaded. As she pushed her hands into his hair, the hair on the nape of her neck rose, tingling, as Evan's hands began gliding over her body. Natalia felt the heat rise in her cheeks and wondered at how different a kiss could be. James kissed her gently, with great tenderness. James! Natalia pushed Evan away, shaking her head.

She hadn't kissed anyone but James in eleven years. But when was the last time James had really kissed her? Had he ever kissed her like that? She couldn't remember.

"No, Evan. Just go," whispered Natalia.

The world was spinning. Natalia watched as Evan stood, frozen in surprise for a moment, before he angrily threw on his clothes and left the room. Natalia lay in bed, her thoughts reeling. An image of Evan standing in his underwear in front of her, the remembrance of the heat of his lips on hers, caused Natalia to hide her face, burrowing it under the covers. What had she done? She needed to talk with James and confess everything right away. Or did she? Should she tell him?

How could Evan take the kids swimming if James was out to brunch with the children, his parents, and Eva? What was going on? Where was James this morning anyway, at the gym? Why had Evan been at her house so early, and on further thought, where were Evan and Eva's kids this morning? Were they at brunch too? And who were those other children in her family room this morning?

Furrowing her brow, heart racing, Natalia thought back on her conversation with James. Why had he said that he would see her at her office tomorrow? What office and why wouldn't she see him tonight? Sighing, Natalia decided there must be a perfectly reasonable explanation for everything.

She thought about calling her dad but reconsidered; it would be the middle of the night in Oregon.

Evan and the children made a great deal of noise downstairs putting on their shoes and exiting the house.

As silence descended Natalia felt her eyes grow heavy and in a few moments, she felt herself slipping into sleep.